John Wesley Hales

Folia litteraria

Essays and notes on English literature

John Wesley Hales

Folia litteraria
Essays and notes on English literature

ISBN/EAN: 9783337203382

Printed in Europe, USA, Canada, Australia, Japan

Cover: Foto ©Andreas Hilbeck / pixelio.de

More available books at **www.hansebooks.com**

FOLIA LITTERARIA

ESSAYS AND NOTES

ON ENGLISH LITERATURE

BY

JOHN W. HALES, M.A.

PROFESSOR OF ENGLISH LITERATURE IN KING'S COLLEGE, LONDON ;
EXAMINER IN ENGLISH AT LONDON UNIVERSITY ;
CLARK LECTURER AT TRINITY COLLEGE,
AND LATE FELLOW OF CHRIST'S COLLEGE, CAMBRIDGE ;
AUTHOR OF 'ESSAYS AND NOTES ON SHAKESPEARE.'

LONDON
SEELEY AND CO. LIMITED
ESSEX STREET, STRAND
1893

King's College, London,
Whitsuntide, 1893.

My dear Peile,

Your high distinction as the Master of a Cambridge College, as the Vice-Chancellor of the University, and as a Scholar, might well make me shrink from dedicating to you, even with your so cheerfully given consent, the present volume with all its faults and shortcomings. But after all it is as a friend that I for my part do and must always first think of you. We were Undergraduates and Fellows and Assistant Tutors of the same College at the same time; we have often travelled together both at home and abroad; few men, indeed, have known or know each other more intimately. And, not to speak of your intellectual gifts, my remembrance of you during all these years presents an unbroken record of wonderful kindliness, and of perpetual thought for everybody but yourself. Of our long and close friendship, please accept the association of your name with this book as a most sincere, however inadequate, memorial.

Ever affectionately yours,

John W. Hales.

To

.JOHN PEILE, M.A.,

LITT. D., CAMBRIDGE AND DUBLIN,

Master of Christ's College, Cambridge;

Vice-Chancellor of the University of Cambridge.

NOTE

—

I HAVE to thank the Editors of *The Nineteenth Century*, *The Contemporary Review*, *Fraser's Magazine*, *The Athenæum*, *The Academy*, *Macmillan's Magazine*, *The St James' Gazette*, *The Gentleman's Magazine*, and other Publications, for permission kindly given to reprint certain contributions of mine.

The Article on Victorian Literature contains the substance of four lectures I had the honour of giving, at the Royal Institution, just six years ago. That entitled 'Milton's Macbeth' is an expansion of part of one of my Clark Lectures at Cambridge.

J. W. H.

CONTENTS

———o———

FOLIA LITTERARIA

I

OLD ENGLISH METRICAL ROMANCES

(From *Fraser's Magazine* for September, 1875)

THE word Romance denoted originally any one of the various forms assumed by the Latin language towards the close of the Dark Ages, so called, in those provinces of Western Europe upon which the influence of Rome had been most deeply impressed. The ancient Hispania and Gallia had resigned themselves altogether to Roman culture; their barbarian eyes had been dazzled by the splendour of their imperial conquerors; they eagerly forsook the language of their race, and endeavoured to adopt that of Italy. The word Romance, slightly modified, is still used in a certain district of Switzerland to denote a Latin-descended speech. In process of time this word came to be applied especially to the Roman dialect spoken in France, perhaps because the earliest cultivation of a modern language for literary purposes would seem to have been attempted there, and must have rendered the tongue of that land famous throughout the contiguous countries; also because the central position of France, with regard to England, Italy and Spain, must have made its speech more generally known than that

of any one of the other Romance-speaking provinces.   Thus
French became pre-eminently *the* Romance.   When Northern
France, some two centuries after the settlement of the
Normans upon its coast, began to show signs of a higher
life than that of mere predation and turbulence, then the
term Romance acquired a new meaning.   It was applied to
the poetical offspring of that higher life—to a sort of rude
narrative poem picturing the life and the spirit that were dear
to the Northern-French people at that time.   Such a poem
was called a Romance.   Presently such stories as were told
by such poems were narrated in prose.   Then prose works
too were styled Romances.   Such are the derivation and
the earliest literary significance of the word Romance.

Various theories have been entertained as to the origin
of this literary form. 'Scholars have referred it to the
Arabians in Spain, to the Scandinavians, to the Classical
writers, to the Britons of Brittany.   We do not care now
to weigh the comparative merits of these several views, or to
point out their superfluousness.   We are content with the
significant fact, that the oldest Romances of which we know
or can hear anything were written in Norman-French.
Whatever earliest Romances are found elsewhere are but
translations of Norman-French ones.   The first themes that
were sung of by the Romancers of Spain and of Germany were themes that had been previously handled by
the Trouvères.   The epical life of modern Europe first
quickened amongst a Norman-French speaking people—
that is to say, in Northern France and in England.   Each
member of that great Teutonic family which reformed and
revivified Western Europe between th fifth and the twelfth
centuries was possessed of its own rich store of traditions—
of the seeds, and much more than the seeds, of a national
Epopeia ; each member of it had its share of the rich imagi-

nation that constituted the most magnificent heritage of the race ; each member did, in course of time, produce great works not unworthy of its spiritual lineage ; but the one member which gave the first signs that epic poetry was not dead and buried for ever, which produced the earliest Iliads and Odysseys of the Middle Ages, was that North-born people which had established itself in Neustria early in the tenth century, and called the province they had seized after their own name.

These Northmen were characterised by a spirit of high daring and adventure. They had made themselves the terror of all the coasts of Western Europe. Charlemagne, in his old age—when, as he fondly thought, he had accomplished the great work of his heart, and suppressed the marauders who, ever since the fall of Rome, had incessantly plagued and confounded the western provinces of the broken empire—saw strange sails hovering about the shores of Southern France, and wept, they say, to think that the labour of his life threatened to prove a mere vanity. Many a church had added to its litany the agonised appeal, 'From the fury of the Normans, good Lord, deliver us.' For some three centuries these Northmen were the imperial spirits of Europe. They made themselves admired and feared from Antioch to Sicily, from Sicily to London. They were the life and soul of the earlier Crusades. They were ever in the front of their times, both as fighters and as scholars. Those who fixed their seat in the fairest district of Northern France were brought there into contact with a Keltic people, amongst whom the traces of Roman civilisation had never been obliterated. This Keltic people had indeed been subdued by a barbarian inroad some four centuries before the Normans overran Neustria ; but these barbarians had not settled amongst them in overwhelming numbers, nor had they been able to resist the contagion of a superior civilisation. The native Kelts, themselves thoroughly Romanised, in the end Romanised their Frankish masters. With this amalgamated nation the Normans were brought into contact. With a facility characteristic of their race, they submitted themselves to its influence. They, too, as the Franks before them, adopted the Roman tongue ; and in no long time these splendid pupils surpassed their teachers in the ease and power with which they wielded the language thus taught them. They adopted also the legends of the two races who formed the population of Northern France ; and in no long time sung or told those alien tales with a force and a beauty never dreamt of by their original possessors.

In the latter half of the eleventh century the heart of Christendom was filled with that wonderful enthusiasm, whose fruit was the Crusades. We need not speak now of the follies and the crimes which sooner or later marked these wars, or of the deadly spirit of intolerance which grew out of them and smote the countries that waged them like some revengeful pestilence. These were the hideous children born of them ; but far other was the spirit in which they were conceived. They were the first wars waged by Europe in any higher spirit than that of mere piracy and plunder—the first with any nobler motive than mere acquisition and conquest. Moreover, they were the first wars in which the idea of a grand Christian confederacy was in any sort embodied. It could not be but that the intellectual spirit of Europe was stirred and ennobled by these more generous impulses. It was kindled into a higher excitement and energy than it had before known ; it felt pulsations that were new and strange : and then, at last, it spake with its tongue.

We have said that the Normans were ever foremost in

these wars, and that their life previous to them had abounded with adventurous enterprises. It had been of a kind to warm and inflame the imagination with its retrospect. Then, shortly before the Crusades, a famous Duke had won himself a crown—the crown of England. What wonder if at this time poetry sprang up amongst them? They had gathered together a vast store of legends, both national and originally belonging to others with whom they had been brought into association; they had gained experience far and wide; they, if any people, could look back upon their career with eyes of elation and triumph; they, in a special degree, were inspired and excited by the powerful sentiment which sent forth the bravest sons of the West to fight and fall in the mysterious far-away East.

What are called *Romances* began, probably, to be produced after some fashion even in the eleventh century. Even then, probably enough, there was current some kind of rude metrical legends—of Rollo and other old Norman heroes, many a one far older than Rollo. Certainly, Charlemagne and his Paladins were already in that century the themes of song; for we are told that at the battle of Senlac, commonly called Hastings, Taillefer, said to have been a minstrel knight—a warrior poet such as was Richard Cœur de Lion in after days—advanced to the charge singing a song of Roland. In the course of the following century—in the twelfth century—when all those motive powers we have mentioned above acted upon the Norman mind with their full force, then the Age of Romances fully dawned. In or about the year 1138 appeared that great original storehouse of Arthurian legend—a storehouse supplied in part at least from genuine British fable—Geoffrey of Monmouth's *History of the Britons*. The corresponding source of information regarding Charlemagne—Turpin's life of that famous monarch

—was no long time after circulating in France. Additional legendary treasures were being brought back from foreign countries by the crusaders. By the close of the twelfth century, Norman-French romance was in full flower. During the thirteenth it continued to bloom and blossom. It was in this latter century, we may remember, that Gothic architecture attained its most exquisite development. The ostentatious strength and solidity of the Norman style were then completely superseded by the grace and refinement of the Early-Pointed. The cathedrals of Notre Dame, of Amiens, of Salisbury, of Westminster, rose into being in all their ineffable loveliness just at the time when the Norman-French romances, whose origin we have briefly sketched, were enjoying their widest popularity.

In other ways, besides, that was a century of vast movement, both here in England and abroad. It was a century of great intellectual and religious agitations. It witnessed the rise of two great orders in the Church, who devoted themselves to the revival both of piety and of erudition. It witnessed a general ardour in quest of learning, royal recognition of the great seats of education by charters granted, the establishment of colleges in connection with these seats by the zeal and munificence of private persons, and an immense thronging from all parts of Europe of students, eager to partake of the benefits of the universities so chartered, so endowed. It was then, in stirring times for Europe, that the old Romances reached their maturity. In our own country the thirteenth century was made memorable by political events of extraordinary importance: by the passing of the Great Charter, by the meeting of the first House of Commons, by vigorous, and for a while seemingly successful efforts after an insular unity, and, to mention last because of its present interest to us, what comes first in chronological order, by the loss of Normandy. The loss of that province—the splendid heir-loom of our Norman kings—did, in fact, sever the intimate connection between this country and France; for the possessions we retained for more than two centuries afterwards in Guienne were too distant to affect our national life as Normandy had affected it. The complete amalgamation of the jarring elements which made up our nation, was greatly accelerated and perfected by what our ancestors of the time regarded as a most bitter misfortune, and one to be repaired at the earliest opportunity. But we have not now to speak of the general results of that great forfeiture. The one result which concerns our present purpose, is the gradual restoration to its proper honour and currency of the English language; the reinstatement in its due position of the English mind. Of all the barbarian peoples which demolished the Roman Empire, the one that settled in this country was the first to bring its native language into a state of literary culture; the earliest vernacular Teutonic Christian poet was Caedmon, an Englishman; the first prince who cultivated a so-called barbarian language, and fostered a vernacular literature, was our Alfred. But those bright promises of the seventh and following centuries were not doomed to be fulfilled. A certain blight, partly, it would seem, engendered at home, partly brought on by external causes, fell upon the land. At the time of the Norman Conquest the intellectual life of the English was deplorably feeble, but it was not extinct. During the two centuries which ensued, it did not go out; but in process of time it gathered new strength. It still beat in many a monastery, in many a retired country district—on the banks of the Severn, in the Cloisters of Peterborough. Norman-French was the language of the Court and all who held on to the skirts of the Court; in all high and mighty circles Norman-French literature was all popular; there the songs of Provence and the infant epics of the *Langue d'oui*, were ever on the lip or in the ear; but beyond the courtly precincts the people clung to the language of their forefathers; they sang their old songs as in the old days ere William landed—songs of Alfred, of Athelstane, of Guy, of Havelok, and many another old English hero: songs not preserved to us in their native form, but whose faint echoes whoso will may hear, as he pores over the pages of William of Malmesbury and other Latin Chronicle writers; in a word, they adhered steadfastly, with a tenacity said to be characteristic, to the tongue and the traditions of their race. In the course of years these persistent natives grew bolder; they even ventured to apply their language to satirical uses; one of the earliest English lyrics written after the Norman Conquest now extant, is a song written evidently by a partisan of Simon De Montfort in derision of the king and his brother and his son, whom that great earl had recently defeated at Lewes. But we cannot now relate in detail how the English language, so long dethroned, so to say, and driven into banishment, at last returned from exile and regained its old dominion. That long period of its suppression had produced many changes in it; it had altered its accent in many respects; it had profoundly modified its word-forms; it had widely extended its vocabulary. In fact, that period of suppression ended not so much in the total overthrow and ejection of the suppressor, as in a certain reconciliation with him—in a certain acknowledgment and confession of his claims and prerogatives: it ended as the struggle of the races who spoke the two contending languages ended—in a sort of fusion, the English tongue predominant and supreme.

Towards the close, probably, of that memorable thirteenth

century, the Norman-French Romances began to be translated into English.   A large society, to which the Norman-
French was but dimly intelligible, had by that time grown
into sufficient importance to call for attention from the
intellectual-food purveyors of the age.   It, too, had its thirsts
that from the soul did rise.   For it the one favourite literary
form of the Early Middle Ages was now adapted; the
already current Norman-French romances were Englished.
And now at last came the day of what are called Early
English Metrical Romances.

The greatest prosperity of these English Romances—their
most sovereign popularity and acceptance—belongs to the
reigns of Edward the Second and his famous son.   It synchronises therefore with the brightest age of Chivalry in
England.   It synchronises also with the later years of Dante
and the lives of Petrarch and Boccaccio; in Italy a fuller,
maturer literature was arising (in light, presently to shine
stronger, reflected from the old classical world) when the
Romance was reaching its greatest glory in England.

In the fourteenth century, then, these Romances were the
great reading, or rather hearing, of English men.   They reflected in some sort the life of the time, and the life of the
time delighted to observe its image mirrored in them.   They
formed a great part of such libraries as there then were, they
were recited or sung at all great festivals—as, for example,
at the banquets that concluded jousts and tournaments;
they inflamed the courage of campaigning knights; they
occupied the minds and the fingers of the fair ladies who sat at
home, and worked in tapestry the stories narrated by them.

They were for the most part translations from the Norman
French.   *King Horn* is not so, for a comparison of it with
the French poem celebrating that hero seems to show that
the French poem was translated from it, and not it from the

French poem. *King Havelok* is certainly, Sir Fred. Madden thinks, an original English work. With regard to those—the great majority, as we have said—which were undoubtedly rendered into English from the French, let it be noted that the legends on which they were founded were by no means always of Norman-French origin. Sir Guy and Sir Bevis were certainly not so. These were indigenous English heroes, whom the Norman-French *Trouvère* adopted for his themes. Very possibly many of the *Trouvères* were of English blood, and so had treasured in their memories many an old English tale. It is certain that very many of them belonged to the Anglo-Norman Court, and produced their works on English soil. Very many of the Norman-French Romances therefore were anything but foreign productions. They were bone of our bone, and flesh of our flesh, albeit they were costumed in no native fashion. The English people would recognise in them, so soon as the dress of them was altered and they could be perused, the children of their own national or ancestral imagination.

England, then, in the fourteenth century, abounded in Romances in the English tongue. No doubt Romances in Norman-French would still find an audience in a certain rank; but with the country at large the vernacular versions found general and increasing favour. Arthur and all his knights were sung of from one end of the land to the other in the native English tongue, and so were the other multifarious Romance heroes—heroes drawn from all the four winds—Alexander, Robert of Sicily, Perceval of Galles, The Soudan of Babylon, Eglamour of Artois, Richard Cœur de Lion, Roland, and many another. We have not time now to explain how such various personages came to be enlisted in one and the same service. It must suffice to say that the medieval minstrels were eminently catholic in their selection of heroes; they were quite devoid of all historical sense of the difference between one age and another; they could not conceive of an age without the crown of knighthood: therefore all famous men that were or ever had been were regarded as knights. One old poet, without any profanity in his soul, we may be sure, describes Pilate as a knight, and speaks of his jousting with Jesus.

Having thus briefly shown under what circumstances, at what time, and with what origin our old Romances first made their appearance, we propose now attempting a slight sketch of what popularity they enjoyed subsequently to the middle of the fourteenth century, when their popularity was supreme. What we wish especially, however shortly, to observe, is the influence they have had upon our literature, from Chaucer's time downwards to Tennyson.

Chaucer, born probably about 1340, grew up at a time, when, as we have seen, the English Romances of chivalry were in their prime—when they formed the main part of the *répertoire* of every minstrel—when they constituted the chief intellectual diet of Squire, and Knight, and Lady. His youthful ears must have been extremely familiar with them in all their tenderness, their prolixity, their extravagance, their simplicity and their ignorance. He has left us amongst his Canterbury Tales, as we shall see, an unmistakable evidence of this familiarity. Chaucer's contemporary, Gower, tells us how—

> Mine ear with a good pitance
> Is fed of reading of romance
> Of Idoyne and of Amadas,
> That whilome were in case;
> And eke of others many a score
> That loved long ere I was bore.

But it is unnecessary to collect instances of this sort. We will now turn to that evidence of his close acquaintance with the chivalrous Romances which Chaucer exhibits, because that evidence, while it shows how widely well known the Romances were, shows also that a term was threatened to their popularity.

We all remember how, as the pilgrims are riding towards Canterbury and telling their tales under the direction of mine host of the Tabard, the poet himself is called to the front and ordered to take his turn.

Then he begins with a piece which is in fact a most cunning and accurate parody of a Romance of Chivalry. As has been remarked by an editor of Chaucer, 'Sir Thopas appears to be the *beau idéal* of an knight; he does everything which a knight should do according to the most approved plan. Even the forest through which he rides is a "model" forest, in which the most incongruous species of birds sport and sing; and nutmegs, cloves, and cinnamon grow spontaneously. The knight himself, as in duty bound, falls on "love-longing," but no earthly beauty being worthy of him, he must love an "elf-queen." Then comes the meeting with the giant, the challenge, the arming of the knight, which is described, even to his putting on of his shirt and breeches, all conducted, according to rule, to the sound of music and the recitation of "Romances that ben reales." His disdain, after the example of Sir Percival, of the luxury of bed and his repose under the canopy of Heaven, with his helmet for a pillow, and water from the well for his drink, while his horse feeds beside him "on herbes fine," are all indispensable to his character.' The piece is written in a favourite Romance metre—in the metre which, with certain modifications, Sir Walter Scott employed in his *Marmion*. Not only are its metre and its incidents pure mimicry, but also its style and language. It opens in the most orthodox manner:

> Listen, lordings, in good intent
> And I will tellè verament
> Of mirthè and solace;
> All of a knight was fair and gent
> In battle and in tournament;
> His name was Sir Thopas.

The following passage is important to us as mentioning some at least of the most popular poems of the day:

> Men speaken of Romauns of price
> Of Horn Child and of Ypotis,
> Of Bevis and Sir Guy,
> Of Sir Libeaux and Pleindamour?
> But Sir Thopas beareth the flour
> Of real chivalry.

Then the story of Sir Thopas is resumed until mine host's patience is completely exhausted:

> No more of this, for Goddes dignity!

And the poet, thus peremptorily rebuked, proceeds to narrate in prose *The Tale of Melibeus*.

Chaucer thus laughed at the old Romances in which, as we have seen, his century abounded, and laughed at them on the strength of no imperfect knowledge. Already the idea of something weightier and more dignified in form, more finished and artistic in spirit, had presented itself to his mind, and found a welcome there. The two great foreign literatures of his time were those of France and of Italy. In the France of his day, the age of chivalrous Romances was going or gone by. Norman France had wearied of its old loves. Their great era in that country was as has been stated, the thirteenth century. A new style of literature had in part at least superseded them in the fourteenth. By far the most famous poem produced in

France in the fourteenth century was the *Roman de la Rose*—an allegorical, satirical, didactic work. This poem[1] Chaucer translated into English. He was therefore intimately acquainted with the French taste of his time, and there can be little doubt was greatly influenced by it, especially in his earlier manhood. In his later years, he was still more profoundly influenced by the literature of Italy—the first great literature of modern Europe. Dante's supreme work was written, or begun to be written, probably some two score years before Chaucer was born; Petrarch and Boccaccio were respectively some thirty-five years and twenty-five years Chaucer's seniors. It is most probable that our poet was personally acquainted with the former at least. He was dispatched to Italy on a diplomatic mission, and, even if there were no evidence on the matter, we might be fairly sure he would seek to see his great fellow-genius. But whether there was any personal friendship or not between him and Petrarch, it is certain, from testimony furnished by his works, that he had acquired an intimate knowledge of the great new-born Italian literature. He refers several times to Dante, and imitates him; he refers to, and quotes from, Petrarch; he translates, after his own fashion, whole works of Boccaccio. In Italy the traditions of the old classical period had never wholly expired; the light of the Augustan age had never utterly died out; the memory of Vergil had never been totally obliterated. During the centuries when chivalrous Romances flourished, as we have seen, in France and in England, when they flourished vigorously in Suabia, even so late as their flourishing in Spain, they found little encouragement in Italy. The long-lived pervading influence of Rome had checked the growth and

---

[1] It is doubted, with good reason, whether the extant version is all of it Chaucer's work.

blossoming of the legends which the barbarians who crossed the Alps carried with them, no less than those who had passed over the Pyrenees, the Rhine, the Northern Sea. Moreover, Italy for certain reasons was less affected by the Crusades than any other country of Western Europe, except perhaps Spain, which had a crusade to carry on at home. The influence of the Troubadours upon Northern Italy was no doubt considerable; by them, beyond controversy, all its three great writers of the fourteenth century were deeply impressed; but, at least in the times of which we now speak, the works of the *Trouvères* had gained but feeble hold upon Italy. The land of Vergil cared very little for what Chaucer makes the host call their 'doggerel rimes.' It aspired after poetical forms less slight and flimsy. Eventually it adopted for its material legends of the Carlovingian Cycle; but to the end it rejected the form in which they circulated in their native country. With Italy's fine scorn for the light measures of the Romancers, Chaucer was penetrated. The striking contrast between his earlier and later works may be accounted for by considering the impressions of this Italian influence upon him. In fact, he heard in Italy the first sounds of that Revival of Ancient Learning and Literature, which no long time after his death changed the face of Europe. And we have dwelt so long on this Italian influence, and its power over Chaucer, because it was in reality but the prelude of an influence which eventually proved fatal to the popularity of the Romances of Chivalry. Already then, towards the close of the fourteenth century, the breath of ridicule had been breathed on the simple nursery epics, which the Early Middle Ages had produced. And yet they were not to be utterly laughed down for many a long day. They were to undergo many metamorphoses, but in some sort they were to live on for many a century.

The spirit of chivalry died hard ; not less easily passed away the works embodying that spirit.

We ought, perhaps, just to mention here two species of the Chivalrous Romance which appeared in the fourteenth century. These are what are called by Warton, in his History of English Poetry, the Historical and the Heraldic Romance. In the one, historical events of the day, or of a day only just set, are treated in the Romance style. Perhaps the poem written by the North British Poet Barbour, in honour of Bruce, is the greatest work of this kind. How easy the transition from History to Romance, anyone may see who reads *Froissart's Chronicles.* At an earlier period such a work would have provided material for a host of Romance-writers. The Black Prince is just such an one as the soul of the old Romancer would have loved. The other species of Romance named above, the Heraldic, pays special attention to the description of coats of armour, costume, precedence, and other such matters as the fashion of its day conceived to be of interest.

One more remark must be made before we quit the fourteenth century—the culminating century of the Middle Ages. We must point out how, side by side with the Chivalrous Romances, there was growing up a sort of rude Popular Romance. *Knighthood* was the grand subject of the former, *Yeomanry* of the latter. The yeomen, too, would have their ideal hero, and their cycle of songs about him. Their hero —the common people's Arthur—was ROBIN HOOD, the famous archer. The poetic form in which his cycle is composed, is yet slighter and more careless than that in which his courtly prototype is celebrated. There is another people's hero whom it is right to mention here. This is PIERS THE PLOUGHMAN, the hero of the more serious and earnest among the common people. One of the most powerful poems the Middle Ages have bequeathed to us is devoted to his celebration. His name was well known amongst the leaders of the great popular movement which broke out in the reign of Richard the Second. When the lower classes of this country were learning to work out for themselves their political salvation, when they were awaking to the necessity of self-reliance, and daring to make conditions with their masters, the picture of Piers the Ploughman presented to them in Langland's poem of the Ploughman able to guide into the way of truth, when all the professional guides proved miserably at fault, must have been eminently suggestive. The number of early MS. copies of that poem is very great; and it is noticed of them for the most part that they are executed on inferior material, as if for the use of no wealthy readers. Other poems appeared subsequently, with this same Ploughman as their centre and hero.

And now we come to that century in whose process the Middle Ages ended and modern times began. It was a century, not of great literary production, but rather of preparation, both here and in the kingdoms of the Continent. For the Chivalrous Romances, they were still generally popular throughout it, though less so at the end than at the beginning. The popular rival of the Romance—the ballad—was gradually encroaching on their monopoly. However, Romances were still written, still adapted from the French. But the times were rapidly changing; earthquake was following earthquake; pictures of life which had once some truth in them were now becoming false—false in fact, false in sentiment. The society of which the romances of chivalry were once to some extent the reflections, was breaking up. The old order was giving place to a new; the literature peculiar to it was losing all its force and meaning. Chivalry was decaying, with all its glories, with all its vanities, with all its fantasies.

> Ah ! my Lord Arthur, whither shall I go?
> Where shall I hide my forehead and my eyes?
> For now I see the true old times are dead,
> When every morning brought a noble chance,
> And every chance brought out a noble knight.
> Such times have been not since the light that led
> The holy elders with the gift of myrrh.
> But now the whole Round Table is dissolved,
> Which was an image of the mighty world ;
> And I, the last, go forth companionless,
> And the days darken round me, and the years
> Among new men, strange faces, other minds.

Caxton exclaimed, when he saw the customs of chivalry falling into desuetude and oblivion :

Oh, ye knights of England, where is the custom and usage of noble chivalry that was used in those days? What do ye now but go to the baynes and play at dice? And some, not well advised, use not honest and good rule, against all order of knighthood. Leave this, leave it ! and read the noble volumes of St Graal, of Lancelot, of Galaad, of Trystram, of Perse Forest, of Percyval, of Gawayn, and many more ; there shall ye see manhood, courtesy and gentleness. And look in latter days of the noble acts sith the Conquest, as in King Richard days Cœur de Lion, Edward I. and III., and his noble sons, Sir Robert Knolles, Sir John Hawkwode, Sir John Chandos, and Sir Gueltiare Marny. Read Froissart ; and also behold that victorious and noble King Harry V. and the captains under him, his noble brethren the Earls of Salisbury, Montagu, and many other whose names shine gloriously by their virtuous noblesse and acts that they did in the order of chivalry. Alas, what do ye but sleep and take ease, and are all disordered from chivalry?

But these, and such clamours to recall a departing era, profited nothing. There is no staying the wheels of time. And he who uttered these laments and adjurations was himself, however unconsciously, more than any other

Englishman of his time, expediting the change he so zealously deplored. The old Romances of Chivalry received a fatal blow from the printing-press—a blow which could not be healed by any appeals to men's better feelings, or any printed editions of the old works. Then that revival of learning, whose early prognostics we observed in Italy in Petrarch's time, which duly reached its full development in the fifteenth and sixteenth centuries, was by no means favourable to this artless literature. There were other events equally hostile to it. Probably no fresh Romances were written after the reign of Henry VI.

But the old Romances were re-written. No other general literature had yet arisen to take their place. The day, whose breaking Chaucer had seemed to herald, had not yet fully dawned. Towards the close of the fifteenth century, and in the earlier course of the sixteenth, the Romances of Chivalry were reproduced in prose. Numerous prose versions issued from the printing-presses of France in the reign of Charles VIII. and his immediate successors. In England, in the year 1485, there came from Caxton's press that most memorable work, the *Histories of King Arthur*, commonly known as the *Morte d'Arthur*—a comprehensive digest of the Arthurian Cycle—a work which, from the year of its appearance, has never, except, perhaps, for some years of the last century, wholly lost its popularity : a work most familiar to Spenser, to Milton, and to certain great poetical spirits of our fathers' and our own times. Caxton's successor, Wynkyn de Worde, twice reprinted this famous compilation, in 1498 and in 1529. Three other editions appeared in the sixteenth century, one from the press of Copeland in 1557, two from that of East. A seventh edition appeared in 1634. Some six or seven editions have come out in this century. 'After that I had accomplished and finished divers histories,' says Caxton in his Prologue to his edition, which, as we have said, was published in 1485, the year of the Battle of Bosworth,

as well of contemplation as of other historical and worldly acts of great conquerors and princes, and also certain books of ensamples and doctrine, many noble and divers gentlemen of this realm of England came and demanded me many and ofttimes, wherefore that I have not had made and emprinted the noble history of the Saint Graal, and of the most renowned Christian King, first and chief of the three best Christian and worthy, King Arthur, which ought most to be remembered among us Englishmen before all other Christian kings.

(The other two chief and worthy kings are Charlemagne and Godfrey of Boulogne.) The printer did not consent to the urging of these divers and noble gentlemen, till they had given him what he thought convincing proofs that Arthur was no fable, but a real, historical personage. Then 'after the simple cunning that God had sent to him, under the favour of all noble lords and gentlemen,' he 'emprised to imprint a book of the noble histories of the said King Arthur and of certain of his knights, after a copy unto me delivered, which copy Sir Thomas Malory did take out of certain books of French and reduced it into English.' Malory's version, as we learn from the conclusion of it, was finished in 1469 or early in the following year. But the French works which mainly formed its basis were composed in the reigns of Henry the Second and Henry the Third; so that in fact it carries us back in some sense to the twelfth century, and as the French works were themselves but the transcripts of yet older legends, to yet earlier centuries. We say in 'some sense,' because much of the spirit which actuates Malory's work certainly belongs to the close and not to the opening years of the Middle Ages. The spirit is of the sunset, not of the sunrise: it is that of a requiem, not of a nativity hymn. It looks back with tender, wistful, regretting eyes on days bygone for ever—not forward with any gaiety of hope to what may be coming, or around it with any exultant pride at what is present. The times portrayed in this work were dead, the picture given of them is, as might be expected, softened and idealised. Those times were now to be used to point a moral. Caxton, in another passage of that Prologue from which we have given an extract above, speaks of Malory's account of them in very much the same tone as that in which Spenser thought of it, and reproduced it. Roger Ascham, who died some fifteen years after Spenser was born, perused the work with cold, unfascinated eyes, in a very different fashion from Spenser. Being a man deeply versed in the new learning, he had but little sympathy with such un-lettered productions,—'which, as some say,' to quote his own words, 'were made in monasteries by idle monks or wanton Chanons;' he recognised nothing in the *Morte d'Arthur* but licentiousness and slaughter.

This is good stuff (he exclaims with bitter irony) for wise men to laugh at or honest men to take pleasure at. Yet I know when God's Bible was banished the Court, and *Morte Arthure* received into the Prince's chamber. What toys the daily reading of such a book may work in the will of a young gentleman or a young maid that liveth wealthily and idly, wise men can judge, and honest men do pity.

Not less bitterly does he inveigh against them in the preface of his *Toxophilus*, addressed to all the gentlemen and yeomen of England. But it may be Ascham is blinded by his own conceit, when he talks after this manner. No pure soul was ever tainted by the reading of the *Morte d'Arthur*. Whatever the incidents of the book, the moral tone is high and reproachless; in this respect the unreality of the book gives security. But it is saying enough, and infinitely more than enough, for the defence of the *Morte d'Arthur*, that it was a favourite work with Spenser and with Milton.

Spenser derived his materials for his great poem mainly from this great quarry, though he was acquainted also with what other Romances of Chivalry were current in his days—with Bevis of Hampton and others. The Arthurian Cycle, as preserved there, was to him what the Carlovingian Cycle was to Ariosto, what that of Amadis to Cervantes. It might be interesting to consider and contrast the different treatments of the Chivalrous Romances by these three great masters. The Italian adopts them for their story's sake, and deals with them accordingly; whatever moral professions he may make, he has no ulterior purpose at heart. The realistic Cervantes is struck by their want of truthfulness to nature—by the great gulf that divides them from actual life; he laughs them to scorn, not without occasional twinges of remorse, and almost involuntary admissions of certain charms still clinging to their faded forms. Lastly our Spenser, a poet of no dramatic nature, and not alienated from them, but perhaps rather drawn towards them, by that very unreality which provoked the genial laughter of the Spaniard—our Spenser recognised in them a most apt vehicle for those lofty ethical lessons which he made it his high business to diffuse. That taste for allegory which was dominant in the crowning century of the Middle Ages, had not died out in Spenser's time. It had been cultivated continuously; it had imbued the productions of our rising drama; it powerfully affected Spenser. In his hands the Arthurian court became but a grand allegory. The stout old knights-errant were refined into mere qualities; they became mere moral spectres, virtuous shadows, exemplary ideas.

Before we leave the sixteenth century, we must mention that though all through it the prose translations of the old

Romances were gradually surpassing the poetic versions in popularity, yet the poetic versions were not yet forgotten. Many of them were printed by the successors of Caxton. Very many of them were abridged, to suit the taste of the day. The Romances of the fourteenth and fifteenth centuries were contracted into ballads in the latter half of the sixteenth, and in this shape enjoyed a most extensive circulation. How well they were known is very clearly shown by the dramatists ; allusions and quotations abound in their plays. We can all recall to mind the 'When Arthur first in Court began,' 'Child Roland to the dark tower came,' and other scraps of the balladry of the time in Shakespeare. These popular abridgments were sung up and down the country by the minstrel, and by his successor the ballad-singer. One Richard Sheal is sometimes called the last of the minstrels ; and certainly, if an extant original piece of his may be taken as a specimen of the style and talents of the fraternity, he altogether deserved to be the last. Gentlemen of his profession became more and more superfluous as ability to read became a more common virtue.

We come now to the seventeenth century. Milton, in his earlier years, when looking round for a worthy subject for the great poem which it was the darling purpose of his life to compose, for whose composition he unweariedly prepared and matured himself through many years, turned his regard first to that same great Arthurian legend that had so deeply charmed the soul of his great master, 'our sage and serious Poet Spenser,' as he calls him, whom he dared be known to think a ' better teacher than Scotus and Aquinas.' In two of his Latin poems, written in or about 1639, he announces fully the theme that then attracted him. Elsewhere, sketching his early life, in answer to the audacious slanders of an unscrupulous enemy, he tells whither 'his young feet wandered.   I betook me,' he writes, 'among those lofty fables and romances which recount in solemn cantos the deeds of knighthood founded by our victorious kings, and from hence had in renown all over Christendom.'   In *Il Penseroso* he refers to Chaucer's Squire's tale with evident admiration—a tale left half-told by Chaucer, but completed, it is to be noted, by Spenser—and would have called up for himself and resung other poetry also of that strain,

> If aught else great bards beside
> In sage and solemn tunes have sung,
> Of turneys and of trophies hung ;
> Of forests and enchantments drear,
> When more is meant than meets the ear.

The great epic poem was at last composed with a far different subject than that originally proposed by its author ; the fascination of the old Romances was in part dispelled ; Milton made his final election truthfully to his own nature and his own moral and spiritual environment.   Yet we can see what knowledge he had gathered, what pictures his imagination had conceived of the old days of chivalry, when he speaks of

> What resounds
> In fable or romance of Uther's son,
> Begirt with British and Armoric knights ;

or when he compares the hall of Pandemonium to

> A covered field where champions bold
> Wont ride in arm'd and at the Soldan's chair
> Defied the best of Panim chivalry
> To mortal combat or career with lance.

Dryden's earlier plays are, in a word, as Scott describes them, dramatised metrical Romances.   The Romances most popular in his day, and, indeed, for some time before were of Spanish origin, belonging to the cycle of Amadis de Gaul, which, though primarily in all probability of Portuguese extraction, had been abundantly cultivated and expanded in Spain. There is a highly amusing evidence of the favour enjoyed by the knightly fictions of the Peninsula in a play by Beaumont and Fletcher, called *The Knight of the Burning Pestle*. There a young grocer called Ralph appears perusing *Palmerin of England* (it should have been *Palmerin d'Oliva*, for from it, not *Palmerin of England*, the passages quoted come), and presently, to the intense delight of an old grocer and his wife, determines to turn grocer-errant. 'What brave spirit,' exclaims the high-minded youth, 'could be content to sit in his shop with a flappet of wood and a blue apron before him, selling mithridatum, that might pursue feats of arms, and through his noble achievements procure such a famous history to be written of his heroic prowess?' So he furnishes himself with a pair of squires in the shape of two apprentices, and sets forth. He gets into some difficulty about his hotel bills; for the times were unenthusiastic, and innkeepers objected to knights-errant that did not pay their way; but he manages to perform some great exploits.

> George (says the old grocer's wife), let Ralph travel over great hills, and let him be very weary, and come to the King of Cracovia's house covered with velvet, and there let the king's daughter stand in her window all in beaten gold, combing her golden locks with a comb of ivory; and let her spy Ralph and fall in love with him, and come down to him and carry him into her father's house, and then let Ralph talk with her!

This play may suggest, perhaps, a suspicion of what, in fact, befell the Romances of Chivalry both in their metrical and their prose shapes. They were abandoned by the better educated classes to the admiration of the common people. They fell from the high estate they had held in the world of letters; they were banished from the fine society which had once so eagerly countenanced and caressed them; they found a welcome with less well-lettered, simpler folk. It is certain that the air in which the author of the *Pilgrim's Progress* grew up was resonant with the songs and stories of Romance. Ballad singers were going to and fro about the country, furnished no doubt with songs of an immediate political import—for ballads in those days did in some sort the work which newspaper articles do now—but furnished also with many a rhymed legend of the olden time, to which unlearned crowds listened with rapt ears. Bunyan may have made one of many such a crowd in various parts of the country visited by him with the itinerant tinker his father, and with half unconscious delight ·heard old ditties which were to bear fruit in him passing wonderful. Moreover, these same old pieces—these fragments of a decaying literature—were circulating in Bunyan's time in the form of cheap books. His immortal allegory is, like the *Faerie Queene*, but a spiritual romance; it overflows in the same incidents, adventures, enterprises that compose the medieval tales, curiously interwoven with the life-scenery of the Commonwealth and the Restoration.

Not again did the seeds of Romance, sown by the wayside, fall into such soil as the mind of Bunyan.

We can now, when our space is so nearly exhausted, only just remind our readers of the once famous popular Heroic Romances, and of the famous Comic Romances which were born of the old Romances of Chivalry, whose history we have been cursorily reviewing. The old prose Romance, interwedded with what was called the Pastoral Romance—a form of literature in part originated in the Middle Ages, in the main imitated from certain late Greek productions—reappeared in the form of such works as Montemayor's *Diana*, and Sydney's *Arcadia*. From these works the heroic romance was directly descended. We suppose no living person has indulged himself in the complete perusal of the twelve volumes of *Cléopatre* or of *Pharamond;* the ten of *Clélie;* the 'twelve huge' ones of the *Grand Cyrus*. Yet these were the favourite reading of ladies and gentleman for near a hundred years—from about the middle of the seventeenth to that of the eighteenth century. Their leading characteristics are defined, by one who in her day, as she says, 'drudged through them,' and was 'still alive,' to be unnatural representations of the passions, false sentiments, false precepts, false honour, and false modesty, with a strange heap of improbable, unnatural incidents, mixed up with true history, and fastened upon some of the great names of antiquity. In a word, there was but slight connection between them and life: they were rife with affectations; they were dyed deep with a sort of mental euphuism. Molière laughed at them; Boileau exposed and derided them. Not being founded on the rock of truth to nature, they soon showed signs of decay, soon tottered and fell. Their downfall was completed in the year 1740 by the outcoming of a book called *Pamela*—a book written with no lofty design of overthrowing the literary dynasty then in power and founding a new one; and yet these were the remarkable feats it achieved. From that day the novel dethroned the Heroic Romance.

As for the Comic Romance, that naturally enough sprung up by the side of the Serious one. The preposterous unreality of the Chivalrous Romances, especially when the lives of the old poems were prolonged into an age for which they were not born—into an age that had little and decreasing sympathy with the sentiments out of which they had arisen —soon awakened laughter. We have seen how Chaucer, who lived near the time of their greatest prosperity, himself parodied them, though his contemporaries, perhaps, sympathised little with his ridicule. No wonder if in later ages, Rabelais, Cervantes, Scarron, all laughed them to scorn. Still less wonder if other writers thought it no profanity to use the form and machinery of them for their own purposes, as eminently Butler used them—with much derision, by the way—when he sketched the famous knight Sir Hudibras, in that memorable mock-romance called, with all propriety, after its hero. The arguments of that work are merely perverted inventories, so to say, of the contents of many an old Romance of Chivalry.

To return, for one last moment, to the Chivalrous Romances themselves. We have now traced their career from the time of their rise and their glory to the age of their decay and obscurity; from the time when kings' palaces and baronial halls resounded with them, to that when they found favour only with the simplest and rudest classes of society; from the time when they were sung by the medieval minstrel, in all his pride and splendour, to the gayest audiences, to when, in marred, mutilated form, they were trolled forth by the vagrant balladmonger to the humblest crowds in the bye-lanes and among the hedges of the country. In the last century there arose generations that knew not King Arthur and his Knights. The Romances of Chivalry sank into deep neglect. To be brief, out of this obscurity they were brought once more into the light by the vital change of literary taste and feeling which inevitably accompanied the tremendous political revolutions in the midst of which the eighteenth century closed. About the beginning of this present century Europe began to recall the 'Old Romances sung beside her in her youth.' The long forgotten old poems were in some sort brought back into the knowledge of men by one who, in a word, as a poet, aspired to be a ninteenth-century *Trouvère*. Scott was the first minstrel, to use the word as he uses it, of a modern school of Romance. He not only wrote himself pieces in imitation of the old style, but he put within reach genuine pieces of the old literature. Since his time both the form and the subjects of the ancient Romances have been repeatedly set before us by Coleridge, Leigh Hunt, Byron, Tennyson, Morris, and many others,— sometimes with the spirit also, but often in a purely modern fashion.

And now this rapid historical survey must be concluded ; nor is there time now to speak of the character of this old literature. We think it could easily have been shown that it possesses certain intrinsic merits besides those extrinsic ones which it has been my present object to consider ; that amidst many weaknesses, such as must be looked for in a poetry that was mainly oral, many exuberances, many rusti-cities, it could yet show for itself many graces such as can never cease to be winning ; that there is a certain tenderness and pathos in the voice of it such as cannot but still move the heart of him who hears it crying in the far-away wilder-nesses of past time. Ancient years live again for us, as we listen to this voice ; the faces of old centuries look up blooming and bright. But of such power in the old Chival-rous Romances we may not now speak. It is perhaps a sufficing testimony for them that they thus have won the ear of successive generations of great men. Thus in a high sense has been fulfilled the prophecy contained in the line on the famous tombstone said to have been exhumed at Glastonbury :—

> Hic jacet Arturus, rex olim, rexque futurus.
> Here Arthur lies, King once, and King to be

II

THE LAY OF HAVELOK THE DANE

(From *The Athenæum* for February 23, 1889)

AS it is impossible that the histories of our language and literature, or of any language and literature, can be accurately written until the dates of the extant specimens are satisfactorily settled, I trust I may without apology proceed to make some suggestions as to the date of *Havelok the Dane.* Sir Fred. Madden assigns it to the year 1280 or thereabouts; and Prof. Skeat in his valuable reissue of Sir Frederick's excellent edition is content to follow so good an authority. But I venture to think that there are several things in this romance that point to a later year—to a year certainly not earlier than 1296, and possibly as late as 1300.

Perhaps the most decisive of these arguments is the curious mentions of Roxburgh that occur. When Athelwold feels that his death is at hand, and is eager to make some arrangement for the safety of his young daughter, we are told that he

> Sende writes sone onon
> After his erles euere-ich on,
> And after hise baruns riche and poure
> Fro Rokesburw al into Douere.

And further on, when Athelwold is dead and Godrich is

beginning his regency with vigour and credit, it is said that

> Justises dede he maken newe
> Al Engelond to faren þorw
> Fro Douere into Rokesborw.

Strangely enough, Sir F. Madden overlooks the importance of these mentions. But surely it is a highly pertinent question why Roxburgh should be thus named as the northern limit of Godrich's dominion. It has been suggested, as Prof. Skeat states in his *Index of Names*, that Rokesborw means Rokeby; but how could Rokeby come to be written Rokesborw, and why should Rokeby, of all places, be selected as a boundary town? There can be no doubt that Roxburgh is the place meant, and a glance at the history of the period at once makes clear why Roxburgh is mentioned in this way. From the year 1296 the name of Roxburgh became thoroughly familiar to the Southern ear, as in fact the name of King Edward's northern border fortress—the name of the limit of English rule in that part of the island. It is difficult, indeed, to imagine that any one before that year could have mentioned it along with Dover, as it is mentioned in the romance of *Havelok*. One could imagine such a phrase as from Dover to Norham, or as from Dover to Wark; in the French romance (*Le Lai d'Avelok*) Havelok's English kingdom is said to extend 'de Holande desq'en Gloucestre.' But that a place well on the further side of the English march, and one of the chief Scottish border fortresses, should be linked with Dover to denote an extremity of an English kingdom would surely be quite incomprehensible. When the Scottish troubles were beginning, and the arbitration of King Edward was invoked, one of his first requests was that certain national fortresses should be given up to him, and one of these was Roxburgh. Dr Robert Chambers in his *History of Scotland* brings out the fact that while the king held these fortresses in 1292, the Court of King's Bench sat for some time at Roxburgh. After this temporary occupation the castles were, when King Edward gave his award, restored to the Scots. When at last war broke out between the two nations, one of Edward's first acts in his first invasion of Scotland in 1296 was to seize Roxburgh: 'accessit rex castrum Rokesburgiæ quod statim redditum est ei a Senescallo Scotiæ,' says Walsingham, 'Hist. Ang.,' *s.a.* 1296. See also Harding's *Chronicle :*—

> To Ronkesburgh the kyng Edward so held
> That sone was yelde to hym without stryfe,
> Their good saufe also and theyr lyfe.

And for many years it remained in the hands of the English : indeed, with intervals, it remained in our hands till the year 1460, when, the Scotch again regaining it, it was levelled to the ground.

It was besieged vainly by Wallace in 1298; it was the English mustering place in 1303 (apud Rokesburgiam...... exercitum adunavit). So it was from the year 1296 that Roxburgh became, for a time at least, the boundary fortress of England. And assuredly not till then might such a phrase as 'from Dover to Roxburgh' be expected to suggest itself. But clearly before 1291 it can scarcely be conceived as occurring.

And several other details seem to agree with a date later than 1280.

Thus the several passages in which the suppression of robbers and the vigorous establishment of order throughout the country are so specially described must surely contain reference to the vigorous administration of him who has been called 'the greatest of the Plantagenets.' See ll. 39-43 :—

> Wreiers and wrobberes made he falle,
> And hated hem so man doth galle ;

> Vtlawes and theues made he bynde,
> Alle that he micthe fynde,
> And heye hangen on galwetre.

And ll. 266-9 :—

> Schireues he sette, bedels and greyues,
> Grith sergeans, wit longe gleyues
> To yemen wilde wodes and paþes
> Fro wicke men that wolde don scaþes.

It seems impossible not to connect these passages with the Statute of Winchester passed in 1285, and the Commissions of Trailbaston first issued in 1292. The object of the Statute of Winchester was 'to put down the lawless bands of club-men, old soldiers, outlaws, and sturdy beggars who had taken to robbing in gangs and living upon the country.' But it was ill observed till, says Lingard, 'the king issued a commission to certain knights in every shire, authorising them to enforce the provisions of the Act, and to call to their aid the posse of the sheriff as often as it might be requisite. The utility of these commissioners was soon ascertained ; they were gradually armed with more extensive powers ; and instead of conservators were at last styled justices of the peace.' See the second of the two passages quoted above for the mention of Roxburgh. The illustrations Sir F. Madden and Dr Skeat refer to *apud* Otterbourne, Guillaume de Jumièges, Dudon de Saint Quentin, and Beda are faint and feeble by the side of the exact parallel the history of Edward I.'s domestic policy provides.

Scarcely less significant is the stress which the romance-writer lays on the incorruptibility with which the law was administered. 'For hem,' *i.e.*, for trangressors, 'ne yede gold ne fe,' *i.e.*, bribes in their behalf went for nothing (for this way of speaking compare l. 1430 : 'hauede go for him gold ne fe'). Now in 1289 the king took the most energetic measures to purify the law courts. When he returned to England from the Continent in that year, 'all the judges were apprehended, and indicted for bribery. Two only were acquitted'—John of Methingham and Elias de Bockingham. Weyland, the Chief Justice of the King's Bench, Stratton, the Chief Baron of the Exchequer, Sir Ralph de Hengham, the Grand Justiciary and regent during the king's absence, and their fellow culprits were all severely punished. What point this contemporary fact would give, and gives, to the romancer's verse!

Again, observe line 2808:—

> Quot Hauelok: ' Hwan þat ye it wite,
> Nu wile ich þat ye doun site ;
> And after Godrich haues wrouht,
> þat haues in sorwe himself brouht,
> Lokes þat ye demen him rith,
> *For dom ne spared clerk ne knith.*'

Surely this last line cannot but be associated not only with the First Statute of Westminster, 1275, but with the decree and the writ of *Circumspecte agatis*, 1285. The First Statute of Westminster declares, amongst other things, that common justice shall be done without respect of persons. As to the writ of *Circumspecte agatis*, it defines the sphere of the spiritual courts. To quote Dr Stubbs, it 'recognises their right to hold pleas on matters merely spiritual, such as offences for which penance was due, tithes, mortuaries, churches and churchyards, injuries done to clerks, perjury, and defamation.' The clerk as well as the knight, says Havelok, is amenable to the common law ; there is no such immunity as the Church is perpetually striving after. And this is just what Edward I. had been insisting upon.

To take another point : when Godrich hears that Havelok is landed in England :—

> He dide sone ferd ut bidde
> þat al þat euere mouhte o stede
> Ride, or helm on heued bere, .
> Brini on bac and sheld and spere
> Or ani oþer wepne bere,
> Hand-ax, syþe, gisarm or spere
> Or aunlaz and god long knif
> þat als he louede leme or lif,
> þat þey sholden comen him to, &c.
>
> Ll. 2548-56.

Surely another note of the time is audible here in this description of the fyrd ; for the fyrd was revived by the Statute of Winchester in 1285.   'The Statute of Winchester,' says Dr Stubbs, 'carries us back to the earliest institutions of the race ; it revives and refines [*sic ;* defines ?] the action of the hundred, hue and cry, watch and ward, the fyrd and the assize of arms.'   In 1297 this statute was put in force in respect of the fyrd.   In that year there was made a military levy of the whole kingdom—exactly such a levy as Godrich appoints.

Is it likely that the following account could have been given of a Parliament before the year 1295, the year of the first complete and model Parliament of the Three Estates?

> In þat time al Hengelond
> þerl Godrich hauede in his hond,
> And he gart komen into þe tun
> Mani erl and mani barun,
> And alle [men] þat liues were
> In Eng [e]lond þanne wer þere,
> þat þey haueden after sent
> To ben þer at þe parlement.—Ll. 999-1006.

That is, this Parliament was composed of earls and barons, and men sent by the people at large ; for this is what the somewhat obscure latter lines seem to mean.   And this Parliament was held at Lincoln.   Now Edward I. held a

Parliament at Lincoln in 1301. This curious coincidence, as it is to say the least, is of course noted, as we shall see, by Sir F. Madden; but, inclining as he does to the year 1280 for the date of the romance, he attaches less importance to it than it may deserve.

I cannot but suspect that in the charming picture of matrimonial bliss the old poet draws when he describes the married life of Havelok and Goldborough, he has in his mind the famous contemporary example of a happy marriage. He is reflecting the devoted mutual attachment of his king and queen—a love whose touching memorials yet present themselves in the three Eleanor Crosses that still in some sort survive. And this description is more likely to have been written late in the eighties than early—perhaps most likely to have been written after 1290, in which year the queen died, when the king's great grief for his irreparable loss made especially evident to his people the depth of his devotion. The date of the Eleanor Crosses is 1291-4.

> So mikel loue was hem bitwene
> þat al þe werd spak of hem two.
> He louede hire, and she him so,
> þat neyþer oþe[r] mithe be
> For [fro ?] oþer, ne no ioie se
> But yf he were togidere boþe.
> Neuere yete ne weren he wroþe,
> For here loue was ay newe;
> Neuere yete wordes ne grewe
> Bitwene hem, hwarof ne lathe
> Mithe rise, ne no wrathe.—Ll. 2967-77.

A nation is fortunate that can find its domestic ideal realised on the throne; and that good fortune was England's in the times of King Edward and Queen Eleanor, as recently in our own.

I think it will be allowed that if we put all these things

together—they might be further enforced and reinforced if space permitted—we have good reason for placing the composition of ' Havelok ' nearer to the year 1300 than the year 1280. On some of them, if they stood quite alone, I would not insist ; but, taken altogether, they form a powerful argument in favour of the later date. The Roxburgh inference is strong enough to stand alone. It appears almost certain that those mentions could not have been made before 1296.

It is important to observe that the passages to which attention has been called belong specially to the English version of the Romance. There is no trace of them in *Le Lai d'Avelok*, nor in Gaimar's abridgment of the 'Lay.' Of course, as both these French versions belong to the first half of the twelfth century, any trace of the suggested allusions there would at once disprove their Edwardian connexion. In fact, the passages to which attention is here called are the significant additions or variations of the English paraphrast, or, as the English version is so largely independent of the previous ones, we may rather say the English composer.

Sir Frederick Madden—in one, at least, of his notes—is not unwilling to entertain the idea of a later date than that he adopts. 'If,' he writes, commenting on l. 2521, 'the connexion between this foundation [which he describes as "the Augustine Friary of Black Monks," founded at Whitby in 1280] and the one recorded in the poem ["of monckes blake a priorie"] be considered valid, the date of the composition must be referred to rather a later period than we wish to admit.' But elsewhere he remarks : 'If we could suppose that the author of the romance alluded to this very Parliament [that of Lincoln, "1303"; he should say 1301], it would reduce the period of the poem's composition to a later date than either the style or the writing of the MS. will possibly admit of.   It is, therefore, far more probable the writer here makes use of a poetical and very pardonable licence in transferring the Parliament to the chief city of the county in which he was evidently born or brought up, without any reference whatever to historical data.'   So Sir Frederick relies upon the style and the writing. Now, is our knowledge of palæography so precise and exact that any one could positively assert of any special document that it belongs certainly to 1280 rather than 1300?   And if palæographic science has attained such excellence—perhaps it has; I speak with the utmost humility on the matter— then do our present authorities in this line ratify Sir Frederick's statement?   Are they prepared to maintain that the Bodleian MS. that concerns us cannot have been written later than 1280?   If they are, then there remains an argument for 1280 that cannot be ignored.   But as to Sir Frederick's argument from 'style,' I must venture to think that our knowledge of Middle English even now—it has made great advances since 1828, when Sir Frederick's edition of 'Havelok' appeared—is not such as to justify any such confident insistence on any special year, or the imme- diate neighbourhood of any special year—on the year 1280 or thereabouts rather than the year 1300 or thereabouts.   I doubt whether any of our chief living scholars would be so daring.   The fact is that the difficulties of the subject are more fully realised than they were sixty years ago; the com- plexity and perplexity of such questions are better under- stood.   An increase of knowledge often, at first at least, makes positiveness impossible.   And the time has not yet come when English scholarship can say the last word as to the date of any medieval composition, when there is nothing but 'style' on which to base a conclusion. ·

I will just add that the English romance is quoted in

1303 by Robert of Brunne (see Skeat's *Spec. of Eng.*, part
ii. p. 301, ed. 1884).   The first certain reference to it noted
by Sir F. Madden belongs to the year 1310.   It is made by
Meistre Rauf de Bonn in his chronicle called *Le Bruit
Dengleterre*, or otherwise *Le Petit Bruit*.

III

EGER AND GRIME [1]

(From the printed Edition of *Bishop Percy's Folio MS.*)

OF this once popular, and deservedly popular romance, there are two copies known—the following one of the Folio, now printed from the Folio for the first time; and a copy printed at Aberdeen in 1711,[2] of which an abstract is given by Mr Ellis in his *Specimens of Early English Metrical Romances*, and a reprint, by Mr Laing, in his *Early Metrical Tales*, in 1826. The latter copy is evidently a much diluted version of the old romance. 'The printer,' says Mr Ellis, 'has evidently followed a very imperfect MS., with which also he seems to have taken great liberties; and the story, as it now stands, is so obscurely told, that the catastrophe is quite unintelligible, and has been in the present abstract supplied by conjecture.'

The diffuseness of the said copy may be appreciated when we state that it consists of 2860 lines, of which 2782 contain the story given in the Folio in 1473 lines, in little more

---

[1] This Old Piece is not much Inferior to one of Ariosto's Gates.—P.

[2] Mr Laing kindly informs us that he possesses an edition twenty-four years earlier than this one. 'It was a bequest,' he writes, 'by my old friend Charles Kirkpatrick Sharpe, Esq., and has this title: " *The History of Sir Eger, Sir Grahame, and Sir Gray-Steel.* Printed in the year 1687.' It is a little 18mo, pp. 72, black letter, without either the place of printing or printer's name.

than half the space. The last 60 furnish a feeble continuation of the original story. Sir Graham (so Sir Grime is called there) dies; Sir Eger's bride discovers the trick that has been played upon her, and betakes herself to a religious life. Sir Eger fights in Holy Land. Returning, and finding his affronted wife dead, he marries Sir Graham's widow. 'This romance,' says Mr Ellis, 'is by no means deficient in merit; but I do not know of its existence in a perfect state, either in MS. or in print, unless it be preserved entire in Bishop Percy's folio.'

Everyone who cares for old romances will, we think, find pleasure in the Folio version now at last brought to the light. We see no reason for suspecting that it deviates from the original romance in respect of its story. The spelling and the language are considerably corrupted or modernised; but the incidents and circumstances remain as they were. The frame of the picture is damaged; but the picture lives. In the later editions of his *Reliques*, in his list of Ancient Metrical Romances, Bishop Percy just mentions his copy. In 1800 he communicated an account of it to Dr Robert Anderson, for the information of Sir Walter (then plain Walter) Scott, the substance of which is reproduced by Dr Leyden in his remarks on the romances mentioned in the *Complaint of Scotland* (edited by him in 1801). It is printed *verbatim* in Mr Laing's Preface to his reprint of the romance.

Sir Walter Scott, after speaking of 'Gawen and Galogras,' 'Galoran of Galloway,' and 'Sir Tristrem,' as romances in which 'there does not appear the least trace of a French original,' and probably 'compiled by Scottish authors from the Celtic traditions which still floated amongst their countrymen,' subjoins the hypothesis, that, 'to this list we might perhaps be authorised in adding the *History of Sir*

Edgar and Sir Grime; for although only a modernised copy is now known to exist, the language is unquestionably Scottish, and the scene is laid in Carrick in Ayrshire.' We see no reason for referring it to Celtic traditions. But it may, perhaps, be of domestic growth. Certainly this romance enjoyed an early and extensive popularity in Scotland. Perhaps the earliest mention [1] of it belongs to the year 1497; when the Treasurer's accounts inform us: 'ixs' was paid to 'twa fithelaris [2] that Sang Gray Steil to the king,' James IV., then holding his court at Stirling. James V., as we learn from Hume of Godscroft's history of the family of Douglas, 'when he was young, loved' Archibald Douglas of Kilspendie 'singularly well, for his ability of body, and was wont to call him Gray Steill.' Then, as we have already intimated, the romance is referred to in the *Complaynt of Scotland*, 1549, as one well and widely known. Sir David Lyndsay, about the same time—who indeed has been put forward by some critics as the author of the *Complaynt*—mentions it more than once: as in his 'Squire Meldrum'—

> I wate he faucht that day als weill
> As did Schir Gryme againes Gray Steill—

in his Interlude of 'The Auld Man and his Wife'—

> This is the sword that slew Gray Steill
> Necht half a myle beyond Kinneill.

A poem, written in 1574, by John Davidson, then one of the ministers of Edinburgh, published twenty-one years afterwards at Edinburgh, says that poets have in all time delighted to celebrate worthy persons:

[1] See Leyden's *Comp. of Sc.* and Mr Laing's Preface to his reprint.

[2] *Not* 'Sachelaris.' That reading is, as Mr Laing informs us, a transcriber's blunder.

> Even of Gray Steill, who list to luke,
> Their is set foorth a meikle buke.

'William, first Earl of Gowrie,' says Mr Laing, 'is denominated Gray Steill in one of Logan's letters, produced as a proof of that alleged and mysterious conspiracy, which in all probability shall [*Anglicè* will] remain a question of doubtful interpretation.' Subsequently, allusions to our romance abound. 'In a curious MS. volume,' to quote again from Mr Laing's valuable Preface, 'formerly in the possession of Dr Burney, entitled *An Playing Booke for the Lute*, " Noted and collected" at Aberdeen by Robert Gordon, in the year 1627, is the air of "Gray Steel," and there is a satirical poem on the Marquis of Argyle, printed in 1686, which is said "to be composed in Scottish rhyme," and is "appointed to be sung according to the tune of Old Gray Steel."'

'Besides these allusions,' adds Mr Laing, 'other evidence of the popularity of this Romance might have been adduced from common sayings and proverbial expressions which are current to this day in various parts of the country, although all knowledge of the hero and his exploits have long since ceased to be remembered. Indeed, this romance would seem, along with the poems of Sir David Lyndsay, and the histories of Robert the Bruce, and of Sir William Wallace, to have formed the standard productions of the vernacular literature of the country. The author of the "Scots Hudibras," originally printed at London, 1681, under the title of "A Mock Poem, or the Whigg's Supplication," in describing Ralph's Library says :

> And here lyes books, and there lyes ballads,
> As Davie Lindsay, and Gray-Steel,
> Squire Meldrum, Bevis, and Adam Bell,
> There Bruce and Wallace.

'To this effect, John Taylor, "the water poet," a noted

character in the reign of Charles I., speaks of Sir Degre, Sir Grime, and Sir Gray-Steele, as having the same popularity in Scotland that the heroes of other romances enjoyed in their respective countries "filling (as he quaintly says) whole volumes with the ayrie imaginations of their unknowne and unmatchable worths." [1]

The reader will not, we think, be surprised at the wide popularity these many allusions imply. The poem is not only valuable for its faithful picture of medieval life, with its adventures and gallantry, and that mysterious atmosphere we called 'romantic,' but for the force and beauty of its story. It has charms beyond those which attract the antiquarian, or the historical eye. The subject of the piece is the true and tried friendship of Sir Eger and Sir Grime. Such a friendship was a favourite subject with the old romance-writers. See 'Amys and Amylion,' and 'Athelstan' (printed from a Caius College MS. in *Reliquiæ Antiquæ*). What Damon and Pythias were to each other, and Pylades and Orestes, and Theseus and Peirithous, that were Eger and Grime.

> They were fellows good & fine ;
> They were nothing sib of blood,
> But they were Sworn Brethren good ;
> They kept a chamber together at home ;
> Better love loved there never none.

Of such a kind was the fast friendship of Wallace and Graham, the recollection of which, perhaps, may have induced later Scotch reciters or editors of the story to change Grime's name into Graham. Graham had become to them the ideal representative of the friend that sticks closer than a brother.

This romance then, like the Fourth Book of the 'Fairy

---

[1] Argument to the verses in praise of the Great O'Toole, originally printed 1623, 8vo, and included in Taylor's works, 1634, folio, sign. Bb 2.

Queen,' sings of friendship. It sings how a true knight
stood faithfully by his friend when misfortune overtook him,
and fought his battle, and won it, and was rewarded with
the same happiness which he had so nobly striven to secure
for his friend—success in love. The causes of his friend's
misfortune are highly characteristic of the age in which the
romance was probably composed—the end of the fourteenth
or beginning of the fifteenth century. They are: (1) Sir
Eger's own adventurous spirit. He is a younger brother,
who, 'large of blood and bone,' but possessing no broad
lands, has to fight his way in the world. 'Ever he justs and
he fights.' Ever unvanquished, he wins the love of Wing
laine, Earl Bragas' daughter, who has set her heart on
marrying such an one. But with her love pledged to him,
and with all his honours, he cannot rest from seeking adventure. He hears of a fresh enemy; he sets off in quest
of him.

> Upon a time Eger he would forth fare
> To win him worship, as he did see ;
> Whereby that he might praised be
> Above all knights of high degree.

(2) Winglaine's inflexible resolve to give her hand to one
who had never been overthrown. The new enemy, against
whom her lover is gone, is the formidable Sir Gray-Steel.
The lover comes back from his encounter with him stained
with defeat.

> So he came home upon a night
> Sore wounded, & ill was he dight ;
> His knife was forth, his sheath was gone ;
> His scabbard by his thigh was done ;
> A truncheon of a spear he bore,
> And other weapons he bare no more.
> On his bedside he set him down ;
> He siked sore, & feel in swoon.

Winglaine overhears the miserable story he gives his much sorrowing friend of his expedition ; and her heart is hardened against him.   He has committed what is in her eyes an unpardonable offence—he has been beaten.   She laughs to scorn the version of the affair, which the *fidus Achates* circulates, to protect his friend's fair fame.   She listens to Sir Grime's intercession with supreme obduracy.   She will no longer lay any commands of hers upon him, she says.

> All that while Eger was the knight
> That wan the degree in every fight,
> For his sake verily
> Many a better I have put by.
> Therefore I will not bid him ride,
> Nor at home I will not bid him abide ;
> Nor of his marriage I have nothing ado :
> I wot not, Grime, what thou sayest thereto.

But poor, wounded Eger loves her as intensely as ever. Such is the terrible distress from which friendship delivers him.   If Eger can yet subdue Gray-Steel, or be believed by Winglaine to have subdued him, all may yet be well.   The friend determines himself to go forth against the enemy, but to persuade the lady that her lover has gone.   His generous scheme succeeds.   He returns triumphant ; and makes everybody believe that it is Eger returning so. Winglaine now relents, as she thinks Sir Eger has redeemed his honour ; and, after some show on his part of feigned indifference to her overtures, *prisca redit venus*, and the happy day is fixed.

> The Earl & Countess accorded soon ;
> The Earl sent forth his messenger
> To great lords far and near,
> That they should come by the 15th day
> To the marriage of his daughter gay.
> And then Sir Eger, that noble knight,
> Married Winglaine, that lady bright.

> The feast it lasted forty days
> With lords & ladies in royal arrays ;
> And at the forty days' end
> Every man to his own home wend.

And in due time

> Winglaine bare to Sir Eger
> Fifteen children that were fair ;
> Ten of them were sonnes wight,
> And five, daughters fair in sight.

Such is the outline of this charming old tale. The central scene is the land of Beam. But the expeditions against Sir Gray-Steel into the Forbidden Country are described at great length and with excellent effect. The introduction of the maiden who entertains and nurses, or advises the knights when engaged in them, and who eventually marries Sir Grime, is accompanied with most pleasant and graphic pictures of the lady's bower of chivalric times. As Winglaine represents the sterner side of the female character, Loosepain represents the gentler. Says Sir Eger :—

> The Moon shone fair, the stars cast light ;
> Then of a Castle I got a sight;
> Of a Castle & a Town ;
> And by an arbour side I light down ;
> And there I saw fast me by
> The fairest bower that ever saw I.
> A little while I tarried there,
> And a lady came forth of a fresh Arbour ;
> She came forth of that garden green,
> And in that bower fain would have been.
> She was clad in scarlet red
> And all of fresh gold shone her head ;
> Her rud was red as rose in rain,
> A fairer creature never seen.
> *Methought her coming did me good.*

She is full of gentle consideration for the wounded and

vanquished knight—for his wounded spirit as well as for his pierced and bruised body.

> The Lady lovesome under line
> With her white hands she did wash mine;
> And when she saw my right hand bare,
> Alas! my shame is much the mair!
> The glove was whole, the hand was nomen;
> Thereby she might well see I was overcomen;
> And *she perceived that I thought shame;*
> *Therefore she would not ask me my name.*
> *Nor at that word she said no mair,*
> *But all good easements I had there.*

This gentle-souled lady proves an excellent doctor—

> Why was she called Loosepain?
> A better leech was none certain.—

(see vv. 243–328), and a most kindly nurse. *Haud ignara mali*—her betrothed had been slain by Sir Gray-Steel, and her brother also, in striving to avenge him—she endeavours to forget her own griefs while she "succours" the miserable Sir Eger; but ever and anon, in the midst of her tender, gracious nursing of him, they recur to her, and she must needs weep. The old romances paint few more beautiful touching pictures than this one :—

> She sat down by the bedside,
> She laid a psalter on her knee;
> Thereon she played full lovesomely;
> *And yet for all her sweet playing,*
> *Ofttimes she had full still mourning;*
> And her two maidens sweetly sang,
> And oft they wept, and their hands wrang;
> But I heard never so sweet playing,
> And ever amongst so sore siking.
> In the night she came to me oft,
> And asked me whether I would ought;
> But always I said her nay,
> Till it drew near the break of day.

No wonder Sir Eger describes her afterwards as

> .   .   .   the gentlest of heart & will
> That ever man came until.

She receives Sir Grime with the same sweet hospitality—happily he did not need experience her leechcraft, either before or after his combat with Gray-Steel—disturbed by the same irrepressible sorrow.

> Meat nor drink none would he,
> He was so enamoured of that fair lady.

He discovers the secret of her tears.

> 'Sir,' she said, 'I must never be weel
> Till I be avenged of Graysteel,
> For he slew my brother, my father's heir,
> And also my own lord both fresh & fair;
> For Sir Attelstan shold me have wedd,
> But I came never in his bed.'

So Sir Grime rides forth against Sir Gray-Steel, not only as Eger's friend, but as Loosepain's lover.   He rides with a lighter heart, therefore; around him the small birds singing, the flowers springing.   The lady Loosepain, sitting at home in her chamber, thinks of him gone to the Forbidden Country

> At supper where she was set;
> But never a morsel might she eat.
> 'Ah!' she said, 'now I think on that knight,
> That went from me when the day was light!
> Yesternight to the chamber I him led;
> This night Graysteel has made his bed.
> Alas! he is foul lost on him!   ·
> That is much pity for his kin!
> For he is large of blood and bone;
> And goodly nurture lacketh he none.
> And he is fair in arms to fold;
> He is worth to her his weight in gold;

> *Woe is me for his love in his country!*
> She may think long or she him see!'
> With that she thought on her Lord Attelstan
> That the water out of her eyen ran.

Who is so hard-hearted as not to rejoice when at this juncture—

> . . . Grime knocked at the chamber door,
> And a maiden stood there on the floor.
> 'O madam!' she said, 'Now is come that knight
> That went hence when the day was light!'
> And hastily from the board she rise,
> And kissed him twenty sithe.
> 'How have you faren on your journey?'
> 'Full well, my love,' Sir Grime did say.

Of course the old, old, never wearisome *finale* follows. The brave, true, virgin knight

> ('I had never wife,' he says, 'nor yet lady.
> I tell you truly by Saint John,
> I had never wife nor yet leman.')

marries the sweet tender-hearted lady. The betrothal—the hand-fasting—takes place at once; the marriage, after Sir Grime has revisited the land of Beam, and ensured the happiness of his friend, returning to Earl Gare's land—

> There Sir Grime, that noble knight,
> Married Loosepain, that lady bright,
>
> . . . .
>
> A royal wedding was made there.

The third knight of the poem is Sir Gray-Steel. He is described as

> . . . . . 'A venturous knight,
> That kept a forbidden country both day & night,
> And a fresh island by the sea,
> Where castles were with towers hie.

The Forbidden Country was made an island by a river and the sea together. It was well furnished with parks, and palaces, and castles, and towers, and with watchmen. For the lord of it, his shield and spear were red; his steed so big as to make Sir Eger's by the side of it look but a foal; his spear was great and long. In the four quarters of his shield were a dragon, an unicorn, a bear, and a wild boar; in the midst "a ramping lion that would bite sore." His armour is of wonderful and lavish magnificence, made of silver and gold, and precious stones. He carries a golden mace with a topaz at the end of it. His horse's furniture is of the same splendid sort—reins of silk hung with bells of gold, saddle of 'selcamar,' fretted with golden bars, breastplate of Indian silk. Moreover, his strength ebbed and flowed, being greatest at noon, least at midnight. He fought better on horseback than on foot. He was believed to be invincible. With his hands too he had

> . . . A hundred knights & mo,
> Shamefully driven them to dead
> Without succour or any remed,

and made their ladies captive. He was wont to cut off the little finger of the right hand of those he slew or overthrew, probably for some purpose of sorcery.[1] The brilliant opulence of Gray-Steel's appearance and his practice of witchcraft both point to an Oriental origin. He is a terrible infidel. At a later time, when an allegorical application of the old romances was the fashion; when they were being turned to uses never dreamt of by their prime authors, and it was insisted that "more was meant than met the ear"; when those tendencies were working that produced their

---

[1] Compare the Hand of Glory in *The Antiquary;* in *Thalaba,* book v. Fingers seem to have been used in a similar way.

most glorious result in the 'Fairy Queen'; when men were
attempting to use for new thoughts the old forms of expression, just as they were retaining for Protestantism the
cathedrals that had so long re-echoed the liturgy of Rome—
at this time the 'Forbidden Country' and Sir Gray-Steel
may have had assigned them a fresh significance.   The
religious interpretation of them is obvious.   The edition of
1711 reads for the Forbidden Country 'The Land of Doubt.'
This latter title cannot fail to remind us, if the former did,
of certain adventures that befall the hero of the *Pilgrim's
Progress*.   Bunyan must have been well familiar with the
common versions circulating in his time of the old romances.
Perhaps he may have heard a version of this very one from
one of the many Scotchmen who for various reasons overran
this country in the seventeenth century.

A supposed difficulty remains.   We have seen that James,
in his youthful days, nick-named a Douglas, whom he then
loved, his 'Gray Steill.'   'There might be some reason as to
Lord Gowrie's nick-name,' writes Mr C. K. Sharpe, *apud*
Mr Laing's Preface, 'for it is plain that Gray Steill was a
sort of magician; and Spottiswood says that Gowrie "was
too curious, and said to have consulted with wizards," etc.;
but for Lord Eglintoun, it is only known that he fought
stoutly for the Solemn League and Covenant, was never
vanquished by Sir Grime, and had no deeper dealings with
the devil than the rest of his fellow Puritans.'   With regard
to Douglas, we should conjecture that the name was given
him in banter.   Affection often uses the seemingly most inapt
terms.[1]   It expresses itself contrariously.   It is much given to
irony.   It can convert the hardest names into terms of en-
dearment.   It can make the rudest speeches civil, the harshest
titles complimentary.   So, perhaps, there is no such great

---

[1] See Coleridge's *Christabel*, the conclusion to Part II.

difficulty in James giving his favourite such a hard name.
As to Lord Eglintone, if it is only 'known that he fought
stoutly for the Solemn League and Covenant,' quite enough
is known to prepare us for the application of the most
abusive terms to him. What with the great differences, and
the endless bitter little differences that distracted his age, he
must have been a very unique person indeed if he did not
get called by every possible bad name at one time or
another.

Naturally enough the popular taste, requiring brevity in a
title, and fascinated by the mystery and weird air that sur-
round Sir Gray-Steel, attached his name to the romance,
though it celebrates him and two others; and so, as we
have seen, it is often referred to as 'Graysteel.'

We think our readers will agree with Percy's verdict that
'it is one of the best of the ancient epic tales' preserved in
the Folio—will perhaps extend their praise. It is, indeed,
a poem of very high excellence, vivid, picturesque, terse,
delicate, tender, vigorous. It breathes the very spirit of
romance, and re-creates for us the old sights and scenes of
romantic life in all their strange grotesque beauty. The
knight-errant in his pride, and in his fall; the Forbidden
Land with its weird lord; the castle standing out in the
moonshine, as the broken knight rides away from the field
of his shame; the scarlet-clad, gold-tiara'd lady who meets,
and greets, and doctors, and nurses him; the wilderness
and the forest; the wonderful sword Egeking, of whose
'guider' 'no man ever of woman born durst abide the face
beforn'; Sir Eger in 'a window,' reading books of romance;
Winglaine on the walls seeing the waygate of her lover; Sir
Grime taking his inn at a burgess's house; Loosepain playing her guest to sleep; the avenger riding about the plain
in quest of the oppressor; the oppressor rushing on the

avenger like a lion 'in his woodest time'; the fighting 'together fell and sore, the space of a mile and something more'; the hacking, and swooning, and dying; the steeds left to themselves when their masters are dismounted, fighting furiously together after the example of their furiously fighting masters; the castle of stone hard by the terrible field, where the victor sees and hears 'ladies, many a one, wringing, and wailing, and riving their hair, striking, and crying with voices full clear'; the lady doing off his armour and searching his wounds, and 'never so sound as when she saw he had no death wound'—these are some of the pictures that our romance gives us; that teach us how unlike, and how like we are the men who played their parts some five centuries ago on the stage we now are occupying.

IV

THE HERE PROPHECY

(From the Academy for Dec. 4, 1886)

THERE is extant so little English of the latter half of the twelfth century that the Here Prophecy, as it undoubtedly belongs to that period, deserves, as a specimen of our language, special attention, more attention certainly than it could claim as a piece of literature. It is, indeed, quoted by the writer known as 'Benedictus Abbas' (Benedictus was the transcriber or director of the transcription, the real author being perhaps Richard Fitzneal as Dr Stubbs suggests), and after him by Hoveden, as something ancient —'antiquitus scriptum.' But what I wish now particularly to point out is, that it, in fact, must belong, as its predictions show, to the very time at which it was said to be discovered ('inveniebatur'); that is to the end of the year 1190, or rather to the beginning of 1191. Thus, as 'Benedictus Abbas' was certainly contemporary with King Richard I., we have, in the Here Prophecy, a genuine specimen of English just at that time—unless, indeed, the 'inventor' archaised his style, which I do not think very likely, several things considered. And so, as it is so very seldom possible *to date precisely, to assign to any exact year*, any piece of medieval English, this 'vaticinium' has, for us, a singular value.

55

To refresh the reader's memory, I will first quote it as appears in Dr Stubbs's edition of Benedictus Abbas :

> Zan zu seches in here hert yreret,
> Zan sulen Hengles in þre be ydeled :
> Zat han sale into Hyrlande alto lade waya ;
> Zat hozer in to Poile mid pride bileve ;
> Ze thirde in hayre haughen hert all . . . ydreghe.

In the last line Hoveden, who, in his history, follows Benedictus very closely, gives 'wreken' before 'ydreghe.' The meaning seems to be :

> When thou seest in Here a hart set up,
> Then shall the English be divided into three :
> The one shall go entirely into Ireland ;
> The second in Apulia shall proudly stay ;
> The third shall suffer all manner of misery in their own land.

Here is here a place-name, as we shall see; but it is also an Anglo-Saxon common noun, meaning 'a host, a multitude.' And there seems to be in these lines a play—a pun—on the two meanings of the word, the secondary sense being, 'When thou *seest* a hart *in the midst of men*,' which would be a startling phenomenon, suggestive to a person of a prophetic or an omen-mongering turn; as if one should say, 'When you see a hind at *Mob*-berley' (there is such a place in Cheshire), or a Latin writer should speak of seeing one at *Populo*-nia.

It has been doubted whether there was a place called Here, and *here* has been taken to be a pronoun (Anglo-Saxon *heora*, answering to our modern 'their'). The participle at the end of the first line has been altered into *y-ueret*, and the line translated, 'When thou seest the English terrified in their heart,' etc.

Now, does not this translation destroy altogether the point of the so-called prophecy, and entirely ignore the Latin chronicler's words. Benedictus speaks of a 'villa regis Angliae quae dicitur Here,' which King Henry (no doubt Henry II.) had given to Ranulf (Hoveden says William), the son of Stephen—that is, to Ralph Fitzstephen—and informs us that this Ralph built there a great house, 'in cujus pinnaculo effigiem cervi statuit.'

There is really no reason why this story should not be accepted. I say the first line loses its point without it. It becomes wholly irrelevant and common-place. Then to substitute the form *y-ueret* for the quite satisfactory word that occurs in the original is surely an unnecessary interference with the text. Moreover, I cannot but doubt whether such a Southern form as *y-ueret* would be likely to be found in what is surely not Southern English—in a version current at Peterborough, and, I suppose, in South Yorkshire. The forms *sal, sees, sulen,* point northwards; and as the prefixes in *yneret, ydelet,* and *ydrighe* are consistent with a twelfth-century Midland origin, the dialect is North-East Midland. So would not the Southern *y-ueret* be out of place here? It would be a difficulty if we found it in such a context. And certainly difficulties do not need 'bespeaking.' There are enough ready-made.

As to identifying the town—the 'villa'—of Here, we need not yet despair, if, indeed, the matter is worth much trouble. Dr Stubbs points out that some Fitzstephens were connected with *Harford,* in Devonshire, a town some ten miles west of Totnes, on the southern edge of Dartmoor. And, in this case, the *original* form of this prophecy would be Southern, which might make for the conjectured reading *yneret.* The particular family may, I think, be identified by the fact that Benedictus names a Ralph, and Hoveden a William. Now Ralph Fitzstephen, a person of some distinction, in Henry II.'s reign—he acted as a justice itinerant in 1174—had a brother William, also a person of some distinction, a justice itinerant in 1190. These Fitzstephens, according to Foss's *Judges of England*, were specially connected with Gloucestershire, one or the other being sheriff of that county for many years (from 18 Henry II. to 1 Richard I.). Ralph possessed property also in the counties of Warwick, Leicester, and Northampton. If a medieval Here could be discovered in Northamptonshire or thereabouts this would exactly meet the case. It would neatly agree with the prophecy being preserved in a Peterborough document. Had any Fitzstephen ever any property at Market *Har*borough or at *Har*grave? Foss does not connect either of these brothers with Devonshire.

In l. 4 the rendering of Benedictus's version seems to be 'al to lead way,' 'al to' being used as an adverb in the sense of 'altogether, entirely' just as in the *Owl and Nightingale*, ll. 837-8:

> Abid, abid, þe ule seide;
> þu gest *al to* mid Swikelhede,

and elsewhere. Hoveden gives 'al to late waie,' *i.e.*, 'all too late turn,' if, as Prof. Skeat plausibly suggests, *waie* is bad spelling for *waiue* or *weue*.

In the last line Hoveden's version has *herd*, which Prof. Skeat happily identifies with *erd*, Anglo-Saxon *eard*, 'native land.' And probably *hert* is a variant of the same word— does not equal 'heart.'

As I have said, the predictions uttered in these curious lines connect them straightaway with the years 1190-1. The allusion to Apulia is too precise to permit us assigning them to an earlier year, in spite of Benedictus's 'antiquitus scriptum.' Prophecy seems to have been much in vogue in the latter half of the twelfth century—πολλὰ λόγια ἐλέγετο, as

Thucydides says of the beginning of the Peloponnesian War —as it is still with some newspapers of our own day, which predict the result of a policy as positively as if they were edited by the Pythian priestess herself. The utterer of certain views gave them a special emphasis and solemnity by passing them off for prophecies. Certainly prophecies abounded. Giraldus Cambrensis wrote a Vaticinal History of the conquest of Ireland. Merlin's prophecies were then in full currency, and in Ireland those of Columbcille; and so some Northamptonshire wiseacre, as we may plausibly suppose, wishing to express his ideas of English prospects at that time, produced them in the shape of an oracle inscribed 'in tabulis lapideis'—an inscription just as genuine, no doubt, as that on the tombstone of King Arthur, then recently 'discovered' at Glastonbury—as genuine as the famous prophecy that was 'found in a bog,' 'Ireland shall be rul'd by an ass and a dog.'

He might well think England was in a poor way at that time. But this prophet's prophecies are grotesque enough. Two-thirds of the English, it seems, were to find homes elsewhere, and those that remained were to be utterly miserable. This was typified by the exaltation of the hart in a town's midst. The nation was to lose its spirit; the $\varkappa\rho\alpha\delta\acute{\iota}\eta$ $\grave{\epsilon}\lambda\acute{\alpha}\varphi o\iota o$ was to possess its bosom. One part might prosper, but it would be far away. Another would pass into Ireland; of their fate our seer judiciously hints nothing. The other would 'dree their weird,' and a most wretched weird, in their own land.

What suggested the Apulian reference was undoubtedly Richard's successes just at this time in South Italy and Sicily. On his way to Palestine he wintered in those parts. He was there from September 23, 1190, to April 10, 1191. No doubt the prophet had heard of his seizing La Bagnara, a castle in Calabria; of his occupying a monastery on the straits of Messina; of his building close by Messina ('extra muros Messinae') his stout fortress of Mategriffon; of the splendid style in which he kept Christmas in that castle, and how generally, the Griffons well suppressed, 'gens Angliae in maxima habebatur reverentia in regno Siciliae'; and, hearing of these things, he rashly concluded—such is the manner of prophets—that the king would never come back, but would establish himself permanently in his new quarters, and leave his England to look after itself. The date of this allusion must certainly be some early month in 1191.

The reference to Ireland is curious. Just twenty years before our veracious oracle spoke, a full beginning had been made of our unfortunate relations with that country. In November 1171—some seven centuries ago!—Henry II. had been acknowledged King at Cashel. But the conquest was far from complete. In 1177 Prince John was declared lord of Ireland, and the whole country was allotted to various nobles and knights, who undertook to complete it. In 1185, that worthless person—he, says an old poet,

> Quo pejor in orbe
> Non fuit, omnimoda vacuus virtute, Johannes—

himself visited the country, only to irritate the native chiefs by his insolence, plucking their beards—a deadly insult—when they offered him the kiss of peace. He was soon recalled. The thorough conquest of Ireland was never to be accomplished, but it was still talked of and planned. Perhaps our prophet thought that he who retained the title of Lord of Ireland would justify his title by a second visit that should be really effective. At all events the general feeling of the age, which the Here prophecy represents, is well brought before us by what Giraldus says in his 'last preface' to his *Conquest of Ireland*—the preface in which he dedicates the new edition of his work to his old pupil, who was by that time king:

It has pleased God and your good fortune [thus he addresses King John] to send you several sons, both natural and legitimate, and you may have more hereafter. Two of these you may raise to the thrones of two kingdoms, and under them you amply provide for numbers of your followers by new grants of lands, especially in Ireland, a country which is still in a wild and unsettled state, *a very small part of it being yet occupied and inhabited by our people.*

As in the Elizabethan age, so then, the English looked upon Ireland as a country not only to be annexed, but to be taken possession of—as a land whose native inhabitants were not more to be considered than the natives of Australia or Tasmania have been considered in later times. So a third part of the English people was to occupy and inhabit Ireland.

As to the last part of the prophecy—a prophet was scarcely needed to tell England its outlook was not good in the year 1191. Its knight-errant of a king, after raising money by all and every means, had gone a crusading, not to return, as the event proved, for nearly four years. His intriguing brother John had been forbidden the country; but it was not to be hoped he would heed the prohibition longer than he could help; nor did he. And men's hearts might well sink within them. And those who looked facts in the face might confidently promise the land 'all manner of misery.'

The date of the Here prophecy then is the year 1191, near the beginning of it.

V

ROBERT OF BRUNNE

(From the *Academy*, Jan. 8, 1887)

SIR FREDERICK MADDEN writes that 'it appears to us, from a long and attentive consideration' of the autobiographical passages in the *Handlyng Synne* and the *Chronicle*, 'that Robert Mannyng was born at Brunne, . . . was a Canon of the Gilbertine Order, and for fifteen years—that is, from 1288 to 1303—professed in the Priory of Sempringham, . . . and that he afterwards removed to Brymwake in Kestevene, six miles from Sempringham, where he wrote the prologue to his first work.' And subsequent historians of literature have faithfully followed so distinguished an authority. Yet Sir Frederic's statement needs revision.

It does not seem to have occurred to him to verify the existence of Brymwake. Was there ever such a place? And, if so, where?

Now that the Brym is identical with Brunne, and the Wake some defining addition is an obvious suggestion; what is more, it is the fact. So I am assured by one who was mentioned to me as the best antiquarian authority on the part of Lincolnshire concerned—by the Bishop of Nottingham, whom I have the pleasure of now heartily thanking for the courtesy and kindness with which he has answered my inquiries. 'Your "Brimwake,"' says Dr Trollope, 'is undoubtedly "Bourn-wake," so called from its lord Hugh Wac and his successors in days of old, as the Wake Deeping Estate is still called Deeping-Wake or Wakes, although this has passed into other hands. . . . There may have been this distinction between the terms Brymwake and Brun—viz., that the first represented the Wak lordship of Brun, and the second the remainder of the land in the parish—as you no doubt know that through the wisdom of the Conqueror he seldom included the whole of a parish in his grants of lordships to his adherents, although he often granted several lordships in different localities to one person.' Thus the name Brimwake may be compared with such place-names as Stoke-Mandeville, Ashby-de-la-Zouch, Min-shull-Vernon, Hurst-Monceaux, Witton-Gilbert, etc. And so Brimwake and Brunne in fact denote the same locality.

Now in this locality there was only one monastery—viz., that—I, again quote Bishop Trollope—'founded by Bald-win Fitz-Gislebert or Gilbert (father of Emma, married to Hugo Wak or Wake) for Canons Regular, of St Austin, in 1138.' So that if Robert Manning was ever a member of Brunne or Brimwake Monastery, Madden errs when he asserts that he never changed his Order—that he was al-ways a Gilbertine.

But does Robert Manning inform us that he ever belonged to Brunne or Bourn Monastery? I think not, if we read his words carefully, and do not punctuate them as is com-monly done. The words from the prologue to his *Handlyng Synne* are these:

> To alle Crystyn men vndir Sunne
> And to gode men of Brunne
> And speciali alle be name
> Þe felaushepe of Symprynghame

(5) Roberd of Brunne greteþ ȝow
     In al godenesse þat may to prow
     Of Brymwake yn Kesteuene
     Syxe myle be syde Sympryngham euene
     Y dwelled yn þe pryorye
(10) Fyftene ȝere yn cumpanye
     In þe tyme of gode dane Jone
     Of Camelton þat now ys gone, etc.

Now, Madden and others connect lines seven and eight with line nine. I propose to connect them with the lines that precede—to take them as in apposition to Brunne, as 'epexegetic' of Brunne in line five. Then all is well. He, a Brunne man, more precisely a Brimwake man, greets his fellow canons of Sempringham, and goes on to describe his association with them. In other words, I would put a full stop after 'euene,' instead of after 'prow.' We should call Bourn some eight miles from Sempringham, not six; but I do not think that difference need trouble us, or set anyone against my present suggestion. Possibly the Brimwake Estate was to the north of Bourn, and so a mile or two nearer Sempringham. At all events, let any objector produce a Brimwake of his own at the specified distance.

Robert of Brunne is in his age a writer of so much importance and merit that no Old English scholar will, I think, grudge thus much time and space to clearing up a detail of his life.

VI

DANTE IN ENGLAND

(From the *Bibliographer* for Jan. 1882)

I DO not think the question when Dante's and the older Italian poetry first became known in England has ever yet been thoroughly discussed ; nor do I propose now to fully discuss it ; but I wish to make one or two remarks on the subject.

It is, it need scarcely be said, a matter of considerable interest to ascertain when the works of the supreme poet of medieval Europe first influenced us and our literature. A new era of the poetic art begins with the *Divina Commedia.* The Troubadours and the Trouvères had sung in the infancy of modern Europe, with a grace and sweetness that still claim and deserve a hearing ; but their song seemed and seems a child's note when the noble melody of Dante was and is heard. It was Dante who first showed that the modern literature was at least to equal ancient, and from him must be dated the resurrection of poetry.

It seems to be commonly supposed that this great master was not at all known in England till Chaucer's return from his sojourn in Italy, in the years 1372 and '73. I wish to suggest for consideration that he was probably known here before that date.

E

It is a question of general interest, and also of particular —viz., in respect of Chaucer; for in Chaucerian criticism it is almost invariably presumed that he knew nothing of the Italian masterpieces before his famous visit in 1372; and decisions as to the dates of some of his works are made to rest upon this presumption.

The *Inferno* was certainly completed, as we are told, by the close of 1308; the *Purgatorio* by the close of 1314, or early in the following year; the *Paradiso* in 1321. How far each part was put in circulation—was published, as we should say—as soon as it was finished, is a matter of controversy. Certainly some cantos of the *Inferno* were seen and known before the whole part was finished. Without dispute, not to speak of the *Vita Nuova* and the *Convito*, the *Divina Commedia* was known as a whole in Italy some half-century before Chaucer's visit. And however widely or narrowly the separate parts, as they issued, may have been known, the popularity of the work as a completed work was immense. 'Never,' says Cary, 'did any poem rise so suddenly into notice after the death of the author [Dante died in 1321], or engage the public attention more powerfully, than the *Divina Commedia.*'

Now, the intercourse between Italy and England in the Middle Ages was extensive and continuous. Of course the close ecclesiastical connection involved a constant interchange of communications and of visits. Many of our 'livings' were held by Italians. No doubt these worthies were mostly absentees; but their receiving English tithes must have brought them, directly or indirectly, into contact with this country. Then the custom of pilgrimage took an annual train of visitors to Italian shrines, and brought visitors to England. The 'Wife of Bath' had been at Rome; and we may be sure that very social person did not go alone—we may be sure she represents the habit of the century. Then our commercial relation with Italy was at that time intimate, and of great importance. Venice and Genoa were then amongst the chief commercial cities of Europe. It was to arrange and improve our relations with Genoa that Chaucer was sent out, in 1372, as one of a commission. Then—and this especially concerns our inquiry—there was much passing to and fro between the universities of the Middle Ages. Students wandered from Oxford to Paris, and into southern France, and to the colleges of Italy, to Bologna, *Mater Studiorum*, and elsewhere. Dante, for instance, after studying at several places in his own country —at Florence, at Bologna, at Padua—studied also at Paris. He was there just after he had finished the *Inferno;* and there is some ground for believing that he passed on into England. Boccaccio, no mean authority on the matter, says, as is well known, that he visited *Parisios dudum extremosque Britannos.* Certainly, whether or not the great poet ever himself visited England, compatriots of his studied at Oxford; and without doubt Englishmen studied at Bologna and elsewhere in Italy. Lastly, let us remember the friars and such gentry, who were perpetually traversing medieval Europe, and carrying news and many another thing from one land to another. They mixed with all degrees and sorts of society, and no doubt considered how to make themselves generally agreeable—agreeable to clerks and scholars, as well as to 'fair wives.' The pardoner, who came with a stock of pardons from Rome 'all hot,' might occasionally have in his wallet, side by side with such miserable trumpery, something of real value—haply one of Petrarch's sonnets, or a canto of the *Divine Comedy.*

Surely, with so many various and constant contacts between Italy and England, it is unlikely that Dante's poetry was unknown here till Chaucer brought it home—brought it probably in manuscript, certainly in his head and heart.

Possibly a minute search in our public libraries might discover some early copy of part, or the whole, of the great Italian poem. Says the Count Cesare Balbo: 'The manuscript copies of the *Commedia* belonging to the fourteenth century, which are numerous in all the libraries of Italy, France, Germany and England, give us a tangible proof how this work had been diffused.' In a note he refers to Pelli for an account of these MSS. ; and adds, 'A catalogue of these manuscripts is desirable, and if possible a description of them, distinguishing those which have been investigated. It is well known that Karl Witte, the deserving editor of Dante's letters, has been for many years occupied on this labour *in Germany!*'

Dante himself, in the *Convito*, speaks as if his *Canzoni* were known, or were sure to be known, in England. Explaining why he has used Italian for his Commentary rather than Latin, he says : 'The Latin would have explained the Canzoni better to foreigners, as to the Germans, the English, and others ; but then it must have expounded their sense without the power of at the same time transferring their beauty.'

I have said this question has a particular interest with regard to Chaucer; for his introduction to the Italian poetry was the artistic turning-point of his life. It is usually supposed that he learnt the Italian language when he visited Italy as a commissioner ; but it may be very reasonably conjectured, as before now it has been, that he was appointed one of that commission because he knew Italian.

Possibly his acquaintance with Dante and the great Italian party may date from 1368—the year in which Prince Lionel married the Lady Violante, daughter of the Duke of Milan. We need not insist that he formed one of the marriage train, though he may have done so. We know that he was acquainted with Prince Lionel, for he was once a page in the household of the prince's first wife ; and it is very difficult to believe that the prince and his friends had, when they returned, nothing to report of Dante ; for Italy was then ringing with his fame.

'In the year 1350,' says Sismondi, 'Giovanni Visconti, Archbishop and Prince of Milan, engaged a number of learned men in the laborious task of illustrating and explaining the obscure passages of the *Divina Commedia*. Six distinguished scholars, two theologians, two men of science, and two Florentine antiquaries united their talents in this undertaking.' And it was only a few years after Prince Lionel's marriage that public lectures on his great poem were founded at Florence, Bologna, Pisa, Piacenza, and Venice. Surely in 1368, if not before, a copy of the *Divine Comedy* reached England.

Valuable light would be cast on this question, if it could be settled (1) whether the extant translation of the *Roman de la Rose* is by Chaucer, and (2) what is the date of this translation ; for it is generally supposed that the famous interpolation in the extant version, as to what is true gentleness—to the effect that a churl is to be judged by his deed, and that he only is a gentleman who 'doth as longeth to a gentleman'—was inspired by Dante,—I suppose by the famous passage in the *Convito*. The same thought, from the same source in all probability, occurs in the *Wife of Bath's Prologue*, and, if the extant translation of the *Roman* could be shown to be as late as 1390, one might suspect it borrowed this conception from that *Prologue*. If, however, the translation belongs to the decade 1360-70, as some scholars hold, then we have in it the earliest ascertained reference to Dante in English Literature.

VII

CHAUCER AT WOODSTOCK

(From *The Gentleman's Magazine* for April 1882)

THE distance of time that lies between us and the past seems itself to be lessened, if we lessen the distance of space—if we stand on the very site of the actions that interest us, on the very ground that our heroes have trodden. As we stand so, the imagination is quickened, and the knowledge of old days that we have gathered receives a new life. And so, local associations have for us all a very special value. Intelligently appreciated, they may do for us no slight service in helping us to realise what has come and gone long before our time. Therefore it is worth while to ascertain and establish such an association; and we propose now trying to prove the connection of the poet Chaucer with the Park at Woodstock.

We know so little about Chaucer, that nothing that casts light on him and his life is to be disregarded. It is with London that he was more closely connected. He was probably born in the heart of the City; his official work drew him for many years to the wharves just below London Bridge. He lived for some time in one of the old City-gates; he died in Westminster. But all those scenes have changed so utterly that it is difficult indeed to picture the London of

Chaucer's age and Chaucer in the midst of it ; most difficult
to obey the mandate of a sweet singer of our own time,
when he bids us—

> Forget six counties overhung with smoke,
> Forget the snorting steam and piston stroke,
> Forget the spreading of the hideous town ;
> Think rather of the pack-horse on the down,
> And dream of London small, and white, and clean,
> The clear Thames bordered by its gardens green ;
> Think that below bridge the green lapping waves
> Smite some few keels that bear Levantine staves
> Cut from the yew wood on the burnt-up hill,
> And pointed jars that Greek hands toiled to fill,
> And treasured scanty spice from some far sea,
> Florence gold cloth and Ypres napery,
> And cloth of Bruges and hogsheads of Guienne,
> While nigh the thronged wharf Geoffrey Chaucer's pen
> Moves over bills of lading.

There are places in the country, far away from London,
that have been associated with Chaucer, as Donnington, in
Berkshire. But their claims do not bear investigation. The
Chaucer really connected with them is not Geoffrey, but
Thomas, a son of Geoffrey.

And Chaucer's connection with Woodstock has been
doubted or denied for the same reason ; that is, it has been
urged that it was Thomas, and not Geoffrey, that had a
house at Woodstock. Now, it is quite true that Thomas
had a house there ; and the first formal connection of the
name Chaucer with Woodstock is of the date 1411, eleven
years after the poet's death, and appears in a grant made by
the Queen to Thomas Chaucer of the farm of the manors of
Woodstock, Hanbrugh, Wotton, and Stanfield, with the
hundred of Wotton. But of course it cannot be argued that
because Thomas was there, therefore Geoffrey cannot have
been. The presence of the one is not incompatible with the

presence of the other; it may even make the presence of the other probable, when the date permits. In the present case there is good evidence for connecting Geoffrey also with Woodstock.

The evidence is to be found in one of Chaucer's undoubted works—in the *Parliament of Fowls*. The scene of that poem is undoubtedly Woodstock Park.

This 'Parliament of Fowls,' or 'Assembly of Birds,' professes to recount a certain memorable dream that had visited the poet. He had spent the day amongst the books he loved—amongst the books that 'of usage' he read, 'what for lust and what for lore,' that is, partly for delight and partly for instruction, and in the especial perusal of the *Somnium Scipionis;* and,

> Fulfilled of thought and busy heaviness,

had retired to rest. In his sleep, as it seemed, the great Roman, whose apparition his book had narrated, stood by his bed's side, and promised to requite him for all his study of the old tattered volume that spoke of him ('our old book all to torn').

> This foresaid African me hent anon,
> And forthwith him unto *a gate* me brought,
> Right *of a park walled with greenè stone.*

This description at once distinguishes the locality Chaucer has in his mind. From the time of Henry I. to the Elizabethan age, and later still, this stone wall is specially mentioned in connection with Woodstock, and as one of its striking features. Let us first quote Fuller, as he refers to older authorities. 'Why,' he asks in his *Worthies of England,* 'should he speak of fallow deer in Oxfordshire? Why not rather in Northamptonshire, where there be the most, or in Yorkshire, where there be the greatest parkes in England? It is because John Rous, of Warwick, telleth me that at Woodstock, in this county, was the most ancient park in the whole land, encompassed with a stone wall by King Henry the First. Let us premise a line or two concerning Parks—the case before we come to what is contained therein : 1. The word *parcus* appears in Varro (derived no doubt [?] *à parcendo*, to spare or save) for a place wherein such cattle are preserved. 2. There is mention once or twice in Domesday-book of *parcus sylvestris bestiarum*, which proveth parks in England before the Conquest. 3. Probably such ancient parks (to keep J. Rous in credit and countenance) were only paled, and Woodstock the first that was walled about. 4. Parks are since so multiplied that there be more in England than in all Europe besides.'

Rous does not actually mention the building of the wall, though he gives some account of the making of the park—unless, as Fuller suggests, he means to refer to this form of cincture when he says the park formed at Woodstock 'erat *primus parcus Angliæ*.' Nor does Knighton mention the wall, briefly stating 'hoc anno [1110?] rex Henricus apud Villam de Wodestoke fecit magnum parcum.' But it is fairly certain that the wall was built by Henry I. ; for this king collected a menagerie at Woodstock—the first menagerie in England, we presume—and probably built the wall for additional security, in case any of his wild beasts should escape from the enclosure devoted to them. ('The menagerie' is marked in an early eighteenth century plan of Blenheim Park, given in Mr Marshall's supplement History to his *Early History of Woodstock Manor*; it stood a little south-east of the old manor-house, Henry I.'s palace). 'Our king,' writes William of Malmesbury, 'was extremely fond of the wonders of distant countries, begging with great delight, as I have observed, from foreign kings, lions, leopards, lynxes, or camels; animals which England does not produce; and he had a park at Woodstock, in which he used to foster his favourites of this kind. He had placed there also a creature called a porcupine, sent him by William of Montpellier, of which animal, Pliny the elder, in the eighth book of his Natural History, and Isidorus on Etymologies, relate that there is a creature in Africa which the inhabitants call of the urchin kind, covered with prickly bristles, which it darts at will against the dogs when pursuing it. The bristles which I have seen are more than a span long, sharp at each extremity, like the quills of a goose where the feather ceases, but rather thicker, and speckled, as it were, with black and white.'

Plot speaks of Henry I. as ''tis like the first that enclosed the park with a wall, though not for deer, but all foreign wild beasts, such as lions, leopards, camels, linxes, which he procured abroad of other princes.' He speaks as if these beasts were allowed to run loose within the park, which is absurd enough. Probably there were already deer on the spot: a deer-fold is mentioned at an early date, certainly as early as 1123; and certainly there was constantly there the court and its retinue, who would have found such freedom somewhat overpowering. The menagerie with its cages no doubt occupied a certain limited space in the park, perhaps with a wall of its own (if so, the foundations must be traceable); but the stone wall that bounded the whole park was probably raised, as we have said, for additional security, in case of any animal escaping, not only for the sake of the dwellers in the neighbouring country, but for the better detention of favourites so rare and so precious.

To pass on to a later time: Hentzner, who travelled in England in 1598, visited Woodstock, among other places. 'This palace,' he says, 'abounding in magnificence, was built by Henry I., to which he joined a very large park, enclosed with a stone wall; according to John Rosse, the first park in England.'

In the account of 'a Topographical Excursion' made in the year 1634, a special notice is given of Woodstock and the walled park with its handsome lodges.

We may conclude, then, with some confidence, even if there were nothing else to guide us, that by 'the park walled with green stone' Chaucer denotes Woodstock.

We may add that in a poem that used to be attributed to Chaucer, but which is certainly by Lydgate—*The Complaint of the Black Knight*—there is mention of this same park with its green stone wall. *The Complaint of the Black Knight* contains several imitations and reminiscences of Chaucer's *Parliament of Fowls*, and of his *Book of the Duchess*—and this reference to Woodstock is one of these, as its form seems to show; though, indeed, Lydgate, who was acquainted with Thomas Chaucer (see his lines on Sir Thomas' going on an embassy to France), probably had seen the place with his own eyes. This is the passage:

> And by a river forth I gan costay [walk at the side]
> Of water clear as beryl or cristal,
> Till, at the last, I found a little way
> Toward a park enclosed with a wall
> In compass round, and by a gatè small
> Who so that would might freely gone
> Into this park wallèd with grenè stone.

The Parliament of Fowls has other points that associate it with Woodstock Park—that justify us in saying that in describing the park of his vision, Chaucer is in fact describing the park of Woodstock. It makes mention of a river, of a wear or fishpond, and of a well. Add these three features to the one already discussed, and the identification may, we think, be said to be fully demonstrated.

First for the river and the fish-ponds. Describing the interior of the park, into which the Africanus of his dream has conducted him, the poet writes thus:

> A garden saw I full of blossomed bowes
> Upon a river in a grenè mead,
> There as sweetness evermore enough is
> With flowers white, blue, yellow, and red,
> And coldè wellè stremes nothing dead,
> And swimming full of smalè fishes light,
> With finnes red, and scalès silver bright.

Now, this description applies well enough to Woodstock Park, with the river Glyme flowing through it. But what gives special value to this passage for the purpose of identification is, that in the original which Chaucer here, as is well known, translates, nothing whatever is said of any river. We quote from one of the Chaucer Society volumes Mr W. M. Rossetti's literal version of the stanza of Boccaccio's 'Teseide' which Chaucer has reproduced:

> With whom going forward she saw that   [Mount Cithæron]
> In every view suave and charming;
> In guise of a garden bosky and beautiful,
> And greenest full of plants,
> Of fresh grass and every new flower;
> And therein rose fountains living and clear;
> And among the other plants it abounded in
> Myrtle seemed to her more than other.

Clearly, the English poet was adapting the Italian picture to suit his own remembrance.

Of course, the river in the old days before the achievements of 'Capability' Brown presented a very different aspect from that it now presents; but even then it was not left altogether to nature. The fish that swam in it were too well appreciated to be given up to their own devices. So here and there 'wears,' or fish-ponds, were formed. Two are marked in the early eighteenth-century map already mentioned. And hence we have a capital illustration of the following lines in the *Parliament of Fowls*, or, to speak from our present point of view, we have in the *Parliament of Fowls* a detail evidently suggested by the dams in the river Glyme:

> This stream you leadeth unto the sorrowful wear
> There as the fish in prison is all day.

Chaucer sees also 'a well,' and of the well in Woodstock Park there are many mentions. It was associated with the story of Fair Rosamond, and known as Rosamond's Well. 'Rosamond's Labyrinth,' says Drayton, 'whose ruins, together with her well, being paved with square stones in the bottom, and also the bower from which the labyrinth did run, are yet remaining, being vaults arched and walled with stone and brick, almost inextricably wound within one another, by which, if at any time her lodging were laid about by the Queen, she might easily avoid peril imminent, and, if need be, by secret issues, take the air abroad many furlongs about Woodstock, in Oxfordshire.' The Topographical Excursionist of 1634 mentions the ruins of her bower, and 'many strong and strange winding walks and turnings, and a dainty, clear, paved well, knee deep, wherein this beautiful creature did sometimes wash and bathe herself.' In this matter, however, Boccaccio's picture may have been suggestive, for the corresponding lines are to this effect:

> Among the bushes beside a fountain
> She saw Cupid forging arrows.

If, in addition to these various coincidences, we remember that the manor-house at Woodstock was a favourite residence of Edward III. and his Court—two of his sons (the Black

Prince and Thomas) were born there—and that Chaucer was a member of that Court—at one time *dilectus noster valettus*, at a later *scutiger regis*—we think that anyone who, in visiting Woodstock Park, likes to imagine Chaucer there, may certainly do so without misgiving.

There is another poem by Chaucer that may very reasonably be associated with Woodstock; but the proof is less commanding than that we have considered. This is the *Book of the Duchess*. We may be sure that the scene of that poem is either Woodstock or Windsor; and, on the whole, the probability is in favour of Woodstock—a probability which is increased by the established connection of the *Parliament of Fowls*. Certainly, Chaucer's words—

> A long castle with walles white
> By Sainct Johan on a rich hill,

seem to correspond admirably with those of the Excursionist of 1634, who speaks of Woodstock as 'that famous court and princely castle and palace, which as I found it ancient, strong, large, and magnificent, so it was sweet, delightful, and sumptuous, and situated on a fair hill.'

Murray's Guide to Oxfordshire informs us that 'the poet Chaucer resided at Woodstock, and is supposed to have taken much of the scenery of "The Dream" from the neighbouring park.' But the poem called 'Chaucer's Dream' is undoubtedly not by Chaucer; and, in the second place, whoever wrote it, the scenery there described is not that of Woodstock. Possibly the *Guide* meant the *Book of the Duchess;* for that was once known, mistakenly, by the title of 'Chaucer's Dream.'

We will just add that Woodstock is mentioned by name in 'The Cuckoo and Nightingale.' This poem is certainly not by Chaucer; but it is one of those attributed to him—

one of those belonging to the Chaucerian circle, and evidently to some extent inspired by the fond perusal of his writings ; so the naming of Woodstock there encourages the view here maintained.   The author, whoever it was, follows his master in the localisation of his story.

VIII

CHAUCER NOTES

(1.) *ROMAUNT OF THE ROSE*

(From the *Athenæum* for Nov. 12, 1881)

WITHOUT now going into the question whether the extant English version of the famous *Roman de la Rose* is by Chaucer or not, there are one or two prevalent misstatements that it may be useful to correct for the benefit of the ordinary reader, if for no one else.   These now to be mentioned occur one, or other, in some of the best current books about Chaucer.

(1.) It is commonly said that what is translated from Jean de Meung's part of the romance is abridged.   It is sometimes inferred that Chaucer's genius was much less in sympathy with Jean de Meung the keen and critical, than with his more romantic predecessor Guillaume de Loris. We are told, for instance, that 'Chaucer reproduces only one-half of the part contributed by Jean de Meung, and again condenses this half to one-third of its length.'   Now, in fact, the English version renders only some 3000 lines, (exactly 3060 in M. Francisque Michel's edition of the Roman) of Jean de Meung's 18,000 (exactly 18,148)—that is, only one-sixth ; and secondly, what is rendered is not

condensed.   The passages, in the original, consist together
of 3000 lines ; in the translation, of 3266.

(2.) The translation mentions 'the lordes son of Wynde-
sore,' the Lord of Windsor's son, as we should say in Modern
English.   By the side of Dame Franchise :

> daunced a bachelere ;
> I cannot tell you what he highte ;
> But faire he was of good highte,
> Alle hadde he be, I sey no more,
> The lordis sonne of Wyndesore.

And this has been taken to be a compliment to Chaucer's
friend and patron John of Gaunt, and of course to confirm
the notion that the translation is by Chaucer.   But, alas !
the line is but a faithful rendering of De Lorris's original,
which runs thus :—

> Uns bachelers jones s'estoit
> Pris à Franchise lez à lez.
> Ne soi comment ert apelé,
> Mès biaus estoit, se il fust ores
> Fiez au Seignor de Gundesores.

And it seems fairly certain that this Lord of Windsor's
son is not John of Gaunt, who was born some eighty years
after De Lorris's death, but, as my friend and colleague
Professor Gardiner has suggested to me, Richard, Earl of
Cornwall, King of the Romans.   A quotation from the
Annals of England will suffice my present purpose : 'He
served with reputation and success both in France and the
Holy Land : and he was in many respects a perfect contrast
to his brother the king, being wise, valiant and rich . . .
Richard was induced to aspire to the imperial dignity, and
bore the title of the King of the Romans, but derived little
else from his profuse expenditure of money abroad.'   I have
read somewhere—I hope presently to verify the recollection

—that special mention is made of him and his magnificence in some French chronicler or chroniclers of the thirteenth century—that is, by some contemporary of De Lorris.   The lord of Windsor, then, is King John.   He 'frequently resided' at Windsor; 'and hence his grant of Magna Charta at Runymede—'

3. Cf. Wicked Tongue (Malebouche) when he sees the lover and Bialacoil together, the translation says :—

> He myghte not his tunge withstonde
> Worse to reporte than he fonde,
> He was so fulle of cursed rage ;
> It satte hym welle of his lynage,
> For hym an Irish womman bare ;
> His tunge was fyled sharpe and square,
> Poygnaunt and right kervyng.
> And wonder bitter in spekyng :

—a passage that cannot but be read with a special painful interest just now.   'Writing not far from the time' remarks one of Chaucer's biographers, 'when the Statute of Kilkenny was passed, he (Chaucer) cannot lose the opportunity of inventing an Irish parentage for Wicked-tongue.'   But alas ! here, too, the translator, whoever he was, followed conscientiously the words of the original, where occurs the line,

> Qu'il fu filz d'une vieille Irese.

Mr Robert Bell thinks that 'irese' here does not denote the lady's nation, but her disposition, as being given to lie. But I presume M. Francisque Michel is right in glossing the word by Irlandaise and in his annotation :   'Les Irlandais ont toujours eu chez nous la plus détestable réputation, même avant les evénements qui en jetèrent sur notre sol un si grand nombre.'

He goes on to give an illustration of this statement, dated 1606. Something earlier would have been more to the purpose.

----

(2) *ECLYMPASTEYRE*

(From *The Athenæum* for April 8, 1882)

There these goddys lay and slepe,
Morpheus and *Eclympasteyre*,
That was the god of slepes eyre,
That slepe and dide noon other werke.
Boke of the Duchesse, 166-9.

Mais la déesse noble et chière
Tramist puis sa messagiere
Pour moi au noble dieu dormant.
Et le doulc dieu fit son commant ;
Car il envoya parmi l'air
L'un de ses fils *Enclimpostair.*
Froissart's *Paradis d'Amour.*

TYRWHITT, as is well known, gives up this strange word, which is known to occur only in these two passages. The annotator in the edition connected with the name of Robert Bell 'ventures to consider it a Greek word ($\dot{\epsilon}\varkappa\lambda\iota\mu\pi\acute{a}\sigma\tau\omega\rho$), which cannot, however, be traced to classical authors, formed from $\dot{\epsilon}\varkappa\lambda\iota\mu\pi\acute{a}\nu\omega$, a rare form of $\dot{\epsilon}\varkappa\lambda\epsilon\acute{\iota}\pi\omega$, one of the meanings of which is to cease, to die,' etc. This, is indeed, being venturesome—it is reckless audacity. To make no other objection, how could such a form as $\dot{\epsilon}\varkappa\lambda\iota\mu\pi\acute{a}\sigma\tau\omega\rho$ be drawn from $\dot{\epsilon}\varkappa\lambda\iota\mu\pi\acute{a}\nu\omega$? Not of more value—of less, if possible—is M. Sandras's suggestion that the word in question is compounded of *engle* (= *ange*) *imposteur.* Nor yet satisfactory are the derivations from $\dot{\epsilon}\varkappa\lambda\upsilon\pi\eta\tau\acute{\eta}\rho$ or $\dot{\epsilon}\gamma\varkappa\alpha\lambda\upsilon\pi\tau\acute{\eta}\rho$. Nor does Dr. ten Brink seem as happy as his excellent scholarship might lead us to hope when he solves the difficulty by supposing that 'pasteyre' is a corruption of 'Phobetora,' undoubtedly right as I believe him to be in his interpretation of 'Eclym,' which he takes to be 'Ikelon.'

The passage in Ovid, which Chaucer is more or less following, runs as follows, 'Met.' xi. 633-48 :—

> At pater [Somnus] e populo natorum mille suorum
> Excitat artificem simulatoremque figuræ
> Morphea.   Non illo jussos sollertius alter
> Exprimit incessus, vultumque sonumque loquendi ;
> Adjicit et vestes et consuetissima cuique
> Verba.   Sed hic solos homines imitatur ; at alter
> Fit fera, fit volucris, fit longo corpore serpens.
> Hunc Ikelon superi, mortale Phobetora vulgus
> Nominat.   Est etiam diversæ tertius artis,
> Phantasos.   Ille in humum saxumque undamque trabemque
> Quæque vacant anima fallaciter omnia transit.
> Regibus hi ducibusque suos ostendere vultus
> Nocte solent ; populos alii plebemque pererrant.
> Præterit hos senior ; cunctisque e fratribus unum
> Morphea qui peragat Thaumantidos edita, Somnus
> Eligit.

Dr. ten Brink, it will be seen, links together the celestial and the mortal names of the second of these thousand sons of Sleep; and so 'Eclympasteyre' would mean Like-Scarer. This is a somewhat awkward combination, as if one were to speak of Reuchlin-Capnio, Gerrit-Erasmus, etc.   Still it is not impossible, especially as Chaucer's scholarship was not of the most accurate kind.   But a graver, if not a fatal, objection to this explanation is the difficulty of that corruption of *Phobetora* into *Pasteyre*.

I now beg to propose a new solution of this perplexing term.   I hold that it is a compound of *Ikelon* and *plastor* or *plaster*, and so means simply likeness-maker, semblance-moulder.   Thus it exactly contains the idea of Ovid's phrase,

'Artificem simulatoremque figuræ,' and of a line immediately preceding those quoted, viz. :—

Somnia quæ veras æquent imitamine formas.

This is, indeed, the dominant idea of the passage, and is well expressed by such a compound as *Ikelo-plastor*.

Every one, I think, will agree that this formation would readily, would quite naturally, yield *Eclympasteyre*. *Ikelon* would so easily become Iklon, and this Eklon, Eklin, and through the influence of the *p*, Eklim, or Eklym, or Eclym. And *plastor* would so easily drop its *l*, for phonetic reasons, through the influence of the *l* in Eclym; and would inevitably corrupt its termination.

If it is objected that Chaucer could not know Greek enough to make such a compound, I answer, without going into the question how much Greek was known in England in the fourteenth century—a question on which something might well be said, if there were any need, or if the occasion served—that both *Ikelon* and *plastor* were accessible enough, if no Greek whatever was known to Chaucer and his contemporaries. *Ikelon*, as we have seen, he would find in Ovid; and derivatives of πλάσσω were sufficiently common in Latin. Thus Pliny has *plastes;* and *plasso* itself, *plasticator*, *plasticus*, as well as *plasma* and *plasmo*, occur in Latin writers of one age or another in post-classical literature. Ducange registers *plastaria*, *plasteria*, *plastrarius*, *plastrierius*, etc. Perhaps the identical form in Chaucer's mind was one of these latter. The stem must also have been familiar to Chaucer in various French derivatives. As to the meaning, Pliny uses *plastes* in the sense of a modeller, a statuary, and quotes a saying that *plastice* was 'mater statuariæ scalpturæque et cælaturæ.' Chaucer's acquaintance with the *Historia Naturalis* is well known.

(3) '*THE DRY SEA*'

(From *The Academy* for Jan. 28, 1882)

THERE has been, and is, much doubt as to what is meant by 'the dry sea' in Chaucer's *Book of the Duchess*. A writer in *The Saturday Review* plausibly suggested the desert of the Great Sahara; and there are current several other suggestions of more or less value. But I am much inclined to think that the phrase may be best explained by a reference to *Mandeville's Travels*—a book that must have been thoroughly familiar to Chaucer—and to the account given by that veracious writer of a *Sea of Sand*. See Mr Halliwell-Phillipps' edition of *Voiage and Travaile of Sir John Maundeville*, Knt., pp. 27-28 :—

And he (Prester John) hathe in his Lordscipes many grete marveyles. For in his Contre is the See that men clepen the Gravely See that is all Gravelle and Sand with outen ony drope of Watre ; and it ebbethe and flowethe in grete waives as other Sees don ; and it is never stille ne in pes in no maner cesoun. And no man may passe that See be navye ne be no maner of craft ; and therefore may no man knowe what Land is beyond that See. And alle be it that it have no Watre, yit men fynden there in and on the Bankes fulle gode Fissche of other maner of kynde and schappe thanne men fynden in ony other See ; and thei ben of righte goode tast, and delycious to mannes mete.

Here is 'a dry sea' with a vengeance. Surely this is what Chaucer means. The author who called himself Mandeville, seems to have derived his account of this remarkable phenomenon from Cedric of Portenau. See, however, Prof. Skeat's note in his valuable edition of Chaucer's *Minor Poems* (1891).

(4) *CHAUCER AT ALDGATE*

(From *The Academy* for Dec. 6, 1879)

IN our dearth of information about Chaucer's life the slightest new fact or observation is welcome, and so what is now pointed out for the first time, I believe, may be worth notice. It relates to the length of his residence in Aldgate—that is, in the gate of Aldgate.

It is well known that that dwelling-place was leased to the poet in May 1374. I find that the same premises were granted to one Richard Foster in October 1386. Thus the poet lived in the old Gate-house certainly not much more than twelve years. That he lived there nearly, if not quite, all these twelve years is fairly certain, if we consider that a chief reason for the selection of such a locality must have been its neighbourhood to the scene of his daily business as Controller of the Customs, and that it was not till February 1385 that he was allowed to nominate a permanent deputy. When first appointed he was ordered to write the rolls with his own hand, to be always on the spot, and perform his duties personally. This was in June 1374. We may safely conclude that his taking the Gate-house in that same year and his leaving it some eleven or twelve years afterwards were both connected with that appointment of his. For eleven years the rigorous terms of it necessitated his living near his office ; and then he was free to move, and move he soon did.

Probably enough, his going into Parliament was already mooted in 1385. Certainly he was one of the knights of the shire for Kent in the Parliament that sat through October 1386. And if he had not left Aldgate in 1385, we might expect to find him leaving it when his parliamentary duties called for his frequent presence in Westminster.

However this may be, in October 1386 'the dwelling-house above the gate of Aldgate' was granted by the Corporation to one Richard Forster, possibly identical with the 'Richard Forrester' who was one of Chaucer's proxies when he went abroad for a time in May 1378.

In that old tower of Aldgate, then, where the poet lived for some dozen years, with temporary absences, as when he was employed abroad on the royal service, most of the works of what may be called his Middle Period were in all probability written. It was there he studied and wrote with the zeal he describes in *The House of Fame.* There he composed his Life of St Cecilia (afterwards used for the Second Nun's Tale), his stories of Griselda, of Constance, of the Christian boy the Jews murdered (afterwards used, the first with additions, for the Clerk's Tale, the Man of Law's, and the Prioress'), *Palamon and Arcite* (the first draught of what we know as the Knight's Tale), his *Troilus and Cressida*, and his *House of Fame*, besides his translation of Boethius' *Consolation of Philosophy.*

The Book of the Duchess was written five years before he went there, when it appears from the poem that he was living, or staying, at Windsor or at Woodstock.

The Legend of Good Women was written after he had moved away, probably very shortly afterwards, likely enough in the spring or summer of 1386; for, probably enough, he ceased to reside in the Gate-house a little time before he ceased to be the lessee. Probably his moving brought him into a closer connexion with the Court, and the dedication of *The Legend* may be regarded as a sign of this increased intimacy. Anyhow—and the remark may be of use towards settling the date of it—the house he mentions in *The Legend*

can scarcely have been his tower in Aldgate (Aldine
edition, v. 282):—

> When that the sun out of the south gon weste,
> And that this flower gon close and go to reste
> For darkness of the night, for which she dredde,
> Home to mine house full swiftly I me spedde,
> To go to rest and early for to rise,
> To see this flower spread, as I devise;
> And in a little arbour that I have
> That benched was on turves fresh ygrave,
> I bad men shoulde me my couche make,
> For dainty of the newe summer's sake,
> I bad them strawen flowers on my bed.

I must express my gratitude to Dr Sharp, the Records
Clerk, for his valuable assistance in searching certain letter-
books now in his keeping at the Guildhall. For permission
to inspect them I have to thank the Town Clerk.

---

(5) *THE CLERK'S TALE*

(From a publication of the Chaucer Society, 1875)

CHAUCER has followed Petrarch's version very closely
throughout his poem, noticeably in his treatment of
Lord Walter, and in the comment towards the end:

> This story is sayd, not for that wyves scholde, etc.

Petrarch's version, though mainly founded on that of Boccaccio, as he expressly states, differs from that 'Novel' in
several important ways.

For the mere form the 'novel' is certainly to be preferred.
Petrarch's Latinity is by no means faultless. Sometimes it
is marred by grave solecisms; seldom, or never, does it

attain any complete fluency and grace. He is not, nor was it in the nature of things that he should be, absolute master of an instrument that was, in fact, foreign to his hands. His own conceptions of his Latin skill were a delusion. Would that he had had the wisdom of David, who declined moving to battle in arms he had not proved! A translation of the old story that stirred him so deeply—'quæ ita mihi placuit meque detinuit ut inter tot curas quæ pene mei ipsius immemorem facem illam memoriæ mandare voiuerim ut et ipse eam animo quotiens vellem, non sine voluntate repeterem et amicis ut sit confabulantibus renarrem, si quando tale accidisset'—if given metrically in his mother tongue, could scarcely have failed to have added glory to his own renown, and to that of the literature of which he was, and is, so brilliant an ornament. But even through the not immaculate medium of Early Renaissance Latin the exquisite beauty of the old story shines out with a piercing effulgence, just, indeed, as the fairness of the heroine herself, when we first see her, could not be hid for all the mean cottage in which she lived obscurely with her father, and the sordid dress that marked and befitted her humble rank. And certainly it was from that version that Chaucer formed his rendering, whether or not he had previously been attracted to the tale by any *viva voce* recital of it heard in some personal interview with Petrarch.

For the spirit, Petrarch seems to have entered more profoundly into the proper motive of the tale than did Boccaccio. Boccaccio grows somewhat impatient and angry with Gualtieri, even as Ellis in a misapprehending contrast he draws between *Griselda* and *the Nut Brown Maid*. Probably Chaucer, too, when maturer, would not have tolerated him; but Chaucer, when he wrote the *Clerkes Tale*, had not yet acquired that breadth and comprehension of view—that wide and catholic survey—that habit of independent realisation, which characterise his more perfect works; he still wrote with the subservience of the disciple rather than with the authority of the master; he took what good the gods provided, or seemed to provide, and aimed at an obeisant and faithful reproduction. Petrarch retold the story in the medieval spirit in which he had originally found it; for the *Decamerone* revived it in his mind, not first made it known; when the *Decamerone* reached him, he bethought him how 'mihi semper ante multos annos audita placuisset.' And in that same spirit Chaucer accepted, and echoed it. Now it is the characteristic of the unsophisticated medieval littérateur that he deals with one idea at a time. It would often lead to a highly injurious conclusion to attach at all equal moral importance, or rather any moral importance, to the subordinate parts of what he sets forth. The central lesson is kept well in view; the others must look to themselves. The principal figure is brought into relief with enthusiasm; on the mere surroundings and background little or no care is spent. Thus many of the stories the Knight of the Tour Landry tells his daughters are sound enough at the core; but as wholes they are anything but edifying—are not only non-moral, but immoral and contra-moral. The mind of the hearer, as of the reciter, is supposed to be fixed on the main notion, and so incapable of seduction by any lateral matters of a less exemplary sort. So, when the Trouvère sang of Friendship in *Eger and Grime*, he did not, when concentrated on that noble theme, deem it his concern to see that other virtues were not violated, provided that one was honoured and glorified. And so in the story of Griselda, if we would read it in the spirit of the day when it became current, we should not vex ourselves into any righteous indignation against the immediate author of her most touching distresses. The old story does not make the Marquis a monster in human shape; indeed, it represents him as a man of a noble and loveable nature; if he is not so, then even in the end Griselda reaps no earthly reward in permanently securing his admiration and love. And yet this Marquis perpetrates inexpressible cruelties; he is a very wolf, ruthlessly teasing and tearing the gentlest of lambs. The explanation is in accordance with what has just been said; the patience of Griselda is the one theme of the tale, and nothing else is to be regarded. In relation to her the Marquis has no moral being; he is a mere means of showing forth her supreme excellence, a mere mechanical expedient. He is no more morally than a thorn in the saint's footpath, or a wheel, or a cross. Surely it is vain to be wroth with him; who rages against the mere fire that enfolds the Martyr, or the nails that pierce the hands of a crucified Believer? Indeed, nothing in the tale is of any ethical moment but the carriage of the heroine herself. The eyes and the heart of the old century when she first appeared were fastened devoutly on that single form, and let all else go by. She is wifely obedience itself, nothing else. Before that virtue all other virtues bow. It enjoys a complete monopoly, an absolute sway. Other moral life is suspended in this representation of it. She has but one function—to obey; for her there is but one sin possible, and that is to murmur. She is all meekness, all yielding, all resignation.

Such a figure has comparatively few charms for us of these latter days. But it pleased the world once—even down to Shakespeare's time, who himself portrayed it in one of his earliest plays: Catherine at the end of the *Taming of the Shrew*, is a phase of Griselda. Perhaps in ages when much most ignorant abuse of women prevailed in literature—

abuse springing mainly out of the vile prejudices and super-
stitions of the medieval Church—some such figure might
have been expected to arise. It is the figure of a reaction.
The hearts of men refused to accept the dishonouring pictures so often drawn of their fellow mortals. They rose in
a loyal insurrection against lying fables of essential wanton-
ness and of shameful obstinacy. To such chivalrous rebels
the pale, sad, constant face of Griselda showed itself as the
image of far other experiences and histories ; and they gazed
on it as on the face of their saint. With an infinite reverence they saw her still calm and quiet in the midst of
anguishes, with heart breaking, but lips uttering no ill word,
with eyes that through the tears with which kindly nature of
herself would relieve the terrible drought of sorrow still
looked nothing but inalienable tenderness and love.

In Prof. Child's *English and Scottish Ballads*, vol. iv.,
may be found the ballad of *Patient Grissel*. (Prof. Child
is certainly wrong in saying that Boccaccio derived the incidents from Petrarch.) This ballad is the work of Thomas
Deloney, a mere day-labourer in verse-making of Queen
Elizabeth's time, and is worthy of its author. A play on
this subject, written by Dekker, Chettle, and Haughton, has
been printed by the Shakespeare Society. Another play of
earlier date is lost ; as also probably an older ballad than
that by Deloney.

With the incidents in the third temptation of Griselda,
when she 'waits' at the new wedding of her husband, and at
last finds that the supposed bride is her own daughter,
should be compared the old ballad of *Fair Annie*. There,
too, the heroine performs a like service, not without much
weeping, for a fair lady who has come from over the sea to
wed the Fair Annie's lover. At last it is found that this

new comer is the Fair Annie's sister, who nobly refuses to marry at her expense; and so all is made well.   See *Lord Thomas and Fair Annie* in the *Minstrelsy of the Scottish Border;* see also Herd's, Motherwell's, and Chambers' Collections.   Scott points out that 'the tale is much the same with the Breton romance called *Lai le Frain,* or the Song of the Ash.'   He also states that 'a ballad agreeing in every respect with that which follows exists in the Danish Collection of ancient songs entitled *Kæmpe Viser.* It is called *Skiæn Anna, i.e.,* Fair Annie, and has been translated literally by my learned friend, Mr Robert Jamieson. See his *Popular Ballads,* Edin., 1806, vol. ii. p. 100.'   See *Lay le Freine,* 305, in Weber's *Metrical Romances,* vol. i. See a translation of the Danish ballad in Prior's *Ancient Danish Ballads,* iii. 298-306, and Appendix H. in that volume.

------

(6) '*LYMOTE*'

(From *The Athenæum* for April 9, 1887)

THE name 'Lymote' in Chaucer's *House of Fame* (iii. 184), to adopt for the nonce the spelling of Caxton and Thynne (the Fairfax MS. spells it 'Limete,' the Bodleian 'Lumete,' according to Dr Furnivall's parallel-text edition), has never yet, I believe, been identified. I venture to suggest that it is a corruption of ' Elymas.'

This suggestion rests on the facts (1) that Lymote is mentioned by Chaucer in connexion with Simon Magus, and (2) that Simon Magus and Elymas are frequently associated. The stories of both men are to be found not far from each other in the Acts of the Apostles (see chaps. viii. and xiii.), and so, naturally enough, they are often linked together elsewhere; for instance, in Tertullian's *De Anima* (chap. lvii.): 'Multa utique et adversus apostolos Simon dedit et Elymas magi; sed plaga cœcitatis de præstigiis non fuit.'

'Nor, perhaps, are the words 'Lymote' and 'Elymas' so difficult to identify as at first it might seem. The Greek form is Ἐλύμας (ἀνθίστατο δὲ αὐτοῖς Ἐλύμας), *i.e.*, the accented syllable is not the first, as in our pronunciation, but the penultimate. Therefore the unaccented E would easily drop off, just as 'Apulia' becomes 'Poyle' (from 'Pulia); *incensoir*, censer; *episcopus*, bishop; *hydrópsis*, dropsy, etc. Thus 'Elymas' would become 'Lymas.'

To explain the termination of Chaucer's form one can only conjecture that the Ἐλύμας was declined like ἐλέφας and such words. This would give a crude form Ἐλύμαντ, which by absorption of the ν and modification of the vowel might produce 'Lumot,' or, with transliteration, 'Lymot.' Or, with less precise scholarship, it might be declined like κέρας; and so there would be a stem Ἐλύματ, whence might come 'Lumat.' Compare Chaucer's and Spenser's 'Mart' for Mars. But I must confess that in the only passage in which I have found the word inflected—not that I have searched far and wide for its inflected occurrences—it is declined as of 'the first declension.' At least, 'Elyma' is the ablative in the index to chap. xiii. of the Acts in the Vulgate, 'Elyma mago......excæcato.'

---

(7) *THE PARLIAMENT OF FOWLS*
(From *The Academy*, Nov. 19, 1881)

THE obligations of Chaucer in his *Parliament of Fowls* to Cicero, Ovid, and Boccaccio have been sufficiently noticed. But scarcely so his obligations to Alanus de

Insulis, though he mentions him by name, and, instead of describing 'the noble goddess Nature' himself, refers the reader to Alanus' description of her:

> 'And right as Aleyn in the Pleynt of Kynde
> Deuyseth Nature in suche array & face:
> In swich aray men myghte hire there yfynde.'

Yet it is well worth noticing that it is from the work here named—the *De Conquestu vel Planctu Naturae* (a work modelled in some respects on that favourite medieval writing, Boethius' *De Consolatione Philosophiae*)—Chaucer derived the somewhat fantastic title given to his poem, as well as some ideas.

Alanus describes at great length the form and costume of Nature as she appears approaching him. On her robe, he says—a robe of tissue so 'subtilized' and fine 'ut ejus aerisque eandem crederes esse naturam'—'prout oculis pictura imaginabatur, *animalium celebratur concilium*,' *i.e.*, 'There is held a Parliament of Animals.' Here, clearly, is the suggestion of the name of Chaucer's poem, and of something more. 'Concilium,' says Maigne d'Arnis' *Ducange*, is used for 'Parliamentum apud Anglicos Scriptores.'

This poem is variously styled the Parliament of Fowls, The Parliament of Birds, The Assembly of Fowls, and The Assembly of Birds. In the Prologue to the Legend of Good Women it is styled the "Parliament of Foules;' in the *Preces de Chauceres*, at the end of the Parson's Tale, it is spoken of as 'the book of Seint Valentines day and of the Parliment of briddes.' Lydgate writes :—

> Of fowles also he wrote the Parlyment,
> Therein remembrynge of ryall Egles three
> Howe in their choyse they felt adversite ;

> Tofore Nature profered the batayle
> Eche for his partye, if he wolde avayle.

Spenser, in a stanza we will venture to quote, for everybody will like to be reminded of it, speaks of the *Foules Parley* :—

> So hard it is for any living wight
>   All her array & vestiments to tell
> That old Dan Geffrey (in whose gentle spright
>   The pure well head of Poesie did dwell)
> In his *Foules parley* durst not with it mell,
>   But it transferd to Alane who he thought
> Had in his *Plaint of kinde* describ'd it well ;
>   Which who will read set forth so as it ought,
> Go seek he out that Alane where he may be sought.

In the MSS. it is commonly called either the Parliament of Fowls, or the Parliament of Birds.

Of course the term Parliament may be used here in its old general sense of a conference—a 'colloquium,' expressed in medieval Latin by *Parliamentum* as well as by *concilium* and *consilium*. But likely enough Chaucer may have had in his mind, as he went on with his story, the then comparatively new idea of Parliament as a representative assembly. This thought may have suggested to him the appointment of delegates to offer their opinion and advice on the delicate question to whom the formel's hand is to be given ; and so we have four M.P.'s or spokes-birds to represent respectively the fowl of raven or birds of prey, the water-fowl, the worm-fowl, and the seed-fowl.

Though Alan speaks of a 'Concilium Animalium,' what he goes on to describe is a Concilium Avium, a Bird Parliament. It is interesting to compare his list with Chaucer's. On the whole, there is more difference than likeness ; but Chaucer has probably taken one or two hints from the earlier writer. At all events, Chaucer may be illustrated from him.

Chaucer speaks of 'the Coward Kite.' Alan's words are curious, 'Illic milvus, venatoris induens personam, venatione furtiva larvam gerebat ancipitris.'

And compare the following pairs of quotations :—

> 'There was the tiraunt with his fethres donne
> And greye, I mene the goshauk that doth pyne
> To bryddis for his outrageous ravyne.'

'Illic ancipiter, civitatis praefêctus aeriae, violenta tyrannide a subditis redditus exposcebat.'

> 'The jalous swan ayens his deth that singeth.'

'Illic olor, sui funeris praeco, citherizationis organo vitae prophetabat apocopam.'

> 'The oule eek that of dethe the bode bringeth.'

'Illic bubo, propheta miseriae, psalmodias funereae lamentationis praecinebat.'

> 'The crane, the geaunt, with his trompes soun.'

'Grus . . . giganteae quantitatis evadebat excessum.'

> 'The thef the chogh.'

'Illic monedula, latrocinio laudabili reculas thesaurizans, innatae avaritiae argumenta monstrabat.'

> 'The jangling pye.'

'Illic pica, dubio picturata colore, curam logices perennabat insomnem.'

> 'The cok that orloge is of thorpes lyte.'

'Illic gallus, tanquam vulgaris astrologus, suæ vocis horologio horarum loquebatur discrimina.'

> 'The wedded turtel with her herte trewe.'

'Illic turtur, suo viduata consorte, amorem epilogare dedignans, in altero bigamiae refutabat solatia.'

> 'The pecok with his aungels fethers bright.'

'Illic in pavone tantum pulcritudinis compluit Natura thesaurum ut eam postea crederes mendicasse.'

> 'The raven wys.'

'Illic corvus, zelotypiae abhorrens dedecus, suos foetus non sua esse pignora fatebatur, usque dum comperto nigri argumento coloris, hoc quasi secum disputans comprobat.' [This is an excellent illustration of Chaucer's epithet, though the proof that contents the observant and reflecting bird would scarcely satisfy a judicial mind, unless ravens are communistic in respect of their mates.]

' The crow with voice of care.'
' Illic cornix ventura prognosticans, nugatorio concitabatur garritu.'

A careful comparison of these two *catalogues raisonnés*—the lists are by no means identical any more than the descriptions—certainly casts light on Chaucer's genius. One can scarcely doubt that his taste appreciated duly the affected and far-fetched style of the older writer. And certainly one may see how he was not content to behold Nature merely through the spectacles of books, but loved to gaze on her face to face. Dear as his old books were to him—'totorn' with faithful use (see l. 110 of the *P. of F.*)—dearer yet was Nature. Sweet were the old songs on the daisy; but the daisy itself was still sweeter. Entertaining and learned were the accounts to be found in literature of his fellow-creatures the birds ; but better than hearing of them he enjoyed hearing them and watching their humours—for they, too, have their humours—with an eye at once merry and kindly. Birds, no less than men, he observed keenly, portrayed wittily, and with all the gentleness of a most gentle heart.

(8.) *THE DATE OF THE CANTERBURY TALES*

(From *The Athenæum* for April 8th, 1893)

AS a really satisfactory study of Chaucer's art and mind cannot be made till the chronological order of his works is to some considerable extent discovered and established, it is a matter of congratulation that in the last few years so much has been done in this latter direction, and that as to the date of many poems, though by no means of all, there is now a fairly general agreement amongst really competent scholars. Of course the most interesting and important of all such questions is the date of the Prologue to *The Canterbury Tales*. It has been, and is by some still placed as late as 1393. But the evidence for placing it so late is extremely slight, if, indeed, there is any at all that bears investigation; whereas assuredly many things point to the year 1387 or thereabouts, as the year of the pilgrimage and of Chaucer's immortal description of it. I do not now propose to discuss this matter at large, but only to call attention to an argument in favour of the earlier date which has, I think, not yet been noticed, and which, if it has not a decisive, has certainly a corroborative value.

We are told of the merchant that

> He wolde the sea were kept for anything
> Bitwixe Middelburgh and Orewelle,

that he thought it of prime moment that the passage from Harwich to Middelburgh should be swept clear of pirates. Why Middelburgh? The answer to this query gives a curious confirmation of the date 1387 or thereabouts; it proves that the Prologue must have been written not before 1384 and not later than 1388. In the year 1384 the wool-staple was removed from Calais and established at Middelburgh; in 1388 it was fixed once more at Calais (see Craik's *History of British Commerce*, 1. 123.) The said woolstaple led a somewhat nomad life in the fourteenth century; it was at different times established at Bruges, and Antwerp, not to mention various towns in England. But its only sojourn at Middelburgh was that in the years 1384–8; and so only just at that time could the merchant's words have their full significance—have a special pointedness.

A careful examination of the case makes it highly improbable that the Prologue was written early in those four or five years. We know it was not till February 1385 that Chaucer was released from the drudgery of daily personal attendance at the Custom House, where he held two appointments, being (since 1374) the Comptroller of the Wool Customs, and also (since 1382) the Comptroller of the Petty Customs—appointments, by the way, that must have made him very familiar with the merchants of the day. There is good reason for believing that the first literary product of his days of comparative leisure was the 'Legend of Good Women.' That work, doomed never to be finished, was still in hand (and probably becoming somewhat burdensome to him through the monotony of the subject matter) when the larger and happier and more congenial idea of the Canterbury pilgrimage occurred to him. Thus it was probably after 1386—probably immediately after—that he composed the Prologue.

One convenience of his new and admirable design, was that it permitted him to use up much old material—to slightly revise and to bring into a series, sundry tales he had composed many years before—as those of Griselda, of Constance, of St Cecily, and of the Christian Boy, whom the Jews were said to have murdered, and possibly other pieces. But except, perhaps, 'The Tale of Melibeus,' and the 'Parson's Tale,' all the new tales—the tales that were written in the first instance for a place in the Canterbury sequence—were probably produced very shortly after the Prologue, *i.e.*, in the latter part of 1387, and in the four or five following years. Certainly in 1393, if that date is accepted for the *Compleynt of Venus*, and it is probable enough

(see Prof. Skeat's excellent edition of the *Minor Poems*)
Chaucer felt or seemed to feel, his right hand losing its
cunning. Possibly later on he recovered health and spirits,
for 1393 he was only some fifty-three years old, and he was
to live to near the end of the century. But it is scarcely
likely his admirable comic vein ever again flowed so freely
as in 1387, and the three or four following years. That is
the supreme period of his humorous and his dramatic
power. At all events in 1393—just five hundred years ago
—in presenting his *Compleynt of Venus* to a princess,
probably the Duchess of York, he speaks of his 'litel suffi-
same.'

> For eld that in my spirit dulleth me,
> Hath of endyting al the soteltie
> Wel ny bereft out of my remembraunce.

(9.) *THE PRIORESS'S 'GREATEST OATH'*

(From *The Athenæum* for Jan. 10, 1891)

IN his description of the Prioress in the Prologue to
the *Canterbury Tales*, Chaucer informs us that 'Her
greatest oath was but by St Loy' ('Hir gretteste ooth was but
by Seynt Loy.') And there has been much discussion as to
why this good lady should swear by St Loy of all the saints
in the calendar, inasmuch as St Loy or Eloy—for Loy
appears to be a clipped and more familiar form of the name
Eloy, which is the French form of Eligius—is commonly
known as the patron of 'goldsmiths, blacksmiths, and
all workers in metals, also of farriers and horses' (Mrs
Jameson's *Sacred and Legendary Art*, vol. ii. 728-32, ed.
1863.) It is natural enough, then, that the carter in 'The

Friar's Tale' should invoke God and St Loy when his horse is struggling to pull his cart out of the slough. But what is his saintship to the Prioress, or she to his saintship?

An attempt has been made to get out of the difficulty by suggesting that by St Loy is meant St Louis; but such a solution creates other difficulties not less formidable than the one it aims at solving, as, *e.g.*, why should the carter swear by St Louis of France? 'Warton's notion that Loy was a form of Louis,' observes Dr Skeat, 'only shows how utterly unknown in his time were the phonetic laws of Old French.' Again, it has been suggested that Loy is simply the French *loi* = law, and that what Chaucer means is that the Prioress never used a stronger expletive than 'par sa loi,' which Roquefort, we are reminded, interprets as equivalent to 'par sa foi, en bonne foi, en honnête homme.' And this would give good sense enough—gives, I think, the real sense; but such a phrase as 'Seynt loi' or 'Seynte loi' (for which there is the authority of one MS.) seems scarcely plausible; at all events, it cannot be accepted without further support than has yet been furnished for it. Moreover, the form Loy undoubtedly occurs elsewhere as a variant of Eloy. Thus there is a half-ruined chapel near Exeter dedicated to St Eligius or St Eloy, which is commonly known as St Loy's. Again, Barnaby Googe writes, 'And *Loye* the Smith doth look to horse, and smithes of all degree,' etc.; and many other proofs of this identity could be quoted if necessary. In this connection it should be remembered that, however strange his name to us, St Eloy was extremely well known in the Middle Ages. According to Sir Thomas More, his day (December 1st) came to be more thought of than Easter Day itself. A correspondent in the pages of a contemporary journal remarks that St Loy or Eloy was almost as popular in France in the Middle Ages as either

St Denis or St Remi, and also exceedingly popular in England.'

Various are the conjectures of those that insist, as I think rightly, on the identity of St Loi and St Eloi. *E.g.*, says one distinguished scholar: 'The phrase seems to be an ejaculation, or rather invocation, of St Eloi by a nervous rider in the sense of "marry come up."' Says another of yet greater note: 'Perhaps she invoked St Loy as being the patron saint of goldsmiths; for she seems to have been a little given to a love of gold and corals; see ll. 158-162.'

May I venture to suggest a quite different explanation? I believe the reference is to the fact that on a certain famous occasion, St Eloy refused to take an oath—firmly declined to swear. And thus we arrive at what I have already said appears to be the real sense of the words, viz., the Prioress never swore at all.

The story is given at full length by St Ouen, the contemporary and friend of St Eligius, in his *Vita Sti Eligii*, though, oddly enough, Alban Butler in his rendering of that biography omits it. It will be found, however, in Maitland's *Dark Ages*, pp. 83-4, ed. 1853. King Dagobert, on appointing Eligius to some confidential situation, or being about to employ him in some business of state, desired him to take an oath on the relics of the saints. Eligius 'respectfully but firmly' refused, 'divinum intuitum verens,' *i.e.*, fearing the judgment of Heaven (*intuitus* in medieval Latin is used in the sense of *arbitrium, sententia, judicium*), or perhaps having respect for the promptings of Heaven, *i.e.*, for the voice of conscience. The king insisted; Eligius, in a dire extremity, 'burst into tears. The king had the good sense to give way, to speak to him in a kind and soothing manner, and to dismiss him with a cheerful countenance and an assurance that he should feel more confidence in him than if he had sworn all sorts of oaths—"pollicens se plus eum ex hoc jam crediturum quam si multimoda tunc dedisset juramenta ! "'

The habit of garnishing talk with 'good mouth-filling oaths' was certainly very prevalent in the Middle Ages. The ordinary person probably felt as great a contempt for such weakly phrases as 'in good sooth' as Hotspur himself. Mine host Harry Bailey at once 'smells a loller in the wind' when the Parson, outraged by his 'Goddes bones' and 'Goddes dignitee,'

> him answered : ' Benedicite !
> What eileth the man so sinfully to swere ?

But even then some natures, *e.g.*, the Parson just quoted, resented this current violence of language, this wild excess of affirmation and denial, and contented themselves with a milder vocabulary. St Eloy was haply one of these. At all events, he forswore swearing, so to speak ; and so an oath by Eloy would mean an oath according to his usage, *i.e.*, an oath such as he might have uttered or approved, *i.e.*, no oath at all.

It is consistent with this interpretation, though it may not confirm it, that the Prioress in her Prologue uses no adjurations such as prevail more or less in other parts of the *Canterbury Tales*.

Lastly, such a way of speaking is just after Chaucer's manner. It is inspired by just the same dry humour that dictates the well-known lines in the description of the Shipman :—

> If that he faught and hadde the heier hond,
> *By water he sente hem hoom to every lond.*

———

(10.) '*THE PREESTES THREE*'

(From *The Academy* for Jan. 31, 1875)

MR FURNIVALL has certainly increased the already great obligations of all Chaucer students to him, by the Illustrations of the *Prologue* he has lately drawn from the paper survey of the Abbey of St Mary's, Winchester, and from *Ducange*, of which an account is given in the last number of *The Academy*. Certain features in the portrait of the Prioress are for the first time explained : the term Chaplain, as applied to a Nun, is satisfactorily defended, and it is shown that there might be several attendant priests, yet it may remain, and in my opinion it does remain, a question whether we have the original text in l. 164.

Was not Tyrwhitt right after all as to that question, however he may have erred in condemning *Chaplain*? See his valuable note in his *Introductory Discourse*. The facts to be considered are these :—

(1.) Chaucer in the proem of the *Prologue*, undertakes to describe for us the condition, the quality and degree, and the array of each one of his pilgrims. And this programme it may be said, he carries out in every instance, except in those of the Nun, and of the 'Preestes three.' Surely this imperfection excites and justifies a suspicion that the text has been disturbed? Let any one who knows the *Prologue* decide for himself, whether there is not a perceptible and unusual abruptness in this couplet :—

> Another Nonne also with hire hadde she
> That was her chapelleine, and Preestes three.

Does not everybody feel that the sketch of the Nun is maimed and mutilated? Chaucer is just beginning a portrait that might have held artistic rank with his other masterpieces, when something or other knocks the brush out of his hand; or more probably, he had finished the portrait, when somebody's sponge, possibly his own, for a reason that may be conjectured, descends ruthlessly on the canvas, and leaves nothing but the first strokes.

(2.) There is not elsewhere, a trace of more than one priest. See the *Nonnes Preestes Prologue* :—

> Then speke our hoste with rude speeche and bold
> And sayd unto *the Nonnes Preest* anon :
> Come here *thou Preest*, come hither thou Sire John.

Is it satisfactory to say that the host picks out Sir John, as being the chief of the priests?

(3.) We are expressly told that there were twenty-nine pilgrims assembled at the Tabard. Now, if we admit the Preestes three, there were thirty-one. And it seems absurd to say, as has been said, that twenty-nine must be taken as a round number. What, then, is an unround number? Chaucer is always singularly exact in details; and when he says twenty-nine it must be taken to mean twenty-nine.

(11.) *THE NAME PALAMON IN THE KNIGHT'S TALE*

(From *The Academy* for Jan. 17, 1874)

THAT the ultimate original of the *Knight's Tale* is a Greek story, there can be little question. The whole poem is marked by Greek features, though seen for the most part through an atmosphere of romance. One may easily believe that Boccaccio's authority was one of those scholars who, already in the fourteenth century, began to leave the sinking Constantinople, and find a welcome in the country destined to be the nurse of the Renaissance.

Evidently the names Palamon and Arcite are corruptions of old Greek names. The Middle Ages gave strange shapes to many a well-known classical form. See, for instance, the catalogue of worthies in Chaucer's *House of Fame*. It was no violent exercise of this science that converted *Archytes* (Αρχύτας) into *Arcite*. The name *Palamon* is the more interesting because it may be shown to be significant of the person who bears it. It is a modification in form and accent of the Greek *Palæmon* (Παλαίμων) a name borne by several celebrated ancients. Spenser, it may be noted in passing, living at a time when scholarship was beginning to pay more attention to accuracy, more correctly writes Palémon (See *Colin Clout's Come Home Again*, line 396). If we look at the radical force of this name, we shall see its appropriateness in the *Teseide*, and the Canterbury Tale founded on the *Teseide*. It means properly 'the wrestler,' and in this sense is applied to Hercules by Sycophron of Alexandria. It is in fact equivalent to παλαιστής. But παλαιστής is used metaphorically to denote a 'suitor,' and what I suggest is, that this is less the meaning of παλαίμων as borne by the 'servant' of the Lady Ewing.

Palamon is emphatically the lover—the lover pure and simple. He is 'all for love!' Arcite is the *protégé* of Mars; but Palamon of Venus. See his prayer to his goddess:

> Fairest of faire, O lady myn Venus,
>
> .　.　.　.　.　.　.　.
>
> Allas! I'ne have no langage for to telle
> Theffectes ne the tormentz of myn helle.
>
> .　.　.　.　.　.　.　.
>
> Considere al this, and rewe upon my sore
> As wisly as I shal for evermore

> Emforth my might thi trewe servant be.
>
> .   .   .   .
>
> I kepe noght of armes for to yelpe
> Ne I ne axe to morwe to haue victorie,
> Ne renown in this caas, ne veyne glorie,
> Of pris of armes, blowen up and doun
> But I wolde have fully possessioun
> Of Emelye, and dye in thi servise ;
> Fynd thou the manere how, and in what wyse
> I recche not but it may bettre be,
> To have victorie of hem, or they of me,
> So that I have my lady in myn armes.

For him, as for King Pharamond, 'love is enough.'

For παλαιστής itself, see Æsch. *Agam.* 1206, where Kassandra says of Apollo :

$$\text{ἀλλ' ἦν παλαιστὴς κάρτ' ἐμοι πνέων χάριν.}$$

Compare *As You Like It*, I. iii.

Celia. Come, come, *wrestle* with thy affections.
Roselind. O ! they take the part of a better *wrestler* than myself.
Celia. O ! a good wish upon you, you will try in time in spite of a fall.

Where the double intention of 'wrestler' is to be noted. If one may speak of 'Adam Cupid,' Cupid the archer,

> 'That shot so trim
> When King Cophetua loved the beggar-maid,'

why not of Cupid the wrestler ?

———

(12.) *GEOFFREY AND THOMAS CHAUCER*

(From *The Athenæum* for March 31, 1888)

THERE has always been fair reason for believing that Thomas Chaucer was a son of the poet, and the belief has been rendered yet more probable by the fact to which

Mr Selby called attention in these columns some eighteen months ago, that Thomas succeeded Geoffrey as forester of North Petherton Park, Somersetshire. I wish now further to corroborate, if not finally to establish it, by quoting the statement of a contemporary authority. It has been quoted before, once at least—by Chalmers in his *British Poets*—but not in this connection, and seems of late years to have been entirely overlooked.

It is to be found in Gascoigne's *Theological Dictionary*. This work, existing in MS. in the library of Lincoln College, Oxford, has not yet been printed as a whole. The volume of extracts from it, edited a few years ago by Prof. Thorold Rogers, does not contain the passage that concerns us, which occurs on p. 377 of *Pars Secunda ;* nor, so far as I know, has all this passage been exactly printed before, though it was certainly known to Anthony Wood. My friend the Rector of Lincoln has been so very good as to verify the sentence given by Chalmers, and to copy out the words that immediately precede it.

Gascoigne is speaking of too late repentances. Our Lord, he says, tells us to pray that our flight may not be in the winter or on the Sabbath day, and then ingeniously interprets such flight in this way: 'Fugit in hyeme qui optat fugere a malo consequente peccatum, quum non potest illud fugere nec illud cavere.' He then illustrates his meaning by the instances of Judas and (may Heaven forgive him for such an unkindly conjunction !) of the poet Chaucer. 'Sic plures,' he goes on after recounting Judas's fate, 'penitere se postea dicunt, quando mala sua et mala per eos [= se ?] inducta destruere non possunt ; sicut Chawserus ante mortem suam sepe clamavit.' 'Ve michi ! ve michi ! quia revocare nec destruere jam potero illa quæ male scripsi de malo et turpissimo amore hominum ad mulieres, et jam de homine

in hominem continuabuntur. Velim! Nolim!' [*i.e.*, I wish
I could destroy them! I wish I had never written them!]
Et sic plangens mortuus.' And then come the words of
biographical importance: 'Fuit idem Chawserus pater Thome
Chawserus [*sic*] armigeri, qui Thomas sepelitur in Nuhelm
[Ewelme] juxta Oxoniam.'

Now Gascoigne was a junior contemporary of Thomas
Chaucer, their lives overlapping for some thirty years. Gascoigne died in 1458; Thomas Chaucer in 1434. 'It
appears,' says Mr Rogers in his excellent introduction to the
Locie Libro Veritatum, 'that from his matriculation to
his death, Gascoigne resided almost constantly in' Oxford.'
And he was a distinguished figure there, reaching, in 1434,
(Thomas Chaucer's death-year) the distinction of the Chan-
cellorship—a distinction again enjoyed in 1442, 1443 and
1445. Thomas Chaucer, too, must have been well known,
not only by report, but personally, at Oxford; for he had
residences both at Woodstock, some seven miles north, and
at Ewelme, some fifteen miles south-west, the direct road
between Woodstock and Ewelme passing through Oxford.
Surely, then, we have in Gascoigne's statement fairly decisive
authority for declaring Thomas to be the son of the poet.

Perhaps some persons may think that Gascoigne's credit
is somewhat impaired by the story of the poet's remorse
with which his statement is associated. But that story is
fully supported by the well-known passage in the paragraph
at the end of the *Canterbury Tales* headed 'Preces de
Chauceres,' which it seems difficult to explain altogether
away, as Tyrwhitt and others have attempted to do. There
is no denying that Chaucer has written some lines which
dying he might well 'wish to blot'; and even if the *ipsis-
sima verba* at the close of the 'Parson's Tale' are those of
a scribe or some father confessor, and are far too com-

prehensive, yet it is credible enough they represent some actual expressions of regret. Possibly the poet's fixing his last abode where he did, so close to the Abbey of West-minster—I do not forget it was also near one of the royal palaces—may suggest that some ascetic tendency or turn marked his declining years. Such things have happened both before and since. Men's judgments have decayed, and they have formed a morbid estimate of their life and works. Certainly Chaucer on his deathbed might, if his mind were healthy, look back to much good service done for 'truth and honour, freedom and curtesy.' The world was the·better for him while he lived, and has been the better for him ever since he was laid in 'the corner' that was to be called 'the Poets'.' But probably enough in those last hours he remembered only, and even exaggerated, his errors, and in his humility could not then perceive that his not professedly religious writings did yet in their way, with whatever defects, make for virtue and goodness even more effectively than those written in the name of religion. What-ever view is taken of this psychological problem, I do not think Gascoigne's evidence on the filial question is to be rejected because of his attitude towards it.

Thus, if there was always fair reason for believing Thomas was Geoffrey's son, surely this relationship may now be taken as proved. But the exact details of it are not absolutely ascertained. Assuredly difficulties yet remain. Speght tells us that in his day, *temp*. Elizabeth, 'some held opinion that Thomas Chaucer was not the son of Geoffrey;' and, says Tyrwhitt, 'there are certainly many circumstances that might incline us to that opinion.' Mr Edward Walford, in an interesting paper on 'Ewelme and the Chaucer Tombs, lately contributed to the *Gentleman's Magazine*, assures us 'that it is now the general opinion of historians and genealogists that this Thomas Chaucer was in reality a son of John of Gaunt by a sister of Catherine Swinford, the same who afterwards married Geoffrey Chaucer; and if this supposition is true, then Thomas Chaucer was the illegitimate son of Geoffrey Chaucer's wife, and therefore not the poet's son, but his stepson, after a fashion.' Now, on what facts is this opinion founded? Is it founded on any? Or is it merely an hypothesis? As an hypothesis it would undoubtedly solve many difficulties; but it would in their place create a difficulty yet more perplexing with regard to Chaucer's character. To suppose that the poet married a cast-off mistress of his patron's, or, still worse, that after his marriage Philippa continued to be, or became his patron's mistress, are obviously not suppositions easy to reconcile with personal respect and admiration.

For the present at least Chaucer's married life is involved in obscurity. That it was not a success there are many indications; but the causes of its unhappiness have not hitherto been discovered—are, perhaps, undiscoverable.

I will just add that it seems extremely probable that the Elizabeth Chaucer, for whose novitiate in the Abbey of Barking John of Gaunt paid 51*l.* 8*s.* 2*d.* in 1381, was a daughter of Geoffrey.

IX

THE 'CONFESSIO AMANTIS

(From *The Athenæum* for Dec. 24, 1881)

TO say nothing of the interest of the question as it relates to Gower himself, the date of the *Confessio Amantis* has a special importance for Chaucerian students. As there are several stories that are told by both poets, the settlement of this date may decide, if there seem to be obligations, which is the obliged person. And as the following lines in Gower are often quoted in connexion with the controversy as to the time of Chaucer's birth, it is obviously of some moment to ascertain the date of the work containing them :

Gower represents Venus speaking to him in this wise :

> And grete wel Chaucer, when ye mete,
> As my disciple and my poete ;
> For in the floures of his youthe
> In sondry wise, as he wel couthe,
> Of dytees and of songes glade
> The whiche he for my sake made,
> The land fulfilled is over al,
> Whereof to him in special
> Above alle other I am most holde.
> Forthy now in his dayes olde
> Thou shalt him telle this message :
> That he upon his latter age,

> To sette an end of al his werke,
> As he whiche is myn owne clerke
> Do make his Testament of Love,
> As thou hast doon thy shrift above,
> So that my court it may recorde.

And yet the statements current in most books dealing with the subject are for the most part careless and inaccurate. Often it is said that the second version or edition of the *Confessio*—it is well known there were two editions—was not presented to Henry of Lancaster till he became king—that is, was not presented before 1399. It is generally taken for granted in discussing Chaucer's birth-year that the above-quoted lines of Gower belong to the year 1393, whereas, as I hope to show, they were probably written nine or ten years earlier. The omission of those lines in the second edition is sometimes explained, by those who are unwilling to allow that the friendship of the two poets was ever disturbed, as due to the fact that Chaucer was in extreme old age, beyond the power of dictating any 'Testament' for Venus, or any testament but his own, if, indeed, he was equal to that, when the revised version appeared. But the revised version was certainly finished, in 1393.

These and other like errors are still widely prevalent, although years ago—nearly a quarter of a century ago—Dr. Pauli pointed out that 1392-3 is the date of the second version, and that the first must have been written some years earlier. This view of Dr. Pauli's, to be found in the introduction to his edition of the *Confessio Amantis*, published in 1857, I propose now not only to call attention to, but to enforce and support with fresh illustrations.

Let it, then, be carefully observed that Gower himself tells us that the version dedicated to Henry of Lancaster was completed in the sixteenth year of Richard II., and that the lines containing Venus's message to Chaucer, as well as the passages that express loyalty to the reigning sovereign, are not found in it. These lines are found only in the other version, which the very slightest consideration of the facts of the case will show to be the earlier—the earlier by several years: six or seven as Dr. Pauli thinks, but perhaps, as I incline to think, by nine or ten.

(1.) Let us, then, first consider the date of the first version of the *Confessio Amantis*. This is Gower's account of its suggestion and origin :—

> In our Englishe I thenke make
> A boke for King Richardes sake,
> To whom belongeth my legeaunce
> With all min hertes obeisaunce
> In all that ever a lege man
> Unto his king may done or can ;
> So ferforth and me recommaunde
> To him which all me may commaunde
> Preiend unto the highe regne,
> Which causeth every king to regne,
> That his corone longe stonde.

And he goes on to describe how one day, as he was rowing, or being rowed, along the Thames, 'under the town of New Troy'—that is, by London—his liege lord met him and called him into his barge, and, amongst other things then said, bade him 'book some new thing to his high worthiness'—*i.e.*, compose some new writing and dedicate it to his Majesty. Gower was eager to act on the royal bidding. He had 'sickness on hand,' and long had had, he tells us ; but, fervent royalist as he was, he determined to 'travail' in the king's service, and so he set to work

> To make a boke after his heste
> And write in such a maner wise,

> Which may be wisdom to the wise
> And play to hem that list to play.

The result was the *Confessio Amantis*.

This interview with the king is often enough referred to, but quite wrongly it is ordinarily assigned to the regnal year 1392-3. In 1392-3, as we shall see, Gower had utterly ceased to believe in Richard II. or expect anything good from him, and had turned to one who seemed better to justify his hope and trust.

If the prologue of the *Confessio* gives us nothing more definite in the way of date than that it was written when its author was a devoted adherent of King Richard, we may, I think, gather more precise information from the epilogue; and this is a point not yet noticed, so far as I know.

The poem concludes by telling us how Venus, after sending her famous message to Chaucer, all suddenly passed up into heaven, and the poet betook himself home, resolved, his beads in hand, ever to pray for all true lovers. And so his work is done; the poem his Majesty ordered is written. And he epilogizes in these Latin lines, followed by some English octo syllabics :—

> Ad laudem Christi, quem tu virgo peperisti,
> Sit laus Ricardi, quem sceptra colunt leopardi.
> *Ad sua precepta complevi carmine cepta,*
> Que Bruti nata legat Anglia perpetuata.

The English lines that follow are filled with the same spirit that inspired the prologue. Gower is not yet disillusioned. Upon his bare knees he prays God to 'convey'—ever to escort, so to speak—'my worthy king'

> Richard by name the Secounde
> In whom hath ever yet be founde
> Justice medled with pite,
> Largesse forth with charite.

> In his persone it may be shewed
> What is a king to be well thewed,
> Touching of pite namely,
> For he yet never unpetously
> Ayein the leges of his londe,
> For no defaute which he fonde
> Through cruelte vengeance sought.

And he continues to chant at length his praises.

Now, Dr. Pauli has remarked that this enthusiastic language towards King Richard must precede 1386. 'The date,' he says, 'when Gower began to write the *Confessio Amantis*, would fall before the year 1386, and before the young king, who had just become of age, developed those dangerous qualities which estranged from him amongst others the poet, who, as he states himself, composed his work in English [better "his English work"] in consequence of an invitation from his sovereign.' The soundness of this view will be doubted by no one who studies Gower's political writings or understands his political temper. He was of a thoroughly loyal nature and habit, but he had a keen sense of a king's duties as well as of his prerogatives. He expected a king to act like a king. For a mere reckless pleasure-lover—for a royal profligate who wasted his substance in riotous living —he felt no respect or reverence. What he wanted in the State was government and order, and of these things there presently seemed a plentiful lack. Possibly enough he may have been even harsh in his judgment of the king. Certainly what was generous and lovable in the king's personal character—such elements were undoubtedly there— seemed to him of trifling value as compared with a firm, strong will and a firm, strong hand to execute it, such as the convulsed and quaking condition of English society at that time made peculiarly needful. Probably what in the first instance fanned, I do not say kindled, the flame of his loyalty towards King Richard, was the vigour and spirit the young prince displayed in dealing with the insurgent peasants in an early year of his reign. The time was out of joint; and here seemed one who was able 'to set it right,' a youth brave and prompt and resolute.

It was when this welcome belief was in all its strength in Gower's heart, ere yet had dawned on him any suspicion how inconstant, headstrong, violent, was in fact the prince's nature, that both the prologue and the epilogue were written; and in the epilogue we have definite allusions to matters of the time.

In the lines just now quoted, Gower is assuredly referring to the king's conduct in the peasants' insurrection. When he speaks of 'justice meddled with pity,' and says he never yet pitilessly exacted vengeance from his lieges for their default, he cannot but be referring to the suppression of that tumult. We of to-day may perhaps think there were excessive severity and flagrant injustice shown then; but Gower did not look at the action of his Government with our eyes; he did not sympathise with ' the villains' so far as we do; and certainly, if in the autumn of 1381 there were many executions, in 1382 there were many pardons issued; indeed, the insurgents—such as survived—were pardoned, with certain exceptions.

There is another reference in the epilogue, which enables us to date the conclusion of the first version of the *Confessio*, yet more exactly :—

> My worthy prince, of whom I write,
> Thus [*i.e.*, like the sun] stant he with him selve clere,
> And doth what lith in his powere,
> Nought only here at home to seke
> Love and accorde, but outward eke,
> As he that save his people wolde.
> So ben we alle well beholde

> To do service and obeisaunce
> To him, which of his high suffraunce
> Hath many a great debate appesed
> To make his lege men ben esed ;
> Wherefore that his cronique shall
> For ever be memoriall
> To the loenge of that he doth.
> For this wote every man in soth
> What king that so desireth pees,
> He taketh the way which Criste ches ;
> And who that Cristes weies sueth
> It proveth well that he escheueth
> The vices and is vertuous ;
> Whereof he mot be gracious
> Toward his god and acceptable.

I venture to hold that Gower here refers to the negotiations for peace with France in the year 1383. They did not succeed; but in the beginning of 1384 a truce was made to last till Michaelmas; it was then prolonged to the following spring. To show how much needed and welcome a boon it was to both countries we have the testimony of Walsingham :—

'Quæ treugæ quantum contulerunt utrique regno, regna manifesta suis commodis persenserunt. Nam Anglia per Gallicos et maxime per Normannos, sequente Quadrigesima referta est cunctis necessariis mercibus, puta vino, fructibus diversi generis, speciebus, atque piscibus ; adeo affluenter, ut admirationi foret incolis vilitas rerum venalium, præcipue in illis partibus ad quas accessus esse poterat Normannorum. Francia et Normannia lætatæ sunt, quia argentum et aurum prompte perceperunt ex Anglicis pro suis mercimoniis, et abundantius multo quam in suis partibus pro tantillo commercio percepissent. *Unde ab utriusque regni incolis et maxime communibus pax est ardentissime concupita.*'

The epilogue, then, could not have been written later

than the beginning of 1385. But the praise of the truce with the French is scarcely likely to have been sung towards the close of it, when already new irritations were being felt, and it was understood that our enemy, Scotland, was expecting French aid. So we can go so far as to say the epilogue was not written later than 1384. We may go yet further, and say it may have been written as early as the close of 1383, when negotiations for something more permanent than a truce were being carried on, and when, no doubt, as a little later in 1389, the proposal of peace required the support of sensible men against anti-French 'patriotism.'

Of these negotiations there is some account given by Froissart. They would seem to have lasted some time. The Duke of Brittany conceived the idea. He suggested it it to certain English knights, who were to suggest it to the English King. But, not content with this arrangement, he sent over to England two of his own knights, the Lord de la Houssaye and the Lord de Mailly; who 'managed matters so well that the Duke of Lancaster, the Earl of Buckingham, the Bishop of Hereford, the Lord John Holland, brother to the king, the Lord Thomas Percy, and others of the king's council, were ordered to Calais, having full powers from the King of England to conclude a peace or truce, according to their pleasure. On the other hand, there came to Boulogne the Duke of Berry, the Duke of Burgundy, the Bishop of Laon, and the Chancellor of France, having also full powers from the King of France and his council to conclude either a peace or a truce.' These plenipotentiaries were presently joined by a bishop, a dean, and two knights on the part of the King of Spain. The conference was transferred to a village that had a church half way between Calais and Boulogne, called 'Bolinges.' Thither all the parties went, and the lords with their council were together many days. The Duke of Brittany and the Earl of Flanders were present; and the great tent of Bruges was pitched, wherein the earl entertained at dinner the Duke of Lancaster, the Earl of Buckingham, and other English lords. Each negotiator kept up a great state, but, notwithstanding, there were many conferences holden, yet could they not agree upon a peace, for the French wanted the English to give up Calais, Guines, and all the fortresses which they possessed in Normandy, Brittany, Poitou, Saintonge, and La Rochelle, as far as the river Garonne. But the English would not any way listen to such a proposal; nor would they ever consent to give back such places as Calais, Guines, Cherbourg, or Brest. These conferences lasted three weeks, in which they or their councils discussed these matters daily. With some difficulty the lords who held so many conferences at Bolinges concluded a truce between the King of France and England and their allies.

Gower's lines may well have been written at the very time of these conferences. It may be noticed that he speaks of the king 'seeking' for 'love and accord' at home and abroad, as if things were yet unsettled; and below he speaks of the king as 'desiring' peace, as if it were not secured. To lay any great stress on these words would perhaps be special pleading; but certainly, to say nothing more, they are happily consistent with the view here suggested, that the lines in which they occur were penned in 1383, while a peace was in discussion.

At all events, these lines were not written after 1384, and, as we have seen, they form part of the epilogue of the first version of the poem, whose date we are endeavouring to discover.

There is a passage in the main part of book viii. which must

have been written at no great distance of time from January
1382, when the advent of a Bohemian princess, to be
married to King Richard, brought in certain Bohemian
fashions :—

> Min eye and[1] as I caste aboutes
> To know among them who was who
> I sigh when lusty youthe tho
> As he, which was a capitein,
> To-fore all other upon the plein,
> Stood with his route well begon,
> Her hedes kempt, and thereupon
> Garlondes, nought of o colour,
> Some of the lefe, some of the floure,
> And some of grete perles were.
> *The newe guise of Beawme* there
> With sondry thinges well devised
> I sigh, whereof they be queintised.

Such a settlement as is here advocated will, of course,
create a new aspect of several Chaucerian questions.   I will
now refer to one only, the date of Chaucer's birth.   The
well-known lines which speak of Chaucer's 'dayes olde'
and 'his latter age' are generally quoted, as I have said, as
written in the year 1393 ; now in fact they occur in the first
version of the poem, and so must have been written some
ten years before the date usually assigned.   Could he, then,
have been born so late as 1340, as is now commonly held ?
Or are those who adhere to the date 1328, after all, in the
right ?   Or was he born in some year between 1328 and
1340 ?   I do not now propose to discuss these questions.
I only point out that they must arise if the view here maintained is accepted.

(2.) We will proceed now to consider the date of the

---

[1] Gower often places *and* in the second or third place in the sentence, in
the Latin manner, where in our usage it ought to stand first ; see, *e.g.*, his
account of Medea's incantations, also the first extract given above.

second version of the *Confessio Amantis*, or, rather, to quote the definite statement on the subject made by Gower himself, and to illustrate it from other passages in his poem.

In the Prologue of this version he says he thinks to make

> A boke for Englondes sake
> The yere sixtenthe of King Richard,

i.e., between June 1392 and June 1393. The marginal note runs in this wise: 'Hic in principio libri declarat qualiter in anno Regis Ricardi secundi sextodecimo Johannes Gower presentem libellum composuit et finaliter complevit, quem strenuissimo domino suo Domino Henrico de Lancastria tunc[1] Derbiæ comiti cum omni reverencia specialiter destinavit.' We may well compare the 'finaliter complevit' here with the 'complevi' of the lines that precede the epilogue of the other version. The 'finaliter' clearly denotes that the edition of 1392-3 is the revised edition.

After some general remarks on the 'reversed' state of the world and its constant changing, so that it is difficult to imagine the past, and on the services of books in preserving the memory of it, he thus continues :—

> But for my wittes ben to smale
> To tellen every man his tale,
> This boke upon amendement
> To stonde at his commaundement.
> With whom my heart is of accorde,
> I send unto min owne lorde,
> Which of Lancastre is Henry named.
> The highe god him hath proclamed
> Full of knighthod and alle grace ;
> So wol I now this werke embrace
> With hol truste and with hol beleve.
> God graunte I mote it well acheve.

---

[1] 'The Earl of Derby' was a 'courtesy' title, derived from his grandfather, Henry Grismond. In 1397 he was created Duke of Hereford.

Let us note here first what is surely a very interesting allusion to the *Canterbury Tales*. Gower, knowing his own lack of the dramatic power in which the genius of his great contemporary so richly abounded, cannot attempt to paint a group of persons such as Chaucer painted, and let each person speak for himself in his own natural or habitual tone and manner. The allusion, be it observed, is compliment-ary. And perhaps, after all, the reason why Venus's message is omitted in this second version is because Chaucer had then taken up with such splendid success a line so different from that enjoined by Venus, as Gower interprets her wishes—was busy with his *Canterbury Tales* and so not in the way of writing any 'Testament of Love' such as Gower suggested. But to return to the passage now before us : let us note secondly the words 'upon amendement,' which must mean 'corrected,' 'revised.' This revised version he formally dedicates to Henry of Lancaster, and to him he professes his sincere attachment and fidelity.

From the king in whom he trusted when he wrote the earlier prologue he had now long been alienated. We are able to trace the history of this alienation in Gower's *Tripartite Chronicle*, written about the close of the century, when the career of him that was once his hope and trust had closed in misery and shame. There is no reason to suspect Gower's integrity. He behaved as a high-minded gentleman well might—as, it may be, a true patriot was bound to behave. He had endeavoured to excite in the king a sense of his great office and how it should he filled, but the king had no ears for such sober addresses.

> In gallant trim the gilded vessel goes,
>   Youth on the prow, and Pleasure at the helm,
> Regardless of the sweeping Whirlwind's sway,
> That, hush'd in grim repose expects his evening prey.

The whirlwind arose duly, and the king and his court were laid low. Gower viewed the miserable ruin with stern eyes, and, like some prophet who sees in degradation and death but the proper fruits of heedlessness and riot, he thus summed up the tragic story :—

> Chronica Ricardi, qui sceptra tulit leopardi,
> Ut patet, est dicta populo sed non benedicta.
> Ut speculum mundi quo lux nequit ulla refundi,
> Sic vacuus transit ; sibi nil nisi culpa remansit.
> Unde superbus erat, modo si præconia quærat,
> Ejus honor sordet, laus culpat, gloria mordet.
> Hoc concernentes caveant qui sunt sapientes ;
> Nam male viventes Deus odit in orbe regentes.
> Est qui peccator non esse potest dominator ;
> Ricardo teste, finis probat hoc manifeste.
> Post sua demerita periit sua pompa sopita.
> Qualis erat vita, chronica stabit ita.

To return to the prologue : the poet proceeds next to describe the troubled condition of the age. 'De statu regnorum,' runs the gloss, 'ut dicunt secundum temporalia, videlicet tempore regis Ricardi secundi, anno regni sui sextodecimo.' He praises the old days, and deplores the present :—

> Now stant the crope under the rote ;
> The worlde is chaunged overall,
> And thereof most in speciall
> That love is falle into discorde.

It is so, he says, all over the world, and he goes on to lament the corruptions of the Church, the restlessness of the common people, the instability of all worldly things.

Turning to the epilogue of the second version, we find the same change of tone. Here, too, we have the poet distressed by the condition of his country :—

> Upon my bare knees I praie
> That he this londe in siker waie
> Woll set upon good governaunce.

He urges the king frankly enough to alter his course. After
mentioning his claim to the allegiance

> Of clerke, of knight, of man of lawe,

and how

> Under his honde all is forthdrawn,
> The merchaunt and the laborer,

he adds :—

> But though that he such power have,
> And that his mightes ben so large,
> He hath hem nought withouten charge
> To which that every king is swore.
> So were it good that he therefore
> First unto rightwisnesse entende ;
> Whereof that he himself amende
> Toward his god, and leve vice,
> Whiche is the chefe of his office—
> And after all the remenaunt
> He shall upon his covenaunt
> Governe and lede in such a wise,
> So that there be no tirannise,
> Whereof that he his people greve ;
> Or elles may he nought acheve
> That longeth to his regalie.

The work is concluded with these Latin lines :—

> Explicit iste liber, qui transeat obsecro liber,
> Ut sine livore vigeat lectoris in ore.
> Qui sedet in scamnis celi det, ut ista Johannis
> Perpetuis omnis stet pagina grata Britannis,
> *Derbeie comiti, recolunt quem laude periti,*
> *Vade liber purus, sub eo requiesce futurus.*

X

CHEVY CHASE

(From *The Gentleman's Magazine* for April 1889)

IT is common to say that the ballads known as the 'Battle of Otterbourne' and the 'Hunting of the Cheviot' commemorate one and the same event. But it is quite certain that they commemorate two quite different events. The confusion of them is of early date; it is found in the earliest extant version of the latter ballad, which belongs to the time of Queen Elizabeth; but a confusion it is so to correlate them. And if one would properly understand their historical value, and in other respects fully enjoy them, one should keep them separate and distinct. I propose in this paper to point out more completely than I think has yet been done, how separate and distinct they in fact are. They are connected with different localities, are based upon different incidents, and represent different features in the old Border life.

Of course this diversity is not now suggested for the first time. It was recognised long ago in the early seventeenth century by Hume of Godscroft, when he wrote: 'That which is commonly sung of the "Hunting of the Cheviot" seemeth indeed poetical and a mere fiction, perhaps to stir up virtue; yet a fiction, whereof there is no mention either in Scottish or English chronicle.' That it has no immediate and particular historical basis is not so indubitable as this writer supposes; but he is right enough in not identifying the occasion of it with the famous battle of Otterbourne. And Bishop Percy saw that it was of different origin, and others have seen it. But commonly, as I said to begin with, in spite of these noticeable authorities, the two ballads are regarded as merely various accounts of one and the same action. Even so excellent a ballad-scholar as Professor Child remarks in his introduction to the 'Hunting,' in his *English and Scottish Ballads*, 1861, that the 'Hunting' 'is founded on the same event' as the 'Battle of Otterbourne.'

I trust that no apology is needed for an attempt to clear up this matter. We profess to be proud of our ballad poetry, and the ballads now to be briefly discussed are amongst its masterpieces. Let us try to make our pride really intelligent by a careful study of its object. There is certainly much effusive praise of our poetry that is based on the slightest possible knowledge. If we wish to indulge in the boast *Cives Romani sumus*, let us understand what is denoted by the '*civitas*' we claim and proclaim. If we would entitle ourselves to the right of lauding our literature, let us obtain some accurate familiarity with it. If we dislike the noisy raptures of the ignorant chauvinist, let us make sure that our appreciation of what we say we admire is really founded on fact—make sure that our zeal is without indiscretion, is well-informed and sensible, is the offspring of a cultivated intelligence. Thus, even a brief scrutiny of a few old ballads may be of service; it may improve our habits of accuracy, increase our powers of enjoyment, help us to be more truthful and sincere in our enthusiasms.

Let us turn first to the ballads that undoubtedly have for

their theme the ' Battle of Otterbourne.' Of these there are three—the one given in Percy's *Reliques of Ancient English Poetry*, the one in Scott's *Minstrelsy of the Scottish Border*, the one in Herd's *Scottish Songs*.

Of the battle itself we have many accounts. It was one of the most famous in the history of the Borders, and the chroniclers glory in its narration. Froissart describes it minutely, and, as he tells us, on good authority.

I was made acquainted [he says, in Johnes' translation] with all the particulars of this battle by knights and squires, who had been actors in it on each side. There were also with the English two valiant knights from the country of Foix, whom I had the good fortune to meet at Orthès, the year after this battle had been fought [*i.e.* 1389]. Their names were Sir John de Châteauneuf and John de Cautiron. On my return from Foix, I met likewise at Avignon a knight and two squires of Scotland of the party of Earl Douglas. They knew me again from the recollections I brought to their minds of their own country ; for in my youth I, the author of this history, travelled all through Scotland, and was full fifteen days resident with William, Earl of Douglas, father of Earl James of whom we are now speaking, at his castle of Dalkeith, five miles distant from Edinburgh. Earl James was then very young, but a promising youth, and he had a sister called Blanche [Isabel ?] I had my information, therefore, from both parties, who agree that it was the hardest and most obstinate battle that ever was fought. This I readily believe, for the English and Scots are excellent men-at-arms, and whenever they meet in battle, they do not spare each other ; nor is there any check in their courage so long as their weapons endure.

And the next paragraph must be quoted, because it gives the very spirit of these old Border wars, and enables us to understand how it was that poetry could flourish in the percincts of such incessant anarchy and bloodshed. One might have reasonably expected that the Muses would have been scared far away from a region that appears at the first glance merely turbulent and savage—to which Buchanan's words concerning the very expedition that was distinguished by the battle of Otterbourne so frequently apply ; ' Quicquid

ferro flammaque fœdari potuit, corrumpunt ac diruunt '—
where more than once the invader boasted, as in 1532, there
was not ' one peel, gentleman's house, nor grange unburnt
and destroyed,' *i.e.*, undestroyed—where at times, as in 1570,
the ' riders were wont to harry, burn, and slay, and take
prisoners, and use all misorder, and cruelty, not only used
in war, but detestable to all barbar and wild Tartars.'   The
following are the words of the old French chronicler that go
so far to solve this strange enigma :—

When they [the English and the Scots] have well beaten each other
and one party is victorious, they are so proud of their conquest that they
ransom their prisoners instantly and in such courteous manner to those
who have been taken that on their departure they return them their
thanks.   However, when in battle, there is no boy's play between them,
nor do they shrink from the combat ; and you will see in the further
detail of this battle as excellent deeds as were ever performed.

And with a quite Homeric delight he proceeds to describe
so glorious an encounter of foemen so keen and fierce and
yet so chivalrous !   But, indeed, even the dullest chronicler
is thrilled with some emotion as he tells the story of this
famous conflict.   Border warfare never before or afterwards
showed so glorious as on the field of Otterbourne.

The ' Raid,' of which it formed so splendid an incident,
was undertaken in revenge of the invasion of Scotland by
King Richard the Second in 1387.   It was made in two
directions.   The main body, under the command of the
Earl of Fife, one of the King's—King Robert the Second
—sons, advanced south-westward, and ravaged the western
borders of England.   The other division, under the command
of the Earl of Douglas, marched swiftly over the Cheviots,
through the south of Northumberland into Durham, where
their presence was soon proclaimed by fire and flame.

The Scottish ballad tells us how the 'doughty Douglas'

> has burn'd the dales of Tyne
> And part of Bambroughshire;
> And three good towns on Reidswire fells,
> He left them all on fire.

The English ballad informs us of the earlier stages of their route.

> Over Ottercap hill they came in,
>   And so down by Rodclyffe crag;
> Upon Green Leyton they lighted down
>   Stirand many a stag;
> And boldly brent Northumberland,
>   And harried many a town.
> They did our Englishmen great wrang,
>   To battle that were not bown.

So they entered England by the Redswire pass, and advanced down Reedsdale, passing the spot that was to be made so famous as they returned, on to Kirkwhelpington, into Hartburn parish. There is in the neighbourhood of Kirkwhelpington a place that still bears the name of Scot's Gap; it is some eight or nine miles south of Rothley Crags. No doubt this was one of the expeditions that gave that place its name. The invaders were now on the high road to Newcastle, but they presently turned aside due south, and crossing the Tyne some miles—about three leagues, says Froissart—above Newcastle, probably at Newburn, flung themselves with fury upon the county of Durham, 'destroying and burning all before them.' 'There was not a town in all this district, unless well enclosed, that was not burnt.' Then, having triumphantly accomplished all the mischief that was possible, they recrossed the Tyne, and halted before Newcastle. And then it was, after some skirmishing, that, according to the ballad, Douglas made a tryst to meet Percy at Otterbourne.

'Where shall I bide thee?' said the Douglas,
  'Or where wilt thou come to me
At Otterbourne in the highway,
  There mayst thou well lodged be.

'There shall I bide thee,' said the Douglas,
  'By the faith of my body;'
'Thither shall I come,' said Sir Henry Percy,
  'My truth I plight to thee.'

Such is the minstrel's translation of the facts recorded by the chroniclers, which are that in one of the encounters 'at the barriers' before Newcastle, Douglas had gained possession of Percy's (Shakespeare's Hotspur) lance with his pennon attached to it, and that Percy had vowed to recover it before Douglas quitted England, and that, Percy having failed to achieve his vow before Douglas marched away from before Newcastle, Douglas resolved to linger at Otterbourne, and so give him another chance of doing so. 'Sir Henry Percy on hearing this was greatly rejoiced, and cried out: "To horse! to horse! For by the faith I owe to God, and to my lord and father, I will seek to recover my pennon and beat up their quarters this night." Such knights and squires in Newcastle as learnt this were willing to be of the party and make themselves ready.' Some thirty miles—not eight, as Buchanan says, inaccurately following Froissart, who is himself inaccurate in putting the distance at 'eight short leagues'—had to be traversed. And there, at last, under the moon (*luna prope pernox lucis diurnæ usum præbebat*), towards the dawning of the day, Douglas and Percy met to fight it out, met to drink 'delight of battle' with 'their peers.'

χάρμῃ γηθόσυνοι τήν σφιν θεὸς ἔμβαλε θυμῷ.

The battle now raged; great was the pushing of lances, and very many of each party were struck down at the first onset. The Earl of

Douglas, being young and impatient to gain renown in arms, ordered his banner to advance, shouting 'Douglas! Douglas!' Sir Henry and Sir Ralph Percy [Shakespeare's Hotspur and his brother], indignant for the affront the Earl of Douglas had put on them by conquering their pennon and desirous of meeting him, hastened to the place from which the sounds came, calling out 'Percy! Percy!' The two banners met, and many gallant deeds of arms ensued.

'Dux Scotorum præcipuus, Willelmus Duglas,' writes Walsingham, excited beyond his wont—even far away, in the cloisters of St Alban's, the monk's pulse quickened as he told the tale—

qui et ipse fuit juvenis ambitiosus, videns rem mille votis petitam, Henricum Percy videlicet, intra castra, alacriter equitat contra eum. Erat ibidem cernere pulchrum spectaculum duos tam præclaros juvenes manus conserere et pro gloria decertare.

A fair spectacle, indeed, O monk! and no wonder the ballad writer should be stirred by it, if your monkship is thus moved. 'Pugnatum igitur acerrime,' so run the words of Buchanan, 'ut inter homines utrinque nobiles et de gloria magis quam de vita sollicitos. Percius ignominiam delere, Duglassus partum decus novo facinore illustrare contendebat.'

> There was no freke that there wold fly,
>   But stiffly in stour can stond,
> Each one hewyng on other while they might drie
>   With many a baleful brond.

The death of Douglas is more fully and finely given in the 'Minstrelsy' ballad, which is indeed as a whole more highly poetical. The ballad of the 'Reliques,' that is the English ballad, is matter of fact enough at this point as at others.

> The Percy was a man of strength,
>   I tell you in this stound ;
> He smote the Douglas at the swordes length,
>   That he fell to the ground.

> The sword was sharp and sore can bite,
>   I tell you in certain ;
> To the heart he coud him smite ;
>   Thus was the Douglas slain.
>
> The standards stood still on each side
>   With many a grievous groan ;
> There they fought the day and all the night,
>   And many a doughty man was slain.

Contrast the Scottish version of this catastrophe :

> But Percy with his good broad sword,
>   That could so sharply wound,
> Has wounded Douglas on the brow
>   Till he fell to the ground.
>
> Then he call'd on his little footpage,
>   And said : ' Run speedily,
> And fetch my ain dear sister's son,
>   Sir Hugh Montgomery.'
>
> ' My nephew good,' the Douglas said,
>   ' What recks the death of ane ?
> Last night I dream'd a dreary dream,
>   And I ken the day's thy ain.'

(In his ' dreary dream ' he saw a dead man win a fight, and thought the man was himself.)

> ' My wound is deep, I fain would sleep,
>   Take thou the vanguard of the three ;
> And hide me by the braken bush,
>   That grows on yonder lilye lea.'

(A favourite stanza that of Sir Walter Scott's, as it well might be.)

> ' O bury me by the braken bush,
>   Beneath the blooming brier ;
> Let never living mortal ken
>   That e'er a kindly Scot lies here.'

> He lifted up that noble lord
> Wi' the saut tear in his e'e ;
> He hid him in the braken bush,
> That his merrie men might not see.

He was buried in fact at Melrose ; but the true ballad does not care for historical detail—'spernit humum fugiente penna.'

> The moon was clear, the day drew near,
> The spears in flinders flew,
> But mony a gallant Englishman
> Ere day the Scotsman slew.

In the other Scottish ballad, that given by Herd, Douglas's death is assigned to treachery—a Scottish page assassinates him ; but in other respects we find but an abridgment of the passage just quoted :

> The boy's ta'en out his little penknife,
> That hanget low down by his gare,
> And he gae Earl Douglas a deadly wound,
> Alas ! a deep wound and sare !

> Earl Douglas said to Sir Hugh Montgomery,
> ' Tak' thou the vanguard o' the three ;
> And bury me at yon braken bush,
> That stands upon yon lily lea.'

But yet to us more interesting and more striking is a saying which the ballads omit from their last speech of the hero, but which is reported by the chroniclers. According to them, Douglas is not struck to death by Percy in the Homeric manner, but, having thrown himself into the midst of the enemy, is borne down by three English spears, thrust by unknown and unknowing hands—thrust, that is, by men whose names are not known, and who had no idea who it was they were bearing down. And then his head was cleft with a battle-axe.

There was a great crowd round him ; and he could not raise himself, for the blow on his head was mortal. His men had followed him as closely as they were able ; and there came to him his cousins, Sir James Lindsay, Sir John and Sir Walter Sinclair, with other knights and squires. They found by his side a gallant knight that had constantly attended him, who was his chaplain, and had at this time exchanged his profession for that of a valiant man-at-arms.

And we are told how the reverend gentleman had been wielding a battle-axe all night with tremendous effect. And then Froissart resumes his story of Douglas's last moments :

When these knights came to the Earl of Douglas, they found him in a melancholy state, as well as one of his knights, Sir Robert Hart, who had fought by his side the whole of the night and now lay beside him covered with fifteen wounds from lances and other weapons. Sir John Sinclair asked the Earl : 'Cousin, how fares it with you ? ' 'But so so,' replied he. [Only so so in one sense, but in another it seems excellent well.] *' Thanks to God there are but few of my ancestors who have died in chambers or in their beds.* I bid you therefore revenge my death, for I have but little hope of living, as my heart becomes more faint every minute. Do you, Walter and Sir John Sinclair, raise up my banner, for certainly it is on the ground from the death of David Campbell, that valiant squire, who bore it, and who refused knighthood from my hands this day, though equal to the most eminent knights for courage and loyalty ; and continue to shout " Douglas ! " but do not tell friend or foe whether I am in your company or not, for should the enemy know the truth they will be greatly rejoiced.' The two brothers Sinclair and Sir John Lindsay obeyed his orders. . . . The Scots, by their valiantly driving the enemy beyond the spot where the Earl of Douglas lay dead, for he had expired on giving his last orders, arrived at his banner, which was borne by Sir John Sinclair.

Buchanan's version is worth quoting as of the same tone :

In hoc statu [when the Douglas lay ' tribus lethalibus plagis saucius atque humi dejectus '] propinqui ejus Joannes Lindesius, Joannes et Valterus Sinclari de eo cum rogassent ecquid valeret, ' *Ego,*' inquit, ' *recte valeo ; morior enim non in lecto segni fato sed quemadmodum omnes prope mei majores.* Illa vero a vobis postrema peto : primum ut mortem meam et nostros et hostes celetis ; deinde ne vexillum meum dejectum sinatis ; demum, ut meam cædem ulciscamini. Hæc si sperem ita fore, cetera aequo animo feram.'

So he died happy in the old Northern belief that no deathbed is so to be desired as the field of battle—that no heroes are so welcome to the gods as those whose spirits come straight from the midst of fighting and slaughter.

How thoroughly the genuine passion of these old stories may be weakened away may be well seen in the accounts Boece and his metrical translator furnish of the same scenes. Boece 'flourished' about the beginning of the sixteenth century. By that time the atmosphere had changed. We may be sure, from the spirit of them, if from nothing else, that the ballads we are considering are of an earlier age— are not, in point of date, far from the time of the events themselves.

There now stands, near Otterbourne, a cross called Percy's Cross, and tradition blunderingly asserts that it marks the spot where Percy fell, who did not fall, but, after a splendid resistance, was taken prisoner. Possibly it, or whatever monument preceded it, may mark the spot where Douglas fell. How pleasant it would be to believe that it was called Percy's Cross because it was erected by Percy in honour of his gallant enemy! There is no external authority for the suggestion, but such a sense would satisfactorily explain a title which otherwise is perverse and false.[1]

To sum up these remarks on the Otterbourne pieces: they deal with a famous 'Warden's Raid,' the details of which are precisely known, and are recorded in these ballads with as much exactness as can reasonably be expected. In this case Douglas is the aggressor. The locality of the final struggle is in Reedsdale; the time, a Wednesday night and Thursday morning, as we are specially informed.

---

[1] The other Percy's Cross—that near Hedgeley Moor—does mark the spot where a Percy fell, having 'saved the bird in his bosom.'

The result is the captivity of Percy and the death of Douglas.

Now let us turn to the Chevy Chase ballads, or, to speak more exactly, to the Chevy Chase ballad in its older form and in its newer. In its older, which must have been written in the fifteenth century, it is entitled 'The Hunting of the Cheviot'; in its later, which must have been produced in the seventeenth century, it bears the familiar name of 'Chevy Chase.'

Now, in 'The Hunting of the Cheviot,' it is not a raid but a great hunting expedition, that is the theme. Percy is the aggressor, and not Douglas; the struggle does not take place in Reedsdale, nor anywhere in England, but in Scotland, across, though close by, the frontier. The day was a Monday, and before the moon rose, as we are specially informed, and the result is the deaths of both Percy and Douglas. Finally, this ballad, if based at all upon any special historical occurrence, allows itself the utmost freedom of treatment; whereas the Otterbourne ballads, as we have seen, adhere to the facts with fair precision. It seems certain there was no border battle in which both a Percy and a Douglas were slain as here described. The ballad is historical in a very important sense; that is, it reflects with admirable truthfulness the habits and feelings and ideas of a certain age and a certain district. But it is not strictly and literally historical in the narrower sense—in the sense in which the Otterbourne ballads are so.

And yet these two sets of ballads are, as I remarked at the beginning of this paper, perpetually confused and confounded. Let us now consider a little more particularly the above-mentioned dissimilarities and distinctions.

In the first place, then, the occasions differ. In the

Otterbourne ballads the feature of Border life that is cele-brated is the Raid, and a raid of a most important kind—what was commonly called a Warden's Raid[1]:

> The doughty Douglas bound him to ride
> In England to take a prey;

or, 'to drive a prey,' as the 'Minstrelsy' version has it; 'to fetch a prey,' as that in Herd's *Scottish Songs*. In the Cheviot ballad, the occasion of the encounter is Percy's deliberate defiance of a well-known March law, viz., that the Scottish and English borderers were not to hunt in one another's territory without express permission from the warden whose province was concerned or his representative. It is exactly not what some ingenious person would fain make the name Chevy Chase mean—it is not a *chivachie*.

For some ingenious person or other has, with brilliant but wholly wasted acuteness, maintained that the name Chevy Chase is a corruption of chivachie !

Πολλὰ τὰ δεινὰ κοὐδὲν ἀνθρώπου δεινότερον πέλει.

And it may be confidently averred that man's δεινότης is nowhere more gloriously exhibited than in the domains of etymology. Whatever comes into his head is accepted for an inspiration. History may be offended, phonetic laws violated, probability defied, but the etymological amateur idolises his 'happy thought'; he follows his own royal road; he can only pity those who will investigate and verify. In the present case his notable cleverness is sadly thrown away; for there can be no reasonable doubt that Chevy Chase is simply a corruption—a corruption, probably, of the late sixteenth or of the seventeenth century—of Cheviot Chase, a phrase which occurs in the older ballad, 'chase'

[1] See *Lay of the Last Minstrel*, iv. 4.

here meaning a hunting ground, or 'forest,' as often in old English, and still in many place-names, as, for instance, in Cannock Chase. The original title is, as we know, 'The Hunting of the Cheviot'; and the original ballad again and again reminds us that the scene is 'in the mountains of Cheviot,' 'in Cheviot, the hills so high,' 'in Cheviot, the hills above,' '*in this Cheviot Chase*,' 'in Cheviot, the hills aboon,' 'Cheviot within.' Douglas's expedition, which resulted in the battle of Otterbourne, might properly be called a chivachie; but not so this of Percy's, that is balladised in 'The Hunting of the Cheviot.'

> The Percy out of Northomberland
> And a vow to God made he,
> That he wold hunt in the mountains
> Of Cheviot within days three,
> In the mauger of doughty Douglas
> And all that ever with him be.

A vigorous beginning, which Macaulay has closely followed in his *Lay of Horatius*.

> The fattest harts in all Cheviot
> He said he wold kill and carry them away.
> 'By my faith,' said the doughty Douglas again,
> 'I will let that hunting if that I may!'

Thus Percy defies Douglas, and, in fact, challenges him to a combat by hunting without leave on Douglas's side of the Border. 'Concordatum est,' runs an old March law, 'quod . . . nullus unius partis vel alterius ingrediatur terras, boschas, forrestas, warrenas, loca, dominia quæcunque alicujus partis alterius subditi [a curious use of *subditi*] causa venandi, piscandi, aucupandi, disportum aut solatium in eisdem [exercendi] aliave quacunque de causa absque licentia ejus . . . ad quem . . . loca . . . pertinent aut de deputatis suis prius capta et obtenta.' An excellent illustration of this point is to be found in the *Memoirs* of Carey, Earl of Monmouth, who was one of the March Wardens in the reign of Queen Mary. The passage is referred to by Percy; and I had the satisfaction of quoting it at length in the introduction to Chevy Chase in the edition of *Bishop Percy's Folio MS.* published some years ago. But as it is not well known, and is extremely pertinent, I venture to reproduce it once more :

There had been an ancient custom of the Borders, when they were quiet, for the opposite Border to send to the warden of the middle march to desire leave that they might come into the Borders of England and hunt with their greyhounds for deer towards the end of summer, which was denied them. Towards the end of Sir John Foster's government, they would, without asking leave, come into England and hunt at their pleasure and stay their own time. I wrote to Farnehurst, the warden over against me, that I was no way willing to hinder them of their accustomed sports, and that if according to the ancient custom they would send to me for leave they should have all the contentment I could give them; if otherwise they would continue their wonted course, I would do my best to hinder them [to 'let that hunting ']. Within a month after, they came and hunted, as they used to do, without leave, and cut down wood and carried it away. Towards the end of summer they came again to their wonted sports. I sent my two deputies with all the speed they could make, and they took along with them such gentlemen as were in their way with my forty horse, and about one o'clock they came up to them and set upon them. [This situation is precisely like that presented in our ballad.] Some hurt was done, but I gave especial order they should do as little hurt and shed as little blood as possible they could. They took a dozen of the principal gentlemen that were there, and brought them to me at Witherington where I then lay. I made them welcome, and gave them the best entertainment I could. They lay in the castle two or three days, and so I sent them home, they assuring me that they would never hunt again without leave. The Scots King complained to Queen Elizabeth very grievously of this fact [*i.e.*, deed, as often in Shakespeare].

The occasion, then, of the 'Chevy Chase' battle was a deliberate act of bravado on Percy's part. ' That tear began this spurn,' as the old ballad curiously puts it. War was the great Border game in the Middle Ages ; and there was never a lack of pretext for it or of opportunity.   Deadly encounters were as common and as welcome as football matches of wrestling bouts now-a-days.   The mutual irritability of the borderers, and especially of the retainers of the houses of Percy and Douglas, was not less keen than that of the Montagues and the Capulets, and of many another pair of families in Italy ; and often the streets of Edinburgh and the highways of the Marches recall the fierce discords of Verona.

> There was never a time on the March-partes
> Sen the Douglas and the Persy met;
> But it was marvel an the red blood ran not
> As the rain does in the street.

Mercutio was not more inflammable and more delighted to be inflamed than those passionate Border gentry.   Shakespeare's picture of Hotspur is excellently true in this respect; he has portrayed perfectly the fiery Border temperament. Hotspur, as we all know, is intolerant of the slightest rebuke or check.   The least opposition drives him into a furious rage.   He is a Borderer of the Borderers.

In 'The Hunting of the Cheviot,' Percy, as already noticed, is the aggressor, the provoker, the challenger.   Perhaps we may regard this ballad as a sort of pendant to 'The Battle of Otterbourne.'   Here Percy repays the compliment presented him by Douglas's visit and its conflagration.   In the ballad of 'Kinmont Willie,' when the bold keeper Buccleugh has rescued his retainer and got him safely across the Eden

> He turn'd him on the other side [*i.e.* towards Carlisle]
> And at Lord Scroop his glove flung he ;
> ' If he like na my visit in merry England,
> In fair Scotland come visit me.'

Such invitations were only too readily and heartily accepted; such 'calls' only too greedily and fiercely 'returned.'   And as a ballad had sung of the Douglas' inroad, a ballad must needs set forth a no less daring and insolent trespass of the Percy.

The locality of the 'Hunting' battle is less certainly ascertainable than that of the other ballads. But there are indications that may be of use. Clearly, as is said above, it is on the Scottish side of the Border; otherwise, there is no point in Percy's sport, no insult is offered to a Scottish warden; and, therefore, it cannot but be a long way from Otterbourne, which is some fifteen miles and more from the Border line. No weight can be attached to the stanza which identifies the two battles, for it is clearly the uncouth interpolation of some minstrel—of some midland minstrel— observe the form *knowen*—haply of Richard Sheal himself, whose particular copy is the one preserved—who knew nothing personally of the country concerned, and followed authorities who knew scarcely more:

> Old men that knowen the ground well enough
> Call it the Battle of Otterburn.

No, they did not know the ground well enough, these patriarchs, whoever they were. They must be 'plucked' in geography, these greybeards. Assuredly we must not go into Reedsdale if we wish to localise the 'Hunting' battle. But perhaps the attempt is idle; poets often make their own maps, and are greatly superior to the latitudes and longitudes of ordinary atlases. However, if the attempt is to be made it seems fairly clear the battle was fought, or imagined to be fought, in or near the Forest of Cheviot. Now the Forest of Cheviot [1] 'formerly covered the lower slopes of' Cheviot itself—the particular hill so called—'was chiefly on the side fronting Scotland,

---

[1] See M. Tomlinson's *Comprehensive Guide to Northumberland*, a very excellent handbook, p. 483.

and the remains of it may be seen in the oaks and birches along the Colledge Valley.' The ballad seems certainly to point to some spot near the north-west corner of Northumberland as the scene of the adventures it celebrates. We are specially told that Percy started from Bamborough, that he drew his forces from the northern district :

> Then the Percy out of Bamborough came,
>   With him a mighty many ;
> With fifteen hondreth archers bold of blood and bone ;
>   They were chosen out of shires three.

The shires three were Islandshire or Holy Island, Norehamshire, and Bamboroughshire. One can scarcely doubt he marched, or was supposed to march, across from Bamborough *viâ* Belford, Wooler, Kirk Newton, and so passing just to the south of Flodden, whose name was to become ' a household word' in the following century, and just to the north of Mount Cheviot, to enter Scotland at a point some seven or eight miles due east of Kelso and Roxburgh. It may also be noticed that the opposing troops came from Tweedside. The words are :

> They were borne along by the water o' Tweed,
>   I' th' bounds of Tividale.

Which are translated in the later version :

> All men of pleasant Tividale
> Fast by the river Tweed.

Undoubtedly, these phrases point to the north-east corner of Roxburghshire, and so agree satisfactorily with the hints given us as to Percy's movements, as a glance at a map will at once show.

The consideration of the locality is of course closely connected with this question of the historical basis of the ballad we are studying. Now, we find that in the immediate neighbourhood at which, for plausible reasons, we have just arrived, there was fought a notable Border battle, with a Percy and a Douglas in it. This was the battle of Piperden, fought in 1435, or possibly, as Bower says, in 1436. And the suggestion made by the editor of the *Reliques*, though by no means generally adopted, though very often forgotten or ignored—the suggestion that the ' Hunting,' so far as it is, has a particular historical foundation, relates to the battle of Piperden—appears to be well worth consideration. Piper-den is, indeed, in England, but it is close by the frontier ; and a battle to which it gave a name might well have spread across the frontier. In respect of position, Piperden exactly suits the requirements of the case. And in other respects it is, though not altogether suitable, yet perhaps as much so as can be expected, the freedom of balladry remembered.

The English invasion that was signalised by the battle of Piperden, or Pepperden, as Ridpath spells it, was, according to the Scottish accounts at least, peculiarly unprovoked and wanton. I will quote Stewart's rendering of the story as given by Boece :

> This beand done as I haif said yow heir.

He has just narrated the marriage of the Dauphin Louis and Margaret, daughter of James I. of Scotland, which took place in 1436 :

> Sir Henrie Persie in the samin yeir
> Quhat wes the caus I can nocht to yow schaw,
> Agane promit without ordour of law
> With four thousand all into armour bricht,
> In Scotland come sone efter on ane nycht,
> His appetite syne for to satisfie
> With fyre and blude, haifond no caus or quhy.
> The Erle of Angus in the tyme that was,
> The quhilk to name hecht William of Douglas,
> With equall nummer under speir and scheild
> Met with the Persie then and gaif him feild ;

> And in that battell so baldie tha baid,
> On euerie syde quhill greit slauchter wes maid.
> The Scottismen so worthie war and wycht,
> The Inglismen on force has tane the flycht,
> And in the feild na langar mycht remane ;
> On euerie syde richt mony than wes slane.
> That da thair deit on the Scottis syde
> Gude Elphinstoun ane nobill of great pryde ;
> Of commoun pepill tha hundreth also
> Departit than and tuke thair leif till go.
> Of Inglismen into the feild did faill
> Ane greit nobill, Henrie of Cliddisdail,
> Richard Persie and Johnne Ogill also,
> Knichtes all thre with mony other mo ;
> Of commoun pepill that tyme young and ald
> Four hundreth into the tyme war told.

So that Boece describes this expedition as a raid—as a chivachic—which in the ballad it is not ; and so Buchanan : 'Angli terra marique e Scotia prædas agere cœperunt, duce Percio, Northumbriæ regulo. Adversus eos missus Gulielmus Duglassus, Angusiæ comes,' etc.

Boece, however, does admit it was possibly a private and not an authorised enterprise : 'Incertum cujus auctoritate an privata an regia.' Gregory's *Chronicle of London* states that in the year 1436 'the Erle of Northehomberlande made a viage in-to Scotlande, and there he made a nobylle jorney.' On the whole, this identification, though it cannot be insisted upon, is not to be roughly rejected. Possibly we must be content, as we well may be, to take the ' Hunting ' as of general historical value rather than particular. Anyhow, it does not reflect the battle of Otterbourne, as is so commonly stated. Meanwhile, the fight at Piperden answers better than any other that has been suggested for a nucleus. If the tourist would fain realise the scene in his imagination with the aid of the *genius loci*, or local spirit, let him try the neighbourhood here readvocated. At all events he will find himself in a haunted land—a land abounding in memories of

old unhappy [and happy] far-off things
And battles long ago.

On the west side of Piper's Hill were buried many of those who fell in the terrible fight of Flodden close by, and at no great distance are Humbleton, Yeavering, Wark, Kelso, Roxburgh, and many less-known places with associations of various interest. Indeed, all that part has been all one great battlefield. It was the favourite cockpit of the Borders.

It must be observed that the chronology of the ballad as we have it is all confused; but it is never consistent with the Otterbourne theory. The Kings of England and Scotland in 1388 were respectively Richard II. and Robert II. The kings mentioned in the ballad are King Henry the Fourth and, in 'Eddenburrowe,' King James, who did not in fact reign at the same time. For it was not till 1424 that James was set free from his long English durance, and actually ascended the Scottish throne. The mention of the battle of Homildon, fought in 1402, makes the confusion worse confounded. These blunders may be due not to the ignorance of the original writer, but to that of successive minstrels, 'the crouders, with no rougher voice than rude style,' who took great liberties with their texts, omitting, modifying, adding at their own sweet will, very much as the old Anglo-Saxon glee-men had done, whence certain difficulties in *Beowulf*—as probably did the ancient reciters, the ῥαψῳδοί or στιχῳδοί of the Homeric ballads, whence certain difficulties that pervade the *Iliad*. The old poetry is sometimes 'evil appareled in the dust and cobwebs of "uncivil" reporters.' In the present case a diaskeuast would in some sort restore order, if for 'Henry the Fourth' he read

Henry the Sixth,' and if he maintained ll. 155-72 to be an interpolation. It is in this dubious passage that the clumsy stanza occurs as to 'the old men' and their knowledge of 'the ground,' which has been extracted above.

As to the date of composition, we may be sure that both the Otterbourne and the Chevy Chase ballads belong to about the same period. Probably those relating to the Otterbourne battle are the older, though the 'Hunting' has, as it happens, been preserved in a more primitive shape. The Otterbourne ballads must surely have been written shortly after the event described; and the 'Hunting' was probably written no long time after them.

But after all it must not be forgotten that such questions and matters as have been discussed here, though they have a real interest for the careful student of literature, are yet of secondary importance. The great thing—the saving grace—is not to know about poems, but to know them themselves, and to bear in mind that antiquarian and critical and suchlike disquisitions are only helps, or intended helps, towards that supreme knowledge. The great thing is that we should keep our ears clear to catch those trumpet notes that so moved Sidney's heart as he heard them rudely sounded in the Elizabethan streets, that we should duly feel with and for the heroes of those old songs, and recognise in them men of like passions with ourselves, or recognise in ourselves men of like passions with them. How vigorously they lived while they lived! With what a will they charged and thrust and struck!

> At last the Douglas and the Percy met
> Like to captains of might and of main;
> They swapt together till they both swat,
> With swords that were of fine Milon.

How infinite their boldness! 'Dare, Madam!' exclaimed one of them, the bold Buccleugh, when Queen Elizabeth, greatly irritated by his breaking into her castle of Carlisle and carrying off one of her prisoners—an exploit we have already referred to—asked him how he dared do such a thing. 'Dare, Madam!' he exclaimed, 'what dare not a man dare?' And they died not less resolutely and dauntlessly than they lived. They fought to the last, these Marchmen, and submitted to fate without a murmur, even with joy, when their hour came.

> With that there came an arrow hastily
>   Forth of a mighty wane;[1]
> It hath stricken the yearl Douglas
>   In at the breast bane.
>
> Thorough liver and lungs both
> The sharp arrow is gane,
> That never after in all his life-days
> He spake mo words but ane:
> 'Fight ye, my merry men, while ye may;
> For my life-days ben gane.'

Fight while ye may !—such was his rule of life. Not *carpe diem*, not 'Soul, take thine ease,' but *Fight while ye may!* The dying Borderer asks for no favour, not even for such an one as Hector vainly begs as he lies in the dust at the feet of Achilles—that his conquerer may be willing to receive ransom money for his body.

> σῶμα δὲ οἴκαδ' ἐμὸν δόμεναι πάλιν ὄφρα πυρός με
> Τρῶες καὶ Τρώων ἄλοχοι λελάχωσι θάνοντα.

Nor, as we have seen, does his spirit pass—

> ὃν πότμον γοόωσα, λιποῦσ' ἀδροτῆτα καὶ ἥβην.

And the pathetic picture of Percy mourning over his fallen foe is a strange contrast to the iron-hearted Greek (σιδήρεος

---

[1] *i.e.*, a number, a shower, a flight.

ἐν φρεσὶ θυμός) binding Hector's corpse to his chariot, and with so shameful an appendage driving exultantly beneath the Walls from which old Priam and Hecuba are looking down on the piteous scene :—

> τοῦ δ'ἦν ἑλκομένοιο κονίσαλος ἀμφὶ δὲ χαῖται
> κυάνεαι πίτναντο, κάρη δ' ἅπαν ἐν κονίῃσι
> κεῖτο πάρος χαρίεν· τότε δὲ Ζεὺς δυσμενέεσσι
> δῶκεν ἀεικίσσασθαι ἑῇ ἐν πατρίδι γαίῃ.

> The Percy leaned on his brand,
>   And saw the Douglas die.
> He took the dead man by the hand,
>   And said 'Wo is me for thee !
>
> To have saved thy life, I would have parted with
>   My lands for years three ;
> For a better man of heart nor of hand
>   Was not in the North Country.'

Happily, the ready shrewdness, the splendid energy, the fearless courage, the chivalrous spirit of the old Borderers are not extinct; though they have changed the forms in which they exhibit themselves. A very remarkable list might be made of their descendants, in whom their old prowess transmitted has been and is conspicuously displayed. The late General Gordon was ultimately of Border lineage. In the centuries to which we have gone back in this paper the name often occurs ; for instance, we read of a John Gordon, who, 'Angliam ingressus cum ingenti hominum pecudumque præda coacta rediret,' is opposed by Sir John Gilburn, and overthrows him. And a note in *A Short Border History* informs us that Coklaw or Ormistown Castle, near Hawick, is 'the peeltower of the Gledstones, a Border family, illustrious now through one of its members, the Right Hon. W. E. Gladstone, M.P.'

XI

WYATT AND SURREY

(From *The Academy* for Dec. 1, 1883)

ALL who wish for an accurate acquaintance with the revival of our literature and the rise of certain literary orms in the second quarter of the sixteenth century, will like to see the lines in which Leland speaks of Wyatt.

Leland's *Naeniae in Mortem Thomae Viati Equitis incomparabilis* is divided into sections (as perhaps the title might lead one to expect)—*i.e.*, into a series of lauds and laments in various metres, hexameters or elegiacs or hondecasyllabics, each with its title. One headed ' Anglus par Italis ' runs thus :—

> Bella suum merito jactet Florentia Dantem ;
> Regia Petrarchae carmina Roma probet.
> His non inferior patrio sermore Viatus,
> Eloquii secum qui decus omne tulit.

Now there is every reason to believe, if we study the biographies of Wyatt and Surrey, that Wyatt, and not Surrey as is so commonly stated, led the way in the work which is associated with their names—that Wyatt, and not Surrey, was the first to attempt the improvement of our metres by Italian example and precedent. As early as 1526, when Surrey was certainly not more than ten years old, perhaps only eight, Leland had 'honoured' Wyatt, then twenty-three, as the most accomplished poet of his time. But it can scarcely be said, I think, that the above lines prove this priority. But there are other passages in Leland's *Naeniae* which do undoubtedly prove it. First, there is the couplet styled 'Lima Viati'—

> Anglica lingua fuit rudis et sine nomine rhythmus ;
> Nunc limam agnoscit, docte Viate, tuam.

And there are two other pieces that may be pronounced fairly decisive. One is headed 'Nobilitas debet Viato'—

> Nobilitas didicit te praeceptore Britanna
> Carmina per varios scribere posse modos.

Can there be any doubt that among these British nobles in Leland's mind as belonging to the 'school' of Wyatt were not only Lord Vaux, Lord Rochfort, Sir Francis Bryan (a nephew of Lord Berners), but eminently and specially Lord Surrey? There can be no doubt at all on this point if we take in this connexion yet another stanza (if I may so use the term) in which Surrey is spoken of as the poetic heir of the great deceased. This stanza is headed 'Vnicus phoenix,' and the words of it are these :—

> Vna dies geminos phoenices non dedit orbi ;
> Mors erit unius, vita sed alterius.
> Rara auis in terris, confectus amore Viatus
> Houardum heredem scripserat ante suum.

It must be remembered that Leland is no mean authority ; and he would seem to have known and admired both poets. Wyatt and he had become friends in their college days at Cambridge—

> Me tibi conjunxit comitem gratissima Granta,
> Granta Camœnarum gloria, fama, deus.

So runs the couplet headed 'Conjunctio animorum,' and the entire 'carmen' is addressed in a tone that implies personal acquaintance and friendship 'ad Henricum Houardum Regnorum comitem juvenem tum nobilissimum tum doctissimum.'

Tulit alter honores. But surely it is time Wyatt had a more general recognition as the first, in time at least, of those 'courtly makers' Puttenham speaks of—the leader in the remarkable Italianised movement which they effected : and should no longer be regarded as a mere follower of one who in fact followed him—as the heir of one whom he himself endowed. It ought to be noticed more than it is that the metrical structure of the sonnet was better understood by him than by Surrey, not one of whose efforts in this kind is according to the Petrarchian model. But, whether this credit is given him or not, surely it is time he should more generally have some credit for having introduced the sonnet into our literature. Yet, in his otherwise admirable remarks on the sonnet in the recently published edition of Milton's Sonnets, Mr Mark Pattison, a singularly accomplished scholar, and a most excellent writer and critic, as all the world knows, does not even mention poor Sir Thomas. *Sic vos non vobis.*

XII

SPENSERIANA

(From *The Academy*, Nov. 28, 1874)

THE important discovery as to the poet Spenser's place of education, made known in the Fourth Report of the Royal Commission on Historical Manuscripts, makes it probable, though not certain, that Spenser was not only born (see the *Prothalamion*) but bred in London ; and so, perhaps, what I ventured to suggest as to the scene of his early life in the *Memoir* prefixed to the Globe edition of his works, published in 1869, may require some modification (see p. xviii. of the *Globe Spenser*), though not necessarily so, if we remember that town and country were not so utterly divorced in the Elizabethan age as now-a-days. What God made, and what man made, as Cowper has it, were not so utterly put asunder but that a man might enjoy both without performing an amazing pedestrian feat. East Smithfield itself was not wholly unrural then. The fields actually touched it ; and the houses did not crowd densely together to make its name a dismal misnomer.

With regard to his connexion with the Merchant Taylors' School, it may, perhaps, be worth noticing that Spenser's choice of St Barnabas's Day for his wedding may indicate a kindly remembrance of his old school life; for that is the great election day at the Merchant Taylors' (Murray's *Handbook of Modern London*). See the *Epithalamion*, the song devoted to the celebration of his own matrimonial bliss :—

> Ring ye the bels, ye yong men of the towne,
>   And leave your wonted labors for this day.
> This day is holy; doe ye write it downe,
>   That ye for ever it remember may.
> This day the sunne is in his chiefest hight,
> With Barnaby the bright,
>   From whence declining daily by degrees,
> He somewhat loseth of his heat and light,
>   When once the Crab behind his back he sees.

Also, may it not now be possible to discover who 'Wrenock' is, mentioned in the *Shepheard's Calender, December?* Certainly, lines 37-42 seem to refer to his school days, as what follows to his University career, when he became acquainted with Gabriel Harvey :—

> And for I was in thilke same looser yeares
>   (Whether the Muse so wrought me from my byrth,
> Or I to much beleeved my shepherd peeres),
>   Somedele ybent to song and musicks mirth,
> A good olde Shephearde, Wrenock was his name,
>   Made me by arte more cunning in the same.

Whether Spenser had visited the North before he went up to Cambridge, or not, the old belief as to his visiting it after he left the University, remains undisturbed. (See *Glosse* to *Shep. Cal., June*). Plausible reasons, as is well known, have been alleged for supposing that the particular part of the North visited was in the neighbourhood of Burnley in East Lancashire (see the *Gentleman's Magazine*, for August, 1842). Probably to those reasons something might be added by a careful study of the language of the *Shepheard's Calender*. Many of the words quoted by Mr T.

T. Wilkinson in his paper on this subject, read before the Historic Society of Lancashire and Cheshire in 1867, are of too general occurrence to be of value in localising the poem; such words, for instance, as *kirk*, *gate* (a road), *wood* (mad), *latch*, *gar* (compel), etc., etc.; and of no word is it shown that it is distinctively East Lancashire. I will only add on this point that, if Spenser passed all his youth in the South country, it is not likely that he writes with complete accuracy the dialect he attempts. His old English is notoriously faulty; and so probably is the language of his Bucolics. A Greek brought up at Athens would be liable to trip in his Doric, if he took to writing in the manner of Theokrites when some six Olympiads old.

Mr F. C. Spenser of Halifax, who first suggested that the neighbourhood of Burnley was the cradle of the poet's race, was of opinion that Hurstwood was the chief seat of the family, but that the branch to which the author of the *Faerie Queene* immediately belonged, was settled on a little property still called 'The Spensers,' near Filly Close, two or three miles to the north of Burnley. Such was his theory; but his practice seems to have been scarcely consistent with it. For he took up his quarters in a house not near Filly Close, but at Hurstwood, and has given currency to a tradition that it was there the poet's own people lived. And the house is now becoming known as 'the poet's house,' and people travel from far to see it. And no doubt soon, if only the soil and climate allow, a mulberry tree planted by Spenser will be pointed out; for, according to the popular fancy, planting mulberry trees was the chief avocation of our great poets. The house is not the principal one in the hamlet—not Hurstwood itself, for that was built for 'Barnardus Townley et Agnes uxor ejus,' as an inscription over the door sets forth; but a house of smaller dimensions, some few yards to the west of the abode of the Townleys.   As the tradition of its being the poet's is now, as I have said, prevailing, and is sure in a few years to be quoted by some biographer, as evidence on the question, I wish here to record that it is, in fact, of altogether modern growth.   In a recent visit to Hurstwood, a friend and I tried to discover the time of its origin, and found that, beyond all question, it dates from Mr F. C. Spenser's visit a generation ago.   We interviewed the three oldest inhabitants we could hear of— they were all said to be eighty-four—that seems a fashionable age with the ancients of Hurstwood—and could find no trace of the Spenser legend in the memories of their earlier life.   But our most decisive witness was the present tenant of the house in question, a thoroughly intelligent and clear-headed man, whose father lived there before him.   He remembered Mr F. C. Spenser's visit, and was quite positive that it was during that visit his father and he first heard of the honour their mansion might boast.   Such traditions so easily take root.   I remember once being assured at Middlewich, in Cheshire, by a man who looked incalculably old, that in the house where he dwelt, John Milton, the poet, 'came a-courting.'   It was an old lath-and-plaster house, inscribed with the names of Edwarde and Prudence Minshull, and of Hvonn and Marie and John Minshull; and from this inscription had sprung the story.   Some one with a little learning, with enough learning to know that Milton's third wife was named Minshull, but not enough to know that she hailed from Nantwich or thereabouts, had leapt to a wrong conclusion; and the popular mind, regarding a formal 'courting' as a necessary preliminary to a marriage, had added a detail of its own, and brought the then blind and feeble poet down in person into Cheshire a-wooing.   In this case also the author of the legend might, I believe, be satisfactorily discovered. Hurstwood is only some three or four miles from Filly Close, so that it may be described as in Spenser's country, and, if the chief seat of his family, may be believed to have been often visited by him ; but there seems no reason for identifying it with his own home.

The great natural feature of the district is Pendle Hill Both at Hurstwood and at Filly Close it is lord of all. Filly Close, indeed, stands in the 'forest' on the south-eastern descent. One interest attaching to this mountain that recalls the poetry of Spenser is that it was the great gathering-place of witches—'the great locale,' saith Murray, ' of the saturnalia of Lancashire witches'—the Brocken of Old England. Several hundreds of these poor creatures were brought to trial and burnt in the early years of the seventeenth century. His native country may well have furnished Spenser with some hints for the pictures he draws of such beings. The original of the following sketch may have been some actual scene in Pendle Forest :—

> There in a gloomy hollow glen she [Florimel] found
> A little cottage, built of stickes and reedes
> In homely wize, and wald with sods around ;
> In which a witch did dwell, in loathly weedes
> And wilfull want, all carelesse of her needes ;
> So choosing solitarie to abide
> Far from all neighbours that her divelish deedes
> And hellish arts from people she might hide,
> And hurt far off unknowne whom ever she envide.
>
> *Faerie Queene*, III. vii. 6.

And there are other passages of a like origin possibly. Duessa herself may have been a Lancashire witch to begin with.

That Rosalind was a Lancashire witch in the modern sense, there can be little doubt. Helps towards her identification are that she was 'the widdowes daughter of the glenne,' that the poet first met her in some 'neighbour town,' that her name 'Rosalinde' is 'a feigned name, which, being well ordered, will bewray the very name of hys love and mistresse whom by that name he coloureth,' (See *Shep. Cal., April and Januarie*, and the *Glosses*.) Suppose her Christian name to be Eliza, could the name of Nord, or any other combination of the four remaining letters, be found in any local register or document?[1] Then perhaps we might discover who was the happy Menalcas who supplanted the poet. (See Argument to *Shep. Cal., June.*) Perhaps she was wise in her generation: for Spenser, late of Pembroke, Cambridge, must have cut a poor figure in those days of his life, waiting wearily for something to turn up, with nothing that could be called his own save a few manuscripts, which I dare say Miss Rosalind could not read. Those who think she was a sister of Daniel the poet must ignore the evidence that connects her with the North Country, for the Daniels were of Somersetshire. One may plausibly believe that 'the neighbour town' was Burnley; for he does not use 'town' here in the old sense—in the sense, for instance, of Chaucer's *Prologue*, l. 478 ('a pore Persoun of a toun')—but evidently he is thinking of Vergils' 'urbs' in the Eclogues, as i. 20 and 34, viii. 68, etc.; and the 'to see' is significant.

> A thousand sithes I curse that carefull hower
>> Wherein I long'd the neighbour towne to see,
> And eke tenne thousand sithes I blesse the stowre
>> Wherein I sawre so fayre a sighte as shee ;
> Yet all for naught ; such sight hath bred my bane.
> Ah God ! that love should breede both joy and payne.

However these things may be, it is certain that he was deeply smitten with her beauty. Fifteen years afterwards the vision of her still haunted him. It was with him in his

---

[1] But see vol. I. of Dr Grosart's edition of *Spenser*, 1884.

castle of Kilcolman, and his heart was as tender towards her as ever, so that he would not hear a word said in her disparagement (see the conclusion of *Colin Clouts come Home again.*)

The registers of St Peter's, Burnley, abound under all the three heads, in entries relating to Spensers. The only one that, in the course of a hasty examination, struck us of possibly immediate importance to the poet, was that of the burial of an Edmund Spenser, November 9, 1577 — an entry seemingly overlooked by Mr F. C. Spenser, if Craik reports him accurately in his *Spenser and His Poetry*, i. 12, ed. 1845. If this was the poet's father, how well it would agree with the poet being then in the North, and also with his leaving it so soon after.

XIII

SIR JOHN DAVIES'S POEMS

(From *the Athenæum* for Sept. 2, 1876)

WE have to thank Dr Grosart for what is probably a quite complete edition of Sir John Davies's Poems. Besides *Nosce Teipsum*, the *Hymns to Astræa*, and other well-known works, he gives us some 200 pages of pieces 'either printed for the first time, or for the first time published among Davies's Poems. These additions are more important for the sake of the completeness of the collection, than for their intrinsic merit. The metaphrase of some of the psalms, printed from a MS. in the possession of Dr David Laing, though superior to some other efforts of the same kind, is yet far from being a success. The work is executed with the editor's characteristic care and accuracy. A few misprints may have escaped him, as in ii. 30. ('He first taught him that keeps the monuments.') We do not know how he would read the second of these two lines:

> Brunns which deems himself a faire sweet youth,
> Is thirty-nine yeares of age at least;

Dyce reads:

> Is nine-and-thirty years of age at least

with a note, 'So MS., except that it has thirtieth, and we

see no reason for altering or retaining the alteration of
'ranging' into 'raging' in the seventeenth Epig. :

> To thoughts of drinking, thriving, duelling, war,
> And borrowing money ranging in his mind.

But, so far as the collection and the text are concerned,
Dr Grosart has done his work well.

Few will deny that it was work worth doing, and doing
well.   It is vain indeed to make definitions of poetry which
would deprive any poet of his well-won title.   Whatever
may be said as to what poetry should be, the fact remains
that the author of *Nosce Teipsum* is a poet.   In the
kingdom of poetry, as has been said, are many mansions,
and undoubtedly one of these belongs to Sir John Davies,
however we may describe it, however we may censure its
style and arrangement.   Far be from us any such critical
or scholastic formulæ as would prevent us from all due
appreciation of such refined, imaginative thought and subtle,
finished workmanship, as mark the first notable philosophical
poem of our literature.

The epigrams possess an interest of a very different kind,
for Davies differed a good deal from himself, to speak in a
Greek manner.   Like Stephano's Monster, he had two
voices.   'His forward voice' is heard when he discourses of
the soul of man and the immortality thereof; 'his backward voice is to utter foul speeches and detract.'   Dr
Grosart, it seems, had 'compunctious visitings' as to re-
publishing these latter utterances; but he had the good
sense to resist them.   Certainly he would have failed to do
his duty had he not resisted them.   And one must be careful not to judge in an exaggerated manner of what there is
of grossness in these pieces.   There are many worse ways

of speaking than plain language. Words that are nauseous to our fine palates had once no bad taste for natures that were certainly as truly healthful and as genuinely refined as we can boast to be. Anyhow, the life pictures these epigrams give are much too precious to be lost or thrown aside. They bring the old Elizabethan London vividly before us, with all its rough humours, its wild wit, its boisterous vitality. They did not play at living, those Elizabethans, but lived hard, and fully and furiously. It was not their way to sip at the cup of enjoyment, they drank deep, and jested loudly, and laughed louder.

Here is a portrait from the gallery :

> Oft in my laughing times, I name a Gull ;
> But this new term will many questions breed ;
> Therefore at first I will express in full,
> Who is a true and perfect Gull indeed.
> A Gull is he who fears a velvet gown,
> And when a wench is brave dares not speak to her.
> A Gull is he which traverseth the town,
> And is for marriage known a common wooer.
> A Gull is he which while he proudly wears
> A silver-hilted rapier by his side,
> Endures the lies and knocks about the ears,
> Whilst in his sheath his sleeping sword doth bide.
> A Gull is he which wears good handsome clothes,
> And stands in Presence stroking up his hair,
> And fills up his imperfect speech with oaths,
> But speaks not one wise word throughout the year.
> But to define a Gull in terms precise ;
> A Gull is he which seems and is not wise.

XIV

THE PILGRIMAGE TO PARNASSUS, WITH THE TWO PARTS OF THE RETURN FROM PARNASSUS[1]

(I.) (From *The Academy* for March 19, 1887)

STUDENTS of the Elizabethan period may well rejoice in the recent addition to their libraries of two such books as Mr Hubert Hall's *Society in the Elizabethan Age* and the volume now before us. Mr Hall's highly interesting and most useful work reproduces 'original matter,' and gives us information that is 'certainly new.' Mr Macray's work is itself a piece, or a set of pieces, of 'original matter.' It consists of three plays, two now printed for the first time, that brings vividly before us a certain phase of Elizabethan life, and might perhaps provide Mr Hall with some illustrations, if to his excellent gallery of the landlord, the burgess, the courtier, and the other persons he portrays, he should presently be inclined to add the literary man.

It is strange, indeed, that the two plays now printed for the first time should not have been discovered before. They

[1] *The Pilgrimage to Parnassus, with the Two Parts of the Return from Parnassus.* Three Comedies performed in St John's College, Cambridge, A.D. MDXCVII.—MDCI. Edited from MSS. by the Rev. W. D. Macray. (Oxford, at the Clarendon Press.)

are referred to in a somewhat obscure passage in the Prologue to what we must now call the second part of *The
Return from Parnassus:*

'*The Pilgrimage to Parnassus and the Returne from Pernassus,*'
says Momus, 'haue stood the honest Stagekeepers in many a crownes
expence for linckes and vizards; purchased many a Sophister a knock
with a clubbe; hindred the buttlers box, and emptied the colledge
barrells; and now vnlesse you know the subject well, you may returne
home as wise as you came; for this last is the last part of the *Returne
from Parnassus,* that is the last time that the authors wit wil turne
vpon the toe in this vaine and at this time the scene is not at Parnassus,
that is, lookes not good invention in the face.'

Which words seem to mean that the preceding plays had
been extremely popular—had often been acted by link-light,
had led to brawls, perhaps, by some at that time unmistakable personalities, greatly diminished the usual Christmas
gambling, and led to the absorption of much college ale by
those whom the performance with its excitement and shouting had made unquenchably thirsty.   But we may presume
the third play was yet more popular: perhaps because in its
satire it appealed to a yet larger circle, and dealt with a
subject about which there was just then much irritation.
Its alternative name is 'the Scourge of Simony;' and among
other things it gives a very full and vigorous picture of the
disreputable traffic in 'livings'—the 'steeple-fairs'—that
then prevailed.   (Are they quite extinct in these 'enlightened'
days?)   However this may be, the third play was twice
printed in 1606, and, though forgotten for a time, has long
been well known and appreciated by Shakespearian scholars;
the famous scene in Act IV., where Philomusus and Studioso in their desperate destitution think of betaking themselves to the stage, and apply to those distinguished
professionals, Burbage and Kempe, and Burbage and Kempe
boast of 'our fellow Shakespeare' and his prowess, having

been quoted again and again. The earlier plays, known only by the mention of them given above, were supposed to have perished till the other day, when Mr Macray unearthed them, in no far-away, scarcely-accessible, retirement, but in the Bodleian Library itself. Perhaps for books and MSS., as for men, the truest solitude is to be found in crowds. To lie in an attic in the Hebrides or at the bottom of a box in Kamchatka—neither of these positions is lonely; but to be well housed in a public library, 'this—this is solitude!' Who can say what may not yet be found, and found within an arm's length of everybody?

The dates of all these plays can happily be fixed with something like certainty. It has been sufficiently shown that the third was acted in December 1601. As to the date of the *Pilgrimage*, Mr Macray's adopted date of 1597 is hardly consistent with his own notes; for they rightly mention that Kinsayder's *Satyres* and also Bastard's *Epigrams*, both which works are named in the text, were not published till 1598. The phrase 'some four years' in Mr Halliwell-Phillipps's MS. copy, denoting the period during which the author has been busy with his two *Individui Vagi* (which seems to mean 'Wandering Individuals'), certainly cannot be pressed to overrule such evidence, or the fact, quoted by a correspondent in a contemporary, that there is a clear allusion to Marlow's *Hero and Leander*, which also was not published till 1598. In the second play, Weaver's *Epigrams* are referred to; and these, as Mr Macray points out, were not published till 1599. If we put these things and others together—Gullio's record of his exploits 'now verie latelie in Irelande,' is worth noting—it would seem fairly certain that the *Pilgrimage* came out at Christmas 1598-9; the *Return*, part i., at Christmas 1599-1600; and part ii. at Christmas 1601-2.

The subject is 'the discontent' of scholars—the misery
of those who, having no private pecuniary means, would
fain devote themselves to poetry and culture. In the
Pilgrimage the two heroes, Philomusus and Studioso, set
out for Parnassus with high hopes and buoyant spirits.
They succeed, these Endymions, in resisting the allurements
of the world, the flesh, and the devil, variously represented
by Madido a sot, Stupido a Puritan, Amoretto a votary of
Venus, and a perhaps yet more dangerous person, one
Ingenioso, a demoralised poet, who is now turning his back
on the country he once sought, having found to his cost
that it is a country stricken with poverty. But the pilgrims
press on, and arrive at last at the haven where they would
be, still sanguine and confident. The *Return* presents
them to us disappointed and crossed. Ingenioso's account
has proved too true. In a stichomythic dialogue they give
voice to their bitterness, and determine to beat a retreat :

> *Phil.* Th' arts are unkind that do their sons neglect.
> *Stud.* Unkinder friends that scholars do reject.
> *Phil.* Dissembling arts looked smoothly on our youth.
> *Stud.* But load our age with discontent and ruth.
> *Phil.* Friends foolishly us to this woe do train.
> *Stud.* Fickle Apollo promised future gain.
> *Phil.* We want the prating coin, the speaking gold.
> *Stud.* Yea, friends are gained by that yellow mould.
> *Phil.* Adieu, Parnassus ! I must pack away.
> *Stud.* Fountains, farewell, where beauteous nymphs do play.
> *Phil.* In Helicon no more I'll dip my quill.
> *Stud.* I'll sing no more upon Parnassus' hill.
> *Phil.* Lets talk no more, since no relief we find.
> *Stud.* In vain to score our losses on the wind.

And so the unhappy youths drift out in the world to live as
they may. Philomusus gets a situation as a village sexton,
Studioso as a private tutor. Both endure much ignominy,
and are at last abruptly dismissed. Then in utter despair

they resolve to go to Rome or Rheims, to turn Papists in the hope of being cherished and made much of by the church to which they should by this movement be 'reconciled.'   And so ends the first part of the *Return*.   The same theme is repeated in the second.

Of special interest among the *personæ* are certainly Ingenioso and Gullio : Gullio for his adoration of 'sweet Mr Shakespeare,' whose poetry he pays the compliment of constantly quoting or appropriating, and whose picture he vows to have in his study at court ; Ingenioso as a 'study' of 'the literary man'—the professional author of the Elizabethan days.

Ingenioso has a wretched time of it.   It was the age of patronage, whose death warrant was not to be signed and sealed for some century and a half, as signed and sealed it was by Dr Johnson in that scathing letter of his to my Lord Chesterfield ; and this distressed man of letters cultivates a patron, who at last presents him with two groats—'a fidler's wages' as the recipient afterwards describes his 'tip'—and a reminder that Homer had scarce so much bestowed upon him in all his lifetime ; 'indeed, our countinance is enough for a scholler, and the sunshine of our favoure yealdes good heate of itselfe.'   And so he will 'live by the printing house ; ' and a miserable livelihood it is he secures in this way, to judge from his subsequent condition.   Mr Walter Besant has just been showing, in his able and eloquent address to the Society of Authors, how far from satisfactory are mostly the pecuniary relations of author and publisher at the present time.   How would he describe such relations as they were in the Elizabethan age ?   The publishers—the 'booksellers,' as they were then called—had it all their own way then ; and certainly it was not a good way for the authors, though one would be sorry to believe that among those publishers there

were not some men of probity and honour, worthy predecessors of the best specimens of 'the trade' in our own
time. There is said to be a good deal of human nature in
man, and I suppose in publishers as well as in other men;
and it is not, as a rule, a good arrangement that one man
should lie at the mercy of another. But that was pretty
much the position of the Elizabethan 'author by profession,'
as of many an author since. Goldsmith's epitaph on Mr
Edward Purden might well have been graven on many a
tombstone, with a change of name:

> Here lies poor Ned Purden, from misery freed,
> Who long was a bookseller's hack;
> He led such a damnable life in this world,
> I don't think he'll wish to come back.

Such a condition of things is represented by the career of
Ingenioso. He starves by the booksellers rather than lives
by them. No doubt he is himself thriftless, but his position
was not likely to encourage habits of thrift. And certainly
he was no mere fiction. There were only too many writers
who might have sat for that portrait. What I wish now to
suggest is that the particular writer who was specially before
the eye and in the mind of the probably Johnian author of
the Parnassus plays was that famous Johnian wit, Thomas
Nash. I do not think anyone will doubt this connexion who
has studied Nash's *Pierce Penniless's Supplication to the
Devil*.

'What, I travel to Parnassus?' shrieks out Ingenioso when the pilgrims
ask him for his company. 'Why, I have burnt my books, split my pen,
rent my papers, and curse the cozening hearts that brought me up to no
better fortune. I, after many years study, having almost brought my
brain into a consumption, looking still when I should meet with some
good Maecenas that liberally would reward my deserts, I fed so long
upon hope till I had almost starved. . . . Go to Parnassus! Alas!
Apollo is bankrupt; there is nothing but silver words and golden phrases

for a man ; his followers want the gold, while tapsters, ostlers, carters and coblers have a foaming pauch [pouch], a belching bag that serves for a chair of estate for *regina pecunia.* . . . Why, would it not grieve a man of a good spirit to see Hobson find more money in the tails of 12 jades than a scholar in 200 books ? Turn home again, unless you mean to be *vacui viatores,* and to curse your witless heads in your old age for taking themselves to no better trades in their youth.'

Compare this passage with the opening pages of *Pierce Penniless: his Supplication:*

I sate up late, and rose early, contended with the colde and con-versed with scarcitie ; for all my labours turned to loss, my vulgar muse was despised and neglected, my pains not regarded or slightly rewarded, and I myself in prime of my best wit laid open to poverty. Whereupon, in a malcontent humour, I accused my fortune, railed on my patrons, bit my pen, rent my papers, and raged in all points like a madman. . . . Thereby I grew to consider how many base men that wanted those parts which I had enjoyed content at will, and had wealth at command. I called to mind a cobbler that was worth five hundred pound, an hostler that had built a goodly inn and might dispend forty pounds yearly by his land, a car-man in a leather pilch that had whipt a thousand pound out of his horse and tail. . . . Thanks be to God, I am *vacuus viator,* and care not though I meet the Commissioners of Newmarket-heath at high midnight, for any crosses, images, or pictures that I carry about me more than needs.

And further parallelisms might be brought forward ; but, perhaps it will be enough to point out that Ingenioso is an admiring student and would-be follower of Juvenal, and that at the end of the third play he informs Academico that writs are out for him to apprehend him for his plays, and that he was bound for the Isle of Dogs, where there seems an evident allusion to Nash's play called the *Isle of Dogs,* which gave such offence in 1597 that Henslow's company which acted it was silenced for a time, and the author put into prison. I do not mean that Ingenioso and Nash are to be identified, for Ingenioso himself, in the third play, speaks of him as past and gone. ' Ay,' he says, after naming Thomas Nash to Judicio, 'here is a fellow, Judicio, that carried the deadly stockado in his pen, whose muse was armed with a gag-tooth, and his pen possest with Hercules' furies'; and the other replies :

> Let all his faults sleep with his mournful chest,
> And there for ever with his ashes rest.
> His style was witty, though it had some gall ;
> Some things he might have mended, so may all.
> Yet this I say that for a mother wit
> Few men have ever seen the like of it.

But clearly Nash illustrates Ingenioso.

These plays exhibit much wit and humour; and, quite apart from their historical interest, are well worth a perusal. The hall at St John's must have rung with justifiable laughter when Goodman Percival appeared to arrange for the comfortable burying of his father, and that without any delay.

' Hark you, Sexton,' says the ' hard heir,' who is already striding about his lands, ' I pray you bury him quickly; for he was a good man, and I know he is in a better place that's fitter for him than this scurvey world, and I would not have him alive again to his hindrance. It will be better for him and me too, for there's a great change with me within this two hours; for the ignorant people that before called me Will, now call me William, and you of the finer sort call me Goodman Percival.'

And there are many other passages and speeches full of excellent fun. Here and there are touches of true poetical feeling and grace, as in the Act III. of the *Pilgrimage*, when the young enthusiasts delight in their journey through the fields of learning and culture. Certainly these plays possess real literary merit, which makes it all the more important that the name of the author should be discovered.

Who was this well-informed and sprightly wit, who on no less than three occasions supplied St John's College, Cambridge, with such admirable fooling? This has always been a mystery; but fresh effort ought now to be made to solve it. The second of the new play seems to say that 'our poet' had suffered from the popularity of his drama, or perhaps of his acting:

> Surely it made our poet a staid man,
> Kept his proud neck from baser lambskin's wear
> > [*i.e.*, from assuming the hood of a Bachelor of Arts.]
> Had like to have made him Senior Sophister
> > [*i.e.*, to have prevented his advancing beyond the status
> > of a third year's man.]
> He was fain to take his course to Germany,
> Ere he could get a silly poor degree.
> He never since durst name a piece of cheese,
> > [My friend, Dr Schoell, informs me that 'Farente
> > Scholaren' were nicknamed 'Käsebettler' and 'Käse-
> > jäger.']
> Though Cheshire seems to privilege his name.
> His look was never sanguine since that day,
> Ne'er since he laughed to see a mimic play.

John Day has been suggested; but, unless the last line but one can be forced into a pun on his name, it is fatal to his pretensions. Moreover, he was of Caius, though this perhaps might be got over; and was he connected with Cheshire? Very little seems made out about the details of his life. It is, perhaps, worth noticing that, though for a time at Cambridge, he does not appear to have graduated there. His claims may deserve further consideration. I will just mention, as nothing ought to be neglected that may be of the slightest use, that Nash seems to have had a friend called Beeston, a name sufficiently redolent of Cheshire; and, I think, what I have said and quoted above justifies the supposition that the writer of the *Parnassus* plays was a friend of Nash. Can anything be found out about 'Maister Apislapis' to whom Nash's confutation of Gabriel

Harvey's *Four Letters* is inscribed? Is he the same as the player Christopher Beeston, first mentioned by Henslow, *s.a.* 1602? The notion of his having anything to do with these plays may prove the worthlessest of worthless conjectures; but it may just be mentioned, if only to be finally refuted and thrown aside.

There are many other points of interest and of importance in these plays; but I will only now heartily thank Mr Macray for having placed within our reach a volume of such real value. He does, indeed, deserve well of the republic of letters.

(2.) (From *Macmillan's Magazine* for May 1887)

EVERY year something is accomplished in our studies of old times : every year something is recovered from oblivion. But it is not often so important an addition is made to the remains of Elizabethan literature as the two plays lately discovered by Mr Macray in one of Thomas Hearne's volumes of miscellaneous collections in the Bodleian Library. It was known that these two plays—*The Pilgrimage to Parnassus*, and a continuation called *The Return from Parnassus*—had been composed ; for they are mentioned in the prologue to a play, also called *The Return from Parnassus*, with the alternative name *The Scourge of Simony*—a play twice printed in the age that produced it, and several times since ; but it was generally supposed they had perished.

For the future, what has been hitherto known as *The Return from Parnassus* must be described as Part II. ; and Mr Macray's *Return* must be described as Part I. Thus we have now a Parnassian trilogy: *The Pilgrimage*, and the *Return* in two parts.

All the three plays show an intimate acquaintance with the literature of the time, and a growing familiarity with the bitterness of a literary man's position, if not indeed a personal experience of it. And certainly they bring clearly before us a man of wit and humour, and no mean dramatic skill, especially if his probable age is considered. But it has not yet been possible to identify him, though with the new facts furnished by Mr Macray's discoveries, it may be hoped this will presently be done. John Day, a well-known play-wright, a colleague of Haughton and Hathway and Chettle and Decker and Wentworth Smith, the sole author of *Peregrinatio Scholastica, or Learning's Pilgrimage*, has been suggested; but, not to dwell on other objections, Day was certainly a writer for the stage in or before 1593, and therefore was not likely to be a Cambridge undergraduate in 1598. Perhaps some vigorous German explorer may be good enough to unearth the name of an Englishman who left Cambridge and took a German degree some time in the year 1599. For the present, at any rate, this question is unsettled.

Putting now on one side all such matters, which after all, though interesting, are of minor importance—for our main consideration concerns the gift, not the giver—concerns the value of what is said rather than the person who says it—let us now see what the plays themselves have to offer us in the way of history, or literary excellence, or criticism of life; that is, as pictures of their age, or as works of art and of wisdom.

Though evidently written by one who was well at home in London, and especially at the London theatres, these plays take us into an old college hall in the midst of Elizabethan Cambridge. We see the University laying aside its severer studies and indulging in its Christmas recreations. The passion for the drama, that just at this time (at the close of the sixteenth century) was at its height in England, prevailed in the cloisters as well as in the town. No wonder that amongst the more distinguished dramatists of the day were many foster-children of Oxford and Cambridge. Delight in some sort of drama had long been a national characteristic. But all through the sixteenth century, from the time the revival of learning affected England, this delight had been quickened and increased. Though it is assuredly a grave mistake to speak of our drama as of classical origin, yet it is undoubtedly true that it was shaped and developed by classical influence. The keen dramatic instinct of the time readily recognised the superiorities of Plautus and Terence, and modified its expression accordingly. And naturally this was particularly the case at the Universities, which, of course, shared with the nation at large in that dramatic instinct. Moreover, it was felt in that period of new-born adoration of the classics, as we are beginning to feel now, that an invaluable help to the study of the classical masterpieces was some sort of representation of them. Such representation satisfied both the dramatic instinct and also the classical enthusiasm. Probably no attempt was made, such as is now made, at archæological exactness at a time of such scanty antiquarian scholarship. But we may believe that the various pieces were rendered with sympathetic energy and intelligence. Possibly, as Mr Mullinger remarks in his history of the University of Cambridge, the precepts of John Sturm, of Strasburg, did much to authorise and encourage this practice. Certainly, about the middle of the century it was well established. 'A statute of Queen's College of the year 1546,' to again quote Mr Mullinger, ' directs that any student refusing to take part in the acting of a comedy or tragedy in the college, and absenting himself from the performance, contrary to the injunctions of the President, shall be expelled from the society.' But the ancient plays were imitated as well as acted; and often, no doubt, much local and much party feeling would find its way into these modern plays. Towards the close of the sixteenth century, and in the beginning of the seventeenth, original plays became common; and sometimes these plays were written in English, or partly in English, in spite of the frowns of the authorities and of a royal prohibitory letter in the second year of King James. The latest performance of the kind seems to have taken place in the hall of Pembroke College in 1747, when and where was acted a comedy called 'A Trip to Cambridge, or the Grateful Fair,' by Mr Christopher Smart, who has lately been revived by Mr Browning as one of the persons of importance with whom it has pleased him to parley.

In the catalogue of these University dramas, the Parnassus plays have a high, if not the highest, place. They were written in the palmiest days of the University drama, and they are a worthy product of those days.

Their theme is the intellectual life, the life of scholarship and culture, its nobleness and its impracticability; how desirable it is, and how for the sake of it much is to be borne and to be forborne. But, on the other hand, how unfavourable are ordinary circumstances; how impossible it is for the aspirant after such a life to find the means of living it; how, lest he should starve, he is compelled to desist from the attempt and to devote himself to the vulgar business of making some sort of income.

The Pilgrimage introduces to us two youthful eager spirits just setting forth in search of learning—just starting for Parnassus. These are the heroes, or central figures, of

the trilogy that is now before us, and are significantly named
Philomusus and Studioso.   The father of the former, who
is called Consiliodorus, is, in the opening scene, just dismiss-
ing his son and his nephew on their journey.   He expresses
his fear that, as

> My winged soul gins scorn this slimy gaol,

(an odd Platonistic phrase for the body, 'this muddy vesture
of decay' as Shakespeare calls it) he may not witness their
return ; but he hopes that, after they have bathed their lips
in Helicon and washed their tongue in Aganippe's well, the
gift of poetry may be secured by them, and they may ravish
the world with their strains, and in triumph and delight may
lead the high life of the poet.   And though poets do not
make pecuniary fortunes, yet they have their reward.

> Though I foreknew that gold runs to the boor,
> I'll be a scholar though I live but poor,

he cries with a fine enthusiasm that is not lost on his ardent
hearers.   Then he warns them of dangers by the way; of
the unthriftiness that makes poor scholars yet poorer, of the
sloth that besets so many, of frivolity and self-indulgence, of
specious false teachers.   And so he bids them step forward.

> Happy I wish may be your pilgrimage !
> Joyful may you return from that fair hill,
> And make the valleys hear with admiration
> Those songs which your refined tongue shall sing.
> But what, do I prolong my studious speech
> Hind'ring the forward hastening of your steps?
> Go, happily with a swift swallow's wing
> To Helicon fair, that pure and happy spring !
> Return triumphant with your laurel boughs ;
> With Phoebus' trees deck your deserving brows !
> Haste, haste with speed unto that loving well ;
> So take from me a loving long farewell,

The route by which they proceed is that of the old Trivium. Supposed to know already something of Grammar, they pass first into Logic land, and press gaily forward, full of heart and hope, never dreaming of failure or of disappointment. Their first tempter meets them in the shape of one Madido, a votary of the wine-cup, compared with whose contents Helicon is but 'puddled water :' one who cares not to travel Parnassus-wards because there is scarce a good tavern or ale-house on that road.

'This Parnassus and Helicon,' he declares, 'are but the fables of the poets. There is no true Parnassus but the third loft in a wine tavern ; no true Helicon but a cup of brown bastard. Will you travel quickly to Parnassus? Do but carry your dry feet into some dry tavern, and straight the drawer will bid you go into the Half-moon or the Rose—that is into Parnassus. Then call for a cup of pure Helicon, and he will bring you a cup of pure hippocras that will make you speak leaping lines and dancing periods. Why, give me but a quart of burnt sack by me, and if I do not with a penniworth of candles make a better poem than Kinsader's *Satires*, Lodge's *Fig for Momus*, Bastard's *Epigrams*, Leichfield's *Trimming of Nash*, I'll give my head to any good fellow to make a *memento mori* of !'

Philomusus is for a while nearly carried away by this gospel of the pint-pot ; but presently he realises its falsehood with his friend's help, and when he sees the gross debauchery, 'the beastly bezoling,' the soul-drowning, in which it duly ends. So again they proceed, and find themselves now in the land of Rhetoric, 'a fair land that it is delightful to traverse ; for the pilgrims have interims and spaces of pleasure and joy . 'Let idle tongues,' cries Studioso.

> Let idle tongues talk of our tedious way ;
> I never saw a more delicious earth,
> A smoother pathway or a sweeter air,
> Than here is in this land of Rhetoric.
> Hark how the birds delight the moving air,

> With pretty tuneful notes and artless lays !
> Hark shrill Don Cicero, how sweet he sings !
> See how the groves wonder at his sweet note,
> And listen unto their sweet nightingale !

But such a respite cannot last long. There encounters them a fresh seduction in the person of Stupido, the representative of the growing Puritanism of the day, one who has come to look upon learning as mere vanity. Better let men study the Mar-prelate tracts, he says, and the Geneva Catechism. To such an effect has his uncle instructed him—a good man 'that never wore cap nor surplice in his life, nor any such popish ornament.' 'Study not,' so had this sagacious relative counselled him, 'those vain arts of Rhetoric, Poetry, and Philosophy; there is no edifying knowledge in them.' 'They are,' Stupido adds, 'more vain than a pair of organs or a morris dance! If you will be good men indeed, go no further in this way. Follow no longer these profane arts that are the rags and parings of learning.' What, asks Philomusus,

> Are then the arts foolish, profane, and vain,
> That gotten are with study, toil, and pain ?

Yes, mere vanity, it seems, in the eyes of a 'zealous professor.' And Stupido would fain lead the pilgrims aside to 'hear a good man's exercise'—to 'sit under' some Puritan fanatic. Thus goodness and learning are presented as antagonistic—as if one or other must be sought after exclusively, and not both together. A dire alternative indeed. Studioso is half minded to listen to this ignorant religionist. But happily Philomusus now repays the service he had himself lately received, and in turn rescues Studioso from a creed so narrow-minded and narrow-hearted, so justly and wholly offensive to all true friends of the higher life.

And so on once more towards their Mountain. But soon a new danger confronts them. The inevitable thought arises whether it would not be well to yield themselves to self-indulgence and enjoyment—whether in the language of one of our greatest poets, who, too, went on a like pilgrimage, it were

> not better done, as others use,
> To sport with Amaryllis in the shade,
> Or with the tangles of Neæra's hair,

—whether, to vary other of Milton's words, it were not good to embrace delights and scorn laborious days. This sore allurement takes the form of one Amoretta, an ardent voluptuary, whose favourite scripture is the *Ars Amoris*. The youthful nature is unwholesomely stirred by the picture he draws of the pleasures within so easy reach.

> Indeed this land hath many a wanton nymph
> That knows always all sportful dalliance.
>
> .   .   .   .
>
> Why should you vainly spend your blooming age
> In sad dull plodding on philosophers,
> Which was ordained for wanton merriments?

And he derides the idea of looking beyond the present hour. He sings the old song with its familiar refrain:

> Crop you the joys of youth while that you may;
> Sorrow and grief will come another day.

For a while the pilgrims surrender themselves to this doctrine of enervation and sloth. But fortunately they soon find such dissipation 'sourly sweet'—that if it yields honey yet it straight doth sting; and having

> nigh made shipwreck of their youth,
> And nipt the blossoms of their budding spring,

they have strength to recall their great purpose, and again

proceed. They now reach the land of Philosophy. As they pass along, Studioso from his recent experience would speak of Poetry disparagingly; but Philomusus eloquently points out that if Poetry degrades and corrupts, it is because of the reader's own grossness of mind and thought—that even the freest-spoken writers of verse may be perused with moral impunity by those that are pure of heart.

> O do not wrong this music of the soul,
> The fairest child that e'er the soul brought forth !
>
> . . . .
>
> Nor think Catullus, Ovid, Martial
> Do teach a chaste mind lewder luxuries.
>
> . . . .
>
> But who reads poets with a chaster mind
> Shall ne'er infected be by poetry.

However, it is certain that they feel more keenly the hardships of their travel after their late evil relaxation. But their perils are not yet exhausted. They now meet Ingenioso, who has turned his back on the famous Hill and urges them to follow his example. He is sick of philosophy; and moreover he has been credibly informed that Parnassus is 'out of silver pitifully pitifully'—that it offers its pilgrims nothing better than starvation for all their pains.

I talked with a friend of mine that lately gave his horse a bottle of hay at the bottom of the hill, who told me that Apollo had sent to Pluto to borrow twenty nobles to pay his commons; he added further that he met coming down from the hill a company of ragged vicars and forlorn schoolmasters who as they walked scratched their unthrifty elbows, and often put their hands into their unpeopled pockets, that had not been possessed with faces this many a day.

But this tempter's counsels they bravely resist. He tells them nothing new. They were aware that in choosing a life of learning they were not to expect great wealth—that riches flowed in other directions.

Ph. Though I fore-knew that dolts possess the gold,
  Yet my intended pilgrimage I'll hold.
St. Within Parnassus dwells all sweet content,
  Nor care I for these excrements of earth.

They press Ingenioso to join them. But in him the sacred fire, if ever it was really kindled, is now quenched. He is the literary man of the Elizabethan age—of an age when a public on whose support an author could depend did not yet exist; and when, therefore, unless he took to writing for the stage, his only hope, if his private means were scanty, lay in private patronage, in winning the ear and opening the purse of some Mæcenas. On the whole, this was a miserable and demoralising state of things for men of letters, though now and then, no doubt, might be found a patron worthy of the rapturous language which it was the necessary custom of the day to employ in dedications, a patron truly appreciative and readily munificent. Ingenioso had discovered that the fine gentlemen, the 'satin suits,' as he calls them, set much more by a 'foggy falconer' than a 'witty scholar.' The carrier (he specially mentions the famous Hobson—Milton's Hobson) and the cobbler could make and bequeath fortunes: the author's fate was starvation, and his children 'must be fain to be kept by the parish.' So he scoffs at the idea of joining the Parnassus Pilgrims: What, I travel to Parnassus? Why, I have burnt my books, splitted my pen, rent my papers, and curst the cozening hearts that brought me up to no better fortune.'

And so the buoyant youths, undepressed by his gloom, press forward alone, exulting in the now immediate nearness of their destination. And anon they arrive at the foot of the Hill. Four years have passed since they started: so that their journey corresponds to the ordinary course of study for a Bachelor's degree.   At the close of the Pilgrimage we see them resting with high delight by the 'Muses Springs,' jubilant and sanguine.

The second Play of the trilogy tells us the sequel.   It is, so to speak, the fourth volume of the novel.   Generally, as we all know, novels conclude with the third volume, at whose close we see the hero and heroine triumphant, their desires attained, and about to live content and happy for ever.   But sometimes, it may be, the prize so long coveted turns out of less value than was fancied.   Do we not read of some who had their desires granted, but into whose souls was sent leanness?   What, if, after all, the Promised Land, whose image has sustained us through weary travellings, should prove as barren as the wilderness itself?   Alas for our bright-spirited pilgrims when the fair radiant form of Hope vanishes, and in her place they behold the hard sombre features of Reality!   Bitter disappointment awaits Studioso and Philomusus.   Not that the land is not lovely, but even in it one must have something to live on, and they have nothing.   One cannot subsist on delightful prospects or the music of falling waters, and when we next see them they are pale and emaciated; and, sad to say, are already bethinking them that they must flee from this land of their aspirations and their efforts, with what speed they may, if they would fain keep body and soul together.   After a few days in the Land of Promise to make for the wilderness again—verily this is a tragical result, though treated in a lighter manner by our poet.   For is there indeed a more tragical spectacle than such a shattering of the ideal life nobly conceived and nobly sought after?   Just as the worshipper has after much grief and pain reached the shrine of his deity, and is kindling the incense, his golden god changes into clay and tumbles to pieces; or the walls of the temple crack and yawn and collapse; or the pilgrims find the expense of his liturgy too great for their resources! Alas for Philomusus and Studioso! They must leave their so hardly-won Paradise.

> *Ph.* Adieu, Parnassus! I must pack away.
> *St.* Fountains, farewell, where beauteous nymphs do play.
> *Ph.* In Helicon no more I'll dip my quill.
> *St.* I'll sing no more upon Parnassus' hill.

At this point, by some confusion in the allegory—it is said, and I think rightly, no allegory is quite free from confusion—Ingenioso again meets them, destitute and thriftless as ever, once more patron-hunting. And we have a ridiculous scene in which is represented an interview between a Great Man and his literary client—a scene that makes one wonder how like in some ways was Elizabethan London to the Imperial Rome of Juvenal. Then comes in another scapegrace, one Luxurioso. And all four persons—Philomusus, Studioso, Ingenioso, Luxurioso—agree to quit together the land they love, but in which they cannot afford to dwell.

Outside those divine precincts they pursue the art of living, or rather of starving, and manage for a while to struggle on in various ways. Philomusus gets a situation as sexton, and is shown in a black frieze coat, carrying keys and a spade, 'dig well and ring well' his instructions. But soon, after some comic experiences, he is summarily dismissed for negligence. In the days of his predecessor, he is told by the Warden: 'The chancell was kept in order, the church swept, and the boards rubbed that thou mightest have seen your face in them, and for my part I never used other looking-glass.' But, for him, he does nothing in this line: he does not even ring the bells, nor whip the dogs out of the church. So a passport, a permit to traverse the country, is handed him, and he is sent to the right-about.

Studioso turns private-tutor in a not very congenial family. He is to have the same food as the household servants, to wait at meals, to work all harvest-time, to make a proper obeisance to his pupil whenever he gives him a lesson, never to flog him when he cannot say his lesson—a peculiar hardship to an Elizabethan teacher, in whose eyes teaching and breeching were as intimately associated in reason as in rhyme; and to receive for his wages five marks a year and some cast-off garments such as a ploughman would scarce accept. He has a lively time of it with young Hopeful, and is at last abruptly cashiered because he would not suffer one of the 'blue coats to perch above' him 'at the latter dinner.' So the Pilgrims do not fare much better outside the Parnassian borders than within them. Luxurioso takes to writing ballads, which his boy sings at markets and fairs; but the pecuniary results are anything but satisfactory.

The main interest in the Second Play attaches rather to Ingenioso, who, as was said above, represents the contemporary man of letters; and in several scenes his relations with one Gullio, an arrant fool and impostor, who poses as a literary patron, are portrayed with much vivacity. Gullio gives Ingenioso an order for some love-verses, to be written 'in two or three diverse veins, in Chaucer's, Gower's, and Spenser's and Mr Shakespeare's,' that he may make his choice. This creature illustrates the Elizabethan age in several ways; but our attention is specially drawn to him by the fact that he is an ardent, if not an intelligent, admirer of 'Mr Shakespeare.' 'We shall have nothing but pure Shakespeare and shreds of poetry that he hath gathered at the theatres,' says Ingenioso as the fop is seen approaching. In the sketch of him may be recognised certain reminiscences of Marston's Satires, published a few months before the play we are considering was acted—of Duceus in the third Satire, and of Luceus in the ninth of *The Scourge of Villany*. Thus of Luceus we are told that from his lips

doth flow
Naught but pure Juliet and Romeo.

The two works with which Gullio is acquainted, to judge by his quotations, are *Romeo and Juliet* and *Venus and Adonis*,' or at least the first two stanzas of *Venus and Adonis*. 'Oh! sweet Mr Shakespeare!' he cries; 'I'll have his picture in my study at the court.' This adoration is no doubt a sign of Shakespeare's popularity, though the adoration of a Gullio may not be a very desirable possession. Probably the author did not mean to pay compliments. He wrote as a University man, with strong prejudices in favour of classical models and dramas that were constructed in accordance with them and with a correspondingly strong suspicion of the popular drama, and of a writer who had not been bred at Cambridge or Oxford. The passage, or passages, in which the Shakespeare-bitten Gullio appears should be read in connexion with the well-known scene in the Second Part of *The Return* (Act iv. Scene iii.) when Burbage and Kemp exalt Shakespeare's fame at the expense of the collegians.

'Few of the University pen play swell,' says Kemp; 'they smell too much of that writer Ovid, and that writer Metamorphosis, and talk too much of Proserpina and Jupiter. Why, here's our fellow Shakespeare puts them all down, ay and Ben Jonson too.'

It has often been noticed that nearly all our early dramatsts were University men, Shakespeare being the notable exception. Thus Marlow was of Corpus Christi College, Cambridge: Green and Nash and Ben Jonson, of St John's: Day, of Caius: Marston and Peel and Massinger belonged to Oxford. Both Universities can claim Lily and Chapman.

There is another point worthy of notice in one of the interviews of Ingenioso with Gullio. Just after the latter has been quoting freely from *Romeo and Juliet*, the former says aside: 'Mark! Romeo and Juliet! O monstrous theft; I think he will run through a whole book of Samuel Daniel's.' This seems to mean that Daniel had helped himself so liberally from the stores of Shakespeare that to run through one of his books was as good as going to Shakespeare's own pages. Or what does it mean? 'Well-languaged' Daniel has been so highly esteemed by many a lover of poetry from his own time down to that of Wordsworth and to our own day that no derogation of his honour is to be lightly allowed. But in the Second Part of *The Return* (Act. i. Scene ii.) Judicio formally warns him against making too free with the writings of his neighbours.

> Sweet honey-dropping Daniel doth wage
> War with the proudest big Italian
> That melts his heart in sugared sonneting.[1]
>
> Only let him more sparingly make use
> Of others' wit, and use his own the more,
> That well may scorn base imitation.

In the *Complaint of Rosamund*, as has been noticed before now by the commentators, occur many lines and phrases that recall Shakespeare. For example,

> And nought-respecting death (the last of pains)
> Placed his pale colours (th' ensign of his might)
> Upon his new-got spoil before his right.
>
> Ah! how methinks I see Death dallying seeks
> To entertain itself in Love's sweet place;
> Decayed roses of discolour'd cheeks
> Do yet retain dear notes of former grace,
> And ugly Death sits fair within her face.

It is beyond doubt that these verses were either suggested

---

[1] That is, is as effective a sonneteer as Petrarch himself. See his Sonnets to Delia.

by certain words in *Romeo and Juliet*, or suggested them ; and the question has been, which alternative was the fact ? Now the newly-discovered play which we have now before us furnishes valuable evidence in this matter. It clearly informs us that by some at least in his own day it was Daniel who was believed to be the borrower. And to decide this question contributes to the decision of the date at or by which *Romeo and Juliet* was written. Daniel's *Rosamund* was first published in 1592; therefore *Romeo and Juliet*, in some shape or other, cannot be later than that year—unless, indeed, those Shakespearian echoes are heard for the first time in the second edition of *Rosamund* which was published two years afterwards, and does, it is said, differ considerably from the first edition. In this latter case *Romeo and Juliet* cannot be later than 1594.

As might be expected, Ingenioso gets little or nothing out of his ridiculous patron. Their relations become all the more irritable because Gullio sets up for a critic, and pretends to revise the other's compositions. To ask for bread and to receive criticism—that is surely beyond any author's endurance. And other difficulties arise. So, in no long time, patron and client quarrel violently ; and the client liberates his soul thus :—

What, you whoreson *tintinnabulum*, thou that are the scorn of all good wits, the ague of all soldiers, that never spokest witty things but out of a play, never heardest the report of a gun without trembling, why, Monsieur Mingo, is your ass's head grown proud with scratching ? Thinkest thou a man of art can endure thy base usage ?

To which Gullio rejoins :—

Terence, thou art a gentleman of thy word : *familiaritas parit contemptum*. Sirrah, Alexander did never strive with any but kings, and Gullio will fight with none but gallants. Farewell, base peasant, and thank God thy fathers were no gentlemen ; else thou shouldest not live an hour longer. Base, base, base peasant, peasant ! So hares may pull dead lions by the beard.'

The best of friends must part, it is said : so, happily, must the worst.

Thus the four comrades, Philomusus, Studioso, Luxurioso, and Ingenioso, are all once more thrown upon the world, penniless and forlorn. Luxurioso resolves to drink himself blind, and to throw himself upon the parish. The others wrap themselves in their virtue, as best they may, and would fain cherish the belief that learning is after all a commodity of price, though the world values it not. Ingenioso determines somehow or other to make his wit maintain him.

The press shall keep me from base beggary.

Studioso and Philomusus will hasten to Rome or Rheims— will turn Papists to 'mend their state,' for perverts were eagerly welcomed and made much of at that time, as often since; and by such a course at least a comfortable subsistence was, they hoped, to be secured.

And so the play ends, in gloom and misery, the actual facts permitting no other conclusion.

> *Ing.* If scholars' wants would end with our short scene,
> 　　　　Then should our little scene end more content ;
> *Stud.* But scholars still must live in discontent.
> 　　　　What reason then our scene should end content ?
> *Phil.* Till then our acts some happier fortune see,
> 　　　　We'll banish from our stage all mirth and glee.
> *Ing.* Whatever scholars
> *Stud.* 　　　　　　　　discontented be
> *Phil.* Let none but them
> *All.* 　　　　　　　　give us a *plaudite.*

The Second Part of *The Return*, as will be remembered, develops what we have shown to be the theme of the First. We see the poor scholars (who have thought better or worse of it, and not gone over to Rome) in the midst of fresh discomfitures and distresses, till at last Ingenioso betakes himself to the Isle of Dogs—goes to the dogs in a double sense—and Philomusus and Studioso adopt a shepherd's life.

With such lively illustrations as *The Pilgrimage* and *The Return* furnish, it would be interesting to study more particularly the position of authors in the Elizabethan age, and to verify the melancholy story that the dramatist lays before us. But space fails, and I will only add that I trust enough has been said to show that these newly-discovered plays have great value not only as excellent specimens of the University drama and as vividly depicting the Elizabethan man of letters, but also for their wit and humour and bright intelligence.

RICHARD BRATHWAITE[1]

(From *The Academy* for Nov. 2, 1878)

LIFE is short; and Brathwaite, like Prynne and Wither, is long, very long. It is not likely that anyone will care to reprint all his works, although he has been lucky enough to find good friends both at the beginning of this century and now in the latter part of it, and may be always lucky in that respect. But we trust no one's passion for him will be so ardent as to reproduce his writings in their entirety. Reproducers must be expected to show some judgment. There are some old books that enjoy quite as much existence as they deserve if the original copies are still preserved in accessible libraries. It is unnecessary to ask them to step out into the world again, and disport themselves in modern raiment. We do not want them to come and stay with us; our houses are overcrowded already. We shall be quite content if we can call on them now and then, without expecting a return visit, from which their age and feebleness excuse them. And, in our opinion, much that the voluminous Brathwaite wrote is of this sort. A

---

[1] *A Strappado for the Devil.* By Richard Brathwaite. With an introduction by the Rev. J. W. Ebsworth, M.A. (Boston, Lincolnshire : Roberts.)

certain vivacity and vigour he certainly has; but he wrote too much, and too hastily, to write well. He was always at it, and, what was worse, always printing his productions, or rather sending them to the press to be printed as they might, for correcting proofs does not seem to have been much in his line. Indeed, with regard to much which he produced, if it were to be judged merely from the artistic point of view, but slight praise could be bestowed upon it, and small thanks would be due to any editor for recalling it to knowledge. It is for the most part—for the most part, we say—the somewhat rude expression of a fervid impulsive nature, that thinks aloud, and whose thoughts, as might be feared, are not always worth hearing, still less preserving.

Happily, in addition to his value as an original author, Brathwaite has a value quite distinct, or he could not have found the favour he has found with certain competent scholars. He is of considerable use for the illustrations he furnishes of contemporary literature; many a Shakespearian phrase and allusion, for instance, have light thrown upon them from his pages; and, secondly, he is of considerable interest as a representative man. The characteristics of the late Elizabethan or Jacobean age show clear in him. He threw himself into the life of his time with a wild enthusiasm. 'A mad world, my masters;' and Brathwaite was at home in it. Passing from Westmoreland (not Lancashire, as Mr Ebsworth says) to Oxford and also to Cambridge, and from the universities to the Inns of Court, he shared with reckless delight in the revelry of his day.

'While roaring was in request,' he writes, long after the uproar of those dissipations had died away in the distance, 'I held it a complete fashion. . . . . I held my pockets sufficiently stored, if they could but bring me off for mine ordinary, and after dinner purchase me a stool on the stage. . . . A long winter night seemed but a midsummer night's dream, being merrily past in a catch of four parts, a deep health to a light mistress, and a knot of brave blades to make up the consort. . . . A weak blast of light fame was a great part of that portion I aimed at. And herein was my madness! I held nothing so likely to make me known to the world, or admired in it, as to be debauched, and to purchase a parasite's praise by my riot.'

He may, perhaps, deepen the colour of his pictures, after the manner of certain religionists who take a fond pleasure in blackening their former complexion, perhaps in order to make their present exceeding fairness the better appreciated— or is it because the 'Old Adam' likes lingering over those old days, and describing, with not unaffectionate emphasis, their once sweet deliriousness?   But probably, even in the midst of his wildnesses, Brathwaite was not without compunctious visitings.   We doubt whether he was ever altogether a re-formed character.   *Barnabae Itinerarium, or Barnabee's Journal,* was not published till 1638, when he was some fifty years of age.   It may have been written in part long before ; but it certainly was not all so.   Anyhow there is no reason for supposing that it was published, when it was published, against the author's will.   Late in life, too, he reprinted one or two not very edifying pieces from the *Strappado : e.g.,* as late as 1665 in his *Comment upon the Two Tales of Our Ancient, Renowned, and Ever living Poet Sir Geoffrey Chaucer, Knight,* the story of how a 'wily wench' 'capri-corned' her husband.   Thus we have in Brathwaite a man of a curiously mixed nature, or rather—for that description would apply to us all—a man who displays his mixedness with a curious frankness and fulness.   We see him in his cups ; we see him at his prayers.   A strange figure this, now reeling, now kneeling.   Do not let us doubt his sincerity : he drinks with zest ; he prays with all earnestness.   He is a vehement, impulsive man, who must still be talking, still unbosoming himself, still giving voice to the passion of the moment. Always hating Puritanism—it had no heartier enemy—he struggles to be religious and to recommend religiousness in what he thought a more liberal spirit than the Puritanic; yet in the midst of his aspirations and efforts there would intrude at times far other thoughts, and all of a sudden the paraphrast of 'The Psalms of David the King and Prophet and of other Holy Prophets' is busy conjugating his favourite verb :—

Sat est, verbum declinavi,
Titubo—titubas—titubavi.

The Psalms of David and the songs of Anacreon, he can sing them both *con amore*, this versatile gentleman. In other writers of the time, as in Herrick, one may see something of the same odd combination, or rather of the same plenary representation, of two different sides of our complex nature; but perhaps in no one so clearly and so abruptly, so to speak, as in the subject of the present notice.

The reprint before us, for which Mr Ebsworth is to be thanked, is of one of his earliest works. It appeared in 1615, the year before Shakespeare's death. The volume consists of two parts : first, the *Strappado for the devil*, and secondly, *Love's Labyrinth : or the True Lover's Knot*, including the disastrous falls of two Star-crost lovers, Pyramus and Thisbe.

The *Strappado* is a miscellany of epigrams, satires, and occasional pieces. The origin of the collection is no doubt sufficiently indicated in his *Spiritual Spicery*, 1638, when he is talking of his early life, how he 'held it in those days an incomparable grace to be styled one of the wits ; where, if at any time invited to a public feast, or some other meeting of the Muses, we hated nothing more than losing time ; reserving even some select hours of that solemnity, to make proof of our Conceits in a present provision of Epigrams,

Anagrams, with other expressive (and many times offensive) fancies. . . By this time I got an eye in the world; and a finger in the streets. There goes an author! One of the wits!' The title should mean, we suppose, a flogging for the Archfiend, a scourge for evil, very much what Wither meant by his *Abuses Stript and Whipt* (1613); but Brathwaite, in a passage in a subsequent volume, leads us to understand that by 'Devil' was thought to be meant especially one particular form of evil—detraction. Whatever is the precise meaning of this fantastic title—it was an age of such—the collection included under it may be briefly described as the characteristic offspring of a young Jacobean wit—of a lively Bohemian of the early seventeenth century. It jokes as men joked then, outspokenly and often coarsely. The epigrams might occasionally have more point, the satires bite more keenly. But, as we said to begin with, Brathwaite has always some vivacity and vigour; he is never utterly dull; now and then he writes with true force and dignity, and he furnishes here many of those illustrations of contemporary life and literature which we have mentioned as giving value to his works. He quotes 'a horse, a kingdom for a horse,' from *Richard III.;* and ' Halloa ye pampered Jades,' from *Tamberlaine the Great,* second part. Here is an early reference to Cervantes' famous romance :—

> If I had lived but in Don Quixote's time,
> His Rozinant had been of little worth;
> For mine was bred within a colder clime,
> And can endure the motion of the earth
> With greater patience; nor will he repine
> At any provender, so mild is he.
> How many men want his humility!

'All true-bred northern sparks' will find something to

interest them in his lines *To the Cottoners.* There he speaks of Wakefield and its Pindar, of Bradford and its 'Souter,' of Kendal and its white coats. Bradford, it seems, was notable for its Puritanism :—

> Bradford, if I should rightly set it forth,
> Style it I might the Banbury of the North ;
> And well this title with the town agrees
> Famous for twanging, Ale, Zeal, Cakes, and Cheese.
>
> But why should I set zeal behind their ale !
> Because zeal is for some, but ale for all ;
> Zealous, indeed, some are (for I do hear
> Of many zealous simpring sister there
> Who love their brothers from their heart i' faith).

The English of the last line but one is noticeable. Brathwaite says 'many sister,' according to the older—the proper —usage : so 'many burden' (p. 67, etc.). Both usages occur in this couplet from Gower :—

> With many an herb and many a stone
> Whereof she hath there many one.

XVI

MILTON'S 'MACBETH'

(From *The Nineteenth Century* for Dec. 1891)

IT is one of the most curious facts in literary history that Milton at one time proposed to write a drama on the story of *Macbeth*—that more than thirty years after Shakespeare's great tragedy had been before the world, Milton proposed to take up the theme already treated with such incomparable power. Such a design seems at first sight to imply a strange want of discernment, or an extraordinary self-confidence, or a reckless audacity; 'for what can the man do that cometh after the King?' But the evidence of its entertainment is decisive; and I wish now to consider what motives could have induced Milton to think of such a thing.

The evidence that he did think of it is to be found in a well-known MS. in his own handwriting, now one of the treasures of the Library of Trinity College, Cambridge. This MS. was in all probability written shortly after his return from his Continental tour, when at last he was leaving his father's roof and beginning an independent life. Till the year 1639, at the close of which he became thirty-one, Milton had been permitted by a highly appreciative and generous father to devote himself to learning and culture, that so he might prepare himself for some great poetical effort.   Everything had been done for his education that could be done.   Not content with the training and the lore imparted by St Paul's School and by Cambridge, he, with his father's sanction and approval, had continued his studies at home for some six years ; and then in 1638 had enjoyed the advantage of a foreign tour, which lasted some ten or eleven months, and acquainted him not only with famous towns and scenes, but also with some of the most distinguished Europeans of his day.   Thus, over thirty years of perpetual and thorough preparation had gone by ; and at last the time seemed come when the fruit of his long 'wearisome labours and studious watchings' should be put forth. Milton himself clearly felt it was so.   He had not been quite at ease that the promise of his youth was so tardy of fulfilment.   He speaks in one of his letters—the only extant one in English—of being 'something suspicious of myself,' and of taking notice of 'a certain belatedness in me': and in another to his friend Diodati ('Damon'), he remarks, 'it is well known, and you well know, that I am naturally slow in writing and averse to write.'   Certainly, when he settled down in lodgings of his own (just off Fleet Street, on part of the site of the 'Punch' office of our time), or a few months later, wanting more room for his books, in a 'garden-house' in Aldersgate Street (on the east side, nor far from Maidenhead Court), he recognised that something must really be done ; and we find him searching for a satisfactory subject.   As late as 1639 his thoughts were set upon King Arthur, as can be proved from two of his Latin poems written in that year, viz. the *Epitaphium Damonis* and the *Mansus*.   But for certain reasons, the chief probably that he had realised the fabulousness of the Arthurian story

('Who Arthur was,' he writes in his *History of Britain*, 'and whether ever any such reigned in Britain, hath been doubted before, and may again with good reason'), he somewhat suddenly as it would seem dismissed that hero, and looked round for a substitute.   In the above-mentioned Trinity College MS., most probably penned just at this period, he makes a long list—a hundred minus one—of subjects that might serve his purpose.   Of these, fifty-three are taken from the old Testament, and among them *Paradise Lost* is unmistakably the favourite; eight are from the New Testament; thirty-three are from British history; and five are 'Scotch stories, or rather British of the North Parts'; and last of these, and so last of the whole ninety-nine, is '*Macbeth*.'   Beginning at the arrival of Malcolm at Macduff.   The matter of Duncan may be expressed by the appearing of his ghost.

Now I propose suggesting and discussing two special reasons for the insertion of *Macbeth* in this list—the one historical, or having reference to the historical facts; the other didactic, or moral.   But before I proceed to these, brief references must be made first to Milton's attitude to the Romantic Drama generally, and to Shakespeare in particular; and secondly, to the state in which Shakespeare's *Macbeth* has come down to us, and the manner in which it was presented in the seventeenth century.

To turn to the first of these points : there is abundant proof that Milton's dramatic sympathies were all in the direction of the classical form.   Late in life, in the prefatory note to *Samson Agonistes* (published in 1671), he issued, as everybody will remember, what we may call a manifesto on this question, so far at least as Tragedy was concerned. After several remarks by no means friendly to the contemporary stage, he names Æschylus, Sophocles, and Euripides as 'the three tragic poets unequalled yet by any, and the best rule to all who endeavour to write tragedy. The circumscription of time,' he adds, 'wherein the whole drama begins and ends, is, according to ancient rule and best example, within the space of twenty-four hours.' And in the work itself that is thus prefaced, he gives us in fact a Greek play in English, a splendid and a still unsurpassed or unequalled monument of Hellenic scholarship and insight. But it would be a mistake to suppose that these convictions, so trenchantly enounced and so nobly illustrated, belonged only to Milton's senescence, or can be explained by his disgust with the theatre of the Restoration. Years and years before Milton had made up his mind on this matter. In the subject-list, drawn up as we have seen when he began seriously and practically to address himself to what he meant to be the achievement of his life, the dramatic form is the prevailing form—nay, the only form—entertained by him ; and it is the classical (*i.e.* the Greek) dramatic form. In several cases he specially mentions the chorus, and of whom it is to consist. In many others the very titles sufficiently indicate the models that are in his thoughts ; thus *Naboth* συκοφαντούμενος, *Eliscæus Hydrochoos*, *Hezechias*, πολιορκούμενος, *Josiah*, αἰαζόμενος, *Herod Massacring* or *Rachel Weeping, Christus Patiens, Christ Risen, Vortiger immured, Hardiknute dying in his cups, Athelstan exposing his brother Edwin to the sea and repenting*, etc., And from the note added to the *Macbeth* entry it is certain that his intention was to treat the subject according to the usage of the Attic stage. Similarly, in one of the most magnificent of the many magnificent passages in his prose writing, in the famous account he renders of himself and his doings and his purposes in *The Reason of Church Government urged against Prelaty*, when he refers to the form his poem may take, whether epic or dramatic, he does not acknowledge or admit under the latter head any other 'constitutions' than those 'wherein Sophocles and Euripides reign.' He discovers the Greek 'constitutions' even in Hebrew literature. He agrees with Origen that 'the Scripture also affords us a divine pastoral drama in the Song of Solomon, consisting of two persons and a double chorus'; and is of opinion, Paræus confirming him, that 'the Apocalypse of St John is the majestic image of a high and stately tragedy shutting up and intermingling her solemn scenes and acts with a sevenfold chorus of hallelujahs and harping sympathies.' Beyond question it was the Greek drama that was meet and right in his eyes; and the modern drama seemed a somewhat dubious growth or creature, with which as an author he meant to have little to do, however he might peruse it as a reader. For that in his younger days at least he read his Shakespeare with immense appreciation and delight, is vividly shown not only by those famous memorial lines beginning 'What needs my Shakespeare for his honoured bones?'—happily, the first lines of Milton's composing that appeared in print—but by a much more significant sign in the shape of numberless allusions and echoes to be observed in his earlier poems—in *L'Allegro* and *Il Penseroso*, and *Comus*. It is wonderful how well Milton knew his *Midsummer Night's Dream*, his *Romeo and Juliet*, his *Tempest*. Often, no doubt, he had seen these plays and others from the same source acted in the Blackfriars Theatre or the Globe.

> Then to the well-trod stage anon,
> If Jonson's learned sock be on,
> Or sweetest Shakespeare, Fancy's child,
> Warble his native woodnotes wild.

> Excipit hinc fessum sinuosi pompa theatri,
> Et vocat ad plausus garrula scena suos.

So he writes in his first 'Elegy,' when he describes his London life during a certain absence from Cambridge. But probably from the very beginning, genuinely and heartily as he appreciated the genius of Shakespeare, in theory he was attached rather to Ben Jonson and his school; and there may be detected in his tone an anticipatory concord with the kind of dramatic criticism which prevailed in Europe till the rise of Lessing, that is, with the habit of crying up Shakespeare's genius, and crying down his art—with the habit of estimating the modern drama by the canons and standard of the classical, instead of recognising it as a new and distinct embodiment of the dramatic spirit. It was Lessing who first led the world to recognise the cardinal fact that Sophocles and Shakespeare represent two quite separate theatres, and that to speak of Shakespeare as a bad Sophocles is as absurd as it would be to speak of Sophocles as a bad Shakespeare. In the seventeenth century this great discovery—for so it was, obvious as what it states now seems to us—had not yet been made; and we must not be surprised or contemptuous if Milton was not in advance of his age in this respect, and so did not understand the exact relation of the Elizabethan playwrights to the Periclean. Brilliant classical scholar as he was, and the classics at that time having such an ascendency, it is no wonder if he was by no means contented with the popular drama of his time.

We must also remember, before we note the two particular reasons that probably led Milton to think of treating, in the classical style, the Macbeth story of all the Shakespearian tragedies, that the play of *Macbeth* seems to have been strangely handled even in its author's lifetime, or, at all events, just after his death. This question cannot here be discussed at length. I can only call attention to the view taken by many competent scholars, and venture to express my thorough agreement with it, that *Macbeth*, as it appears in the first folio, 1623, is not exactly what Shakespeare wrote, but a revised version of what Shakespeare wrote. There are many difficulties about the present shape of this tragedy, as all students and possibly some 'general readers' know; and they are probably best accounted for by the hypothesis that the play, as we have it, has been freely edited and modified by somebody, Middleton very likely, who augmented the lyrical parts and multiplied the dances— operatised it, in short, if I may invent such a verb for the occasion. We may marvel that the right hand that did such a deed did not wither; we may be pleased to fancy that its owner afterwards repented, and, like Cranmer, denounced such an unworthy member. But none the less the deed seems to have been done, and this tremendous tragedy was mixed with baser matter. A further evolution of this curious process is to be seen in Davenant's *Macbeth*, the current form in the Restoration period printed in 1674 (the year in which Milton died). 'From hence' (my Lord Crewe's), writes Mr Pepys in December 1666, 'to the Duke's house, and there saw *Macbeth* most excellently acted, and a most excellent play for *variety*'; and in the following month still more significantly, he notes: 'To the Duke's house, and saw *Macbeth*, which, though I saw it lately, yet appears a most excellent play in all respects, but *especially in diver-tisement*, though it be a deep tragedy, which is a strange per-fection in a tragedy, it being most proper here and suitable; in which sagacious comment many a modern critic would insert just the opposite adjectives. 'The Weird Sisters,' says Lamb, in a passage well known but deserving to be known yet better, 'are serious things. Their presence cannot co-exist with mirth.' Yet, to the audience of Charles the

Second's reign, they had become comic figures, and were greeted with roars of laughter.   Conceive the *Eumenides* of Æschylus presented in like fashion.   Conceive Alecto and her sisterhood as she buffoons, or Pluto 'entering' with the grimaces and the somersaults of a clown !   This vulgarising of *Macbeth*, of which the beginnings are discernible, as we have pointed out, in the earlier half of the century, may surely be pleaded in mitigation of Milton's offence when he dared to meditate a fresh dramatic rendering of a story already set forth by Shakespeare.

Let us now consider those two special reasons that have been suggested above as probably influencing Milton in this matter.   The first has relation to the treatment of historical facts by Shakespeare in *Macbeth*—to the freedom and licence with which they were rearranged and altered. Milton's objection to Shakespeare's *Macbeth* on this score is, I think, suggested and proved by another entry in his subject-list, which has, I believe, never yet been noticed in this connexion, viz. 'Duff and Donewald : A strange story of witchcraft and murder discovered and revenged.'

The principles on which the historical drama and the historical novel should be constructed are by no means easy to define.   Certainly the historian has often resented, and often resents, the intrusion of the fictionist on his domain. And undoubtedly many popular errors are due to the gross inaccuracies or the daring interferences with historical fact that are to be found in most plays and novels that profess to deal with history.   Some writers do not shrink from rewriting what has already been written for ever by the finger of time. The past is not the past with them, but a flexible and manageable present.   They arrogate a power beyond that of Jupiter himself, who, however he may cloud or sun the skies to-morrow,

Non tamen inritum,
Quodcunque retrost, efficiet, neque
Diffinget infectumque reddet,
Quod fugiens semel hora vexit.

And, indeed, if they are verily ' creators,' how, they ask, is their creative power to be limited and fixed?   And they quote, or might quote, for their charter Horace's trite dictum :

Pictoribus atque poetis
Quidlibet audendi semper fuit æqua potestas.

And accordingly *quidlibet audent.*   On the other hand, Aristotle insists ' that it is not the province of a poet to relate things which have happened, but such as might have happened, and such things as are possible according to probability, or would necessarily have happened.   For an historian and a poet do not differ from each other because the one writes in verse and the other in prose; for the history of Herodotus might be written in verse, and yet it would be no less a history with metre than without metre. But they differ in this, that the one speaks of things which have happened, and the other of such as might have happened. Hence poetry is more philosophic and more deserving of attention that history.'   However, the service which writers of imagination—Shakespeare and Scott, above all others— have done in exciting a real interest in distant ages—in mak- ing the dry bones live and ' provoking the silent dust '—is so great and grand that we accept their works with grateful thanks, and think it a comparatively little thing that they are not always found in exact agreement with the contemporary records which the researches of the learned from time to time bring to light.   Now what were Milton's views on this question?   He seems to have held that the poet, if he dealt with historical fact, should faithfully adhere to it; and, what is more, he seems to have held that the poet should deal with historical fact.

'It was necessary for Milton,' as that excellent critic and writer Mr Mark Pattison observes, ' that the events and personages which were to arouse and detain his interests should be real events and personages. The mere play of fancy with the pretty aspects of things could not satisfy him ; he wanted to feel beneath him a substantial world of reality. . . . His imagination is only stirred by real circumstances.' Perhaps we may relevantly refer to Carlyle's insistence on the impressiveness of 'the smallest historical fact' 'as contrasted with the grandest fictitious event.'

All those ninety-nine subjects that, as we know, Milton was revolving in his mind when he was earnestly meditating a great poetical work, are historical. All those stories that attracted him in the Old Testament and in the New seemed to him, whatever conclusions or views about them modern criticism may arrive at or entertain, to be strictly historical, not Hebrew or Christian legends. In the *Reason for Church Government* he tells us how he considered 'what king or knight before the Conquest might be chosen, in whom to lay the pattern of a Christian hero.' As Tasso had chosen an historical person for his hero, finally adopting Godfrey of Boulogne, after some hesitation whether it should be he or Belisarius or Charlemagne, so would Milton select one of our 'ancient stories,' *i.e.*, one of our ancient histories, for the word 'story' is etymologically but a decapitated form of the word 'history,' and in Elizabethan and even later English it is often used in its original sense. As already re-marked, he rejected King Arthur because he found, after careful scrutiny, that he was not historical—that he was mainly, if not wholly, a mere mythical figment. Finally he selected a Biblical subject, having in the Biblical narrative, as he read it, the *terra firma* his genius desired. For he accepted the Biblical narrative *verbatim et literatim ;* in his eyes it not only contained the word of God; it was the word of God. And so, whenever he could, he followed closely the very diction of the Bible; and undoubtedly the comparative inferiority of many parts of *Paradise Lost*, considered as a poem, is due to this very method. It is as if he deliberately restrained the free movement of his wings. In a certain sense, and to a certain degree, he ceases to be a 'poet soaring in the high region of his fancies, with his garland and singing robes about him'; he reproduces and translates and does not create. Invention came to be regarded as of secondary importance. This view of the poet's function grew more and more upon him, and does much to explain the austerity and baldness of his latest style. And indeed, strange as the statement may at first appear, it leads us on to the immediately subsequent periods of our literature, in which poetry became a kind of decorative art—in which formal themes that belonged rather to the province of prose are taken up by the reigning poets, and argued and discussed in metre. The seeds of the school of Dryden and Pope were sown in the middle of the seventeenth century. It is by no mere accident that Pope in the opening of his *Essay on Man* almost exactly repeats certain words in the opening of *Paradise Lost.* In Milton's time the tide of the imagination that reached such a height in the Elizabethan age had not yet completely ebbed; in Pope's time it was gone far down, and often we find ourselves in a sandy tract of metrical essays and treatises, and scarcely 'hear the mighty waters rolling evermore.'

Pope sneers, perhaps not unjustly—if sneering is ever just —at Milton for turning 'God the Father' into a 'School divine'; but it is not less true of Pope and his age that the poet is often transformed into the professor, and when we are listening for a song, we have a lecture inflicted upon us; we look for a vision of Apollo, and behold a doctor of theology or some graduate in metaphysics or in science. I say the movement in this prosaic direction is perceptible in Milton's age, and in Milton's theory at least, and in his practice, so far as he obeyed his theory. The most splendid passages of *Paradise Lost* are, in fact, just those where Milton is delivered from his theory—when he has no such facts to go upon as so often make him 'pedestrian.' In the first two books of his great epic, Milton has to rely only on his imagination; there is no restricting narrative to 'damp' his 'intended wing depressed,' and the result is one of the finest and noblest achievements of the poetical spirit.

And so happily in art, as in the moral world, men are often better than their theories: they do not live down to their creeds. Often, no doubt, it is true that 'the better is seen and the worse is followed,' but, if we may vary Ovid's familiar words, it is also often true—

> Video *pejora* proboque,
> Sed *meliora* sequor.

Nature is stronger than the rules and canons that are formulated for her guidance. The artistic instinct prevails over all the utterances of a self-conscious and a perverse analysis.

But, however this may be, and to whatever degree Milton's greatness and his theories are in harmony, it is certain Milton had a profound respect for historic fact, and was by no means willing to give poetry a charter to ignore or to reconstruct it. The poet might or might not adopt it as his material, and for his part he inclined to adopt it; but assuredly, if the poet did adopt it, he had no right to take liberties with it, he was bound to be faithful to it.　Now what is to be said of Shakespeare's *Macbeth* in this respect ?

Briefly, Shakespeare did just what Milton thought ought not to be done.　Whatever may have been his practice with regard to later periods, which there is no time now to discuss, Shakespeare troubled himself little about the historical details in dealing with the more distant ones, *e.g.*, in dealing with the periods of *Hamlet*, of *King Lear*, of *Cymbeline*, and of *Macbeth*.　He submitted to no such bondage as Milton willingly endured and even gladly welcomed.　Not that he altogether ignored the circumstances of his plots, or wholly forgot with what age they were connected, or said to be connected ; but he was contented with a mere general recognition of the circumstances and the age.　His first and his last thought was to produce a picture of life ; it was not historical, or archæological, or ethical.　Some local and some historical colour might be introduced ; but such considerations were entirely secondary and subordinate.　He would omit, and he would add, even as it pleased him.　He would not attempt to tread precisely in the footsteps of any chronicler, let him chronicle ever so wisely.　It was the book of life he studied, and Hall and Holinshed were valuable only as helps to that supreme study.　And so in his great tragedy of *Macbeth* he drew many of the incidents from a quite different story. Nearly all the details of the murder of Duncan are, it is well known, derived from the story of King Duff's murder by Donwald.　In both narratives a wife appears, who instigates her husband to crime.　But it is from the King Duff narrative that the particulars of the enactment are taken.

The drugging of the chamberlains, the assassination of the too confiding guest as he slept, the pretended unconsciousness—the outraged innocence—of the real criminal, and his slaughter of the royal attendants in a paroxysm of zeal, the wild furious storm which broke over the guilty scene, as if Nature must needs vent her horror at what was so accursedly done ; 'the heavens, as troubled with man's act,' threatening 'his bloody stage'—all these things appertain in the old chronicler whom Shakespeare followed to the murder of King Duff, and not to the death of King Duncan. All that Holinshed reports of this latter event is this short paragraph :

At length, therefore, communicating his purposed intent (to usurp the kingdom by force) with his trusty friends, amongst whom Banquho was the chiefest, upon confidence of their promised aid, he slew the king at Enverness (Inverness), or, as some say, at Botgosvane, in the vj year of his reign.

It would be easy to mention other points in which Shakespeare varied from his nominal authority ;[1] but this single one is enough for our purpose. For I think we may infer from a certain fact that it was this that caused Milton some discontent and annoyance. The fact is that which I have mentioned above, and which, as I remarked, has not before been quoted in this connexion, and so surely not properly understood—viz., that Milton mentions also in his subject-list *Duff and Donwald*. Evidently then in Milton's *Macbeth*, had it ever been written, the story of King Duff would have been kept quite separate from the story of King Duncan ; the two threads which Shakespeare has so boldly intertwined would have been carefully disentangled ; the con-

---

[1] ' With the exception of Duncan's murder[?] in which Macbeth was concerned either as principal or accessory, and the character of Lady Macbeth, there is hardly any point in which the drama coincides with the real history. The single point upon which historians agree is that the reign of Macbeth was one of remarkable prosperity and vigorous government.'—So Messrs Clark and Wright in the Preface to the Clarendon Press edition of *Macbeth*.

fusion of two distinct historical events would have been in no wise permitted.

With the ultimate historical value of Holinshed's chronicle we are not here concerned. Shakespeare's disrespectful use of it did not spring, we may be sure, from any enlightened views as to its accuracy or importance; even the wildest of his idolators will scarcely maintain that he anticipated the results of modern historical criticism and investigation, and so attached but slight weight to what is very largely a tissue of legends. But I may just quote one sentence from Mr Robertson's *Scotland under Her Early Kings*. 'The double failure in Northumberland and Murray[Duncan had made unsuccessful expeditions into England and against Thorfin] hastening the catastrophe of the youthful king, he was assassinated "in the smith's bothy" near Elgin, not far from the scene of his latest battle, the Mormaor Macbeth being the undoubted author of his death.'

On historical grounds then Milton was dissatisfied with Shakespeare's *Macbeth*. Let us now turn to another point of view from which this play seemed to him no less, probably still more, unsatisfactory. Let us turn to the central action and thought of it, and reflect how Milton would regard Shakespeare's treatment of the great question presented.

And, first of all, let it be noticed that no other of Shakespeare's plays comes so near dealing with the very subject of *Paradise Lost*, or we may say does in fact so fully deal with it, as *Macbeth*. The subject of *Paradise Lost* is the Ruin of Man; and what else is the subject of *Macbeth?* Each work in its own manner treats of the origin of evil; each portrays a spiritual decline and fall. Adam represents the human race, but he is also as individual as Milton could make him; Macbeth is an individual, but also he is typical.

Milton formally states the theme which he proposes to set forth.   He bids the heavenly muse sing—

> Of man's first disobedience, and the fruit
> Of that forbidden tree, whose mortal taste
> Brought death into the world, and all our woe,
> With loss of Eden.

Without any such formal enunciation, not less fully, and with far greater power, does Shakespeare paint one of man's later disobediences, the disobedience of a remote son of Adam, and how he too plucked forbidden fruit, and was expelled from his Eden—expelled from the state of happiness, honour, and peace.   For indeed the story of Adam is perpetually repeated ; it is a faithful image of what goes on every day in the world.   Every day in the world paradises are lost, and looking back poor exiles behold their so late

> Happy seat,
> Waved over by that flaming brand ; the gate
> With dreadful faces thronged, and fiery arms ;

and, 'with wandering steps and slow,' they have to traverse the stony tracts that spread far away outside.   Thus the fall of man never ceases being acted on the human stage. Happily, too, his restoration never ceases being acted ; in some sort daily the lost paradises are regained.   But the brighter side of the great human drama does not now claim our consideration.   It is with a tragedy of tragedies that we have now to do—one in which all that makes life worth living is wasted and lost, and he who, when we first see him, 'sits high' in all the people's hearts, is at last cast out into the outer darkness of men's hate and loathing.

Besides the fall of man Milton presents also the fall of Satan, and in his picture he gives us a scene exactly parallel to that in *Macbeth*, where the already demoralised nature of Macbeth receives a fresh strong impulse towards its fatal corruption through the preferment of Malcolm to be Prince of Cumberland.

> The Prince of Cumberland ! That is a step,
> On which I must fall down, or else o'erleap,
> For in my way it lies.   Stars, hide your fires !
> Let not light see my black and deep desires ;
> The eye wink at the hand ! yet let that be,
> Which the eye fears, when it is done, to see.

In *Paradise Lost* the appointment by God of His Son to be His Vicegerent awakes similarly the evil—how strange and unaccountable an inmate !—in the bosom of Satan ; and shortly afterwards he thus addresses him whom we see in another book as his favourite devil :

> Sleep'st thou, companion dear ? What sleep can close
> Thy eyelids, and rememberest what decree
> Of yesterday, so late hath passed the lips
> Of Heaven's Almighty ? . . .
> 　　　. . . New laws thou seest imposed ;
> New laws from him who reigns new minds may raise
> In us who serve—new counsels to debate
> What doubtful may ensue.

And so there is rebellion in Heaven, and in due time rebellion on earth, just as in Macbeth's 'single state of man.'

But, leaving secondary resemblances alone, I wish to dwell on the fact that Shakespeare and Milton are in these great works, each in his own way, thinking of the same transcendent problem, viz., the freedom of man's will.   As to Adam, and as to Macbeth, the old, old questions arise : were they capable of resisting the terrible forces that were arrayed against them ?   Could they have delivered themselves from evil ?   How did they come to fall so miserably ? Whence was engendered the weakness that undid them ? How far were they responsible for such a disastrous debility ?

What is the real parentage of crime? Even such awful and insoluble problems are at once suggested by the careers of Adam and Macbeth. For in neither case do external causes explain the horrible mischief that is depicted. 'A man's foes are those of his own household.' It was the treachery of the defending garrison, not the overwhelming strength of the attack, that produced the overthrow. If Milton's serpent had had no encouragements or alliances in the heart of his victims, he might have charmed in vain. And it is not the witches that work Macbeth's ruin; it is Macbeth's own falseness that works it. When he first appears on the stage, so honoured and trusted and loved, and seemingly so loyal and true, he is already in correspondence and treaty with the powers of darkness. Already he

> Is like a villain with a smiling cheek,
> A goodly apple rotten at the heart.
> O what a goodly outside falsehood hath !

Those wild figures he encounters on the Heath, near Forres, only in fact give voice to the dire imaginings that already have a home in his breast.

> Evil into the mind of God or man
> May come and go, so unapproved, and leave
> No spot or blame behind.

But Macbeth has invited evil to stay and abide with him, and is already saying, 'Evil, be thou my good.'

But the manner in which Shakespeare deals with these dark inscrutable problems is very different from that in which Milton deals with them; and what I have now to suggest is that this manner was far from satisfying Milton, and that Milton's dissatisfaction with it was one chief reason why he was guilty of the impertinence, as it will seem to many persons to be, of proposing to write another dramatic version of the Macbeth story. Briefly, Shakespeare deals with these problems as one who feels their infinite mystery, and that they are 'beyond the reaches of our souls.' Milton, to speak plainly, deals with them in the spirit of a dogmatist—of one who has an exegetic scheme ready drawn up, which he perpetually enforces and reinforces. In this respect Shakespeare's humanity exhibits itself· in all its breadth and depth; and it must be allowed, I think, that Milton, with all his culture and all his greatness, shows by the side of him as one of narrower vision, and a less wide range of sympathy.

The catholicity of Shakespeare's spirit—I use the word, I need scarcely say, in no limited ecclesiastical sense—is nowhere more amply displayed than in *Macbeth*, whatever faults in some respects might be found with this play. As Dryden finely remarks of him, 'he was the man who, of all modern and perhaps ancient poets, had the largest and most comprehensive soul.' We may well apply to him Virgil's untranslatable line:

Sunt lacrymæ rerum, et mentem mortalia tangunt.

He had a profound sense of the pathos of things. 'But yet the pity of it . . . the pity of it.' He certainly does not spare the sinner. He certainly makes us hate his sin; but in him 'the quality of mercy is not strained.' As we watch Macbeth drifting towards the precipice, it is not contempt for his weakness that he excites overpoweringly within us; it is rather a profound compassion; it is not a sense of superiority and pride that we stand firm but a sense of humility—a sense that we are of like passions with him, and might too easily be drifting in a like direction. Pity and terror purify our souls. We feel ourselves face to face with

> those mysteries which Heaven
> Will not have earth to know.

We are conscious of the amazing shallowness of those who 'take upon' them the 'mystery of things, as if' they 'were God's spies.' We perceive with a new vividness that

> There are more things in heaven and earth
> Than are dreamt of in your philosophy;

and that the truest reverence, and it may be that the most exemplary 'faith,' are exhibited in the submissive acceptance of the limitedness of human discovery and knowledge.

In striking contrast is Milton's attitude. He has so clearly, as he believes, reasoned out the matter, that he feels more impatience than pity—more anger than sorrow—as he narrates the fall of man. To him the event appears not so much pathetic as shameful. If I may put it so, he holds a brief for the Almighty as he conceives Him, and is perpetually defending Him from the charge of undue severity. He is always insisting that Adam was made perfectly well able to resist the tempter, had he been so minded. If he fell, he had only himself to blame; his Maker had done everything for him that could be expected—everything that was right. If he fell,

> Whose fault?
> Whose but his own? Ingrate, he had of me
> All he could have; I made him just and right,
> Sufficient to have stood, though free to fall.
> Such I created all the Ethereal Powers
> And Spirits, both them who stood and them who failed;
> Freely they stood who stood, and fell who fell.

Qui s'excuse s'accuse. And Milton's God, scarcely perhaps a Being to attract men's devotion and love, 'protests too much, methinks.' To Milton's intellect, indeed, there is no mystery in what seems to most men so profound a mystery. Everything is amenable to argument, and can be made entirely plain.

> When first this Tempter crossed the gulf for hell,
> I told ye then he should prevail, and speed
> On his bad errand.   Man should be seduced
> And flattered out of all, believing lies
> Against his Maker ; no decree of mine
> Concurring to necessitate his fall,
> Or touch with lightest moment of impulse
> His free will, to his own inclining left
> In even scale.

And so, with scarcely an exception, this merely hard-headed, and therefore obviously limited manner, prevails in Milton's treatment of this terrible tragedy.   He writes for the most part like some inexorable logician, and not like a man conscious of the infirmities of his kind.   Just the same spirit expresses itself in *Samson Agonistes*, especially in the scene between Samson and Dalilah.

> All wickedness is wickedness ; that plea, therefore,
> With God or man will gain thee no remission.

Milton was himself of a singularly lofty and strong character, and lived throughout a life of noble and sustained purposes.

> 'Credible est' illum 'pariter vitiisque locisque
> Altius humanis exseruisse caput.'

And so he found it hard to make allowance—hard to feel any pity—for the weaknesses of ordinary mortals.   He had in a high degree the faults of his virtues.   And, as suggested above, his genius, with all its rich natural endowments, and with all the talents that learning and culture had contributed to it, was yet narrower—less catholic—than that of Shakespeare.

I am not, of course, attempting in this paper to discuss the profound and awful questions that are brought before us in *Paradise Lost* and in *Macbeth*. I am only calling attention to the difference between the manner in which these works, each in its own way so great and so splendid and priceless, present them to us. And I trust I have made it sufficiently clear how Milton would regard Shakespeare's presentment of them as inadequate—would be persuaded that Shakespeare had not enough emphasised the wilfulness of Macbeth's ruin, and so to his thinking had not satisfactorily asserted

> Eternal Providence,
> And justified the ways of God to men.

XVII

MILTON AND GRAY'S INN WALKS

(From the *St James's Gazette* for July 29 and 30, 1891)

EXCEPT the years he spent at Cambridge (1625-32), and the following period (1632-38) which he spent at Horton, near Windsor, and the months of his foreign tour (1638–39), and the weeks he spent at Chalfont St Giles, when the plague was raging in town, and possibly some time when, before he went to St Paul's, he was at some school in Essex, Milton's life was wholly passed in London. All these exceptions would not amount to more than some fifteen years; and during the two longest of them—the Cambridge and the Horton periods — he was perpetually revisiting London, not only during the vacations, but, in one case at least, during term.

> Me tenet urbs reflua quam Thamesis alluit unda ;
> Meque nec invitum patria dulcis habet.
> Jam nec arundiferum mihi cura revisere Camum,
> Nec dudum vetiti me laris angit amor.

So that the connexion of Milton with London is singularly close and intimate, and certainly at one epoch in its history he was proud of the city with which he was thus incessantly associated. And with devoted industry Professor Masson and others have traced his footsteps from one locality to another : from St Bride's Churchyard to Aldersgate Street, and from Aldersgate Street to the Barbican ; and so to Holborn, and to Charing Cross and Whitehall, and to Petty France, Westminster ; and then back to his old neighbourhood, to Holborn, and to Jewin Street in St Giles's, Cripplegate, by the side of the father to whom he was bound by no common sympathy and affection, at no great distance from the house in which, some sixty-six years before, he was born. Thus he was no stranger and sojourner in town, as in a sense Shakespeare was ; and his vicinities have been carefully noted. But there is one London allusion in his works to which attention has not, I think, been yet called ; and as it is of some interest both for lovers of Milton and lovers of London, I propose now to point it out and to illustrate it.

It occurs in the First of what he call his ' Elegies '—the one from which a quotation has already been given. It was written in the spring of 1626, from London, at a time when through some easily intelligible jar with his tutor, the Rev. William Chappell—easily intelligible from what little we know of the reverend gentleman's character, and from what much we know of the character of the pupil in question— the writer seems to have been temporarily ' sent down ' from his university. It is addressed to his old schoolfellow, Charles Deodati ; who, after leaving St Paul's had gone to Oxford, and after leaving Oxford in December, 1625, was residing for a while in Cheshire. It informs us pretty clearly that though this undergraduate was under a cloud, the position did not in the least trouble him. If this is exile, he says, he likes exile ; he is free from care—meaning, probably, unbothered with lectures and such frivolous interruptions of serious study. He wishes Ovid (a favourite poet of his) had never had anything worse to bear than he now has ; then he of Tomi might have rivalled Homer, and have won the first

place amongst the Latins ; for his time is all his own and all
devoted to the Muses, and the books, that are his life, wholly
ravish him.

> Si sit hoc exilium patrios adiisse penates,
>   Et vacuum curis otia grata sequi,
> Non ego vel profugi nomen sortemve recuso,
>   Lætus et exilii conditione fruor.
>
> Tempora nam licet hic placidis dare libera musis,
>   Et totum rapient me, mea vita, libri.

And, when he is weary with reading, he goes to the theatre :

> Excipit hine fessum sinuosi pompi theatri,
>   Et vocat ad plausus garrula scena suos.

He briefly sketches the comedies that delight him ; but
evidently in these sketches he seems to have largely in his
mind the Latin stage and the Cantabrigian, which mainly
imitated the Latin stage, rather than the Elizabethan or
Jacobean.   Then he refers to the tragedies that were to be
seen acted ; and here too his classics haunt him, as, indeed,
they always did ; but along with such memories we find
what may well be allusions to *Romeo and Juliet* and
possibly to *King Richard III.* :—

> Seu peur infelix indelibata reliquit
>   Gaudia, et abrupto flendus amore perit ;
> Seu ferus e tenebris iterat Styga criminis ultor,
>   Conscia funereo pectora torre movens.

But, he proceeds, he does not always lie perdue under a
roof or in the city, or let the springtide hours go by unen-
joyed :—

> Sed neque sub tecto semper nec in urbe latemus,
>   Irrita nec nobis tempora veris eunt.

And now we come to the London passage, which has
hitherto, I believe, not been understood. Dr Garnett, in

his admirable little book on Milton—one of the best little books yet written about him, and, indeed, worth much more than many of the big ones—makes, I venture to think, one slight slip here; and where so much, so nearly all, is so excellent, I trust I may, without offence, suggest a correction.   Dr Garnett supposes the lines that now concern us refer to Milton's residence at Horton; conjecturing, without any other evidence, that Milton *père* had already bought unto himself a country house, and that Milton *fils* is alluding to this purchase.   But I feel sure that a further inspection of this passage will convince Dr Garnett that Milton means some spot in the immediate neighbourhood of London— of Milton's London.   He calls it 'suburban,' and he describes it as haunted by what he elsewhere calls 'a store of ladies,' bright-eyed and fascinating: he is evidently thinking of some fashionable promenade of the day.   Even if he might extend the adjective 'suburban' to include a village some eighteen miles from London, as, indeed, in one of his Latin letters he apparently does, yet he would scarcely speak of this out-of-the-way hamlet as the thronged resort of the reigning beauties.   He might 'chance' see there 'with nymph-like step fair virgin pass,' and

> As one who long in populous city pent,
> Where houses thick and sewers annoy the air,
> Forth issuing on a summer's morn to breathe
> Among the pleasant villages, and farms
> Adjoined, from each thing met conceives delight,
> The smell of grain or tedded grass or kine
> Or dairy, each rural sight, each rural sound ;

yet finds all his joy augmented if some sweet girl's face brightens the landscape :—

> What pleasing seemed for her now pleases more,
> She most and in her looks sums all delight ;

so on Milton sauntering through the green lanes at Horton some such lonely apparition of loveliness might have dawned. But 'bands of virgins'—how were they likely to be disporting themselves there?

It seems to me fairly certain Milton in these lines is referring to Gray's Inn Gardens. The place he describes was suburban, as we have already remarked; so was Gray's Inn at that time. It was planted with elms; so were Gray's Inn Gardens. It was the haunt of 'society;' so again were these gardens. Finally, the context proves that he means some place close to London.

The words are as follows :—

> Nos quoque lucus habet vicina consitus ulmo,
> Atque suburbani nobilis umbra loci.
> Sæpius hic blandas spirantia sidera flammas
> Virgineos videas præteriisse choros.
> Ah! quoties dignæ stupui miracula formæ,
> Quæ possit senium vel reparare Jovis.

And for four couplets this susceptible young man—his susceptibility was one day to cost him dear—raves about the exquisite complexions and figures that he beholds in this favoured and favourite spot. All previous beauties— the Heroids, the Persians, the Danaans, the Trojans, the Italians, must give place to these :—

> Gloria virginibus debetur prima Britannis;
> Extera, sat tibi sit, femina, posse sequi.

London—too happy London—encloses within its walls all the loveliness the world contains. There are not so many stars in the clear sky as there are fair maidens in its streets. For himself, he is preparing to leave these blessed precincts as soon as he may, while yet heart-whole; for it is determined he is to go back to Cambridge. The lines at the end of the poem read as if this decision had been arrived at—as if his peace had been made with Dr Bainbridge, the Master of Christ's, and his transference from the 'side' of Mr Chappell to that of Mr Tovey had been successfully effected—since he wrote the opening passage,

> Tuque urbs, Dardaniis, Londinum, structa colonis
> Turrigerum late conspicienda caput,
> Tu nimium felix intra tua mœnia claudis
> Quicquid formosi pendulus orbis habet.
>
> .   .   .   .   .   .
>
> Ast ego, dum pueri sinit indulgentia cœci,
> Mœnia quam subito linquere fausta paro ;
> Et vitare procul malafidæ infamia Circes
> Atria, divini Molyos usus ope.
> Stat quoque juncosas Cami remeare paludes,
> Atque iterum raucæ murmur adire scholæ.

To the popularity of Gray's Inn Walks, and the elms that threw their shade over them, there are many references in seventeenth-century literature and elsewhere. 'There is good reason for believing,' writes Mr Douthwaite in his interesting volume on *Gray's Inn: Its History and Associations*, that the gardens of Gray's Inn were laid out in the year 1597 under the direction of Bacon. In that year it was ordered "that the summe of £7, 15*s*. 4*d*. [some £35 of our money] due to Mr Bacon for planting trees in the walkes be paid next term."' In the following year another order was made for a further 'supply of more yonge elme trees in the places of such as are decayed, and that a new Rayle and quicksett hedge bee set uppon the upper long walke at the good discretion of Mr Bacon and Mr Wilbraham, soe that the charges thereof does not exceed the sum of seventy pounds.' On the 29th of April, A.D. 1600, it was ordered 'that there shall bee payed and allowed unto Mr Bacon for money disbursed about the garnishing of the walkes,

£60, 6*s.* 8*d.*' . . . The records of the society contain an account of such trees as existed in the year 1583 :—'In the Grene Courte, xi Elmes and iii Walnut trees ; in the Pannyermans Close, v Elmes . . . ; vi Elmes in the Est side of the said Close ; vii Elmes in the North End of the Close ; xx^te Elmes in the West side of the said Close . . . . ; one Elme in Greis Inne Close . . . ; eighteen Elmes standing in and near the Mud Wall and Buyldinges . . . ; xix Elmes in and neare the Walk enclosed, and iii young Elmes in the West end of the Walke and one in the North side, and one younge Ashe near the Seate.' Thus Milton might well speak of these gardens as 'Lucus, vicina consitus ulmo.'

Naturally enough these grounds and terraces, already so richly wooded before the author of the famous essay on 'Gardens' gave them some finishing touches, became 'the most fashionable lounge in London.' The current topographical works give us illustrative quotations from Stowe, from Howell, from Pepys, from Dryden, from Addison. 'I hold your walks,' writes Howell from Venice in 1621—just five years before Milton penned his *Elegy*—to a Gray's Inn friend, 'to be the pleasantest place about London, and that you have there the choicest society.' Mr Pepys's diary record for June 30, 1661, 'Lord's Day,' runs thus :—'Here I to Graye's Inn Walk all alone, and with great pleasure seeing the fine ladies walk there.' Under the date May 4, 1662, the entry is :—'When Church was done, my wife and I walked to Graye's Inn to observe fashions of the ladies, because of my wife's making some clothes.'

As late as 1780 the neighbourhood was fairly rural. Sir Samuel Romilly, to quote again Mr Douthwaite, in a letter to his sister, dated from his chambers in Gray's Inn Square, says : — 'My rooms are exceedingly lively . . . . The moment the sun peeps out I am in the country . . . having only one row of houses between me and Highgate and Hampstead.' And, in one of the Essays of Elia, Lamb speaks with enthusiasm of the beauty of these gardens as he remembered them, 'better than five-and-twenty years ago ;' and adds : 'They are still the best gardens of any of the Inns of Court—my beloved Temple not forgotten—have the gravest character, their aspect being altogether reverend and law-breathing. Bacon has left the impress of his foot upon their gravel walks.'

Yes, the *genius loci* is surely Bacon. We think of all the others as but a slight and fleeting tribe, like the ghosts that gathered round the trench Odysseus dug in the land of Cimmeria :—

αἱ δ' ἀγέροντο
ψυχαὶ ὑπὲξ 'Ερέβευς νεκύων κατατεθνηώτων
νύμφαι τ' ἠίθεοί τε, πολύτλητοί τε γέροντες,
παρθενικαί τ' ἀταλαί.

Amaryllis and those who sported with her in the shade, Neæra with the tangled hair, the busy quidnuncs of many generations, the glittering kings and queens of society, and many another personage once of note and fame—haply all these still in spirit hover about the scene that they made gay and lively with their gossip or their beauty ; certainly, in a bright motley train, their images pass before us as we visit the parterre so familiar to the originals when they had their day. But they melt into thin air when Bacon presents himself to our fancy ; their light badinage dies away as we listen to his voice. He had chambers close by, in what was then called Coney Court, now Gray's Inn Square ; and there many of his works were undoubtedly written. In his earlier days this was his chief London residence, and it was so in his later. 'After he had sold York House and reduced his establishment at Gorhambury, he confined himself chiefly to his lodgings in Gray's Inn.'　Spedding mentions his having a long conversation with Sir Walter Raleigh in Gray's Inn Walks, just before Raleigh's last fatal voyage to the new world.

I trust those who care to look at old places, and picture them radiant with life and movement as they once were, will the next time they visit Gray's Inn Walks or when first they visit them—

> Most sweet it is, with un-uplifted eyes,
> To pace the ground, if path there be or none.
> While a fair region round the traveller lies,
> Which he forbears again to look upon,
> Pleased rather with some soft ideal scene,
> The work of fancy or some happy tone
> Of meditation—

permit the figure of the young Milton to have a place by the side of the ageing Bacon.　There could be no more striking juxtaposition.　Both men were endowed with a passionate love of knowledge and truth, and with noble powers of expression; though in character and in conduct, as also in the directions their geniuses led them, the difference was profound.　At the close of James I.'s reign, Bacon's life lay behind him, Milton's in front; in the one case we have splendid performance, in the other splendid promise.

Professor Masson, in whose investigations the *præfervidum ingenium Scotorum* so fully displays itself, plausibly imagines that, as the Mermaid Tavern, a great resort of the Elizabethan wits, was close to Milton's birthplace—one of its entrances seems to have been in Bread Street, just opposite the sign of the Spread Eagle that marked the shop and the dwelling of Milton's father—Milton, when a boy, may have seen Shakespeare and been seen by him.　Professor Masson supposes that in the 'year 1614, when the dramatist paid his last known visit to London, he may have spent an evening at the Mermaid, and, going down Bread Street with Ben Jonson, on his way may have passed a fair child of six playing at his father's door.'   Assuredly, with not less plausibility, we may conceive Bacon and Milton meeting each other in these Gray's Inn Walks; and, at all events, take for granted that the younger man would gaze with curious interest and respect on the great philosopher with whose writings he perpetually shows his familiarity.   Probably enough, we may believe also that the great philosopher would return the compliment, as the younger man was of so noticeable and attractive an aspect, 'the cynosure of neighbouring eyes.'

But however often they had passed each other in former years, Bacon, at the time when Milton was writing the lines that have suggested this short article, was conspicuous by his absence from the walks which his 'due feet' had for so long never failed to tread.   *Elegia Prima* was probably written in the first half of April 1626.   The Easter Term at Cambridge that year began on the 19th of April, and Milton 'kept' it.   On the 9th of April Bacon died.   About the end of March he had set out from his Gray's Inn Chambers for his home at St Alban's, or possibly only for a drive northwards.   At Highgate 'he took advantage of an unseasonable fall of snow to try whether it would preserve flesh from putrefaction, as salt does.'   He caught a chill, and as he tells us himself in a letter to Lord Arundel, 'when I came to your lordship's house I was not able to go back, and was forced to take up my lodging there, where your housekeeper is very careful and diligent about me.'   The story is that this 'careful and diligent' housekeeper, bent on doing him all honour, put him in the best bed; but the best bed, long unused in the absence of the family, was damp. 'This brought on an attack of what would now be called bronchitis, which lasted some days, and ended (as that complaint so often does with people of all ages) in sudden suffocation.' Early on Easter Sunday morning Lord Bacon, as he is oddly styled, left his 'name and memory' 'to men's charitable speeches and to foreign nations and the next ages.'

Thus, while Milton was composing his sprightly elegiacs hard by Cheapside, on Highgate Hill Bacon lay dying. 'Two jars are there,' says the old Greek poet, 'that stand at the threshold of Zeus, of gifts that he gives—one of evil things and one of good.' But which are which is, after all, not easy to say. 'Above all, believe it the sweetest canticle is 'Nunc Dimittis,' when a man hath obtained worthy ends and expectations. Death has this also: that it openeth the gate to good fame and extinguisheth envy. 'Extinctus amabitur idem.' So Bacon in his celebrated essay.

XVIII

MILTON NOTES

(1) *AN UNEXPLAINED PASSAGE IN 'COMUS'*

(From *The Athenæum* for April 20, 1889)

IT may seem surprising that, after so much industry and acuteness have been given to the elucidation of *Comus* there should yet remain a passage imperfectly or not at all explained. Yet such appears to be the case. The passage occurs in the Lady's Song, when she is lost in the wood :—

> Sweet Echo, sweetest nymph, that livest unseen
> Within thy airy shell,
> By slow Meander's margent green,
> And in the violet-embroidered vale
> Where the love-lorn nightingale
> Nightly to thee her sad song mourneth well.

No one has satisfactorily explained why the Meander is mentioned here; and no one has considered whether there is, or is not, any special local reference in the lines that follow.

1. As to the introduction of the Meander, Keightley of the leading commentators seems to be the only one who makes any suggestion, and the suggestion he makes cannot

be called very valuable. 'It is possible,' he says, 'that he assigns the bank of the Meander as the abode of Echo because its course goes backwards and forwards, returning on itself like the repercussion of an echo.' Surely this is the very type of what are termed far-fetched interpretations. Yet the real reason is obvious enough, if we remember how richly and fully Milton's memory was furnished with the poetry and the lore of the ancient classics. The real reason is that the Meander was a famous haunt of swans, and the swan was a favourite bird with the Greek and Latin writers —one to whose sweet singing they perpetually allude. There are abundant illustrations of these two statements to be found in Æschylus, Plato, Lucretius, Virgil, Horace, Ovid, etc. Here are a few that speak of the swan as a sweet singer : Socrates, when in his last moments, as described in the *Phædo*, he remonstrates with his friends for thinking he regarded his coming fate as a calamity, tells them they seem to give him credit for less divination than swans possess, which, though they have sung in their former days, yet sing most fully and frequently when they rejoice at the prospect of their departure to be with the god whose servants they are; that is, to be with Apollo. Ὡς ἔοικε, τῶν κύκνων δοκῶ φαυλότερος ὑμῖν εἶναι τὴν μαντικήν, οἳ ἐπειδὰν αἴσθωνται ὅτι δεῖ αὐτοὺς ἀποθανεῖν, ᾄδοντες καὶ ἐν τῷ πρόσθεν χρόνῳ, τότε δὴ πλεῖστα καὶ μάλιστα ᾄδουσι, γεγηθότες ὅτι μέλλουσι παρὰ τὸν θεὸν ἀπιέναι οὗπερ θεράποντες. And below in this passage, which should all be read in this connexion, he speaks of the swans as τοῦ ᾽Απόλλωνος ὄντες, μαντικοί, and προειδότες τὰ ἐν Αἴδου ἀγαθα, and that for these reasons they sing on their death-day more excellently (διαφερόντως) than ever before. See Cicero's reproductions of these words in the Tusculan Disputations (i. 30, 73) : 'Cygni qui non sine causa Apollini dicati sunt sed quod ab eo divinationem habere videantur quia providentes quid in morte boni sit cum cantu et voluptate moriantur.' Lucretius contrasts the song of the swan with the cry of the crane ; see iv. 181—the same couplet is repeated below, ll. 910-1 :—

> Parvus ut est cycni melior canor, ille gruum quam
> Clamor in ætheriis dispersus nubibus austri.

And elsewhere with that of the swallow (iii. 6) :

> Quid enim contendat hirundo
> Cycnis ?

With Virgil, too, it is the type of sweet singing, as the owl and the goose of cacophony ; see *Ecl.*, viii. 55 :—

> Certent et cycnis ululæ.

Ecl., ix. 36 :—

> argutos inter strepere anser olores.

Compare *ib*. 29 :—

> Cantantes sublime ferent ad sidera cycni.

In *Æneid*, i. 398, an augury is drawn from certain swans who at first, scared by an eagle, fly earthwards, but at last wing their way aloft :

> Et cætu cinxere polum cantusque dedere.

See Mart., i. 54, 8 :—

> Inter Ledæos ridetur corvus olores.

And such quotations might be endlessly multiplied. And scarcely less abundant are passages of like tenor in the modern poets, especially in those of the Elizabethan age. Thus in Shakespeare's *King John* (V. vii. 21), when the fever-parched monarch has, we are told, broken out into singing, Prince Henry is represented as saying :—

> 'Tis strange that death should sing.
> I am the cygnet to this pale faint swan,
> Who chants a doleful hymn to his own death,
> And from the organ pipe of frailty sings
> His soul and body to their lasting rest.

So *Lucrece*, 1611 :—

> And now this pale swan in her watery nest
> Begins the sad dirge of her certain ending.

And in accordance with the old classical tradition, just as Horace alludes to Pindar as a swan ('Multa Dircæum levat aura cygnum,' *Od.*, iv. 2, 25), and speaks of himself as about to be changed into a swan (*Od.*, ii. 20, 15), so Ben Jonson in his noble memorial lines apostrophizes Shakespeare as the 'Sweet Swan of Avon.' Assuredly the swan myth deserves the attention of folk-lore students. As a fact, according to Mr Harting, this bird 'has no song properly so called,' but it has 'a soft and rather plaintive note, monotonous, but not disagreeable.'

What concerns us further to notice just now is that one of its chief reputed haunts was the Meander. Thus Ovid's *Heroides*, vii. 1 :—

> Sic ubi fata vocant udis abjectus in herbis
> Ad vada Mæandri concinit albus olor.

And that this was a favourite neighbourhood may be illustrated from Homer's *Iliad*, ii. 462, though the river specially named there is the Cayster, which flowed a little to the north of the Meander, just on the other side of the Messogis mountains, which divided Caria from Lydia :—

> Τῶν δ' ὥστ' ὀρνίθων πετεηνῶν ἔθνεα πολλὰ
> χηνῶν ἢ γεράνων ἢ κύκνων δουλιχοδείρων
> Ἀσίῳ ἐν λειμῶνι Καϋστρίου ἀμφὶ ῥέεθρα
> ἔνθα καὶ ἔνθα ποτῶνται ἀγαλλόμενα πτερύγεσσιν,
> κλαγγηδὸν προκαθιζόντων, σμαραγεῖ δέ τε λειμών·
> ὡς τῶν ἔθνεα πολλὰ, κ. τ. λ.

Comp. Virg., *Æn.*, vii. 699 :—

> Ceu quondam nivei liquida inter nubila cycni
> Cum sese e pastu referunt et longa canoros
> Dant per colla modos.   Sonat amnis et Asia longe
> Pulsa palus.

Ovid's *Trist.*, v. 1, 11 :—

> Utque jacens ripa deflere Caystrius ales
>   Dicitur ore suam deficiente necem,
> Sic ego, Sarmaticas longe projectus in oras
>   Efficio, tacitum ne mihi funus eat.

Perhaps it is worth noticing that the modern name of the Cayster is the Little Meinder; Meinder being obviously a corruption of Meander.   Conceivably, therefore, the Cayster was of old known also by the name of Meander.   In any case the rivers are contiguous, and what is said of the swans haunting the one applies also to the other.

Thus in the mention of the Meander by Milton there is no particular reference to the sinuous course of the river, except so far as the epithet 'slow' refers to it.   What he is thinking of is the swanneries that were to be found on its banks and in its vicinity.

2. As he thought of the Meander as the haunt of the swan, what special haunt of the nightingale was in his mind in the lines that follow?   Does he mean no place in particular by 'the violet-embroidered vale'?   Observe the 'the.'   What, then, is the vale that is present to his imagination?

I think there can scarcely be a doubt he is thinking of the woodlands close by Athens to the north-west, through which the Cephissus flowed, and where stood the birthplace of Sophocles,

> Singer of sweet Colonus and its child.

He is thinking of the famous passage in the famous 'chorus'
where Sophocles chants the praises of his native hamlet.   See
Œd. Col., 668 :

> Εὐίππου, ξένε, τᾶσδε χώρας
> ἵκου τὰ κράτιστα γᾶς ἔπαυλα,
> τὸν ἀργῆτα Κολωνὸν, ἔνθ'
> ἁ λίγεια μινύρεται
> θαμίζουσα μάλιστ' ἀηδὼν
> χλωραῖς ὑπὸ βάσσαις,
> τὸν οἰνῶπα νέμουσα κισσὸν
> καὶ τὰν ἄβατον θεοῦ
> φυλλάδα μυριόκκαρπον ἀνήλιον
> ἀνήνεμόν τε πάντων
> χειμώνων·

> Of all the land far famed for goodly steeds
> Thou com'st, O stranger, to the noblest spot,
> Colonus, glistening bright ;
> Where evermore in thickets freshly green
> The clear-voiced nightingale
> Still haunts and pours her song,
> By purpling ivy hid,
> And the thick leafage sacred to the god
> With all its myriad fruits,
> By mortal's foot untouched,
> By sun's hot ray unscathed,
> Sheltered from every blast.—*Plumptre.*

Three things point to this identification : the fame of the
passage, the verb 'mourneth,' and the epithet 'violet-embroidered.'   The passage is so famous that it could scarcely
be absent from Milton's mind when he looked through his
classical stores in search of a nightingale's haunt.   Then
has not the verb 'mourneth' been suggested by Sophocles's
μινύρεται.   The commentators quote Virgil's

> Flet noctem ramoque sedens miserabile carmen
> Integrat.

But μινύρεται, which is best rendered here by 'trills,' might be taken to mean 'utters plaintively'; so μινυρίζειν, to complain in a low tone, Lat. *minurire*. Lastly, surely that epithet 'violet-embroidered' is a translation of the Greek ἰοστέφανος; and ἰοστέφανοι was a current, and, as Aristophanes lets us know (*Acharn.*, 636), a dearly-prized epithet of Athens; and Colonus, as we have seen, is a suburb of Athens. This epithet seems first to have been bestowed by Pindar; see his *Frag.*, No. 46 (p. 346 of Donaldson's edition) :—

> αἵ τε λιπαραὶ καὶ ἰοστέφανοι καὶ ἀοίδιμοι
> Ἑλλάδος ἔρεισμα, κλειναὶ ᾿Αθῆναι, δαιμόνιον
> Πτολίεθρον.

It occurs again in Aristophanes, *Knights*, 1322 :—

> ἐν ταῖσιν ἰοστεφάνοις οἰκεῖ ταις ἀρχαίαισιν
> ᾿Αθήναις.

It may have been given with reference to the violets that abound in the neighbourhood (see the quotation from Murray's *Greece* given below), or to the colour in certain lights of Hymettus and other mountains that stand around the city (see again the quotation just referred to), or it may have arisen from some poetic fantasy. Mr Swinburne finely illustrates it in his glowing lines to the glory of Athens in his *Erechtheus*. A choral ode sings how the gods, arbitrating between certain claimants,

> Gave Pallas the strife's fair stake,
> The lordship and love of the lovely land,
> The grace of the town that hath on it for crown
> But a headband to wear
> Of violets one-hued with her hair.

The 'vale,' then, is the valley of Cephissus. That it is so seems confirmed by certain lines in the description of Athens in *Paradise Regained*, iv. 244-6 :—

> See there the olive grove of Academe,
> Plato's retirement, where the Attic bird
> Trills her thick-warbled notes the summer long.

The Attic bird is certainly the nightingale (see Mart., *Epigr.*, i. 46); for Philomela, as Mr Jerram reminds us in his excellent edition of *Paradise Regained*, was the legendary daughter of Pandion, king of Athens. And the Academy was situated at no great distance from the hill or knoll of Colonus; it was a little to the south-west of it. Plutarch speaks of the district as 'the best wooded of all the suburbs' (δενδροφορωτάτην προαστείων); see again Jerram's *Paradise Regained*.

So very pertinent a quotation is given from 'Mr Hughes' in Murray's *Greece*, ed. 1872, that a few sentences of it must be here reproduced :—

We arrived at the banks of the Cephissus, the ancient rival of Ilissus and its superior in utility, flowing through the fertile plains which it still adorns with verdure, fruits and flowers. A scene more delightful can scarcely be conceived than the gardens on its banks, which extend from the Academy up to the hills of Colonus. . . . In the opening of the year the whole grove is vocal with the melody of nightingales, and the ground is carpeted with violets, those national flowers of Athens ; at its close the purple and yellow clusters, the glory of Bacchus, hang round the trellis work with which the numerous cottages and villas are adorned. . . . Nor can anything be more charming than the views which present themselves to the eye through vistas of dark foliage : the temple-crowned Acropolis, the empurpled summits of Hymettus, Anchesmus, and Pentelicus ; or the waving out-lines of Corydalus, Ægaleos, and Parnes. . . . This paradise owes its chief beauty and fertility to the perennial fountains of the Cephissus (*Œd. Col.*, 685), over whose innumerable rills those soft breezes flow which, according to the ancient muse (Eurip., *Med.*, 835), were wafted by the Cytherean queen herself.

(2) *THE NAME LYCIDAS*

(From *The Athenæum* for Aug. 1, 1891)

OF the many pastoral names at his service, why did Milton select Lycidas to designate his college friend Edward King? Commentators refer us to Virgil's Ninth Eclogue, in which two shepherds—Lycidas and Mœris—discourse on certain ejectments that are taking place, and also on certain things poetical. Both are themselves verse-writers, and gracefully quote each other's songs. Lycidas seems to accept the title of 'poeta,' though he modestly shrinks from that of 'vates' :—

> Et me fecere poetam
> Pierides, sunt et mihi carmina ; me quoque dicunt
> Vatem pastores ; sed non ego credulus illis ;
> Nam neque adhuc Vario videor nec dicere Cinna
> Digna, sed argutos inter strepere anser olores.

And this Vergilian use of the name, probably enough, was in Milton's mind when he wrote his exquisite monody. But still more, I wish now to suggest, was he influenced in his choice by three other poets, with whose works he was certainly well acquainted, and even familiar, viz., Theocritus, and two of the Italian pastoralists, Sannazaro and Giovanni Baptista Amaltei.

In one of the most delightful of Theocritus's idyls we are introduced to a goatherd Lycidas. As Simichidas with his friends Eucritus and Amyntas were on the road to a certain festival, they met another wayfarer ; it was Lycidas, a goatherd, as everybody might see who looked at him :—

> καὶ τιν᾽ ὁδίταν
> ἐσθλὸν σὺν Μοίσαισι Κυδωνικὸν εὕρομες ἄνδρα
> οὔνομα μὲν Λυκίδαν, ἦς δ᾽ αἰπόλος οὐδέ κέ τίς μιν
> ἠγνοίησεν ἰδών, ἐπεὶ αἰπόλῳ ἔξοχ᾽ ἐῴκει.

We learn that he is a well-known minstrel :—

συρικτὰν μεγ' ὑπείροχον ἔν τε νομεῦσιν
ἔν τ' ἀμητήρεσσι

And with little delay Simichidas proposes that they shall
pastoral it together :—

Βουκολιασδώμεσθα· τάχ' ὥτερος ἄλλον ὀνασεῖ.

Lycidas, after deprecating extravagant praise, sings a song,
some of whose echoes may well have attracted Milton's ears
when he was brooding over the loss of a friend by shipwreck,
as certainly they were not forgotten when he wrote the
' Hymn on the Nativity.'   It speaks of one Ageanax, who
is voyaging to Mitylene ; and promises him calm seas, if
only he will deliver Lycidas from the love wherewith he is
consumed :—

Ἔσσεται Ἀγεάνακτι καλὸς πλόος εἰς Μυτιλάναν,
χὥταν ἐφ' ἑσπερίοις ἐρίφοις νότος ὑγρὰ διώκῃ
κύματα, χὥρίων ὅτ' ἐπ' ὠκεανῷ πόδας ἴσχει,
αἴκεν τὸν Λυκίδαν ὀπτώμενον ἐξ Ἀφροδίτας
ῥύσηται·   θερμὸς γὰρ ἔρως αὐτῶ με καταίθει.
χἀλκυόνες στορεσεῦντι τὰ κύματα τάν τε θάλασσαν
τόν τε νότον τόν τ' εὖρον ὃς ἔσχατα φυκία κινεῖ.
ἀλκυόνες γλαυκαῖς Νηρηίσι ταί τε μάλιστα
ὀρνίθων ἐφίληθεν, ὅσαις τέ περ ἐξ ἁλὸς ἄγρα.
ὥρια παντα γένοιτο, καὶ εὔπλοος ὅρμον ἵκοιτο.

An eclogue of Joh. Bapt. Amaltheus is entitled *Lycidas* :—

His deploratum in sylvis nemorumque latebris
Dicemus Lycidæ musam ; quem flumina circum
Quem flevere suo spoliati gramine colles.

Lycidas, it appears, has to leave the land that loves
him,

Jussus terras lustrare repostas ;

and in this his last song bids it adieu :—

> Effudit miseros extremo hoc carmine questus.

The lovely hills and the fields that the Muses haunt, and the liquid fountains and the caves that neighbour the fountains, and the woodland shades—he bids them all adieu. From their embrace the impious fates tear him asunder to traverse 'the monstrous world,'

> Ut videam iratas errantia monstra per undas.

He weeps for the so sweet scenes of so many happy memories, which he must now needs quit. He bethinks him of the gentle breezes amidst which he had sung so gaily, and prays them to be with him on his voyage :—

> Vos placidæ salvete auræ, mecumque per æquor
> Atque per insuetos mecum decurrite campos—
> .   .   .   .
> Nunc vero quoniam superi tot gaudia noctis
> Invidere, trucis tentare pericula ponti,
> Et Pyrenæo considere vertice certum est.

Lastly, a certain eclogue by Actius Syncerus Sannazarius, gave associations to the name Lycidas, which certainly in some degree determined Milton's choice. This is the eclogue entitled Phillis, or Phyllis in the old spelling (which was probably inspired by a false etymology.) Like Milton's poem, it is an elegy. Two shepherds, Lycidas and Mycon, on the anniversary of Phillis's death, recall that sad day and all its distresses :—

> Ecce dies aderat, charam qua Phyllida terræ
> Condidimus, tumuloque pias deflevimus umbras.

Mycon urges Lycidas to testify their grief and their love in some threnody :—

> Sed tu, siquid habes, veteres quod lugeat ignes,
> Quod manes cineresque diu testetur amatos,

> Incipe ; quandoquidem molles tibi littus arenas
> Sternit, et insani posuerunt murmura fluctus.

And standing by Phillis's tomb Lycidas wails his wail. Phillis, it appears, was to have been his bride ; and he cannot live without her.   What place will the sea-gods find for him in their domain, for he cannot but have done with the earth, and will become 'liquidi novus incola ponti ?'   Who, who was it that snatched her from his arms ?   He will seek her in the deep :—

> Nunc juvat immensi fines lustrare profundi ;
> Perque procellosas errare licentius undas
> Tritonum immistum turbis, scopulosaque cete
> Inter et informes horrenti corpore Phocas.

Then, forgetting the swift extinction to which he had just sentenced himself, he vows to build altars and offer sacrifices to his lost love.   Panope and her sisters shall weave dances in her honour.   And she shall become a deity.

> At tu sive altum felix colis æthera, seu jam
> Elysios inter manes cætusque verendos
> [Midst 'solemn troops and sweet societies ']
> Lethæos sequeris per stagna liquentia pisces ;
> Seu legis æternos formoso pollice flores,
> Narcissumque crocumque, et vivaces amaranthos,
> Et violis teneras misces pallentibus algas,
> Adspice nos mitisque veni ; tum numen aquarum
> Semper eris, semper lætum piscantibus omen.

Compare Milton's words :—

> Henceforth thou art the genius of the shore
> In thy large recompense, and shalt be good
> To all that wander in that perilous flood.

P.S.—Since writing the above note, I find with much pleasure that Mr Symonds, in his *Renaissance in Italy*, has called attention to the influence on Milton of the Renaissance Latin verse, though he does not refer to the special poems I have named.

DID MILTON SERVE IN THE PARLIAMENTARY ARMY?

(From *The Academy* for Oct. 31, 1876)

IN the second volume, pp. 472, *et seq.*, of his *Life of Milton*, Professor Masson raises the question whether the poet ever was in arms among the Parliamentarians. He seems to feel that Milton *ought* to have been so; and also he finds in his writings a singularly minute acquaintance with military matters, of which he gives some very interesting illustrations. On the whole, Professor Masson concludes that Milton did not actually serve. 'The proof positive,' he says, 'that Milton was not in the Parliamentary army is furnished by his own hand;' and he presently proceeds to quote the famous sonnet written, 'When the Assault was intended to the City.' Strangely enough, he overlooks a passage in the *Defensio Secunda*, where Milton speaks explicitly and fully on this very point. It would seem that he was conscious that some persons in his own time thought, as his learned biographer in ours, that he ought to have taken his place in the ranks, and he vindicates himself at some length. Possibly he may have suffered some appeals of conscience on the subject. We may be sure he had fully debated the question with himself in that inner 'forum.' He was not the man to shrink from any duty, however distasteful, that he recognised to be a duty, 'were it the meanest under-service, if God by his secretary—conscience—enjoin it, it were sad for me if I should draw back.' The passage from the *Second Defence* is as follows :—

Atque illi quidem (those who took up arms for the laws and religion. Deo perinde confisi, servitutem honestissimis armis pepulere; *cujus*

laudis etsi nullam partem mihi vindico, a reprehensione tamen vel
timiditatis vel ignariæ, siqua infertur, facile ne tueor.

'Neque enim *militiæ labores et pericula sic defugi*, ut non alia ratione
et operam multo utiliorem nec minore cum periculo meis civibus navarim
et animum dubiis in rebus neque demissum unquam neque ullius invidiæ
vel etiam mortis plus æquo metuentem præstiterim. Nam cum ab
adolescentulo humanioribus essem studiis ut qui maxime deditus et
ingenio semper quam corpore validior, posthabita castrensi opera, qua
me gregarius quilibet robustior facile superesset, ad ea me contuli quibus
plus potui ; ut parte mei meliore ac potiore, si saperem, non deteriore,
ad rationes patriæ causamque hanc præstantissimam quantum maxime
possem momentum accederem. Sic itaque existimabam si illos Deus
res gerere tam præclaras voluit, esse itidem alios a quibus gestas dici pro
dignitate atque ornari et defensam armis veritatem ratione etiam (quod
unicum est præsidium vere ac proprie humanum) defendi voluerit. Unde
est ut dum illos invictos acie viros admiror, de mea interim provincia
non querar ; immo mihi gratuler et gratias insuper largitori munerum
cœlesti iterum summas agam obtigisse talem ut aliis invidenda multo
magis quam mihi ullo modo poenitentia videatur.

Relying on the Divine assistance, they used every honourable exer-
tion to break the yoke of slavery ; of the praises of which, though I
claim no share myself, yet I can easily repel any charge which may
be adduced against me, either of want of courage, or want of zeal.

For though I did not participate in the toils or dangers of the war,
yet I was at the same time engaged in a service not less hazardous to
myself, and more beneficial to my fellow citizens ; nor in the adverse
turns of our affairs, did I ever betray any symptoms of pusillanimity
and dejection, or show myself more afraid than became me of malice
or of death.   For since from my youth I was devoted to the pursuits of
literature, and my mind had always been stronger than my body, I did
not court the labours of a camp, in which any common person would
have been of more service than myself, but resorted to that employment
ni which my exertions were likely to be of most avail.   Thus, with the
better part of my frame, I contributed as much as possible to the good
of my country, and to the success of the glorious cause in which we
were engaged ; and I thought that if God willed the success of such
glorious achievements, it was equally His will that there should be
others by whom those achievements should be recorded with dignity
and elegance ; and that the truth, which had been defended by arms,
should also be defended by reason, which is the best and only legitimate

means of defending it. Hence, while I applaud those who were victorious in the field, I will not complain of the province which was assigned me ; but rather congratulate myself upon it, and thank the Author of all Good for having placed me in a station, which may be an object of envy to others rather than of regret to myself.'

XIX

BUNYAN [1]

(From *The Academy* for Feb. 20, 1875)

THE *Pilgrim's Progress* is one of the strangest phenomena of literature; perhaps, indeed, the strangest.
That a man of Bunyan's position, with all its crushing dis-
advantages, should have produced a work that was at once
welcomed and loved by the class out of which its author
sprang, and eventually won the admiration of the best judgments of the nation, is an achievement without a parallel.
The case of Burns is quite different. As compared with the
Bedford tinker, the Ayrshire ploughman was born in favourable circumstances, and in his very youth acquired no mean
culture. Bunyan's high success makes one half doubt the
existence of 'mute inglorious Miltons.' His genius was
absolutely irrepressible. He was 'man and master of his
fate.' At no time of his life did he breathe a truly genial
atmosphere. Even in the society into which he was happily
raised, there were many influences that might have proved
fatal to a less hardy and sovereign spirit. One may see
from his 'Apology' for his book that among his co-religion-

[1] *The Pilgrim's Progress as Originally Published by John Bunyan, being
a Facsimile Reproduction of the First Edition.* (London : Elliot Stock.)

ists there were many who considered his 'feigning' to be of the world worldly. But all lets and hindrances—'the blows of circumstance,' the narrowness of sect, the indifference or contempt of the powers that were—all these 'invidious bars' he broke through, and in some sort found for himself freedom and power. So did 'the foolish things of the world' 'confound the wise.'

To many persons it is a distinct pleasure and a valuable help to peruse a man's writings in the very shape in which he sent them forth; to know his very orthography seems to bring the author nearer. And of course there are cases where the orthography may cast light upon the thought. But it is not only for such reasons that a facsimile reprint of *The Pilgrim's Progress* deserves notice. As we know so little of the growth of Bunyan's genius, a facsimile has special interest from the possibility that it may aid to elucidate that remarkable problem. The assistance may be inconsiderable; but certainly in the instance of Bunyan no assistance, however feeble and meagre, is to be rejected.

Only one copy of the first edition of the First Part of *The Pilgrim's Progress* is extant, so far as is known; and this is a comparatively recent find. It is in the library of H. S. Holford, Esq., of Weston-Birt House, Tetbury, Gloucestershire. It is a significant sign of the popularity of the work that the second edition was issued in the same year as the first, viz. 1678, the date of the Third Part of *Hudibras*, four years after the death of Milton, three years before the publication of *Absalom and Achitophel*. It seems fairly certain that it had been written some years before. One may well accept the common belief that 'the den' was Bedford Gaol; and it was in June, 1672, that Bunyan was released therefrom. Moreover, we may gather from the Apology above mentioned that there was an appreciable interval be-

tween the production and the publication. He was busy,
he says,

Writing of the Way
And Race of Saints in this our Gospel Day,

when he

Fell suddenly into an Allegory
About their journey and the way to Glory.

His ideas 'breed so fast' that he resolved to 'put them
by themselves.'

Well, so I did ; but yet I did not think
To shew to all the World my Pen and Ink
In such a mode ; I only thought to make
I knew not what : nor did I undertake
Thereby to please my neighbour ; no, not I ;
I did it mine own self to gratifie.

When 'mine ends' were thus put together, he consulted
others about them, and it is evident the very life of the
precious MS. was not altogether secure—

Some said Let them live ; some, Let them die ;
Some said, John, print it ; others said Not so ;
Some said It might do good ; others said No.

Thus his book, 'in wors condition than a peccant soul,'
had 'to stand before a Jury ere it' could 'be born to the
world, and undergo yet in darkness the judgment of
Rhadamanth and his colleagues ere it' could 'pass the
ferry backward into light.' In these deliberations probably
some time was spent. So that at the time of the publication
of his pilgrimage, Christian had probably been created at
least some six years The Second Part of the work was
certainly not written till the wide popularity of the First
suggested it. In this case there could be no hesitation as to
printing and publishing ; so that we may believe it was not
written, or finished, till 1683 or 1684. In the latter year it

was given to the world. There was then an interval of at least some twelve years between the composition of the two parts. Something may certainly be gathered as to Bunyan's development by comparing these representatives of two periods of his life. The difference is in many respects very striking. But obviously what the volume before us suggests, is not so much this contrast between the First and Second Parts, as the difference between the early editions of the First Part.

Messrs Unwin, the printers of the volume, inform us that the following are additions that appear in the second issue of 1678 :—

The paragraph descriptive of Bunyan's revealing his distress to his family, and of their bearing towards him ; the interruption and turning aside of Christian by Mr Worldly Wiseman (the former being represented in the first edition as going direct to the Wicket-gate from the Slough of Despond), and all the references to this incident ; the interview between Charity and Christian at the Palace Beautiful ; the meeting of Christian and Faithful with Evangelist, just previous to their entering Vanity Fair ; the list of quaint names, descriptive of the relatives of Byends ; the narrative relating to Lot's wife ; and the conversation between Giant Despair and his wife Diffidence.'[1]

Seven noticeable additions. Messrs Unwin further inform us that ‘ the characters designated Mr Hold-the-world, Mr Money-love, and Mr Save-all, appear for the first time in the third edition.’ All subsequent—eight editions were published before Bunyan's death, in 1638—changes are ‘ confined to orthography, grammar, and idiom, and the addition of fresh notes.’

Thus we learn that *The Pilgrim's Progress*, in the shape in which we have it, was no rapidly improvised production,

---

[1] For a more minute account of the additions see Godwin and Pocock's edition of *The Pilgrim's Progress*, illustrated by H. C. Selous (London, 1844).

but beyond doubt the fruit of 'poetic pains' prolonged and incessant. Like *Romeo and Juliet* and *Hamlet*, it is a growth—an inspiration slowly ripened and perfected so far as might be—a thing whose beauty and joy are no mere accidents, however divine, but the immortal results not only of an overflowing spontaneity but of a faithful loving toil, and a perpetual considerate cherishing. We see that Bunyan was a true artist, not a mere creature of impulse; that he too, with all his ignorances, had in him a fine sense of perfection; that he ever saw before him an ideal towards which he still stretched with devotion his rude-seeming hands, and the light of whose face broke and dispersed the shadows that threatened to close in upon his much-tried soul.

To learn so much about him—to see that he was ever docile as well as ever aspiring, and conscious that his work might be bettered and amended—is indeed something. But it was known, even before the copy of the first edition was discovered, that in the second edition the work was not as we have it. It did not contain, for instance, the Byends passage. What we can now see for ourselves are differences between the first and second editions.

In the Second Part no changes at all were made in the narrative. It was first published in 1684, a second time two years later, and in 1688 Bunyan died.

We have no space now to speak of other matters concerning the author of *The Pilgrim's Progress*. We will only just say, with regard to his sources, that we think his indebtedness to old romances circulating in popular shapes has not yet been sufficiently recognised. It is especially noticeable in the Second Part. What is Mr Greatheart but one of the old knights *sans peur et sans reproche*—a Sir Guy or Sir Bevis—in new surroundings? One thing more. Many who discuss Bunyan's material write as if the idea of pilgrimage was as extinct in Bunyan's age as in our own, or rather, perhaps, as it was in our own till its late grotesque revival.   In fact, the recollection of the custom must have been quite fresh in Bunyan's boyhood.   His own grand-father might have gone on pilgrimage in the good old fashion.   The old tinker, as he probably was, may have formed a not unuseful item in just such a throng as Chaucer portrays in that never-fading picture.

(From *The Academy* for April 17, 1880)[1]

It is not yet a century since Cowper shrank from naming Bunyan, warmly as he admired his great work,

> Lest so despised a name
> Should move a sneer at thy deserved fame.

And now a University Press is treating him as a classic, and he is ranked among our chief 'Men of Letters' by the excellent judgment of Mr John Morley.   This is an advance in critical freedom and catholicity on which our century may be heartily congratulated.   It began with Southey; it was promoted by Macaulay; our own day witnesses its completion.   *The Pilgrim's Progress* is now truly recognised as one of the glories of our literature.   Its value is no longer merely allowed with condescension and pity.   Not less clearly, indeed, are seen its imperfections and weaknesses; but, shining forth with a brightness that makes these com-

----

[1] *Bunyan.* By J. A. Froude. (Macmillan.)
Bunyan: The Pilgrim's Progress, Grace Abounding, and a Relation of His Imprisonment. Edited, with Biographical Introduction and Notes, by Edmund Venables, M.A., Precentor and Canon of Lincoln. (Oxford: Clarendon Press.)

paratively pale and slight, is seen also a genius of real power and brilliancy.

Certainly, in one way, Bunyan must ever be the chief wonder of our literature. No one has done so much with so little help from predecessors or contemporaries. Few works besides the Bible can be mentioned as seriously affecting or informing him. He owed something to the popularised *Romance of Chivalry;* he may have taken an idea or two from Foxe's *Book of Martyrs;* but, on the whole, Foxe probably did him more harm than good. But the Bible was, in fact, his library. The proverb tells us to beware of the man of one book; but proverbs are commonly one-sided and partial. Much depends on who the man is, and what the book. No one can overrate either the literary or the spiritual influence of the Bible upon Bunyan. But, as we have just said, there are few other literary influences worth recording. And it is difficult to conceive how Bunyan could have been brought into contact with the literary culture of his time without being ruined. For it was altogether unfavourable to such intensity and fervour as characterise his nature. The genius of Milton, indeed, flourished, and flourished nobly, in that same age. But Milton's was a personality of almost scornful independence. His soul was 'like a star ; it dwelt apart.' Not so Bunyan's. His was an eager, sympathetic spirit that would have withered in the atmosphere in which that other lived its own glorious life, lonely, exalted, supreme—

Unshaken, unseduced, unterrified.

Moreover, Bunyan was some twenty years the younger ; and the magnificent inheritance of Elizabethan traditions, in which Milton in some sense shared, was well-nigh exhausted when Bunyan grew up. Milton belongs in many respects to the great Elizabethan race. If we take Butler or Dryden as more truly representing the age to which Bunyan belonged, we shall see reason to suspect that it might have gone ill with Bunyan had he moved in their circle. How could his fervid, passionate soul have thriven there? In the midst of cynics and satirists, how could it but have languished and died? Something of the ancient chivalrous spirit lived in the bosom of this Bedfordshire tinker; he had a lingering love for knight errantry and its ways; to him were still dear the old ballads whose simplicity and artlessness had won them the contempt of the Restoration wits. Evidently, Bunyan could not have been Bunyan had he been so unfortunate as to rise in the social scale. One simply cannot imagine Mr John Bunyan, late of Elstow, sipping coffee at Button's!

Not that it is not to be regretted that he was no better educated. We will not be so disloyal to culture as not to believe it might not have vastly benefited and blessed him. But there is culture and culture; and what could have fostered and strengthened his genius was not then anywhere accessible for him.

One laudable service, for which let us ever be grateful, his age performed for him—it put him in prison. One could scarcely have expected from the Restorationists any proceeding so thoroughly sound and judicious. It may be that they did not altogether appreciate their own action; they thought, perhaps, they were taking measures to close his mouth; whereas they opened it. Supreme benefactors to Bunyan and to us, they were in fact preventing the lavish waste of his talents in sermons and such matters, and providing him with the leisure and the retirement necessary for a worthier expression of what his soul yearned to express, and must needs express, in one form or another. They to some extent silenced the preacher, but they gave immortal life and breath to the poet. Such a use of gaols seems now unhappily obsolete. It is impossible to say how many 'public men' of our time might not save their souls alive if only it could be revived—revived with some additional restrictions, such as, for instance, that the supply of writing-paper and of ink should be strictly limited. We all quote with much admiration Lovelace's lines about stone walls not making a prison, nor iron bars a cage; but we do not really believe them nowadays. In the seventeenth century they contained an accepted truth. And some of the most famous 'studies' of that period were prison cells. Famous in this way was Bunyan's place of confinement in Bedford, concerning the locality of which all that is fairly certain is that it was not the 'lock-up' on the bridge. There he was enabled to take council with himself, and depict with undying force the terrible struggles with which his 'little state of man' had been shaken and torn.

The secret of his success, as of all true success, is that he deals with realities. He could dispense with books, and such knowledge as they can give, because he could paint straight from nature. Few men that have lived have had experiences so intense, so protracted, so tremendous. Thus he found in his own history abundant material; and to give this shape became now an imperious desire. The creative instinct awoke in him, and the result was the first part of *The Pilgrim's Progress*. In the 'Author's Apology for his Book' he tells us in his own manner how he wrote it to relieve his overflowing brain. He was busy, he says, writing of 'the way and race of Saints' when he

> Fell suddenly into an allegory
> About their journey and the way to glory
> In more than twenty things which I set down;

> This done, I twenty more had in my crown,
> And they began again to multiply,
> Like sparks that from the coals of fire do fly.
>
> Thus I set pen to paper with delight,
> And quickly had my thoughts in black and white.
> For having now my method by the end
> Still, as I pulled, it came ; and so I penn'd
> It down ; until at last it came to be
> For length and breadth the bigness that you see.

It is the story of a true artist awaking to the consciousness of his gifts and to the joy of their application and use—of a creator feeling at his heart the first divine throbbings of creative energy and might.

Several of the points we have mentioned are ably and eloquently discussed by Mr Froude. But the main interest of his volume lies in its careful study of Bunyan's spiritual history and of Bunyan as the representative and spokesman of seventeenth century Puritanism. Indeed, one might perhaps complain that Mr Froude does not enough consider Bunyan for his own sake, so to speak, but rather makes use of him for the consideration of the religious question. It is here that his volume is faulty ; and it is for this reason that one closes it with Mr Froude on one's mind rather than John Bunyan. Mr Froude is not sufficiently disengaged and unimpassioned to write with due critical calmness and self-suppression of a work that, in certain ways, moves him so deeply as *The Pilgrim's Progress*. He cannot stand outside his subject and, vividly and disinterestedly bringing it before us, let it speak for itself. It is as if, in showing us a portrait, the painter should place his own head close alongside of it, and by his brilliant monologue and in other ways so attract us that we should find ourselves thinking about the painter and not the painted. Mr Froude is one of those persons who must take a side and fight vigorously on it ; and this is not a disposition favourable for the production of sound criticism. Still, there is much to be thankful for, and no admirer of Bunyan must abstain from reading this fresh contribution to the literature that is gathering around Bunyan's name.

The Clarendon Press volume before us provides an excellently printed text of *The Pilgrim's Progress and Grace Abounding*, together with *A Relation of his Imprisonment*. *The Grace Abounding* is well placed by the side of *The Pilgrim's Progress*, for, as Mr Froude well says, the latter work 'is the same story which he has told of himself in *Grace Abounding* thrown out into an objective form.' The 'Biographical Introduction' is well informed and well written. Canon Venables does not settle the question as to which side Bunyan served on in the Civil War, but holds it most probable that it was the side of the Parliament. Certainly Macaulay is scarcely justified in speaking so positively of his enlisting in the Parliamentary army; but we incline to think Mr Froude is wrong in agreeing with those who assign him to the Royalists. For the rest, Mr Venables' notes are, on the whole, useful and illustrative. Now and then they are somewhat irrelevant—that is, if the first purpose of notes is to enlighten the text, and not to convey general information. Thus, *à propos* of 'they will stick like burs,' we are told that 'bur is allied to the French *bourre*,' etc., in a paragraph ten lines long! This, and several other notes, as those on *beshrew, trespass, churl, respit, caitiff*, should, if inserted at all, have been inserted in a glossary at the end of the volume. They really interrupt the study of the text, whatever philological or other value they may have. Mr Venables is disposed to think that Bunyan was acquainted with *The Fairy Queen*. This is a question never yet thoroughly discussed. Indeed, we may say that the general question of Bunyan's sources and models has never yet been fully considered.

His one great quarry was, as we have said, the Bible; but there were other works, few no doubt, but not to be forgotten, if we would understand how his mind was furnished. For instance, we know he had read *Bevis of Hampton;* and something might be said of the influence on him of this and other old romances. *Caught* is *not* a 'strong' preterite (see p. 448), though Mr Venables has many companions in that error. The cockle-shell (p. 482) was not a badge of all pilgrims, but properly of those to Compostella. On p. 291, 1666 is given as the date of the publication of *Grace Abounding,* but in the work itself (see p. 391) Bunyan speaks of having lain in prison 'now complete twelve years,' *i.e.,* is writing in 1672. Mr Venables is 'provoked' by 'the exceeding beauty' of the Shepherd Boy's song in the Valley of Humiliation, 'so unlike the rugged rhymes and halting measure of Bunyan's verse generally,' to doubt whether it was 'really composed by him, and not rather, like the stanzas from the Old Version of the Psalms on p. 218, taken from some other source.' As to such a conjecture, what Mr Froude has to say on pp. 92–95 is well worth reading.

XX

THE REVIVAL OF BALLAD POETRY IN THE EIGHTEENTH CENTURY

(From the printed edition of the *Percy Folio MS.*, 1867)

I DO not now propose to attempt a full description of the great literary revolution which took place in the last century. But I propose confining myself to one particular feature of it—the appreciation of our older literature, and especially of our ballad poetry. The century that had long been fully satisfied with its own productions, at last recognised that the English literature of ages that had preceded it was not wholly barbarous. The century that had given up itself to rules, and reduced the art of poetry to a mechanical trick, at last acknowledged graces beyond the reach of its art. At last it was brought to see that there were more things in heaven and earth than were dreamt of in its philosophy.

It discovered that there were innumerable beauties around it to which it had long been blind. It left its gardens and its elaborate manipulations of nature to see Nature· herself. It gave over refining the lily and gilding the rose to look at the flowers in their simple beauty. It became conscious of the exquisite beauties and glories of Switzerland, of the

258

English lakes, of Wales. New worlds of splendour, and of noble enjoyment, dawned upon it. Not greater discoveries were made by Columbus and his followers four centuries before than were then made. The age, with all its self-complaisance, had been living in a prison. The doors were thrown open, and it came forth to feel and enjoy the fresh breezes and the gracious sunshine. The age saw at the same time that, besides the beauties of nature, there were beauties that the art of former days had bequeathed it. It began to discern the subtle loveliness of old cathedral churches that studded the country. It had long eyed them with much disfavour. It had sadly disfigured them with adornments of its own devising, and according with its own notions. It had deplored them as monstrous relics of a profound barbarism. But at last the scales fell from its eyes, and it saw that these 'tabernacles of the Lord of Hosts' were 'amiable.' It awoke to their supreme, unstinted, refined beautifulness. So with respect to other branches of Gothic art, other fruits of the old Romantic times, it came to a better appreciation of them. Poets and poems that had for many a day been relegated to neglect and oblivion, were more frankly and fairly valued. Voices that had long been silenced or ignored began to find a hearing and a heeding audience. As Classical literature was revived in the fifteenth, so was Romantic in the eighteenth.

A fair criterion of the progress of the century in the recognition of the Romantic ages is its appreciation of Chaucer. The most important event of the century regarding him is the appearance of Tyrwhitt's edition of *The Canterbury Tales* in 1775. Then at last an attempt was made to vindicate his fame from the imputation of rudeness; to show that he, no less than the eighteenth-century poets, had some sense of melody, some talent for character-drawing, some power of language.　Spenser was more readily and continuously accepted.　The age sympathised with the moralising part of his genius, and found pleasure in imitating him. But, as I have said, I propose now considering the history of our ballad poetry ; and to it I turn.

The most signal event regarding it is the publication of Percy's *Reliques of Ancient English Poetry* in 1765.　Let us see how the century was prepared, or had been preparing, for that famous publication.

Our English ballads, though highly popular in the Elizabethan age, as innumerable allusions to them in Shakespeare and the other dramatists, and in the general literature of the time, show, were yet never collected into any volume, save in *Garlands*, till the year 1723.　They wandered up and down the country without even sheepskins or goatskins to protect them.　They flew about like the birds of the air, and sung songs dear to the heart of the common people—songs whose power was sometimes confessed by the 'higher' classes, but not so thoroughly appreciated as to induce them to exert themselves for their preservation.　They were looked down upon as things that were very good in their proper place, but must not be admitted into fashionable society.　They were admired in a condescending manner.　They were much better than could be expected.　But no one thought of them as popular lyrics of great intrinsic value.　Scarcely anyone put forth a hand to save them from perishing.　The custom of covering the walls of houses with them that happily prevailed in the seventeenth century did something for their preservation. So secured, they had a better chance of keeping a place in men's memories, and meeting some day appreciative eyes. Towards the end of the said century were made one or two collections of the broad sheets containing them.　The black letter literature of the people was collected rather for its curiousness than its power or beauty, by antiquaries rather than by poets or enjoyers of poetry. Whatever their motives, let us praise Wood and Harley, Selden[1] and Pepys, Rawlinson, Douce, and Bagford, for their services in gathering together and protecting the frail outcasts from destruction.

There can be no doubt that the powerful mind of Dryden justly appreciated the strength of our old literature, although he so far bows before the spirit of his age as to deface it for the reception of that age. Even when he revised and spoiled Chaucer's works, he felt the power of them. But he resigned his own judgment to that of his contemporaries. This Samson in his captivity consented to make merry and carouse with his captors—to translate the songs he loved into the Philistine dialect. He had a fine appreciation of the old ballads. 'I have heard,' says a *Spectator*, 'that the late Lord Dorset, who had the greatest wit tempered with the greatest candour, and was one of the finest critics as well as the best poets of his age, had a numerous collection of old English ballads, and took a particular pleasure in the reading of them. I can affirm the same of Mr Dryden, and know several of the most refined writers of our present age who are of the same humour.' He is, I think, the first collector of poems who conceded to popular ballads their due place—who admitted them into the society of other poems—poems by the most Eminent Hands—who perceived their excellence, and welcomed them accordingly. To other collectors of that date it was as disgraceful to a poem as to a man to have no father, or to be suspected of a common origin. Dryden rose above this prejudice. He showed one or two ballads the same hospitality as he extended to the poetasters of Oxford and

[1] Tradition says that Pepys 'borrowed' a part of his Collection from Selden, and forgot to return it.—W. Chappell.

Cambridge, whose name was Legion at this time. In the *Miscellany Poems*, edited by him, of which the first volume appeared in 1684, the last in 1708, eight years after his death, are to be found *Little Musgrave and the Lady Bernard*, certainly one of the most vigorous ballads in our language ; *Chevy Chase*, with a rhyming Latin translation ; *Johnnie Armstrong*, *Gilderoy*, *The Miller and the King's Daughters*. But the evil that men do lives after them. Dryden, in his *Knight's Tale* and other works, had set the fashion of imitating and modernising our old poems. That fashion survived him. For more than half a century after his death, with the exception of the insertion of two or three in Playford's[1] *Wit and Mirth, or Pills to purge Melancholy*, and of the *Collection of Old Ballads* above referred to, we have produced in England imitations or adaptations of ballads—no faithful reprint of the genuine thing. The wine that the age had given it to drink was a miserable dilution, or only coloured water. Conspicuous amongst these imitators or adapters were Parnell, Prior, and Tickell. But there were two men in Queen Anne's time who had a genuine relish for old ballads, and who said a good word for them. These were Addison and Rowe. Addison's taste for them had been awakened during his travels on the Continent. 'When I travelled,' he writes, 'I took a particular delight in hearing the songs and fables that are come from father to son, and are most in vogue among the common people of the countries through which I passed ; for it is impossible that anything should be universally tasted and approved by a multitude, though they are only the rabble of a nation, which hath not in it some peculiar apt-

---

[1] This Collection, though generally called D'Urfey's, was Henry Playford's. D'Urfey edited only the last edition (1719), in six volumes. Five were printed in 1714 ; the first volume in 1699.—W. Chappell.

ness to please and gratify the mind of man.' He gives, as is well known, two numbers of the *Spectator* to a consideration of *Chevy Chase*, one to that of the *Children in the Wood.* 'The old song of *Chevy Chase*,' he writes, 'is the favourite ballad of the common people of England, and Ben Jonson used to say he had rather have been the author of it than of all his works.' Then he quotes Sir Philip Sidney's famous words; and then adds, 'For my own part I am so professed an admirer of this antiquated song that I shall give my reader a critick upon it, without any further apology for so doing.' And he proceeds to investigate the poem according to the critical rules of his time. He compares it with other heroic poems, and illustrates it from Virgil and Horace. He read the old ballad in the light of his age— viewed and reviewed it in a somewhat narrow spirit. But he did read it—he did look at it. In spite of the confining criticism and hypercriticism of the day, he did feel and recognise its vigour. 'Thus we see,' his *examen* concludes, 'how the thoughts of this poem, which naturally arise from the subject, are always simple, and sometimes exquisitely noble; that the language is often very sounding, and that the whole is written with a true poetical spirit.' In another paper he calls attention to and expresses the 'most exquisite pleasure' he had received from *The Two Children in the Wood*, which he had encountered pasted upon the wall of some house in the country. He describes it as 'one of the darling songs of the common people,' and as having been 'the delight of most Englishmen in some part of their age;' and then he discusses it after his manner. 'The tale of it is a pretty tragical story, and pleases for no other reason but because it is a copy of nature. There is even a despicable simplicity in the verse; and yet because the sentiments appear genuine and unaffected, they are able to move the mind of the most polite reader with inward meltings of humanity and compassion.'   But he could not bring his contemporaries to sympathise with him.   They would not hear, charmed he never so wisely.   His *Chevy Chase* papers were ridiculed and parodied by Dennis and Wagstaff and similar witlings.   To them, perhaps, he alludes in the concluding words of his notice of the other ballad he reviews: 'As for the little conceited wits of the age,' he writes, 'who can only show their judgment by finding fault, they cannot be supposed to admire those productions which have nothing to recommend them but the beauties of nature, when they do not know how to relish even those compositions that, with all the beauties of nature, have also the additional advantages of art.'   He fought a losing battle.   What appreciation of the old things there was at the beginning of the century was rapidly decaying.   An age of elaborate artificiality, and studied affectation, was dawning.

I have mentioned Rowe as sharing Addison's appreciation of the old ballads.   He takes for one of his plays a subject that was the theme of a widely popular ballad, and in introducing his tragedy, deprecates the adverse prejudices of his audience, and speaks boldly in favour of the older literature, and against the wretched affectations of his time. The Prologue to his *Jane Shore*, first acted in 1713, opens thus :

> To-night, if you have brought your good old taste,
> We'll treat you with a downright English feast,
> A tale which, told long since in homely wise,
> Hath never failed of melting gentle eyes.
> Let no nice sir despise the hapless dame
> Because recording ballads chaunt her name ;
> Those venerable ancient song-enditers
> Soared many a pitch above our modern writers.
> They caterwauled in no romantic ditty,
> Sighing for Philis's or Cloe's pity ;

> Justly they drew the Fair, and spoke her plain,
> And sung her by her Christian name—'twas Jane.
> Our numbers may be more refined than those,
> But what we've gained in verse, we've lost in prose ;
> Their words no shuffling double·meaning knew,
> Their speech was homely, but their hearts were true.
> In such an age immortal Shakespear wrote.
> By no quaint rules nor hampering critics taught,
> With rough majestic force he moved the heart,
> And strength and nature made amends for art,
> Our humble author does his steps pursue ;
> He owns he had the mighty bard in view ;
> And in these scenes has made it more his care
> To rouse the passions than to charm the ear.

But this advocacy, too, of a better taste was doomed to fail. Rowe, as Addison, spoke in vain. The literary dominion of France was growing more and more supreme. Protests in behalf of our old masters were urged fruitlessly. The charms of our ballad poetry were disregarded, were despised.

There were, however, others besides Addison and Rowe who had some slight sense of those charms, as, for instance, those whom we have named—Parnell, Tickell, Prior. Parnell's acquaintance with our older literature is shown in his *Fairy Tale in the Ancient English Style*. It is but a feeble piece, written in a favourite Romance metre—the metre of Chaucer's *Tale of Sir Topas*—and decorated with occasional bits of bad grammar to give it an antique look. Tickell's friendship with Addison could not but have conduced to some familiarity on his part with the old ballads. He seems to have been inspired by them in no ordinary degree. *Apropos* of his *Lucy aud Colin*, Goldsmith remarks : 'Through all Tickell's works there is a strain of ballad-thinking, if I may so express it ; and in this professed ballad he seems to have surpassed himself. It is perhaps the best in our language in this way.' The writer of it has

evidently drunk from the old wells. The story is simple.
It is told in a queer style—a sort of strange compromise
between the simplicity of the old ballad language and the
superfine verbiage that was rising into esteem in Tickell's
own day. Lucy, the reader may remember, is deserted by
her lover for a richer bride. She cannot survive this cruelty,
She says, to quote well-known lines,—

> I hear a voice you cannot hear,
>   Which says I must not stay.
> I see a hand you cannot see,
>   Which beckons me away.

She is buried on the day of her false lover's marriage. The
funeral cortège encounters the hymeneal. The bridegroom's
old passion, too late, revives.

> Confusion, shame, remorse, despair
>   At once his bosom swell;
> The damps of death bedew his brow;
>   He shook, he groaned, he fell.

There is not the true note here, but there is a distant echo
of it. In the handsome folio volume of poems published
by Matthew Prior in 1718 was printed the *Not-Browne
Maide*, not for its own sake, but for the sake of a piece
called *Henry and Emma*, an extremely loose paraphrase of
it, that the reader might see how magic was Mr Prior's
touch, who could transmute so rude an effort into a work so
finely polished. However, Prior deserves some credit for
having brought the old poem forward at all. His *Henry
and Emma* won great applause. What a strange, instructive,
significant fact, that when such a paraphrase and such an
original were placed before them, men should deliberately
choose the paraphrase. No plea that the language was
obscure can be advanced in this case, as for Dryden's and

Pope's versions of some of the *Canterbury Tales*. There is no obscurity in these words :

> O Lorde, what is
> This worldis blisse,
> That chaungeth as the mone !
> The somers day
> In lusty may
> Is derked before the mone.
> I hear you say
> Farewel ! Nay, nay,
> We departe not soo sone ;
> Why say ye so ?
> Wheder wyle ye goo ?
> Alas ! what have ye done ?
> Alle my welfare
> To sorow and care
> Shulde chaunge yf ye were gon ;
> For in my mynde
> Of all mankynde
> I loue but you alone.

But Prior's age did not care for their simple beauty. It could not value that art *quæ celat artem*. To the above delightful speech it preferred the following :—

> What is our bliss, that changeth with the moon,
> And day of life, that darkens ere 'tis noon ?
> What is true passion, if unblest it dies ?
> And where is Emma's joy, if Henry flies ?
> If love, alas ! be pain, the pain I bear
> No thought can figure, and no tongue declare.
> Ne'er faithful woman felt, nor false one feign'd
> The flames which long have in my bosom reign'd ;
> The God of love himself inhabits there,
> With all his rage, and dread, and grief, and care,
> His complement of stores and total war.
> Oh ! cease then coldly to suspect my love,
> And let my deed at least my faith approve.
> Alas ! no youth shall my endearments share,
> Nor day nor night shall interrupt my care ;

No future story shall with truth upbraid
The cold indifference of the nut-brown maid ;
Nor to hard banishment shall Henry run,
While careless Emma sleeps on beds of down.
View me resolved, where'er thou lead'st, to go,
Friend to thy pain, and partner of thy woe ;
For I attest fair Venus and her son,
That I, of all mankind, will love but thee alone.

Early in the reign of George I., then, the old ballads had grown insipid. Men had no longer eyes to see their wild graces. An age of rules was shocked by their fine irregularity. A moralising and sentimentalising age was horrified at their plain-spokenness and objectivity. A didactic age could conceive no interest in such spontaneous songs. It had narrow ideas of what is instructive, and it wanted instructing. It did not understand the singing as the linnet sings. It wanted its theories illustrated, discussed, enforced. In a word, it confounded poetry and morality. It did not cultivate, and it lost the faculty of pure enjoyment. No wonder then, if, finding no response to its ideas in the old ballads, it turned away from them, and would not answer when they called, would not dance when they piped.

But even at this time, when they were rapidly nearing the *nadir* of their popularity, the ballads found a friend. In 1723 appeared a volume of collected ballads, followed three years afterwards by a second, in 1727 by a third. These three volumes formed that first collection of English ballads (there is only one Scotch[1] ballad among them) to which we

---

[1] Songs and ballads of rustic and of humble life were called 'Scotch' from about the middle of the 17th century, and without any intention of imputing to them a Scottish origin, or that they were imitations. The same had before been called 'Northern.' Mr Payne Collier repeatedly reminds the readers of the Registers of the Stationers' Company that this word 'northern' means 'rustic.' (See *Notes and Queries*, Dec. 28, 1861, p. 514; Feb. 8, 1862, p. 106; Feb. 21, 1863, p. 145.) The substitution of 'Scotch' seems

have above adverted.   Denmark had made collections of its ballads in 1591 and in 1695 ; Spain in 1510, 1555, 1566, and 1615.   England—save the earlier *Garlands*—first did so in 1723.   Scotland, without, so far as we know, any knowledge of what had been done in England, in the following year, when Allan Ramsay, a great student of 'the Bruce,' 'the Wallis,' and Lyndsay's works, having 'observed that Readers of the best and most exquisite Discernment frequently complain of our modern Writings as filled with affected Delicacies and studied Refinements, which they would gladly exchange for that natural strength of thought and simplicity of style our Forefathers practised,' published his *Ever-Green*, 'being a collection of Scots Poems wrote by the Ingenious before 1600,' and in the same year *The Tea-Table Miscellany, or a Collection of Scots Sangs*, 'in three volumes.'   All three Collections seem to have enjoyed a fair success.   Who was the author of the English one is not known.[1]

to have commenced during the civil war, and perhaps only after Charles II. had been crowned King of Scots, when 'Scotch' at length became a popular, and even a party word with the Cavaliers.   The first writer in whom I have noted the change is Martin Parker, author of the famous Cavalier ballad 'When the King shall enjoy his own again.'   (See, for instance, 'A pair of turtle doves, or a dainty new Scotch dialogue between a young man and his mistresse,' subscribed Martin Parker, *Pop. Music*, p. 452.)   After him came Tom D'Urfey, and many more.   The use extended till, at length, even ballads relating to the northern counties of England, and so, in every sense 'northern,' were reprinted as Scotch.   (See, for instance, 'Nanny O,' *Pop. Music*, p. 610, note *a*.)   This conventional meaning of 'Scotch' seems to have been accepted in Scotland as well as in England, for in no other sense could Allan Ramsay claim, among others, Gay's ballad, 'Black-ey'd Susan,' in the very first part of 'A Miscellany of Scots Sangs,' or W. Thomson appropriate songs by Ambrose Phillips and other well-known Englishmen, in his *Orpheus Caledonius*.   This remark is necessary, because Percy has, throughout, taken the words 'northern' and 'Scotch' only in their literal local sense.—W. Chappell.

[1] Dr Farmer ascribes it to Ambrose Phillips.   See Lowndes, under 'Ballads.'—W. Chappell.

It is called 'A Collection of Old Ballads corrected from the best and most ancient copies extant, with Introductions, Historical, Critical, or Humorous, illustrated with copper plates.' The editor adopts an apologetic motto for his book—some of the above quoted words of Rowe. He writes, too, in an apologetic vein. 'There are many,' he says, 'who perhaps will think it ridiculous enough to enter seriously into a Dissertation upon Ballads.' He is evidently rather afraid of being thought a frivolous creature by his lofty-minded contemporaries. He is a little uneasy in introducing his protégés to the polished public. But he does his duty by them bravely, only indulging himself now and then in a little superior laugh at their expense. He gives what account he can of the theme of each one, and shows always a thorough interest in his work. But the time was not yet ripe for his labours. The popularity that attended the first appearance of his collection soon ceased. The predominant character of the age was not changed. The old voices could not yet secure a hearing. The age clung to its idols. Its Pharisaic spirit was too strong to be restrained. It could not yet believe that out of the mouth of the common people there was ordained strength.

After the middle of the century some promise was shown of a better era. In Capell's '*Prolusions, or Select Pieces of Antient Poetry*, compil'd with great care from their several Originals, and offer'd to the Publick as Specimens of the Integrity that should be found in the Editions of Worthy Authors,' published in 1760, appeared the *Not-browne Mayde*, no longer accompanied by a modernised version. This book gives hints of the reaction that was coming against the old manipulating method. 'Fidelity to the best Texts' is its watchword. In the same year (1760) appeared Macpherson's Ossian, and produced an immense sensation.

Bishop Percy, with the good wishes and assistance of many then distinguished men—of Shenstone, Garrick, Joseph Warton, Farmer—was supplementing the treasures of his wonderful Folio MS. from other quarters, and preparing the materials of his *Reliques of Ancient English Poetry*. About the same time (1764) appeared Evans's *Specimens of the Poetry of the Antient Welsh Bards*. Mallet's work on *The Remains of the Mythology and Poetry of the Celtes, particularly of Scandinavia*, had already been published some years. About the same time Gray was writing his Welsh and Scandinavian pieces. At the same time Chatterton was striving to satisfy the new taste that was spreading with forgeries of old poems,. The first decade, then, of George III.'s reign is most memorable in the history of the revival of our ballad poetry. Then commenced an appreciation of it which has grown stronger and stronger with the lapse of years. Then it found itself so well supported that it was able to hold up its head in spite of peremptory contemptuous criticism. It feared no more the frowns of the great. Its beauty was no longer to be hid— its light no longer veiled away from men's eyes. 'Even from the tomb the voice of nature cried.' In the midst of conventionalisms and artificialities, Simplicity and Truth asserted themselves. The age was growing sick and weary of its old darlings; growing sensible that there was no salvation in them, no infallibility, no supreme delight in their worships:

Naturam expellas furcâ, tamen usque recurret.

Cinderella had sat by the kitchen fire for many a day. For many a day the elder sisters, tricked out in all the modish finery of the time, every attitude studied, every look elaborated, every movement affected, had possessed the drawing-room in all their fashionable state. Cinderella down in the kitchen had heard the rustle of their fine silks and satins, and the sound of their polite conversation. She had been perplexed by their polished verbiage, and felt her own awkwardness and rusticity. She had never dared to think herself beautiful. No admiring eyes ever came near her in which she might mirror herself. She had never dared to think her voice sweet. No rapt ears ever drank in fondly its accents. She felt herself a plain-faced, dull-souled, uninteresting person not worthy to receive any attention from any one of the fine gentlemen who adored her sisters, or to enter their well-mannered society. But her lowliness was to be regarded. The songs she had sung in the kitchen to the servants—her humble, unpretentious songs—they were to find greater favour than ever did those of her much-complimented sisters. It was about the year 1760 when the possibility of so great a change in her condition became first conceivable. She met with many enemies, who clamoured that the kitchen was her proper place, and vehemently opposed her admission into any higher room. The Prince was long in finding her out. The sisters put many an obstacle between him and her. They could not understand the failure of their own attractions. They could not appreciate the excellence of hers. But at last the Prince found her, and took her in all her simple sweetness to himself. At last, to lay metaphors aside, England acknowledged the power and beauty of the ballads that had suffered for so long a time such grievous neglect.

At the accession of George III., William Whitehead was in the third year of his adornment of the Poet Laureateship. *The Pleasures of Imagination, The Schoolmistress, The Complaint, or Night Thoughts on Life, Death, and Immortality*—works which had been given to the world some sixteen or eighteen years before—were at the zenith of their fame. The general character of our literature at this time was highly didactic. We cannot wonder, then, if the appearance of a poetry that was weighted with no overbearing moral, or other purpose, produced a tremendous effect. We may be prepared to understand the prodigious excitement caused by the publication in 1760 of *The Works of Ossian the Son of Fingal,* 'translated for the Gaelic language by James Macpherson.' With all their magniloquence, they did not sermonise; they expressed some genuine feeling. Amidst all their affected cries there was a true voice audible. Three years subsequently, Bishop Percy, moved by Ossian's popularity, published a translation from the Icelandic language of five pieces of Runic poetry.

In the following year, 1764, appeared 'Some Specimens of the Poetry of the Ancient Welsh Bards translated into English, with Explanatory Notes on the Historical Passages, and a short Account of Men and Places mentioned by the Bards, in order to give the Curious some Idea of the Taste and Sentiments of our Ancestors and their Manner of Writing, by the Rev. Mr Evan Evans, curate of Glenvair Talyhaern, in Denbighshire'—a work with which Gray was familiar. Shortly afterwards appeared Gray's own translations, made from translations, of Norse and Welsh pieces: *The Fatal Sisters, The Descent of Odin, The Triumphs of Owen,* and *The Death of Hoel.* About the time, then, of the appearance of the *Reliques* in 1765, there was dispersed over the country some slight knowledge of the Old Celtic and of Scandinavian poetry.

And now the age was ripe for the reception of such a collection of old ballads as had been published some forty years, but had then, after a short-lived circulation, fallen into neglect. Thomas Percy, the son of a grocer, at Bridgenorth, Shropshire, a graduate of Oxford, vicar of Easton

Maudit, Northamptonshire, was by nature something of an antiquary. When 'very young,' he became possessed of a folio MS. of old ballads and romances. 'This very curious old MS.,' he says, in a memorandum made in the old folio itself, 'in its present mutilated state, but unbound and sadly torn, I rescued from destruction, and begged at the hands of my worthy friend Humphrey Pitt, Esq., then living at Shiffnal in Shropshire, afterwards of Prior Lee near that town; who died very lately at Bath; viz. in Summer 1769. I saw it lying dirty on the floor under a Bureau in ye Parlour, being used by the maids to light the fire. When I first got possession of this MS.,' he says in another entry in the same place, 'I was very young, and being in no degree an Antiquary, I had not then learnt to reverence it; which must be my excuse for the scribble which I then spread over some parts of its margin, and in one or two instances for even taking out the leaves, to save the trouble of transcribing. I have since been more careful.' Besides this famous folio, he possessed also a quarto MS. volume of similar pieces, supposed to be the same as one still in the hands of his family, and containing only copies of printed poems. The folio has remained in the hands of the Bishop's family in the greatest privacy hitherto; Jamieson and Sir F. Madden being (I believe) the only editors who have printed from it, though Dibdin was allowed to catalogue part of it. These volumes had in Percy a (for that time) highly appreciative possessor. He determined to introduce to the public some specimens of their contents. This proposal was promoted by the sympathy of many then distinguished men: of Shenstone, Bird, Grainger, Steevens, Farmer, and by others of still greater and more enduring note—Garrick and Goldsmith. At last, in 1765, appeared *Reliques of Ancient English Poetry*, *consisting of Old Heroic Ballads, Songs, and other pieces of our earlier poets (chiefly of the Lyric kind) together with some few of later date.* The editor, even as the editor of the collection of 1723, of whom we have spoken, has, manifestly, some misgivings about the character of his protégés. He is not quite sure how they will be received by his polite contemporaries. He speaks of them, in his Dedication of his volumes to the Countess of Northumberland (he was extremely ambitious to connect himself with the great Percies of the North), as 'the rude songs of ancient minstrels,' 'the barbarous productions of unpolished ages,' and is troubled for fear lest he should be guilty of some impropriety in hoping that they 'can obtain the approbation or the notice of her, who adorns courts by her presence, and diffuses elegance by her example. But this impropriety, it is presumed, will disappear when it is declared that these poems are presented to your Ladyship, not as labours of art but as effusions of nature, shewing the first efforts of ancient genius, and exhibiting the customs and opinions of remote ages.' In his Preface he says that 'as most of' the contents of his folio MS. 'are of great simplicity, and seem to have been merely written for the people, the possessor was long in doubt, whether in the present state of improved literature they could be deemed worthy the attention of the public. At length the importunity of his friends prevailed.' 'In a polished age, like the present,' he adds, 'I am sensible that many of these reliques of antiquity will require great allowances to be made for them. Yet have they, for the most part, a pleasing simplicity, and many artless graces, which in the opinion of no mean critics [a footnote cites Addison, Dryden, Lord Dorset, etc., and Selden] have been thought to compensate for the want of higher beauties, and if they do not dazzle the imagination [Did *The School-mistress, The Sugar-cane,* dazzle the imagination?] are frequently found to interest the heart.'   Still more striking are the following words: 'To atone for the rudeness of the more obsolete poems, each volume concludes with a few modern attempts in the same kind of writing.'   And then he buttresses his volumes with eminent names—Shenstone, Thomas Warton, Garrick, Johnson (we shall see presently how far Johnson was likely to smile on his undertaking), which 'names of so many men of learning and character, the editor hopes will serve as an amulet, to guard him from every unfavourable censure for having bestowed any attention on a parcel of Old Ballads.   It was at the request of many of these gentlemen, and of others eminent for their genius and taste, that this little work was undertaken.   To prepare it for the press has been the amusement of now and then a vacant hour amid the leisure and retirement of rural life, and hath only served as a relaxation from graver studies.   It hath been taken up and thrown aside for many months during an interval of four or five years.'   With such apologies and antidotes did the Reliques make their *début!*   How strange —what a wonderful tale of altered taste it tells—that in order to make *Chevy Chase*, *Edom o' Gordon*, *Little Musgrave and Lady Barnard* endurable, to reconcile the reader to their rudeness, such charming *chaperones* should be assigned them as *Bryan and Pereene*, a West Indian ballad by Dr Grainger, *Jemmy Dawson*, by Mr Shenstone!   *Bryan and Pereene*, 'founded on a real fact,' narrates how Pereene, 'the pride of Indian dames,' went down to the sea-shore to meet her lover, who after an absence in England of one long long year one month and day, was returning to St Christopher's and his mistress

> Soon as his well-known ship she spied
> She cast her weeds away,

> And to the palmy shore she hied
>   All in her best array.
>
> In sea-green silk, so neatly clad
>   She there impatient stood ;

Bryan, seeing her in the said sea-green silk, impatient also, leapt overboard in the hope of reaching her sooner.

> The crew with wonder saw the lad
>   Repell the foaming flood.
>
> Her hands a handkerchief display'd,
>   Which he at parting gave ;
> Well-pleas'd the token he survey'd,
>   And manlier beat the wave.
>
> Her fair companions one and all
>   Rejoicing crowd the strand ;
> For now her lover swam in call,
>   And almost touch'd the land.
>
> Then through the white surf did she haste,
>   To clasp her lovely swain ;
> When ah ! a shark bit through his waist,
>   His heart's blood dy'd the main.
>
> He shriek'd ! His half sprang from the wave,
>   Streaming with purple gore,
> And soon it found a living grave,
>   And ah ! was seen no more.
>
> Now haste, now haste, ye maids, I pray,
>   Fetch water from the spring ;
> She falls, she swoons, she dies away,
>   And soon her knell they ring.

And so the doleful ditty ends with an injunction to the 'fair' to strew her tomb with fresh flowerets every May morning, to the end that they and their lovers may not come to similar distress. Jemmy Dawson was one of the Manchester rebels who took part in the '45, and was hanged, drawn, and quartered on Kennington Common in 1746.

> Their colours and their sash he wore,
>   And in the fatal dress was found ;
> And now he must that death endure,
>   Which gives the brave the keenest wound.
>
> How pale was then his true love's cheek,
>   When Jemmy's sentence reach'd her ear ;
> For never yet did Alpine snows,
>   So pale, nor yet so chill appear.
>
> With faltering voice she weeping said :
>   Oh ! Dawson, monarch of my heart,
> Think not thy death shall end our loves,
>   For thou and I will never part.

Poor Kitty inflexibly witnesses his execution.

> The dismal scene was o'er and past,
>   The lover's mournful hearse retir'd ;
> The maid drew back her languid head,
>   And sighing forth his name expir'd.

Such were the pieces whose elegance was to make atonement to the readers of a century ago, for the barbarousness of the other components of the *Reliques*.

This barbarousness was further mitigated by an application of a polishing process to the ballads themselves. Percy performed the offices of a sort of tireman for them. He dressed and adorned them to go into polite society. To how great an extent he laboured in their service, is now at last manifested by the publication of the Folio. The old MS. contained many pieces which, it would seem, were considered hopeless. No amount of manipulation could ever make them presentable. It contained many pieces and many fragments—thanks to the anxiety of Mr Humphrey Pitt's servants to light his fires !—which the art of the editorial refiner of the eighteenth century deemed capable of adaptation ; and Percy adapted them. The old ballads could reckon on no genuine sympathy. They were, so to speak, the songs of Zion in a strange land.

Percy, as the extracts we have quoted from his Dedication and Preface have shown, was not free from the prejudices of his time. He was but slightly in advance of them ; but he *was* in advance of them. He *did* recognise the power and beauty of the old poetry, more deeply, perhaps, than he ever dared confess. And, though unconscious of the greatness of the work he was doing, did for us—for Europe—an unutterable service. He was, to the end, curiously unconscious of it. Men are often reminded to be delicately careful in their actions, because they know not what harm they may do. They might sometimes be encouraged by the thought that they know not what good they do. Certainly Percy performed for English literature a far higher service than he ever dreamt of. He always regarded the *Reliques* as something rather frivolous. 'I read *Edwin and Angelina* to Mr Percy some years ago,' writes Goldsmith, in 1767, to the printer of the *St James' Chronicle*, who had assigned Goldsmith's ballad to Percy, 'and he (as we both considered these things as trifles at best) told me, with his usual good-humour, the next time I saw him, that he had taken my plan to form the fragments of Shakespeare into a ballad of his own. He then read me his little cento, if I may so call it, and I highly approved of it.' 'I am so little interested about *the amusements of my youth,*' writes Percy to his publisher in 1794, 'that, had it not been for the benefit of my nephew, I could contentedly have let the *Reliques of Ancient Poetry* remain unpublished.' The great effect the memorable work produced came ' not with observation.'

With all the consideration Percy showed for the prevailing taste, he did not succeed in winning over to his support certain great leaders of it. He was extremely solicitous to secure the approval of the leader of the leaders of it—of that supreme potentate, Dr Johnson. In his Preface he twice mentions him: first, as having urged him to publish a selection from the Folio ('He could refuse nothing,' he says, 'to such judges as the author of the *Rambler*, and the late Mr Shenstone'); and secondly, as having lightened his editorial task with his assistance ('To the friendship of Mr Johnson,' he writes, 'he owes many valuable hints for the conduct of his work'). But, for all these complimentary mentions, Johnson seems to 'have liked neither the work nor its author, as may be seen in *Boswell* again and again; thus: 'The conversation having turned on modern imitations of ancient ballads, and some one having praised their simplicity, he treated them with that ridicule which he always displayed when that subject was mentioned.' The 177th number of the *Rambler* gives a satirical account of a Club of Antiquaries. Hirsute, we are told, had a passion for black-letter books; Ferratus for coins; Chartophylax for gazettes; 'Cantilenus turned all his thoughts upon old ballads, for he considered them as the genuine records of the natural taste. He offered to show me a copy of *The Children of the Wood*, which he firmly believed to be of the first edition, and by the help of which the text might be freed from several corruptions, if this age of barbarity had any claim to such favours from him.' In his *Life of Addison*, after a sarcastic reference to his *Spectators* on *Chevy Chase*, and Wagstaff's ridicule of them, he adds, in modification of Dennis's *reductio ad absurdum* of Addison's canon—that *Chevy Chase* pleases, and ought to please, because it is natural—'In *Chevy Chase* there is not much of either bombast or affectation, but there is chill and lifeless imbecility. The story cannot possibly be told in a manner that shall make less impression on the mind.' With what horror the ghost of Sir Philip Sidney must have been struck if ever it was aware of this crushing dictum ! Still more suggestive are his observations on another old ballad. 'The greatest of all his amorous essays,' he remarks in his *Life of Prior*, 'is Henry and Emma—a dull and tedious dialogue, which excites neither esteem for the man nor tenderness for the woman. The example of Emma, who resolves to follow an outlawed murderer wherever fear and guilt shall drive him, deserves no imitation [would Johnson have said that the *Laocoon*, or the *Venus de Medici*, deserved an imitation ? how could his critical rules have been applied to them ?], and the experiment by which Henry tries the lady's constancy is such as must end either in infamy to her or in disappointment to himself.' With these terrible sentences in our ear, let us read these stanzas :

> Though it be songe
> Of old and yonge,
> That I shold be to blame,
>   Theyrs be the charge
> That speke so large
> In hurtynge of my name ;
> *For I wyll prove*
> *That faythfulle love,*
> *It is devoyd of shame ;*
> In your dystresse,
> And hevynesse,
> To part with you the same ;
> And sure all tho
> That do not so
> True lovers are they none.
> For in my mynde
> Of all mankynde
> I love but you alone.

And,

> I thinke nat nay
> But as ye say,

It is no mayden's lore ;
But love may make
Me for your sake,
As I have sayd before,
To come on foote
Te hunte, to shote
To get us mete in store ;
For so that I
Your compancy
May have, I ask no more.
From which to part,
It makyth my hart
As colde as ony stone ;
For in my mynde
Of all mankynde
I love but you alone.

Read these high, passionate words, and think of Johnson's criticism.[1]　He misses, evidently, the point of the poem—does not see how one noble idea permeates and vivifies every line, and glorifies the self-abandonment confessed.

Here may ye see
That women be
In love, meke kynde, and stable ;
Late never man
Reprove them than,
Or call them variable ;
But rather pray
God that we may
To them be comfortable.

His criticism of the *Nut-brown Maid* makes his dislike of the old ballads intelligible enough.　We can understand

---

[1] *Cf.* Mr Gilpin's (Saurey-Gilpin, an artist, 1733-1807,) remark, *apud* Nichols and Steevens' *Hogarth*, on the seventh plate of the Rake's Progress : ' The episode of the fainting woman might have given way to many circumstances more proper to the occasion.　This is the same woman whom the Rake discards in the first print, by whom he is rescued in the fourth, who is present at his marriage, who follows him into jail, and lastly to Bedlam. The thought is rather unnatural, *and the moral certainly culpable.*'

now how he came to despise and abuse them, and parody their form in this wise :

> The tender infant, meek and mild,
> Fell down upon a stone ;
> The nurse took up the squealing child,
> But still the child squeal'd on.

Warburton, Hurd, and others heartily concurred in his opinion. Warburton thought that the old ballads were utterly despicable by the side of the exalted literature of his own and recent times. He called them 'specious funguses compared to the oak.'

But in the face of this contumely, looked down on and sneered at by the learning and refinement of the age, the old ballads grew dear to the heart of the nation. They stirred emotions that had long lain dormant. They revived fires that had long slumbered. The nation lay in prison like its old Troubadour king; in its durance it heard its minstrel singing beneath the window its old songs, and its heart leapt in its bosom. It recognised the well-known, though long-neglected, strains that it had heard and loved in the days of its youth. The old love revived. The captive could not at once cast off its fetters, and go forth. But a yearning for liberty awoke in it ; a wild, growing, passionate longing for liberty ; for real, not artificial flowers ; for true feeling, not sentimentalism ; for the fresh life-giving breezes of the open country, not the languid airs of enclosed courts.

> As one who long in populous city pent,
> Where houses thick and sewers annoy the air,
> Forth issuing on a summer's morn, to breathe
> Among the pleasant villages and farms
> Adjoin'd, from each thing met conceives delight,
> The smell of grain, or tedded grass, or kine,
> Or dairy, each rural sight, each rural sound,

so did the nation issue forth from its confinement, and conceive truer, more comprehensive joys.

The publication of the *Reliques*, then, constitutes an epoch in the history of the great revival of taste ; it changed the face of literature. After 1765, before the end of the century, numerous collections of old ballads, in Scotland and in England, by Evans, Pinkerton, Hurd, Ritson, were made. The noble reformation, that received so great an impulse in 1765, advanced thenceforward steadily. The taste that was awakened never slumbered again. The recognition of our old life and poetry that the *Reliques* gave, was at last gloriously confirmed and established by Walter Scott. That great minstrel was profoundly influenced by the *Reliques*, both directly and indirectly, through Bürger and others who had drunk deep of its waters.

'Among the valuable acquisitions,' says Scott in his Autobiography, writing of his studies after his leaving Edinburgh High School, 'I made about this time, was an acquaintance with Tasso's *Jerusalem Delivered* through the flat medium of Mr Hoole's translation. But above all I then first became acquainted with Bishop Percy's *Reliques of Ancient Poetry*. As I had been from infancy devoted to legendary lore of this nature, and only reluctantly withdrew my attention from the scarcity of materials and the rudeness of those which I possessed, it may be imagined, but cannot be described, with what delight I saw pieces of the same kind which had amused my childhood, and still continued in secret the Delilahs of my imagination, considered as the subject of sober research, grave commentary, and apt illustration by an editor who showed his practical genius was capable of emulating the best qualities of what his pious labour preserved. I remember well the spot where I read these volumes for the first time. It was beneath a huge plantaine tree, in the ruins of what had been intended for an old-fashioned arbour in the garden I have mentioned. The summer day sped onwards so fast that, notwithstanding the sharp appetite of thirteen, I forgot the hour of dinner, was sought for with anxiety, and was still found entranced in my intellectual banquet. To read and to remember was in this instance the same thing, and henceforth I over-whelmed my schoolfellows and all who would hearken to me with tragical recitations from the ballads of Bishop Percy. The first time too I could scrape a few shillings together, which were not common occurrences with me, I bought unto myself a copy of these beloved volumes ; nor do I believe I ever read a book half so frequently or with half the enthusiasm.'

XXI

THE LAST DECADE OF THE LAST CENTURY

(From *The Contemporary Review* for Sept. 1892)

IT is just a hundred and one years since a certain under-graduate of St John's College, Cambridge, by name Wordsworth, took his Bachelor's Degree and went his way into the world. The studies of the University had not greatly attracted him, at least so as to pursue them in the spirit that wins 'marks' and produces 'Wranglers.' 'William, you may have heard,' writes his sister to her friend, Miss Pollard, in June 1791, 'lost the chance (indeed, the certainty) of a fellowship by not combating his inclinations. He gave way to his natural dislike to study so dry as many parts of mathematics; consequently could not succeed at Cambridge. He reads Italian, Spanish, French, Greek, Latin, and English, but never opens a mathematical book.' And he himself speaks, in a letter to his sister, of his having acquainted his uncle (his mother's brother, the Rev. Dr Cookson) with his having given up 'all thoughts of a fellowship.' Only in a general way did mathematics, which in the Procrustean system of the then Cambridge formed the main occupation of the place, excite his interest and admiration:

> Yet may we not entirely overlook
> The pleasure gathered from the rudiments
> Of geometric science.   Though advanced
> In these enquiries, with regret I speak,
> No farther than the threshold, there I found
> Both elevation and composed delight ;
> With Indian awe and wonder, ignorance pleased
> With its own struggles, did I meditate
> On the relation those abstractions bear
> To Nature's laws, and by what process led,
> Those immaterial agents bowed their heads
> Duly to serve the mind of earth-born man ;
> From star to star, from kindred sphere to sphere,
> From system on to system without end.
>
> More frequently from the same source I drew
> A pleasure quiet and profound, a sense
> Of permanent and universal sway,
> And paramount belief ; there, recognised
> A type, for finite natures, of the one
> Supreme Existence, the surpassing life
> Which—to the boundaries of space and time,
> Of melancholy space and doleful time,
> Superior and incapable of change,
> Nor touched by welterings of passion—is,
> And hath the name of, God.   Transcendent peace
> And silence did await upon these thoughts
> That were a frequent comfort to my youth.
>
> *Prelude*, Bk. vi.

So that it was not so much the spirit of these great studies, as the spirit in which they were prosecuted, that discouraged him from taking them up.   He felt then as he felt and wrote some years afterwards, that there is no real antagonism between Poetry and Science.   'Poetry,' he wrote in the preface to the second edition of the *Lyrical Ballads*, 'is the breath and finer spirit of all knowledge ; it is the impassioned expression which is in the countenance of all science . . . . If the labours of men of science should ever create any material revolution, direct or indirect, in our condition, and in the impressions which we habitually receive, the poet will sleep no more than at present; he will be ready to follow the steps of the men of science, not only in those general indirect effects, but he will be at his side, carrying sensation into the midst of the objects of science itself.'   Thus, after all, the future poet's soul may have found some food and sustenance in the Cambridge atmosphere.   And his experience may be of some significance if any one should thoroughly investigate the striking fact that so many of our chief poetical geniuses from Spenser to Tennyson have been bred in an university especially devoted to 'exact' studies.   Probably there are other respects in which Wordsworth's Cambridge life did more for him than he thought—more, at all events, than he acknowledges in that careful analysis he gives in the *Prelude* of his development and growth, and more than any one of his biographers has yet fully ascertained.   Still, it remains true that during his residence at Cambridge he had no high opinion of the place, which, indeed, was not then at its best; nor had the place any very high opinion of him.   He achieved no academic distinction; he was 'disturbed at times' by

> a strangeness in the mind,
> A feeling that I was not for that hour,
> Nor for that place;

and when he had completed his terms and ceased to

> frequent the college groves
> And tributary walks,

no one dreamt that in the crowd of Bachelors that 'went down' just a century since was one who would in course of time be ranked amongst the most famous of the many famous sons of St John's—one who would make an epoch in English literature.

In that same year (1791) there went 'up' to Jesus College of the same University one Samuel Taylor Coleridge, he, too, not ever to take kindly to the then academic ways and limits, though he was a classical scholar of considerable attainments, and won a University prize for Greek verse. Already a brilliant talker, and, as always, a man of a restlessly active mind and thirsty for new ideas, he availed himself much more than did Wordsworth of the social advantages which are one of the most precious benefits of a University career—I mean the advantages of a thorough interchange and comparison of opinions with his contemporaries, though indeed from the very beginning Coleridge seems to have shone rather in monologue than dialogue, and from the beginning his companions seem to have been ready to sit and listen to his wonderful outpourings. At one time pecuniary and other troubles beset him, partly at least due to his own thoughtlessness ; and he disappeared, and no one at Cambridge or elsewhere knew what had become of him. Presently discovered by his writing a Latin sentence (*Eheu ! quam infortunii miserrimum est fuisse felicem*) on the wall of a stable—he had enlisted as a light dragoon—he came back to the University and 'kept' two more terms ; but as through certain theological scruples, which the kindly Master of his college in vain discussed with him, he could take no degree, he declined the final examination ; and in December 1794 his connection with Cambridge finally ceased. Nor in his case, though he was more highly thought of than Wordsworth, was there any conception that he was to be one of the chief beginners of a new literary age.

Nor, in the last decade of the last century, if Cambridge was so unconscious of the promise and prowess of two such illustrious men, was the world at large better-sighted and better-informed as to the great movement that was then in fact taking place. Works like the *Pleasures of Memory*, published in 1791, Darwin's *Loves of the Plants* (the second part of the *Botanic Garden*), his *Zoonomia or Laws of Organic Life*, and *Physiologia*, published respectively in 1791, 1794-6 and 1799, and the *Pleasures of Hope*, published in 1799, might well leave the impression that the old poetical paths were still being trodden. The 'Kingdom of Heaven,' we are told, 'cometh not with observation.' And the same may be said of other spiritual kingdoms. The world is slow to recognise a new note in poetry; it is slow merely to listen and attend to it. The old songs and the old voices occupy its ear, absorb its interest, monopolise its admiration, and to turn to new singers seems a kind of treason. It has been said that every new poet has to make an audience for himself. Certainly his audience is likely to be but small at first; and for a time the people at large doubt whether the faith of his scanty band of hearers is not a mere craze, or a mere transitory illusion or delusion. And indeed, amidst a great mingling of cries it requires some sensitiveness to select the one that is best worth hearing, and which the coming generations will hear with delight. It is easy to prophesy after the event—to assume the prophetic mantle, and solemnly re-anoint and crown him who is already known to be born a king. Still, contemporary criticism in great periods is for the most part a marvel, and the perusal of it should certainly inspire us in our day with a profound humility and an undogmatic caution.

Looking back to the close of the last century, we nowadays can easily discern, to a large extent at least, the signs of the times. Figures that reached no great height as their age saw them, have become colossal to us; and, *vice versâ*, some figures that were then thought gigantic have become smaller and smaller—have dwindled into the puniest dwarfs.

The keen intelligence of Coleridge separated him from the crowd that received Wordsworth's *Descriptive Sketches*, published in 1793, with indifference and neglect. 'Seldom, if ever,' he wrote, 'was the emergency of an original poetic genius above the literary horizon more evidently announced.' But for many a long year there was no poet whom the public and its ordinary advisers more carefully and contemptuously ignored than Wordsworth. They became ecstatic over Scott, and presently, when Sir Walter ceased to reign in poetry and ascended the throne of prose fiction, over Byron; they gave Wordsworth a frigid reception; and yet, who nowadays would compare in value and in influence what Scott and Byron have added to our poetry with the contributions made by Wordsworth? And not only with regard to men, but with regard to movements, is it difficult for an age to realise what is going on in its midst. I propose now to call attention to some of the tendencies and changes that were working their way in England in the last decade of the last century, and that were profoundly to influence and modify our literature, but which, at the time, were scarcely noticed or perceived.

Some of these movements will be at once indicated if we mention certain other works which came out in the decade 1791-1800—viz.: Mary Wollstonecraft's *Vindication of the Rights of Women*, *The Romance of the Forest*, *Descriptive Sketches*, Godwin's *Political Justice*, Cowper's *Miscellaneous Poems*, *Caleb Williams*, *The Mysteries of Udolpho*, Southey's *Joan of Arc*, Lewis' *Monk*, Landor's *Poems*, *Camilla*, *The Anti-Jacobin*, *The Italian*, Porson's edition of *The Hecuba*, Malthus' *Treatise on Population*, *Lyrical Ballads*, *Gebir* (the English version). Let us further note that John Wesley died in 1791, Gibbon in 1794, Burns in 1796, Cowper in 1800; and that Shelley was born in 1792, Keats in 1796, Macaulay in 1800; and we see clearly enough that the last ten years of the last century were in a special sense, so far as literature is concerned, a time of transition—a time in which old things were passing away, and all things were becoming new—a time of death and a time of birth.

The impulses and energies which I propose to specify, as in an effective way acting upon that decade, and co-operating with each other and with other causes to produce results so noticeable and so far-reaching, are these: the great intellectual vigour and brilliancy of Germany; the deepened influence of Greek literature and art; the revived study and appreciation of our own older poetry; the growing powers of the democratic movement; and, lastly, the new cult of Nature, so to speak—that is, the new enthusiasm with which men regarded the external world, and what we call natural scenery.

Now, it is true that many traces of these tendencies and movements can be recognised in the earlier years of the eighteenth century. Influences that so deeply penetrate and pervade the mind of an age cannot be sudden and abrupt in their action. In the case both of individuals and nations, conduct that seems strange and surprising seems so only because our knowledge of their inner history is so limited and so slight. It is in fact the outcome of suggestions and aspirations and predispositions that have long been rendering it probable and certain. It is only because of our ignorance that nothing happens but the unexpected. Assuredly, if we were better informed, we might rather say that the unexpectable never happens. In literature, long before a great revolution comes to pass, the murmur of its coming may be detected, by subsequent students at least, if we watch and listen carefully. And all through the last century we can now perceive the rise and growth of the movements that did not fully prevail till the end of it. When its own peculiar idols were in all their glory, and all men seemed bowing down on their faces before them, there were yet some persons who dissented from the established worships, some who were beginning to burn incense to other deities. All great movements and great men have had their forerunners, and the voice has been raised in the desert, listen who would, proclaiming that the way should be prepared. A most remarkable figure in this respect is the poet Gray. Of course, he is remarkable also for the exquisiteness of some of his own productions; but he has for the student of literature a very particular interest as having in many ways anticipated the tastes and the devotions of a subsequent age. It is quite curious to notice how powerfully he was affected by four at least of the movements we have specified long before the dawning of their day of triumph. He was a keen and eager Greek scholar. 'I have read Pausanias and Athenæus all through,' he says in one of his letters, 'and Æschylus again. I am now in Pindar and Lysias, for I take verse and prose together, like bread and cheese.' The *Anthologia Græca* was one of his favourite books. His attachment to older English literature was another of his special distinctions; yet another was his fine appreciation of mediæval architecture. His famous *Elegy*—what is it but an expression of profound sympathy with 'the rude forefathers of the hamlet'? He felt the beauty of the English lakes a generation before the great hierophant of them settled at Dove Cottage, Grasmere. And, though the said hierophant had his quarrel with Gray, and thought that his language was often unintelligible, yet scarcely he himself could have written of a sunrise with a faithfuller observation and a more genuine feeling than Gray describes what he saw one daybreak.

I must not close my letter [he writes to his friend Nicolls, in Nov. 1764] without giving you one principal event of my history, which was that (in the course of my late tour) I set out one morning before five o'clock, the moon shining through a dark and misty autumnal air, and got to the sea-coast time enough to be at the sun's *levée*.   I saw the clouds and dark vapours open gradually to right and left, rolling over one another in great smoky wreaths, and the tide (as it flowed gently in upon the sands), first whitening, then slightly tinged with gold and blue ; and all at once (before I can write these five words) was grown to half an orb, and now to a whole one, too glorious to be distinctly seen.   It is very odd it makes no figure on paper, yet I shall remember it as long as the sun, or at least as long as I endure.   I wonder whether anybody ever saw it before ; I hardly believe it.

And before Gray there was Thomson, some at least of whose lines, we know, clung to the memory of Wordsworth :

> I care not, Fortune, what you me deny ;
> You cannot rob me of free Nature's grace ;
> You cannot shut the windows of the sky
> Through which Aurora shows her brightening face ;
> You cannot bar my constant feet to trace
> The woods and lawns by living stream at eve ;
> Let health my nerves and finer fibres brace,
> And I their toys to the great children leave ;
> Of fancy, reason, virtue nought can me bereave.

But, whatever forerunners there may have been of the great movements we are considering, it was certainly not till about the close of the century that these movements began to produce their full effect.

I.

To turn to them briefly one by one: The dominant foreign influence on our literature, through the great part of the eighteenth century, was certainly French.   By this declaration is not at all meant that we did nothing but ape and imitate the French classics, though they were translated or in some way reproduced often enough. What is meant is that the direction and the tone of our literature were to a large extent imparted by France, then, and just before then, at the height of its literary glory. Pope's work is thoroughly his own, and not to be confounded with that of anybody else, at home or abroad; but in many respects that work would have been different, had not Boileau, for instance, preceded him. And so elsewhere we see deeply impressed the influence of Racine, Voltaire, Rousseau. Hence the somewhat extravagant outburst of Keats in his lines entitled 'Sleep and Poetry,' when he denounces the last century versifiers as an

<blockquote>
Ill-fated, impious race,
That blasphemed the bright Lyrist [Apollo himself] to his face,
And did not know it.   No, they went about,
Holding a poor decrepit standard out,
Mark'd with most flimsy mottoes, and in large
The name of one Boileau !
</blockquote>

Among the most wonderful phenomena of literary history are the revival of the German spirit some hundred and thirty years ago, and the supersession by it of this French leadership. The German genius had slept so deeply and so long that the world had arrived at the conviction that no good poetical thing could come from it; and when it began to wake and speak again, its voice was heard with incredulity not unmixed with contempt. No one imagined that a country so long a proverb for literary inferiority and dulness was about to take the foremost place in the world of literature and science and learning. 'The taste for what is German will pass away like the taste for coffee,' cried a French wit, with curious infelicity. How this resurrection came about would be a fascinating subject to discuss, if the space at our disposal permitted. It would be specially in-

teresting to dwell upon the part that England played in its
accomplishment—upon the influence on Germany of Milton,
Shakespeare, Richardson, Goldsmith, Percy's *Reliques of
Ancient Poetry*.   But just now we have only to remind ourselves of the great fact that it was accomplished, and that
whatever Germany owed to us at that time of its so splendid
regeneration, it repaid us, and still repays us, 'good measure,
pressed down and shaken together, and running over.' The
German impulse harmonised with impulses that were already
permeating England, and to these it gave a stronger force
and more successful action.

The influence of Germany clearly exhibits itself in the
works of Coleridge, Scott, Shelley, Byron, not to mention
lesser names.   At first it does not exhibit itself at its best.
The plays of Kotzebue enjoyed in England, as in their
native country, an attention and a popularity they were far
from deserving; and Schiller was more thought of than
Goethe.   The *Robbers* was wildly admired.   The susceptible Coleridge declares :

> I would have wished to die,
> If through the shuddering midnight I had sent
> From the dark dungeon of the tower time-rent,
> That fearful voice, a famished father's cry,
> Lest in some after-moment aught more mean
> Might stamp me mortal !   A triumphant shout
> Black Horror screamed, and all her goblin rout,
> Diminished, shrunk from the more withering scene !
> Ah ! Bard tremendous in sublimity !
> Could I behold thee in thy loftier mood,
> Wandering at eve, with finely frenzied eye,
> Beneath some vast old tempest-swinging wood !
> Awhile with mute awe gazing I would brood,
> Then weep aloud in a wild ecstasy.

And in the preface to *The Fall of Robespierre* he states his
design to develop the chief characters 'on a vast scale of

horror.' Well-pointed and applied was Canning's satire in *The Rovers ;* and the picture of the manacled Rogero was not without justification :

> Whene'er with haggard eyes I view
> This dungeon that I'm rotting in,
> I think of those companions true
> Who studied with me at the U-
> niversity of Gottingen.
> niversity of Gottingen.
>
> Sun, moon, and thou vain world, adieu,
> That kings and priests are plotting in;
> Here doomed to starve on water-gru-
> el, never shall I see the U-
> niversity of Gottingen.
> niversity of Gottingen.

(During the last stanza Rogero dashes his head repeatedly against the walls of his prison, and finally so hard as to produce a visible contusion. He then throws himself on the floor in an agony. The curtain drops, the music still continuing to play till it is wholly fallen.)

But it would be unfair to assign such sensationalism to a wholly foreign origin. It was, in fact, in the air of the time —in the air of England as well as in that of Germany; only Germany, as it happened, gave it the most popular expression, and so a greater vogue than it might otherwise have acquired. But these morbid excesses were soon discredited, and the healthier and purer influences of the new intellectual *régime* soon made themselves felt. Coleridge, who had begun to learn German in the autumn of 1797, in order to read Wieland's *Oberon*, and had practised himself by the translation of Klopstock's *Odes*, 'determined to continue his education in Germany itself;'[1] and in September 1798 sailed from Yarmouth for Hamburg, accompanied by Words-

[1] Brandl's *Coleridge*, Eng. Edition, p. 227.

worth and his sister.　From his sojourn at Goslar the latter poet seems to have derived no special mental benefit—at least, no benefit which he might not have gained anywhere else.　He lived all alone, and he was home-sick:

> I travelled among unknown men,
>   In lands beyond the sea ;
> Nor, England ! did I know till then
>   What love I bore to thee.
>
> 'Tis past, that melancholy dream !
>   Nor will I quit thy shore
> A second time ; for still I seem
>   To love thee more and more.

But to Coleridge, his stay in Germany was far from being a mere melancholy dream ; it was a delightful reality, and he gathered a rich store of new ideas.　The writer that did most for his development at that time was Lessing.　And with that influence began a new era in dramatic criticism.

It was Lessing [he writes in his *Biographia Literaria*, p. 275] who first introduced the name and the works of Shakespeare to the admiration of the Germans ; and I should not perhaps go too far if I add that it was Lessing who first proved to all thinking men, even to Shakespeare's own countrymen, the true nature of his apparent irregularities. These, he demonstrated, were deviations only from the accidents of the Greek tragedy, and from such accidents as hung a heavy weight on the wings of the Greek poets, and narrowed their flight within the limits of what we may call the heroic opera.　He proved that in all the essentials of art, no less than in the truth of nature, the plays of Shakespeare were incomparably more coincident with the principles of Aristotle than the productions of Corneille and Racine, notwith-standing the boasted regularity of the latter.

The influences on Scott of Goethe's early romantic drama, and of Bürger's ballads, were undoubtedly important.　They encouraged and strengthened other influences amidst which he had lived and was living, and, coming just at the crisis of his life, had much to do in determining and shaping his literary career.

It would easily be possible to illustrate this German dominion at length and in detail. But what is now proposed is a general survey of the movements above mentioned, rather than a minute exposition. And as our time and space are emphatically finite, we must pass on briefly to consider the Greek influences on the poetic renascence of a hundred years ago.

I I.

Now the critics and authors of the eighteenth century are for ever talking about the classics; but if we observe their remarks, we shall find for the most part that they mean the Latin classics—that they have little or no real acquaintance with the Greek. It is true that Bentley's life extends from 1662 to 1742; but Bentley is the exception that proves—*i.e.*, tries—the rule, and that verifies it. That his age believed that the so-called *Epistles of Phalaris* were genuine, and that Bentley had the worse in the controversy about them, at once writes down that age as singularly innocent of Greek learning, and, in fact, incompetent to appreciate a real Greek scholar. In this respect Bentley stands all alone, of such lofty stature that his puny contemporaries cannot even conceive the extent of his dimensions. It is true Pope translated Homer; but what is there Homeric, or at all events how much is there that is un-Homeric, and even anti-Homeric, in that brilliant performance!

To turn to another accomplished Augustan. 'Great praise,' says Macaulay,[1] 'is due to the notes which Addison appended to his version of the second and third books of

[1] Essays: *Addison.*

the *Metamorphoses*. Yet those notices, while they show him to have been, in his own domain, an accomplished scholar, show also how confined that domain was. They are rich in apposite references to Virgil, Statius, and Claudian ; but they contain not a single illustration drawn from the Greek poets. . . . All the best ancient works of art at Rome and Florence are Greek. Addison saw them, however, without reading one single verse of Pindar, of Callimachus, or of the Attic dramatists ; but they brought to his recollection innumerable passages of Horace, Juvenal, Statius, and Ovid. The same may be said of the *Treatise on Medals*. We are confident that not a line is quoted from any Greek writer.'

If we cast a glance at the classical tragedies that were in esteem, we find they belong to the school of Seneca rather than that of Sophocles.

It is not easy to exaggerate the importance of the fact that towards the close of the century there arose a classicism better worthy of the name—that the relations of Greek and Latin art and literature were more clearly understood, that the supremacy of the Greek genius was fully felt and acknowledged.[1]   The truth of what the most competent Romans had themselves perceived and confessed came now to be accepted.   Says Horace :

> Vos exemplaria Græca
> Nocturna versate manu, versate diurna.

Says Goethe : ' Let us study Molière, let us study Shakespeare ; but, above all things, the old Greeks and always the Greeks.'   The Germans lent splendid assistance in this Hellenic revival. The perfection of Greek literary forms,

---

[1] Mr Pollard's Introduction to his *Odes from the Greek Dramatists* is well worth reading in this connexion.

and the incomparable beauty of Greek workmanship were studied and appreciated by Western Europe as never before, not even in the period of what is specially called the Renaissance. Nor was it merely an artistic sympathy that was felt. It was a sympathy with the independence and daring of Greek thought—a sympathy with the Greek passion for intellectual freedom and an unfettered spirit, not cribbed and cabined and confined by custom and worldliness and dogma. Those who strove to deliver themselves and their age from the yoke of mere conventionality—to set the soul free, so to speak—drew their inspiration and their strength largely from Attic sources. Shelley, fleeing from what seemed to him the oppressive and stifling air of England, promises his son a home in Italy or Greece, and from his very child-hood a knowledge of Greek history and literature.

> We soon shall dwell by the azure sea
> Of serene and golden Italy,
> Or Greece, the mother of the free ;
> And I will teach thine infant tongue
> To call upon their heroes old
> ·In their own language, and will mould
> Thy growing spirit in the flame
> Of Grecian lore : that by such name
> A patriot's birthright thou mayst claim.

Happily, so far as these Greek studies were concerned, he might well have trained his boy in England; for England was indeed taking a distinguished place in their pursuit. It was in 1793 that Porson was appointed Professor of Greek at Cambridge, and with Porson begins a new era in Greek scholarship. By this Greek influence our literature is widely and deeply penetrated. It is to be observed even in the work of Wordsworth, a poet not readily or commonly ac-cessible to literary stimulations. What Landor says of his

Laodamia may perhaps be somewhat hyperbolical, but there is no little truth in it, and it is very noticeable as coming from such an accomplished Hellenist.   He pronounces it 'a composition such as Sophocles might have exulted to own, and a part of which might have been heard with shouts of rapture in the regions he describes—the Elysian Fields.'[1] But Shelley and Keats are those who most profoundly and abundantly illustrate the mighty power of Greece in the period of our last poetic revival.   Conceive their writings with this power withdrawn.   How deeply the genius of Æschylus, Theocritus, and of Moschus, stirred and moved the genius of Shelley cannot easily be over-estimated; and for Keats, we know indeed that it was Spenser who first woke in him a poetical consciousness, but it was Greek art that thrilled him through and through.   For Greek art came in a sense to abide amongst us, when in 1816 our Government purchased 'The Elgin Marbles,' and these 'marbles' were presently exhibited at the British Museum.   The ancient Greek spirit, as embodied in them, strangely moved the spirit of Keats; and other masterpieces of classical antiquity profoundly affected him.   A new sense of beauty awoke in the bosom of this Londoner of the nineteenth century, and a deep sympathetic joy in the sight of these ancient perfections.   Let us recall his apostrophe to a Grecian urn :

> O Attic shape !   Fair attitude ! with brede
> Of marble men and maidens overwrought,
> With forest branches and the trodden weed ;
> Thou, silent form ! dost tease us out of thought
> As doth eternity.   Cold Pastoral !
> When old age shall this generation waste,
> Thou shalt remain, in midst of other woe
> Than ours, a friend to man, to whom thou sayst,

[1] See *Imaginary Conversations:* Southey and Porson.

'Beauty is truth, truth beauty—that is all
    Ye know on earth, and all ye need to know.'

And this quickening and energic Greek influence has not throughout the century ceased to perform its divine ministry. A poet only recently passed away—one, I suppose, of what are called 'Minor Poets,' but an exquisite one—thus speaks for himself to a friend who wondered how he kept his soul alive in this modern climate:

Who prop, thou ask'st, in these bad days, my mind?
    He much, the old man, who clearest soul'd of men,
    Saw The Wide Prospect and the Asian Fen,
And Tmolus hill and Smyrna bay, though blind.
Much he, whose friendship I not long since won,
    That halting slave who in Nicopolis
    Taught Arrian when Vespasian's brutal son
Clear'd Rome of what most shamed him.   But be his
    My special thanks, whose even-balanced soul
From first youth tested up to extreme old age
Business could not make dull, nor passion wild ;
    Who saw life steadily, and saw it whole ;
The mellow glory of the Attic stage,
Singer of sweet Colonus, and its child.'

I I I.

But we must hasten on, in this most rapid survey, to notice the revival of our older literature some hundred years ago.

Now, the last century, admirable as it was in so many ways, and doing so much good service of which we now reap the benefit, made the mistake of prizing too highly its own literary culture and its own productions, and thinking far too little of the culture and productions of preceding times. People often talked as if English poetry began with Waller ! They made some exception, perhaps, in favour of

Spenser; but for the most part they scarcely thought that our older writers were worth studying, or that the Middle Ages could have anything to offer them in the way of instruction or of delight. The general attitude towards Shakespeare was apologetic. Voltaire had labelled him a 'buffoon,' and there seemed something in it. His best friends allowed he was very 'irregular;' and others spoke with less reserve. Hume, one of the finest intellects of his day, describes him as 'born in a rude age, and educated in the lowest manner, without any instruction from the world or from books,' and finally pronounces that 'a reasonable propriety of thought he cannot for any time uphold.' Other Elizabethans, except possibly Ben Jonson, fared yet worse when brought before such tribunals. Our still older poetry was as good as unknown. As to Chaucer, nothing more need be said, for nothing more significant could be said, than that Dryden's and Pope's versions of certain pieces of his were currently accepted—versions that should be assiduously read by any one who wishes to remain really ignorant of the great Plantagenet poet. That there could be poetry of any high quality in Anglo-Saxon—anything of vigour and power, and having in it some flashes of Homeric fire—this had not yet entered into men's heads to conceive.

Some hundred years ago a complete and a blessed change took place in this respect. The past, and the poetry of the past, began to excite interest and command attention. The national mind refreshed itself by a perusal of the native masterpieces of previous periods. The way for this revival had been happily prepared by Percy's *Reliques of Ancient English Poetry*, and the writings of the Wartons, and the scholarship of Tyrwhitt. And at last men turned with enthusiasm to the Elizabethan literature and to the Middle Ages, both early and late. The result is conspicuous in the works of Scott, of Coleridge, of Keats, to confine ourselves to the greater names. These geniuses delighted to wander amidst the fields of mediæval thought and feeling that were in their time reopened, and to make others share their delight. The contrasts with modern ideas, and the strange likenesses to them, were a perpetual fascination. It was clearly seen that the present had much to learn from the past, and that the attitude of pity and condescension towards it was by no means just or wise. Astonishing and incredible as it might seem, the Middle Ages, however imperfect their civilisation in some respects, were not a mere wilderness of barbarism, but a time of splendid visions and inspirations—of 'fine intelligence,' that could worthily express and embody itself. Have any centuries left behind them more magnificent monuments than the old churches and cathedrals that are yet one of the supreme glories of our land? What are they but noble poems in stone, the epics of architecture, petrifactions of beauty—

> Thoughts whose very sweetness yieldeth proof
> That they were born for immortality?

It was strange indeed that men's eyes should have been so long blind to art-work so exquisite; but at last they saw it, and more and more fully realised its incomparable excellence. How deeply Scott felt the spell of Melrose Abbey, and Wordsworth that of King's College Chapel, each poet, in this respect as in others, a minister of 'the Gothic Revival!' And how fitly does Sir Walter lie in his last long sleep amid the ruins of Dryburgh! Once more men delighted to enter the land of Romance, and marvel at its so long-forgotten flowers, and listen to the sweet weird songs that filled the air of it.

IV.

The fourth movement I wish briefly to point out is the democratic, using the term in the widest sense. The poetry of Pope does not concern itself with the people at large. It is busy with lords and ladies, with wits and *littérateurs*. But a profound social change was slowly accomplishing itself, even from the time of Queen Anne; and this soon began to have some representation in literature. The old exclusiveness gradually disappeared, and was succeeded by a broader conception of society, inspired by a new sense of brotherhood, and a more comprehensive humanity. It was a bold innovation that Richardson should adopt a servant girl for a heroine; but he sufficiently acknowledges the old *régime* when he rewards his sadly persecuted Pamela with the hand of the worthless nobleman who has done his worst to effect her ruin. By the end of the century no writer who was up to date, so to speak—*i.e.*, who really understood the spirit of the age and wrote under its characteristic dictates—would have thought such a finale became the situation. No doubt this expression of sympathy was often marred by what was ill-judged and foolish and grotesque; and Canning's ridiculous picture of the philanthropist who thinks that a needy knife-grinder must necessarily have been, or be, wholly the victim of some proud oppressor, and not at all the victim of himself had its truth and value when he drew it. But on the whole this movement was truly human and humanising. It was good for the mind, and it was good for the soul, that their horizons should be widened. The poetic area was immensely increased. A new world, indeed, was discovered and traversed and annexed. It was finely said of Sir Walter Scott that he spoke to every man as if he were his blood-relation. And not other is the spirit that passed into literature in the great era of the French Revolution, when, in a most important sense, if I may so use St Paul's phrase, not without blood in France itself, the members of each nation were all 'baptised into one body,' whether they were bond or free.   Of this noble extension of its interests literature furnishes us with copious examples.   Perhaps more than any other poet, Wordsworth, however alienated—and not surprisingly—he became from the Revolutionary movement, taught men a more catholic affection for their kind—that all fellow-creatures were to be regarded with interest and respect; at least that rank and position should not be allowed to monopolise respect and interest; that amongst the poorest and the humblest may be found characters of genuine worth, that deserve an unpatronising, a kindly, and even a reverent consideration.   Nowadays these statements sound like vapid commonplaces; but it was not always so, and even now they often need reinforcement.   The commonest circumstances and things, and persons of the least outward note and distinction, moving in the most ordinary environment—around and on these Wordsworth threw a new light, and made visible and clear their hitherto scarcely recognised attractions :

> O reader, had you in your mind
>   Such stores as silent thought can bring,
> O gentle reader ! you will find
>   A tale in everything.

Of the poet he asserts that—

> In common things that round us lie
>   Some random truths he can impart —
> The harvest of a quiet eye,
>   That broods and sleeps on his own heart.

It was a lesson which Wordsworth himself had had to learn

—a revelation that had come to him after and amidst some bitter experiences.   Equable and calm as were his mood and temper when we knew him best, that peace had not been attained without effort, and till after a severe convulsion. There was a certain dark hour of his life when despair nearly overpowered him—despair of mankind and of the world's future.   The horrid orgies of the French Revolution, when it forgot its own prime principles and lost all self-control, profoundly depressed and saddened one who from the first had hailed that movement as the beginning of a better time :

> Bliss was it in that dawn to be alive,
> But to be young was very heaven.

Till 1793 he thought that the best dreams of the best friends of humanity were about to be realised.   Then there befell, as it seemed, a frightful reverse.   And Wordsworth's soul well-nigh died within him ; and for some months his spiritual condition was highly critical.   He was tempted to turn cynic and satirist.   The influences that saved him from such perdition, and so saved and secured for our literature one of its most purifying and strengthening forces, are a very interesting study ; but only one of them can now be mentioned—viz., that happily he was led from the observation of men in masses to the observation of men as individuals. The Parisian mob, with its wild excesses, was no edifying spectacle.   And often it happens that men in large bodies seem to be guided, not by their collective wisdom, but by their collective folly—that not common sense seems to dominate, but common nonsense, and the human race is not shown at its best, but at its worst.   For a mass of men is not merely an accumulation of individuals ; a certain new element is introduced through the very accumulation, and each individual is not exactly himself, but in becoming part of a large conglomeration he is modified and shaped, and to a certain degree transformed. And when conglomerations take a bad turn, then man appears but a wild and hopeless animal. Now, to Wordsworth, the human herd, as he saw it, had ceased to give comfort and pleasure. And he was moved to despair of the Republic. But happily for him, he found in the individual what he so sadly missed in the mob, and so he recovered his faith in his kind. A passage in a letter of his to Fox, the famous statesman, deserves to be quoted in this connexion :—

Necessitated as you have been, from your public situation, to have much to do with men in bodies and in classes, and, accordingly, to contemplate them in that relation, it has been your praise that you have not thereby been prevented from looking upon them as individuals, and that you have habitually left your heart open to be influenced by them in that capacity. This habit [he adds] cannot but have made you dear to poets; and I am sure that if, since your first entrance into public life, there has been a single true poet living in England, he must have loved you.

It was Wordsworth's good fortune to number amongst his intimate friends some persons of singularly fine and excellent disposition and genius; and their society was an infinite blessing to him always, but especially at this time, when his heart was so depressed within him. Not less fortunate was he in discovering amongst the peasantry that lived round his humble home a real dignity of character, a true manliness, a natural nobility. Like the Shepherd-lord in his own exquisite poem,

Love had he found in huts where poor men lie ;

and by the intimate knowledge he acquired of his humble neighbours—of their trials and the fortitude with which they were borne—of their principles and their ambitions and their ideals—he was inspired with a genuine admiration for lives so simple, so unexacting, so brave.   And he was content to celebrate them, and the troubles and the defeats and the victories that darkened or brightened those unostentatious careers :

> Long have I loved what I behold,
>   The night that calms, the day that cheers ;
> The common growth of mother-earth
> Suffices me—her tears, her mirth,
>   Her humblest mirth and tears.
>
> The dragon's wing, the magic ring,
>   I shall not covet for my dower,
> If I along that lowly way
> With sympathetic heart may stray,
>   And with a soul of power.
>
> These given, what more need I desire
>   To stir, to soothe, or elevate ?
> What nobler marvels than the mind
> May in life's daily prospect find,
>   May find, or there create ?
>
> A potent wand doth Sorrow wield ;
>   What spell so strong as guilty Fear ?
> Repentance is a tender Sprite ;
> If aught on earth have heavenly might,
>   'Tis lodged within her silent tear.

In the older poetry we are introduced to shepherds and shepherdesses and other rustics, but they are for the most part fine ladies and gentlemen thinly disguised, provided with dainty crooks and fine-spun blouses from the stores of the costumier.   But now we have before us the real thing— the *bonâ-fide* milkmaid, the dalesman who

>   had been alone
> Amid the heart of many thousand mists,
> That came to him, and left him on the heights,

the Female Vagrant, the Pedlar, the Old Huntsman, the Leechgatherer on the Moor.

It would be easy to illustrate more fully this democratic movement in literature, and from the writings of other poets besides Wordsworth—*e.g.*, of Scott, of Campbell, of Coleridge, of Shelley; but we must now quickly glance at the fifth and last movement which we have specified as marking and directing the literary era that now concerns us.

V.

A very striking difference between this century and the last is presented to us, if we notice the attitudes of the two periods towards external nature—towards natural scenery in its most ordinary, and yet more noticeably in its wilder and grander forms. Very generally in the time of Pope, and by the school of Pope, natural phenomena were described without any real knowledge of them, the eye of the describer not upon the object, to use a phrase of Wordsworth's which is often cited nowadays as invented by Matthew Arnold, who, indeed, borrowed it from Wordsworth. There was little pure delight in nature and the things of nature. There was, indeed, some interest in nature when duly tricked out and arranged in a certain fashion; but nature, not artificially readjusted and so made presentable, had comparatively few friends. The taste for mountains had not yet arisen. Not a word is said in praise of those 'great creatures of God.' 'Our earliest travellers—Ray, the naturalist, one of the first men of his age ; Bishop Burnet and others who had crossed the Alps, or lived some time in Switzerland—are silent upon the sublimity and beauty of those regions ; and Burnet even uses these words, speaking of the Grisons : "When they have made up estates elsewhere, they are glad to leave Italy and the best parts of Germany, and to come and live among those mountains, of which the very sight is enough to fill a man with horror." The accomplished Evelyn, giving an account of his journey from Italy through the Alps, dilates upon the terrible, the melancholy, and the uncomfortable; but till he comes to the fruitful country in the neighbourhood of Geneva not a syllable of praise or delight.' In Defoe's *Tour through the Whole Island of Great Britain*, continued by Richardson, and by 'a gentleman of eminence in the literary world' (seventh edition, 1769), the favourite adjective—the *constans epitheton* — for the mountains is 'frightful.' Westmoreland is spoken of as 'a country eminent only for being the wildest, most barren, and frightful of any that I have passed over in England or in Wales.' Elsewhere we read : 'But notwithstanding the terrible aspect of the hills, when we had passed by Kendal and descended from the frightful mountains, the flat country began to show itself; and we soon found the north and north-east part of the country to be pleasant, rich, fruitful, and, if compared to the other part, may be said to be populous.'[1] In another passage we are informed that the writer and his companion or companions did 'not think it worth our while to go among the hills and cliffs and rocks and terrible precipices of the Stanmore district, in the North Riding.'

Since such views were current, what a revolution in taste has come about ! How complete is the contrast presented by the poetry of Wordsworth, of Scott, of Byron ! The very regions which the typical eighteenth-century man carefully avoided, so far as he could, his successor began to visit and frequent with enthusiasm. A new sense of natural beauty

---

[1] Wordsworth's *Prose Works*, ii. 327.
[2] Defoe's *Tour*, etc., iii. 304. *Ibid.* iii. 161.

developed itself.   Landscapes that once excited only horror were now gazed upon with awe, but also with delight.   The solitudes once thought so forbidding and so gloomy, were hailed as homes of refreshment and peace for the weary spirit.   A veil was withdrawn from the face of Nature, and she showed herself in all her loveliness and in all her majesty. No wonder if those who so beheld her were fascinated by her charms.   The beauty of the earth had never been so keenly realised, and it became a mighty influence.   Things that lay all round, and of which little heed had been taken, were now discerned to be gems of price.   One might almost say that men seemed now to see for the first time, or to see with a new clearness and appreciation, everything that God had made, and 'behold it was very good.'   The visible world was crowned with a new glory, and drew men's eyes and thoughts towards it with a fresh attraction and a new-born ardour :

> The sounding cataract
> Haunted me like a passion ; the tall rock,
> The mountain, and the deep and gloomy wood,
> Their colours and their forms, were then to me
> An appetite ; a feeling, and a love,
> That had no need of a remoter charm,
> By thought supplied, nor any interest
> Unborrowed from the eye.

And, in Wordsworth's mind at least, this delight in the mere external form was followed by a yet deeper delight in what seemed to lie beneath or within it, and be expressed by it :

> For I have learned
> To look on Nature, not as in the hour
> Of thoughtless youth ; but hearing oftentimes
> The still, sad music of humanity,
> Nor harsh nor grating, though of ample power
> To chasten and subdue.   And I have felt

A presence that disturbs me with the joy
Of elevated thoughts ; a sense sublime
Of something far more deeply interfused,
Wwhose delling is the light of setting suns,
And the round ocean, and the living air,
And the blue sky, and in the mind of man ;
A motion and a spirit, that impels
All thinking things, all object of all thought,
And rolls through all things.   Therefore am I still
A lover of the meadows, and the woods,
And mountains ; and of all that we behold
From this green earth ; of all the mighty world
Of eye and ear—both what they half create,
And what perceive ; well pleased to recognise
In nature and the language of the sense
The anchor of my purest thoughts, the nurse,
The guide, the guardian of my heart and soul,
Of all my moral being.'

And such a recognition of Nature and her sway—such a worship of Nature—is perpetually uttered in the poetry of Wordsworth, 'of Nature's inmost shrine . . . the priest.' Thus, to quote the whole of the fine stanza of which I have already in another connexion quoted the first line :

Love had he found in huts where poor men lie ;
His daily teachers had been woods and rills,
The silence that is in the starry sky,
The sleep that is among the lonely hills.

Or, again, in the well-known lines called *The Tables Turned*, where he disparages book-learning by the side of Nature's lessons for those who know how to receive them :

Books ! 'tis a dull and endless strife ;
Come, hear the woodland linnet,
How sweet his music ! On my life,
There's more of wisdom in it.

And hark ! how blithe the throstle sings !
He, too, is no mean preacher ;

> Come forth into the light of things,
>   Let Nature be your teacher.
>
> She has a world of ready wealth,
>   Our minds and hearts to bless—
> Spontaneous wisdom breathed by health,
>   Truth breathed by cheerfulness.
>
> One impulse from a vernal wood
>   May teach you more of man,
> Of moral evil and of good,
>   Than all the sages can.

Of such teachings that to most ears were inarticulate and obscure, Wordsworth was ordained the interpreter; and if at times, like priests in other temples, he was excessive in his commentaries, yet not easily can be overrated the service he performed for his day and generation, and for days and generations to come, in making men feel—not only see, but *feel*—the beauties of the material world in which we live; not only of its rarer and grander sights and shows, but of its every-day and common phenomena. To 'see nothing in Nature that is ours,' and to give 'our hearts away, a sordid boon,' that, he taught us, is a sorry condition, and this a miserable surrender. He taught us that life had ceased to be worth living when we find ourselves without any responsive emotion in the presence of what is lovely and divine, however common the spectacle of it; when a thing of beauty ceases to be a 'joy for ever.'

> My heart leaps up when I behold
>   A rainbow in the sky:
> So was it when my life began;
> So is it now I am a man;
> So be it when I shall grow old,
>   Or let me die!'

Other illustrations of this change in the general attitude

towards Nature might be brought forward in abundance from other contemporary authors ; but this rapid survey must now be concluded. I trust that I have made distinct some at least of the influences that effected such a wonderful transformation in our literature nearly a century ago ; influences whose force is not yet spent, but is still active and beneficent.

XXII

VICTORIAN LITERATURE

(From the *Gentleman's Magazine* for April and May 1888)

IN studying the literature of the nineteenth century, and the life which that literature reflects and represents, we may find it both convenient and accurate to recognise three distinct periods. The first extends from the beginning of the century to the year 1830 or thereabouts ; this is the period of Wordsworth and Shelley. The second extends from the close of the first to about 1870 ; this is the period of Carlyle, Tennyson (if we may venture to omit his title and speak of him in the old familiar way), Browning, Dickens, Thackeray, and 'George Eliot.' The third is now running its course. It can scarcely be said to have brought forward, as yet at least, any writer of equal importance with the great masters that distinguish the preceding periods. It seems a period rather of abundant cleverness than of supreme genius. But it is too early yet to pronounce its character. Possibly, though for certain reasons not probably, some star may arise of surpassing brilliancy, which may illumine these concluding years of the century with a special and enduring glory.

Now in dealing with Victorian literature, it is, of course,

with the two latter periods we are particularly concerned. And I shall first of all point out how these two periods are marked off from the first period. Later on we shall see how they are parted from each other.

If it is true, as certainly it is and cannot but be, that literature, to repeat the phrase already used, reflects and represents the life of the age to which it.belongs, then in defining literary epochs we shall find it serviceable to look at the general history—at the political and social history—of the country whose literature we are surveying. In the present case it can easily be shown that the decade from 1830 to 1840 was one of wide general movement and change, and that the decade from 1860 to 1870 was also remarkable in the same way—that is, that the middle of the three periods named lies between two epochs of noticeable departures. If it is wished to be more precise, we might perhaps take the first two Reform Bills as sufficiently suggestive for our purpose—the Reform Bill of 1832, and that of 1867.

Let us consider a little the decade from 1830 to 1840— the decade that witnessed the Queen's accession. It was a time of singular activity and innovation in all departments of life. The prolonged reaction produced by the wild excesses of the first French Revolution was at last exhausting itself. Ideas of political advance that had been put aside for more than a generation began once more to be ardently and irrepressibly entertained. Democracy began to feel its strength and to make its strength felt. It was clear to all that had eyes to see and ears to hear that things could not go on in the old groove—that the old arrangements must be readjusted and expanded—that for new needs there must be new accommodations. It was no longer possible to resist the clamorous outcry of excluded populations for some share in the government of the country of which they formed so large and rapidly increasing and so important a part. And so the democratic movement in England won its first paramount recognition in the passing of the first Reform Bill. No wonder if there was then much extravagant elation and hope, to be inevitably followed by some disappointment and depression. But, whatever came afterwards, whatever evils and troubles beyond the medical efficacy of Reform Bills, men, to begin with, were elate and hopeful. 'The world's great age' seemed beginning anew; 'the golden years' seemed returning. And in all directions, along with this political energy, both just before and just after 1832, there were accomplished new developments and signal discoveries. It was in the year 1830 that our railway system was started. And since the printing-press, no invention perhaps has exerted an influence comparable with that of the steam-engine; by bringing distant people into close and intimate communication, it has made easily possible full and effective conference on all matters, not only on those of business; and it is by such conferences, such unhampered interchanges of thought and feeling and tendency, that national impulses are quickened and matured. Yet further were the obstacles of space removed by the introduction of the electric telegraph. It was in the year 1837 that that momentous invention was first successfully employed: the first scene, the London and Blackwall railway. In 1838 a steamer crossed the Atlantic, though an eminent savant had proved such a feat absolutely impracticable. Meanwhile, in 1834, we have a substantial proof that the national conscience was awakening to its duty in respect of the education of the people. In that year was made the first education grant. It was but a paltry sum for such a purpose—some £20,000; but its importance is not to be estimated by its amount. In 1836 the newspaper stamp tax was reduced from 4*d.* to 1*d.*; the advertisement tax from 3*s.* 6*d.* to 1*s.* 6*d.* In 1837 the proposal of a penny postage was first brought forward by Rowland Hill; it was adopted two years afterwards. Nor, as illustrating the various activity of the time and the valuable additions then made to our material conveniences and comforts, will any householder think it out of place or *infra dignitatem* if he is reminded or informed that Lucifer matches came into use in 1834.

Much more might be here recorded to show the eventfulness of the decade we are now considering, but perhaps enough has been said for our special purpose. What we have now to note, and what it is our special business to note, is how in literature too, at this time, the old things passed away, and behold all things became new—how the new political and social movement is, as it was bound to be, accompanied and interpreted by a new literary movement.

This decade, in fact, witnesses the final passing away of a great race, and the advent of their successors.

The greatest literary figure of modern days vanished at this time from the ken of Europe: in the spring of 1832 Goethe died. But to confine ourselves to England, at this time there were taken from our midst Scott (in '32), Coleridge (in '34), Lamb (also in '34), not to mention miscellaneously Crabbe ('32,), Mrs Hemans ('35), Hannah More ('33), Hogg ('35), Mackintosh ('32), Jeremy Bentham ('32), James Mill ('36), Malthus ('34), Cobbett ('35), Hazlitt ('30), Wilberforce ('33), Robert Hall (31), Godwin ('36). Some years previously the Italian winds had blown away the ashes of Shelley, and the heart of Keats had ceased to feel its capacity of misery, and Byron had died worthily and nobly, whatever shall be said of his life. There still survived, amongst others of lesser name, Landor, Hallam, Rogers,

Southey, Moore, and he who, as many think, and as may well be thought, is the foremost genius of his generation—Wordsworth. But of all these their best writings had been written. The work of Southey, for instance, was well-nigh done. While he was engaged on his edition of Cowper, a terrible domestic trouble befell him, and presently his health broke down, and, though he lived on till 1843, his intelligence never returned; though he still fondly handled his dearly loved books, he could not gather their meaning. And for Moore, too, an inferior lyrist at the best, a time of similar darkness was coming. Wordsworth lived on in growing honour till 1850, when Tennyson received the laurel

> Greener from the brows
> Of him that uttered nothing base.

But, indeed, his work too was done long before the end came. Not that for him in his latter years the light of reason was ever quenched, as in those other distressing cases, though a severe affliction sorely tried the old man. He still sang on, but his voice had lost its pristine charm. As late as 1837 he wrote *Memorials of a Tour in Italy*, a collection not indeed without interest, for it contains the 'Musings near Aquapendente' and the well-known generous reference to Scott as 'the whole world's darling,' and also indignant references to the fallen state of Italy, and ardent wishes for a new era, which have happily been since accomplished. 'Italia,' he cries, as he stands by the shore of Lago Morto:

> Italia ! on the surface of thy spirit
> (Too aptly emblemed by that torpid lake)
> Shall a few partial breezes only creep?
> Be its depths quickened ; what thou dost inherit
> Of the world's hopes, dare to fulfil ; awake,
> Mother of heroes, from thy death-like sleep.

X

And after 1837 he wrote occasionally, as, for instance, the two sonnets to Miss Fenwick in 1840. But certainly he wrote nothing that increased his fame. Indeed, it was at the end of the eighteenth century and the very beginning of the nineteenth that the genius of Wordsworth was at its best, and produced its most perfect fruit. His reputation would scarcely have been less than it is—it might possibly have been greater—had he kept silence the last half of his life. Still, his venerable figure stands out conspicuous for us in the opening years of the Victorian period. Though to some of the rising generation, as to Mr Browning (see Browning's letter in Grosart's *Wordsworth's Prose Works*), he seemed 'a lost leader,' it was at this time he enjoyed his greatest popularity. Certainly, whether then 'lost' or not, he had been a great leader—a great deliverer. Quite recently he had delivered the soul of a certain John Stuart Mill from a bondage that was becoming intolerable, and was paralysing all his powers—from the bondage of an education that had left half his nature untouched and hard. And for many others he had performed a like inestimable service, so that men looked up to him as something more than a poet in the ordinary use of the term—they looked up to him as a prophet, as a high priest in a wider sense than the ecclesiastical.

> He, too, upon a wintry clime
> Had fallen—on this iron time
> Of doubts, disputes, distractions, fears.
> He found us when the age had bound
> Our souls in its benumbing round.
> He spoke, and loosed our heart in tears.
> He laid us, as we lay at birth,
> On the cool, flowery lap of earth ;
> Smiles broke from us, and we had ease.
> The hills were round us, and the breeze

> Went o'er the sunlit fields again ;
> Our foreheads felt the wind and rain.
> Our youth return'd ; for there was shed
> On spirits that had long been dead,
> Spirits dried up and closely furl'd,
> The freshness of the early world.

'Our youth returned.' What a noble conception of the poet's office this phrase suggests ! It is assuredly his prime business to keep us young in spirit, or make us young again if we have grown secular and old—to keep or make us capable of simple and innocent enjoyments, tender-natured and sensitive, quickly sympathetic. Wordsworth beyond doubt exercised a highly important influence on the generation that succeeded his own—as, for example, on Tennyson—and must be carefully taken into account by anyone who would understand the growth and development of Victorian poetry and Victorian thought. The reverence of his younger contemporaries was some compensation, let us hope, for the loss of coeval friends, which he, like all who grow old, was fated to experience. In a characteristic manner he expressed his sense of loneliness and of the everlasting mystery of life and death in lines which enclose so much literary history that we might well quote them here if space permitted, the lines entitled (Wordsworth was often not very happy in his titles) 'Extempore Effusion upon the Death of James Hogg,' written in November 1835.

So much do our limits permit us to say of the race that was passing in the decade 1830-40. Now let us turn to the race that was advancing, the race to which belong the great masters of the Victorian period—Macaulay, Carlyle, Tennyson, Browning, Dickens, Thackeray, Mill, Whewell, and others, whose names have become 'familiar in our mouths as household words.' Let us notice also the noble band of scientists—Darwin, Lyell, Faraday, the younger (John)

Herschell, Owen, Sedgwick, Murchison.   All these and others were coming to the front some fifty or fifty-five years ago ; and these are they who have given the Victorian age whatever intellectual glory it wears for its crown.

Macaulay and Dickens became famous all at' once.   It was not till after some years of waiting that the voices of Carlyle, of Tennyson, of Browning, of Thackeray won a hearing.   But about the year 1830 all these writers were connected, or becoming connected, with literature ; and by the time of the Queen's accession they had all won some degree of distinction.   Macaulay's Essay on Milton was published in 1825, when he was only just twenty-five years of age ; and by its singular gift of style at once secured him a popularity which went on increasing to the end of his life, and which probably will, to some extent, be retained, though at present suffering, as Dickens's fame too is suffering, from the reaction inevitable from excessive laudation. Carlyle had won his famous battle with the Everlasting No, which under changed names is described in *Sartor Resartus*, and in the year 1830 was vainly endeavouring to persuade London publishers to bring out this now so famous work. It was in 1834 that he finally left his hermitage at Craigenputtoch and settled in the then out-of-the-way street in Chelsea which will be associated with his name for ever, or at least until that day comes when London is a mere heap of ruins, and the planet earth is as extinct and dead as the moon.   *Sartor Resartus* was by that time coming out in *Fraser's Magazine*, to the serious detriment of that serial's sale, so perplexed was the general reader by both the thought and the style of this strange contributor, so utterly unable to recognise the advent of a new great humorist and a great prophet, who was to stir and move his age as no other man stirred and moved it, who above all others in a time that tended to the grossest mammon-worship and to say to its soul, 'Soul, take thine ease, eat, drink, and be merry,' was to excite in the hearts of men a noble rebellion against a life merely mechanical and material, who, in short, was to be one of the most powerful spiritual forces of the Victorian period. Some three years later, in 1837, when his work on the *French Revolution* was published, the supremacy of the genius of this Scottish border peasant began to be perceived, and in no long time he took his throne amongst the intellectual kings of his day. In the year 1830 the energy of Dickens, struggling bravely with adverse fortune, had raised him from surroundings that might well have subdued and prostrated a less vigorous nature to the reporters' gallery in the House of Commons, and made possible for him the brilliant career that was to be his. Presently he applied his hand to sketching scenes from the life he saw around him, and discovered powers of observation and powers of insight into certain types of character and certain ranks of society that made him the founder and the unequalled master of a new novelistic school. His papers, afterwards reprinted as *Sketches by Boz*, began to appear in 1834. At the time of the Queen's accession the *Pickwick Papers* were in the course of publication. Probably there have never been any other years, in the history of England at least, in which people were so convulsed with laughter as in the years 1836 and 1837 ; one seems to hear the incessant roar across the half-century that separates us. We are not so overwhelmed as its first readers were ; but even now can one easily mention a more laughter-moving book than the *Posthumous Papers of the Pickwick Club* ? And is not the moving of laughter, of hearty, healthy, innocent laughter, 'of mirth that after no repentance draws,' an excellent service to perform for the world ? We have it on good authority, if authority is wanted, that there is a time to laugh; but it seems true many persons never remember that delightful fact. They find time to scold, to grumble, to denounce; but they are too busy, they tell us, I suppose with scolding and such vocations, to laugh. Yet a good common laugh is one of the best and hopefullest bonds of good fellowship—one of the most effective solvents of ill-feeling. What the French call 'gaiety' in style may be something superior to the power of moving laughter; but still there are few persons who can make the world laugh heartily. So we do not depreciate the serviceableness of Dickens if we say nothing more of him than that he provided his age with good honest laughter. But he did much more, as we shall presently see. Tennyson may be said, like a preceding master of his craft, to have lisped in numbers. He and one of his six brothers (Charles) published a volume of poems when they were yet in their teens (1827). At Cambridge, in 1829, he performed the dubious feat of writing the successful University Prize Poem on the fascinating subject of 'Timbuctoo.' In the following year he produced his first independent collection of pieces; and in 1832 a second collection. From both these volumes some things were preserved and reproduced ten years later. The main interest of all these earlier efforts is that they bring the future laureate before us in his poetic apprenticeship, and illustrate the curious care and faithful industry with which he trained himself for the noble ministry to which he felt himself called. His individuality of style, already apparent, had to make its own audience—had to create the taste which was to appreciate it. And thus he met with no cordial reception from the current critics; for indeed very few of the so-called critics are at all in advance of the public or whom they cater,—are anything more than the spokesmen of the prevailing schools. Thus the rising Tennyson had but little cause for gratitude—I do not say none, for happily real critics do exist, though they are scarce—to the literary judgments of the day. However, his cold reception probably did him an undesigned service: it made him, to use Wordsworth's phrase, 'a severe critic of himself,' and saved him from the temptation to which great popularity might have exposed him, of writing too fast and profusely. Moreover, a great trouble for a time shrank the streams of his genius. In 1833 Arthur Hallam, his most intimate friend, one of the most brilliant of the brilliant Cambridge set to which the undergraduate poet belonged, was suddenly taken away from what seemed to be the good to come.

> Beneath Vienna's fatal walls
> God's finger touched him, and he slept.

And for a while Tennyson wrestled with this mighty sorrow. It was but slowly that he recovered heart and voice. The chief work of the next following years was that series of 'complaints' and of cryings for the light, not published till long after they were completed or all but completed (it was published in 1850), which is known as the *In Memoriam*, and which amongst Tennyson's longer poems is surely the one that is likely to preserve his memory. We may picture Tennyson, then, in the decade we are surveying as rapidly maturing and perfecting himself in the art of expression, and also gathering in the deep darkness and amidst the lightning flashes of a great affliction the knowledge and the wisdom that were to make his technical mastery of value in giving it worthy themes, the ultimate themes of all literature, the themes of life and death, of endurance and rebellion, of hope and despair.

Among Tennyson's other contemporaries at Cambridge

and at Trinity College was a certain William Makepeace
Thackeray. Thackeray's lively sense of the ridiculous had
already shown itself at the Charterhouse ; but it was long
before he took his proper place amongst the princes of his
time. He, too, noted the subject of the University Prize Poem
in 1829, and professes to print in the *Snob*—an undergraduate
serial so called—some lines that formed part of his own com-
petitive effort, lines that give indications of the facility and
the humour that in fuller forms were to characterise his
masterpieces :

> In Africa (a quarter of the world)
> Men's skins are black, their hair is crisp and curled ;
> And somewhere there, unknown to public view,
> A mighty city lies, called Timbuctoo.
>
> .   .   .   .
>
> There stalks the tiger, there the lion roars,
> Who sometimes eats the luckless blackamoors.
>
> .   .   .   .
>
> Desolate Afric ! thou art lovely yet !
> One heart yet beats which ne'er thee shall forget.
> What though thy maidens are a blackish brown,
> Does virtue dwell in whiter breasts alone?
> Oh no, oh no, oh no, oh no, oh no !
> It shall not, must not, cannot e'er be so.
> The day shall come when Albion's self shall feel
> Stern Afric's wrath, and writhe 'neath Afric's steel.
> I see her tribes the hill of glory mount,
> And sell their sugars on their own account ;
> While round her throne the prostrate nations come,
> Sue for her rice, and barter for her rum !

It was to the readers of *Fraser's Magazine* that Thackeray
first gave a real taste of his quality, but the exact date of
his forming that important connexion seems not at present ascertainable. Anthony Trollope, in the volume on
Thackeray in the 'Men of Letters Series'—a volume
neither for information nor discernment quite worthy of

that excellent series—says that Thackeray is not in the famous symposium picture of January 1835; but surely he is there, the fifth figure on Maginn's right hand. So that the Fraserian connexion must have begun not later than 1834, which, as we have seen, was precisely the year in which Dickens was first attempting original composition. But Dickens quickly outstripped Thackeray in the race for fame. When, on Seymour's death, a new illustrator was needed for the *Pickwick Papers*, Thackeray offered himself in that capacity. His offer was declined, no doubt on just grounds; for Thackeray, though fond of drawing, and putting into his sketches abundant humour, seems never to have had patience and ability to acquire technical accuracy. But at last his *Fraser* papers attracted notice. In 1837 he started the Yellowplush Correspondence; in 1840 appeared *A Shabby Genteel Story*.

Of all this new generation, the most precocious was certainly John Stuart Mill. He began his contributions to the *Westminster Review* in 1824, when he was only some eighteen years of age. Two years subsequently there fell on his spirit that darkness which, as we have seen, the study of Wordsworth dispersed or reduced; and very shortly afterwards, ever bent on some good service for his day and generation, he became one of the noblest and best influences of his time. About the year 1837, stimulated by the perusal of Whewell's *History of the Inductive Sciences*, he was devoting his attention to those studies of *Logic* which resulted in his two memorable volumes in 1843.

But our space forbids our going into further details about the decade 1830-40. We have demonstrated sufficiently for our present purpose how it is one of those important transitional times in which a well-defined era closes, and another not less definite commences.

A few years later the great writers we have named were joined by others of scarcely less note—by Charlotte Brontë, 'George Eliot,' Mr Ruskin, Mr Herbert Spencer, Professors Huxley and Tyndall. Of this distinguished group several, happily, are still with us; but it may be convenient, as we think it would also be exact, to associate them rather with the middle than with the concluding period of the nineteenth century. Charlotte Brontë's three famous novels were all published between 1847 and 1853. 'George Eliot's' best work, with the exception of *Middlemarch*, belongs to the fifties and the sixties, and *Middlemarch* came out early in the seventies. Mr Herbert Spencer's *Social Statics* appeared in 1851; his *Principles of Psychology* in 1855; his *Principles of Biology* in 1864. Huxley was already prominent in the world of science in 1854. It was in 1856 that he and Tyndall made their famous exploration of glaciers.

Let us now consider the literature whose incoming we have pointed out at such lengths as our limits permit.

This may be done in several ways. We might take the different literary departments one by one, and observe how far each has flourished during the period we are studying; or we might adopt the personal method, and pass in review some three or four of the distinguished figures who have done most to express and to direct the tendencies of the age; or we might follow a merely chronological arrangement; or, lastly, we might select some of the leading ideas or characteristics of the time, and try to show what various embodiment these have found in the current literature. It is this last method I propose now to follow.

I will briefly dwell upon what seems to be the special feature of our age—viz., its various and many-sided activity, its incessant and thorough movement, or what, perhaps, might be called its revolutionary character; and then I will illustrate two special phases of this general characteristic—viz., the democratic movement and the scientific.

It can scarcely be doubted, I think, that the nineteenth century will hereafter be regarded as one of the great transitional centuries of history — as a century resembling in this respect the fifteenth or the fifth—a century of dissolution, and also in some sort, let us hope, of reconstruction—a century of transformation. In the last century there was prevailing the idea of stationariness — the idea that the social system could be maintained permanently in the condition at which it had arrived. There was prevailing the idea of finality in politics and in other provinces of thought and of action. For example, men looked back at the Great Revolution of 1688 as if it had done all that wanted doing—as if it had settled and arranged things for ever—as if under the shadow of it they might repose undisturbed and placid. This curious peace of mind was first rudely disturbed by the convulsions that shook France and all the world as the eighteenth century closed. Still, England trusted that by a vigorous policy of restraint and suppression it might manage to keep down the forces that were beginning to make the country tremble and quake—forces whose energy and significance it was then difficult indeed to calculate, and of which the sudden emission might well be deeply dreaded. Happily, with the good practical sense that has saved us from so many a collision that might have been fatal, concessions were presently made; these new forces, which it was impossible to hold in lasting durance, received a judicious recognition ; and we turned over to a new page of our history. Even after the first Reform Bill men could still dream of renewing the old quiet. An eminent statesman could advise his constituents to 'rest and be thankful.' But rest was not yet to be our fortune. We had passed into a period of unrest—into a period of great discontent and uneasiness, of new aspirations and strivings, of death pains and birth pains. Our outward habits were greatly changed. Our being was moved to its inmost depths. Creeds of every kind were questioned and revised or rejected. Beliefs that we thought eternal proved strangely temporary and transient. Indeed, there was nothing in any region of life that could evade the daring, relentless scrutiny of this new era.

Now let us see how our literature reflects and images just such an age. Tennyson, Browning, Dickens, Carlyle, 'George Eliot,' all in one degree or another, in one way or another represent just such an age.

Tennyson in the earlier part of his life and his poetry kept himself in close contact with his time, In his later years he has lost or relinquished such contact. The movements, whose infancy and adolescence he watched without any or with slight apprehension, and cheered with his choicest songs, have now left him behind, so strangely swift has been their pace, so unexpected their developments. Now, in their full strength and vigour, he regards them with but little sympathy; he is like some godfather who is appalled at the manners, and what seems to him the turbulence and recklessness, of the adult whose childish gambols he used to look on with so warm an affection. Compare the laureate's *Locksley Hall Sixty Years After* with the *Locksley Hall* of his youth, and what a tale of change and movement is suggested to us. In both poems he illustrates the temper of his age; but in the earlier one his sanguine spirit exults in the eager activity he sees around him. It exactly recalls for us that stage in the modern movement when all seemed good and promising, and fear of excess was not excited. Disgusted with his lady-love's treason, the hero appeals to his wondrous mother-age, for shelter and succour. He sees keenly the evils around him, but he does not despair; he does not mistrust the future. He is tempted to think there might be calm for him in some distant 'isle of Eden,' far away from the impetuous life that rushes on all sides.

There, methinks, would be enjoyment more than in this march of mind,
In the steamship, in the railway, in the thoughts that shake mankind.

But the idea of stagnation repels him; his old delight in a vital activity returns, and with a hearty cheer he bids the world move on:

Not in vain the distance beacons. Forward, forward let us range.
Let the great world spin for ever down the ringing grooves of change.
Thro' the shadow of the globe we sweep into the younger day:
Better fifty years of Europe than a cycle of Cathay.

Another of Tennyson's poems which it is highly interesting to read in the light of his age is his *Ulysses.* Through the lips of the old Greek he gives voice to the yearnings of his day. Dante, as is well known, had turned the story of Ulysses to the same account. The spirit of the early Renaissance had recognised in it an excellent symbol. But not the less significant for this previous interpretation is the nineteeth-century rendering of it. Certainly, it is true that the nineteenth-century aspirations are often undefined and vague. Longfellow's popular verses called 'Excelsior' may be said perhaps to express this vagueness. The passion for knowledge, for the exploration of its limitless fields, for the annexation of new kingdoms of science and thought is what actuates the modern Ulysses. He is intent—

To follow knowledge like a sinking star,
Beyond the utmost bounds of human thought.

The latter line exactly reminds us of the uncontrollable ambition of the modern mind—its insatiable and implacable thirst for fresh conquests.

> Come, my friends,
> 'Tis not too late to seek a newer world.
> Push off, and sitting well in order smite
> The sounding furrows ; for my purpose holds
> To sail beyond the sunset, and the baths
> Of all the western stars, until I die.

Notice the vast uncertainty of their destination as given in the following lines :—

> It may be that the gulfs will wash us down :
> It may be we shall touch the Happy Isles,
> And see the great Achilles, whom we knew.
> Tho' much is taken, much abides ; and tho'
> We are not now that strength which in old days
> Moved earth and heaven, that which we are, we are ;
> One equal temper of heroic hearts,
> Made weak by time and fate, but *strong in will*
> *To strive, to seek, to find, and not to yield.*

What finer wording could there be of the modern spirit of tireless investigation? But, indeed, throughout his poetry, sympathetically or antipathetically, Tennyson reflects his age with singular faithfulness. I am not sure that any other poet has been so largely and fully the spokesman of his age. To use a Hamletian metaphor, he has been the instrument on which his age has played its various tunes. Nor am I sure that a poet who is so specially the spokesman of his own age and its notions, will not be found of the less value by future ages. The supreme poets are 'not of an age, but for all time,' or, rather, they belong to their respective ages, but to all other ages besides. The lesser poets are limited to their ages. Immersed in the present, for future readers, except for the historical student, they have less interest. Certainly Tennyson mirrors his age in a wonderful manner. But our space permits but one more illustration. How admirably the transitional character of the century is rendered in the famous passage in which King Arthur, with shatter'd casque, his 'brow Striped with dark blood,' his face white and colourless, is placed, disabled and broken, in the barge to go

To the island valley of Avilion !

He is the representative of a great age that is being superseded, of a system, that, after noble service done, is making room for a new system which also shall be nobly serviceable; of a régime that has waxed old as doth a garment, and is being put aside for a vesture new-woven and new-dyed. Sir Bedivere exactly images those persons who hold indiscriminately to the old ideas and the old ways; who cling blindly to the skirts of the past, and can never see that the costume they have admired is threadbare and discoloured, and ragged and rotten. They 'love not wisely but too well.' They cannot conceive that life may be worth living—may be lived nobly—under other forms than those with which they are familiar. In all transitional ages you may hear the piteous outcries of these weak, forlorn brethren. They would forbid and obstruct the departure of their Arthur, although indeed he is dying, and would fondly cherish a mere corpse, from which, alas ! there must needs proceed corruption and plague.

Then loudly cried the bold Sir Bedivere :
'Ah ! my Lord Arthur, whither shall I go ?
Where shall I hide my forehead and my eyes ?
For now I see the true old times are dead,
When every morning brought a noble chance,
And every chance brought out a noble knight.
Such times have been not since the light that led

> The holy Elders with the gift of myrrh.
> But now the whole Round Table is dissolved
> Which was an image of the mighty world,
> And I, the last, go forth companionless,
> And the days darken round me, and the years,
> Among new men, strange faces, other minds.'
>   And slowly answered Arthur from the barge :
> *' The old order changeth, yielding place to new,*
> *And God fulfils Himself in many ways,*
> *Lest one good custom should corrupt the world.'*

In Browning, too, we may easily see reflected the perpetual inquisitiveness and unsettlement of the age. Browning's own religious belief never falters ; but he portrays current scepticisms in such works as the *Death in the Desert*, and *La Saisiaz*. In Paracelsus he gives a memorable enunciation of the idea of progress. It is to be feared that many people confound the ideas of movement and progress, which, obviously, are extremely different. A man may walk, and walk with exemplary vigour, along what is unfortunately quite the wrong road for him, if he has any particular destination in view. He moves, but he does not progress. But we may presume he thinks he is progressing—that his motto is progress. And let us hope that much of the movement of our time is really progressive. Browning thus describes his ideals, and endeavours to guide the impulses of the age accordingly :

> Progress is
> The law of life, man's self is not yet Man !
> Nor shall I deem his object served, his end
> Attained, his genuine strength put fairly forth,
> While only here and there a star dispels
> The darkness, here and there a towering mind
> O'erlooks its prostrate fellows.

And he goes on to dwell sanguinely on the fresh start that life seems making. Of course the words refer, in the first instance, to the early sixteenth century ; but there cannot be a doubt they are largely suggested by the poet's immediate environment.

Prognostics told
Man's near approach ; so in man's self arise
August anticipations, symbols, types
Of a dim splendour ever on before,
In that eternal circle run by life,
For men begin to pass their nature's bound,
And find new hopes and cares which fast supplant
Their proper joys and griefs ; they outgrow all
The narrow creeds of right and wrong, which fade
Before the unmeasured thirst for good ; while peace
Rises within them ever more and more.

The same spirit of movement, of alacrity, and of hope permeates the work of Dickens. He is peculiarly the offspring of the first Reform Bill period. He is full of confidence in himself and his age. He was fond of declaring his reliance on Demos. 'My faith in the people governing,' he said, and said more than once, 'is, on the whole, infinitesimal; my faith in the People governed is, on the whole, illimitable.' And the busy, sanguine temper and radiant optimism of his youth were in him to the last. He attacked in his novels various existing evils with vigour and with considerable success. Thus the *Pickwick Papers*, *Oliver Twist*, *Nicholas Nickleby*, *Bleak House*, *Little Dorrit*, were all in part inspired by a reforming purpose. I am not saying they are the better works of art on this account; the artist and the reformer have very different natures and functions, and their characters cannot be compounded and confounded with impunity. But, happily for Dickens's success as a novelist, the reforming instinct in him was always subordinate to the artistic. Still it was there, and serves at least to remind us of the atmosphere in which his genius grew up. In Macaulay, too, may be

Y

heard to the end the same cheerful, sanguine tone. To him his age seemed the best of ages; he was never tired of dilating upon its virtues and glories; indeed there never was such an age. Its material advances were unrivalled, and he delighted to celebrate them; and he celebrated them with an eloquence and a wit that placed him amongst the masters of language and style. He is the great trumpet-blower of his age, and blows with a will, and with such a power and resonance that we still listen with pleasure to his splendid blasts. But far other did this same vaunted age seem to the eyes of Carlyle—eyes of much deeper insight and penetration than those of Macaulay. For, indeed, Macaulay saw little beneath the surface of life. He had the quickest sense of the picturesque and the external, both in the past and the present; but of the inner meaning of things and their real significance he has not much to tell us. He could have described in an incomparable way the handwriting on the wall in that old Babylonian palace, but he could never have suggested the interpretation. He never dreamt of the insoluble, or at least utterly tangled and intricate, problems that were awaiting the society which seemed to him to be such a glorious success. Carlyle looked deeper and further. It is perhaps true that he did not sufficiently recognise what was good and promising in his age; the effusive optimism of Macaulay and such zealots may have impelled him in the opposite direction; also, there was in his disposition a certain tendency to acerbity and censoriousness; for in this respect, as in so many others, Carlyle is a striking contrast to Macaulay, whose sweetness of nature it would be difficult to overpraise. 'Thomas,' as his mother frankly said, 'was gay ill to·live wi'' or 'to deal wi'' as another version has it; and the accuracy of this maternal verdict his age experienced no less than individuals. But to speak of Carlyle as a mere sharp-tongued dyspeptic anathemiser would be to commit a shameful injustice. Rather he was a great prophet-like figure, not able, indeed, to prophesy smooth things like his buoyant-hearted contemporary, but in the inmost heart of him, to use his own way of speaking, with a profound admiration for what was really noble and worshipful. To him the glories that were so loudly lauded and hymned seemed of but slight and fleeting splendour. To him society seemed profoundly disorganised, and rapidly travelling towards mere anarchy. The aims and triumphs of the prevailing legislature seemed of trivial moment. It was as if a fire brigade should attempt to extinguish Vesuvius, or as if one exposed to a shower of bullets should protect himself with an umbrella. He saw, and saw most truly, as we now too well know, that much of the prosperity that made such a show around him was 'like a green bay tree,' that it would not and could not last. In *Past and Present* there is a remarkable passage that may justly be called prophetic, in which he predicts that a wide expansion of commerce and a great increase of wealth will follow the removal of certain oppressive laws, but that this expansion and this increase will soon reach their limit, and difficulties and distresses will recur, which is precisely what has happened. Since about the year 1870 these difficulties and distresses have direly beset us. As I have never seen these pertinent words pointed out or quoted in this connexion, let me here repeat them. They were written in 1843. 'Yes, were the corn laws ended to-morrow, there is nothing yet ended; there is only room made for all manner of things beginning. The corn laws gone, and trade made free, it is as good as certain this paralysis of industry will pass away. We shall have another period of commercial enterprise, of victory and prosperity, during which it is likely much money will again be made, and all the people may by the extant methods still for a space of years be kept alive and physically fed. The strangling band of famine will be loosened from our necks; we shall have room again to breathe; time to bethink ourselves, to repent, and consider! A precious and thrice precious space of years, wherein to struggle as for life in reforming our foul ways, in alleviating, instructing, regulating our people, seeking, as for life, that something like spiritual food be imparted them, some real governance and guidance be provided them. It will be a priceless time. For our new period, or paroxysm of commercial prosperity, will and can, on the old methods of "Competition and devil take the hindmost," prove but a paroxysm—a new paroxysm, likely enough, if we do not use it better, to be our *last*. In this, of itself, is no salvation. If our trade in twenty years, flourishing as never trade flourished, could double itself, yet then also, by the old *laissezfaire* method, our population is doubled. We shall then be as we are, only twice as many of us, twice and ten times as unmanageable.' Surely this is the voice of a prophet, whether we accept all its utterances or not. And it is a voice that was heard and heeded. Much has been done in that very way of popular instruction that Carlyle advocates and enjoins—much but for which our confusion at this hour would certainly have been worse confounded, our darkness yet thicker and deeper and dawnless. If this prophet could have perceived how the generation to which he preached was not altogether perverse and viperous—that it did in some sort answer to his awful warnings, and made some efforts to flee from the wrath to come of his denunciation, he might have been saved from the rank pessimism to which he abandoned himself in his latter days. While Macaulay complacently blew the trumpet of the age, here was Carlyle, 'his hoary hair' streaming 'like a meteor to the troubled air,' kindling the alarm beacons on the hill tops, and with their fierce blaze and wild roar startling the age from its security and self-satisfaction. But if Macaulay trusted too much, Carlyle trusted too little. Great and grand as he was, there was yet something of the cynic in Carlyle. He would have been greater had he been humbler, less wilful, more tolerant. With respect to much that was excellent in his age he lived in obstinate isolation, and I do not think it can be said he grew wiser as he grew older. He certainly did not understand the capacities and potentialities of his age. He saw with the keenest eyes its dangers and its vices, but the only remedy he could imagine was that of the strong-handed ruler. He was for ever insisting on complete obedience to the God-sent hero as the panacea for all evils, and he declared that his hero would always be sent in time of need. This was Carlyle's great faith, but it cannot but be pronounced transcendental. Is it never the case that an afflicted people scan the heavens in vain for the star that is to indicate the presence of 'a Saviour of society?'—that in the east, whose space they so wistfully and earnestly explore, they can descry no Epiphany? Can an age do nothing for itself? Must it merely pray and wait till its Great Man appears? Does God fulfil himself only in one way? Is it not a gross misstatement to say, as is said in the lectures on Hero-Worship, and as Kingsley echoingly and impetuously says, that 'Universal History is at bottom the history of the Great Men who have worked there?' If it may be asserted that a great man makes his age what it becomes, it may also be asserted that his age makes him what he is. It is great ages that produce great men; and in a highly important sense the great man is the offspring of his age.   He is the special heir of the past out of which that age has proceeded, the special exponent of its mind, the special representative of its character.   We cannot, indeed, fully explain the genesis of genius—there remains something that escapes our present analysis; we cannot thoroughly understand all the circumstances and conditions under which the genius of the age concentrates and culminates in some select individual.   But that a vital relation exists between the individual and his age seems beyond question.   And yet Carlyle treats with contempt and derision the notion that a great man is 'the creation of his time.'[1]   Tennyson's phrase, 'O thou wondrous mother-age,' in the lines referred to above, reminds us of the great truth Carlyle perversely ignored.   Certainly it was not without detriment that 'the Sage of Chelsea' stood aloof from the scientific impulses of his time—that he wrapped himself in his virtue, and fed on his intuitions and visions, despising the Darwins and the humble plodders along the paths of reason and research.   The study of society—of men in combinations and masses—attracted him not at all.   Such investigations as Mr Herbert Spencer has formally initiated in his *Sociology* and other works seemed to him frivolous. What interested him was the individual man of ability and force.   Most men, he maintained, were fools, and the greater number of men you get together, the greater the heap of folly.   That the average of intelligence and wisdom might be raised was not one of his leading conceptions. The idea of a people, as a whole, educated and cultured was not one of his day dreams.   He only thought of the masses as something to be controlled and managed.   In short, he was devoid of sympathy with the democratic movement.

[1] See *Lectures on Heroes*, Lect. I.

And yet the democratic movement is the one great social and political movement of these latter days, and cannot for one instant be ignored by any competent thinker. In some minds it excites no overwhelming fears; it is but a natural evolution of society; it is but a new order, a new system, inevitably arriving. There may be some confusion during its coming and its establishment, but in due time this confusion will cease, and the world will settle down under the new *régime*, not less composedly than under the old, till this, too, shall become old, and in its turn be superseded. But, however we may regard democracy—with horror, or with misgiving, or with confidence, or with exultation—all practical thinkers must accept it. It is one of those facts which Carlyle so eloquently proclaimed it is the mark of greatness to recognise. It cannot be annihilated by the most persistent indifference, or the profoundest disgust, or shutting one's eyes with the utmost pertinacity. In one of Dickens's novels—in *Our Mutual Friend*—there is a certain Mr Podsnap who has the for him happy faculty of believing that what he does not wish to exist does not exist. To ignore a distasteful thing is as good as extirpating and demolishing it. And that gentleman, though perhaps somewhat extravagantly and grotesquely portrayed, as is often the case with Dickens's pictures, is certainly in some degree true to nature. Podsnappery is, in fact, uncommonly common. It is wonderful how many people there are who think that if they will not look at a thing the thing vanishes, and is not. And often enough they only learn better when the said thing falls upon them, and is crushing them. He that hath eyes to see, let him close them—that is perilous advice.

One most striking mark of the democratic movement, to use the phrase in the broadest sense, is the extent to which the people, in the more limited application of the term, have been the subject-matter of literature during the present century, and especially the last fifty years. What a contrast our literature presents in this respect to that of the last century. What different social interests are represented by Pope and by Tennyson. It is true that in one well-known passage it does occur to Pope whether it is quite right that 'the great' should monopolise the poets, and he does proceed to celebrate somebody without a title, but this somebody is what we should call a private gentleman of limited means, which he uses beneficently:

> Yet all our praises why should lords engross?
> Rise, honest Muse, and sing the Man of Ross.

It is true that the heroine of the first novel, properly so called, is a servant-girl; but this was accidental, as could be easily shown; and, moreover, Pamela is in the end married to a lord. In Cowper may be noticed sympathies that comprehend the poor and the humble. The rise of Burns gave a quite new attraction to the 'labouring classes.' That a ploughman should be one of the sweetest and brightest song-writers of his age, and of all ages—here was an amazing phenomenon. Then came Wordsworth with his humble heroes and heroines, to make us feel how in the most ordinary and least illustrious person there may be the possibility, and the reality, of all that makes life noble, and to be desired, and to be admired. And so our interests and sympathies have been broadened and deepened. And this is, perhaps, the supreme distinction of the Victorian period. The sense of brotherhood has been quickened within us. The vast multiplication of manufactures, the huge increase of population, the rapid growth of democracy have inevitably brought before us a knowledge of forms and states of life and experience that has deeply affected the natural conscience, and has widely and variously aroused both shame and pride, condolence and congratulation, both terror and delight. Partitions and walls have been removed; and the different classes of society know each other better than they did, and, let us hope, judge each other more justly. Dives and Lazarus have conversed together. The east and the west of our great towns have interchanged visits. And, if their relations are yet far from being all that could be wished, yet it is something that they are in correspondence, and that they meet. To this deepened and broadened feeling our current literature has given noble utterance. The writings of Dickens, Hood, Tennyson, Thackeray, 'George Eliot,' Mrs Browning, Charlotte Brontë, Carlyle, and of many others whom I would fain name if space permitted, have all in one way or another, directly and indirectly, worthily interpreted and inspired their age in respect of this 'enthusiasm of humanity.' What fine passion and compassion glow in Carlyle's noble words concerning ' the toilworn craftsman that with earth-made implement labouring conquers the earth, and makes her man's. Venerable to me is the hard hand, crooked, coarse; wherein, notwithstanding, lies a cunning virtue, indefeasibly royal, as of the sceptre of this planet. Venerable, too, is the rugged face, all weather tanned, besoiled, with its rude intelligence; for it is the face of a man living manlike. O! but the more venerable for thy rudeness, and even because we must pity as well as love thee; Hardly entreated brother! For us was thy back so bent, for us were thy straight limbs and fingers so deformed; thou wert our conscript, on whom the lot fell, and fighting our battles wert so marred. For in thee lay a God-created form, but it was not to be unfolded; encrusted must it stand, with the thick adhesions and defacements of Labour; and thy body, like thy soul, was not to know freedom. Yet toil on,

toil on ; *thou* art in thy duty, be out of it who may ; thou
toilest for the altogether indispensable, for daily bread.'
Hood might well be content to have inscribed on his tombstone : 'He wrote the Song of a Shirt.' That touching cry
has assuredly not been heard in vain, though yet far away
seems the time when the 'Song of a Shirt' shall be a song of
gladness. Our hearts are deeply stirred, as through the
night it goes up to heaven from yonder attic. But the great
writer, who has done most to enable the rich and well-to-do
classes to understand the poorer, is certainly Charles Dickens.
This is from our present point of view, which is not the
purely artistic, his highest glory, his best jewelled crown.
He undoubtedly fails when he paints the aristocracy, which,
happily, he has had the good sense seldom to attempt. Such
a character as Lord Verisopht is a mere idiotic puppet.
Nor, strangely enough, does he succeed in portraying
satisfactorily his own class—the class in which he moved
when grown up. His ladies and gentlemen are not exactly
the ladies and gentlemen of society in the special sense.
They have their merits, but amongst these is not that
indefinite something, that precise mark of breeding and
manner, which essentially distinguishes this social species.
Nor is Dickens happy in his delineation of the artisan.
'Stephen Blackpool,' truly says Mr Ruskin, is 'a dramatic
perfection instead of a characteristic example of an honest
workman.' It cannot be said that Dickens understood the
industrial problem in all its intricacy, as it lies before us
nowadays ; it was, indeed, in its earlier phases, and not yet
completely articulate when he wrote ; and he is not at ease
and in full command when he approaches it. But he had a
real fellow-feeling with the industrial classes. 'Ah !' he said
to his friend Forster, after visiting Venice, 'when I saw those
places, how I thought that to leave one's hand upon the

time, lastingly upon the time, with one tender touch for the mass of toiling people that nothing could obliterate, would be to lift oneself above the dust of all the Doges in their graves, and stand upon a giant's staircase that Samson could not overthrow.' 'In varying forms,' adds Forster, 'this ambition was in all his life.' *The Chimes* (1844), *Bleak House* (1853), *Hard Times* (1854), are the books in which he specially exhibits this sympathy with the working-man. But his sympathetic knowledge of the poor, of the struggles of men of humble position, of the outcasts of society, is displayed in all his writings. He had in his own youth endured many hardships, and been brought into close contact with much distress and poverty. He knew by bitter experience what a truceless wrestle with troubles life is for many people. But happily he knew also how, on the whole, this battle was fought bravely and manfully. He keenly and heartily recognised the kindliness and the goodness that survived, and even flourished amidst what might have seemed, and perhaps used to be thought to be, quite fatal surroundings. Thus his pictures of what one may call the East End and the Central district of life—pictures painted with the same consummate intimacy which marks Thackeray's pictures of the West End—have real value for their truth and their humanity. He does not visit the regions of Rotherhithe and Saffron Hill in the spirit of a patron, or as some superior being; he goes amongst the people as a man amongst men, as one ready and eager to teach, but not less ready and eager to be taught.

> And gladly would he learn, and gladly teach.

The Pharisee in the parable thanked God he was not as other men, and he draws up a sufficiently forbidding list of what other men are. But should we not rather be thankful we are as other men ?—be proud to be the fellows of other men, when mankind is judged generously and with a sympathetic insight? Dickens joins the East and the West together in a true human league. Even in the criminal class that finds a place everywhere—in the West as well as the East—he makes us all remember that there are seeds and even growths of nobleness, though the seeds have not always ripened, and the growths are sadly stunted. He unseals in us the fountains of pity; if he kindles indignation, it is not against nature, but it is against the evil arrangements and conventions that so often pervert nature. Probably no writer, in England at least, has ever done more in the way of acquainting us with the proletariat—with their manners and customs, their sorrows and their joys, their genuine kindliness and wonderful generosity to each other; and thus no man has ever done more to remove the barriers that ignorance and estrangement set up between the classes of society, and to make us really sensible of our common lineage—to show us how slight are the differences between men, whatever their birth and condition, as compared with the points of likeness and identity. Mrs Gaskell, and many others, have followed faithfully in the steps of Dickens. And Thackeray too, in a different way, has helped to impress on the world the same lesson. If Dickens has told us of the goodness and the excellence that bloom in humble quarters, of the love to be found 'in huts where poor men lie,' Thackeray has mercilessly exposed the meanness and selfishness that abound in the circles of wealth and rank. He has led his readers along the streets and amidst the booths of Vanity Fair, and shows them how much that looks like gold is the merest tinsel. He is not so utterly perverse and inhuman as to forget that even in Vanity Fair truth has its dwellings, that even there nature is not extinct. Happily nature is not easy to extinguish, or no doubt conventionalism would have extinguished it long ago. Even in Vanity Fair, as Thackeray describes it, there is something generous and sincere ; the booths do sometimes contain what the showman outside announces, and promises are not always lies. But undoubtedly the general result of Thackeray's work was to disperse the glamour which had been vulgarly—by such writers as Theodore Hook, for instance—thrown around the tenants of mansions and palaces. He exhibited these tenants as they really were, good, bad, and indifferent, even as other men. And thus he, too, proved there is 'a good deal of human nature in man,' whatever his social status, and reinforced and vivified the old commonplace, that rank and fashion are not invariably associated with goodness and virtue—that, to use Tennyson's phrases, 'kind hearts' and 'coronets' are not always found together, nor yet 'simple faith' and 'Norman blood,' and that, after all—

> 'Tis only noble to be good.
> Kind hearts are more than coronets,
> And simple faith than Norman blood.

Not that Thackeray despised rank and fashion, or that rank and fashion are to be despised—why should they be ?—but that they should be estimated at their proper worth—should not be worshipped blindly and grossly. Amongst his most effective portraits are the figures of those who so worship such comparatively trivial things — of the parasites and hangers on and slaves of 'society'; and here he shows us what real vulgarity is, and that it is not a mere ignorance of etiquette, or some inaccuracy of grammar and language.

Much more might be said of the influence of the democratic movement on literature ; I have only dwelt upon its influence on the subject-matter of it, and the ethical spirit in which that subject-matter has been handled. But to discuss, or try to discuss, the matter more fully—as, for instance, the general relation of democracy and art, how art is likely to thrive in a democratic atmosphere, it being remembered that the modern form of democracy is essentially different from the ancient, from that under which art flourished at Athens—would far exceed our present limits of time and space. And I must now very briefly speak of the scientific movement and its influence.

I do not propose here to celebrate the triumphs of science in the Victorian period, to catalogue the new sciences that have arisen—as, for example, geology and biology—to record the extraordinary advances they have made, and point out the immense influence they have exercised upon all departments of thought; I wish rather, most briefly, to refer to the influence of the scientific spirit outside the domain of what is commonly known as science. Not only have many of the special ideas and discoveries of science, cosmical and other, acted upon our general conception of things, but this scientific spirit has made and is making itself felt everywhere. Let me mention one of those ideas— perhaps the one that has been most active and influential— the idea of evolution. In biology that idea had been form- ing in men's minds from the beginning of the century; ex- cept to correct a popular error, I need not say it is not due to Darwin. It was already in the air, and had already been repeatedly stated years before the *Origin of Species* ap- peared in 1859, which made a great epoch, not by announc- ing the doctrine of evolution, but by explaining the method by which evolution was brought about. One may catch echoes of the doctrine in Tennyson's *In Memoriam* (1850, written as we have seen in the thirties); as where the poet sketches the gradual formation of the solid earth from 'tracts of fluent heat,' till at the last arose the man, 'the herald of a higher race,' if only he

> Move upward, working out the beast,
> And let the ape and tiger die ;

or in the passage when he again looks forward to a yet higher development of humanity to

> The crowning race

> Of those that eye to eye shall look
> On knowledge ; under whose command
> Is Earth and Earth's, and in their hand
> Is Nature like an open book ;

> No longer half akin to brute,
> For all we thought and loved and did,
> And hoped, and suffer'd, is but seed
> Of what in them is flower and fruit ;

> Whereof the man, that with me trod
> This planet, was a noble type
> Appearing ere the times were ripe.

Observe how this idea of evolution is pervading all our studies—our study of history, of language, of society. But, as I have said, let us notice not only the influence of single and special ideas, but of the scientific spirit. What is the scientific spirit? What does the term 'science' mean? Let us remember that science meant originally only knowledge. It is only quite recently that the term has acquired a special and technical sense; when Gray uses it in his *Elegy*, he uses it in the old general sense. But it has come to mean knowledge of a special quality—knowledge that is thorough, systematic, complete, so far as it goes, absolutely and finally demonstrated, wholly sifted from conjecture and assumption.   In *In Memoriam* Tennyson uses the term knowledge in this sense, when he says

> Let knowledge grow from more to more.

If such is the meaning of the term science, we can now realise what is meant by the scientific spirit; and this is a dominant and sovereign spirit in our time.   Observe how it is telling on the aims and methods of history.   Macaulay, with all his vivid style, is falling from the high place he once held, because he did not study and write in this spirit; and so such a work as Carlyle's *French Revolution*, with all its picturesque splendour, though we hear the thunder roll as we read it, and are dazzled by the lightning flashes, fails to satisfy the modern requirements of what a successful historical work should be.   Let the historian describe and narrate graphically if he can; it is no slight service to make the past live again in this way.   But this is not his highest duty; it is not his chief glory to rival or surpass the current novelist, and supply our mental gallery with pictures.   His real work is to interpret the past—not only to make us realise that it existed, but to explain how and why it existed, what it inherited, how it administered its inheritance, and what it bequeathed—not only to show us what it was externally, but what it was essentially—not only to describe its customs, and to chronicle its attitudes and its gestures, but to analyse its mind, to discover precisely the special problems with which it had to grapple.   In short, by knowing an age we mean something different and something more than used to be meant.   In other words, the scientific spirit has taken possession of the department of historical study.   Observe again, how it is influencing the study of philology.   Not so long ago etymology was regarded as a mere matter of guesswork.   One derivation was thought as

good as another. The changes in word forms were held to
be purely arbitrary. Voltaire remarked that the consonants
went for nothing, and the vowels were of no importance.
The application of the scientific spirit to this province of
study makes such a witticism curiously groundless. In all
these letter changes that so transform and disguise words,
the reign of law is being discovered.

' So free ' they ' seem, so fettered fast ' they ' are.'

And one of the most conspicuous of the progresses made by
the century in England — the linguistic and philological
progress — is now being magnificently illustrated in the
appearance of the *New English Dictionary*, which, when
completed, bids fair to be not only a noble monument of
English scholarship, but one of the completest and best
dictionaries the world has yet seen. And in many other
areas of thought and life the presence of the historical spirit
might readily be indicated.

So much, and only so much, our space permits us to
say of the general character of the middle period of the
nineteeth century.

This period may be said to have closed, as I remarked
above, about the year 1867. The great race whom we saw
arise about the year 1832, by that time, with a few honoured
exceptions, had in its turn passed, or was passing, away.
Charlotte Brontë died in 1856, Macaulay in 1859, Thackeray
in 1863, Mrs Browning in 1861, Whewell in 1866, Faraday
in 1867, Dickens and Murchison in 1870, Sir John Herschell
in 1871, Mill and Sidgwick in 1873, Sir Charles Lyell in
1875, Darwin in 1882, Matthew Arnold in 1888. Tennyson,
now (1888) a poet amongst the peers, as always a peer
amongst the poets, is still amongst us, and long may he be !

But it may be doubted whether his reputation, either as a thinker or a poet, has been materially raised by any of his later writings, though seldom indeed has a poetic career extending over some sixty years been so nobly maintained with such constant energy.   Browning, too, is still productive and vigorous; but it is probably by his earlier works—his *Men and Women*, and *Dramatis Personæ*—that Browning holds his honoured and distinguished position.   Carlyle, who died in 1880, produced little of note after his *Life of Frederick*, concluded in 1865, except his *Reminiscences*—a work which shows indeed that his hand has not lost its cunning, but which, written in a morbid hour, by no means fairly reflects the nature or the conduct of the author. Possibly enough he had much to blame himself for—what honest person has not many charges to bring against himself?   But certainly, as he places himself before us sheeted to do his penance, we cannot throw one word of scorn at him—we can only sadly and humbly bow our heads before so pathetic a spectacle — an old honoured leader in so strange a guise.   'George Eliot's' *Middlemarch* (1871) was the last of the great works that charmed the general public. *Daniel Deronda*, though full of thought and power, and increasing the writer's already great influence over certain minds, yet failed to excite a very general interest.

Meanwhile, new forces were beginning to act upon the age, or rather, perhaps, the forces and movements I have mentioned were intensified and accelerated.   For the last quarter of the century seems likely to behold those earlier forces in yet fuller expansion and energy.   As vitally affecting the political and social area, we have to note the foundation of the International Working Men's Association in 1864, the death of Lord Palmerston in 1865, the second Reform Bill in 1867, the great agricultural movement that started in 1872, and the third Reform Bill enfranchising the peasantry in 1884. ·In 1866 the first Atlantic cable was laid. In 1861 was effected the final abolition of taxes on knowledge, 'with the removal of the Paper Duties, which were so oppressive that they amounted to £20,000 on Charles Knight's *Encyclopædia ;* and the effect of their abolition was such · that the newspaper circulation, which averaged 800,000 copies *weekly* at the time of the Queen's accession, rose to $10\frac{1}{2}$ millions in 1864, and is now 32 millions. Cheap editions of the best English authors have found their way into every cottage in the three kingdoms.'[1] But the pre-eminent opening glory of this new period is the establishment, in 1870, of a national system of popular education. That great Act, far too long delayed, disgracefully delayed indeed to the latest moment, has already produced, or helped to produce, results most beneficial and most significant and potent. For instance, juvenile crime since 1869, 'has fallen 53 per cent. ; ' and adult crime has strikingly diminished ; 'instead of building new prisons,' says Mr Mulhall, 'we have recently seen eleven sold by auction.' For, let obstructionists urge what they will, there is some real alliance between cultivation and honesty, and ignorance and crime are close confederates.

Such facts as these sufficiently mark the ushering in of a new era, and a new era must have a new literature—a literature to embody its characteristic ideas and ambitions. Of this new literature it would be premature yet to speak. One may venture, perhaps, to say that the current age is one of great intellectual activity, and that literary ability abounds. It may be questioned whether ever before have lived at the same time so many writers, both of prose and of poetry, of such brilliancy and skill. It would be invidious

[1] Mulhall's *Fifty Years of National Progress.*

to select names from such a crowd of distinguished *littérateurs.* But also, as we have already suggested, it may be
seriously questioned whether we can boast of any writer
of consummate genius: whether amongst our poets we can
point to anyone who is for us, in any comparable degree,
what Tennyson and Browning were for the last generation
—anyone of at all equal originality and power; and in
imaginative prose, whether we have any novelist of the
highest creative faculty, or of the finest penetration and
insight—anyone whose survey of our time is both broad and
deep. And this absence of superior genius in the region
of literary art is probably due to the character of our age.
While there is much to encourage and to cheer us when we
look around, there is undoubtedly much to perturb and to
scare. If the sun shines on us, there are frowning clouds
also—clouds black and theatening. Institutions that we
have regarded as firm and fast for ever are trembling to their
base. There is a sense of uncertainty and of revolution.
Some ears already catch the roar of Niagara, as they think,
and are persuaded we are rapidly drifting towards the
fatal precipice; and others, that are less timorous and hys-
terical, yet warn us of breakers ahead. And, indeed, even
the lightest-hearted are conscious of strange disquiets and
disturbances in the encircling atmosphere. It is a time of
profound agitations and commotions, of spiritual and moral
mutinies and rebellions which may at any time translate
themselves into action—a weary and heavy-laden time.

In the midst of such rumblings and uproars, no wonder
if men fancy themselves on the verge of some portentous
earthquake, and their hearts fail them for fear. No wonder
if they forget how great are the restorative forces of nature,
or how merciful and moderated her processes may be. The
storm breaks and the labours of men and oxen lie in wrack

and ruin ; but the landscape is soon recruited and revived. The changes from summer to winter and to summer again are immense, but are not abrupt. Still, no wonder if our age is perplexed and distressed when its best statesmanship seems baffled by the problems that beset it, and, at so many points, inscrutable difficulties face and obstruct us. Hence the pessimism of our time, which presents in this respect a curious contrast to the buoyancy and sanguineness of the century in some of its earlier years. 'It is very wonderful to me now,' says Mr Ruskin in a note to his *Frondes Agrestes*—a series of selections from his *Modern Painters*— 'to see what hopes I had once ; but Turner was alive then ; and the sun used to shine and rivers to sparkle.' He, too, had some joy in his time, and some hope of it in his old days. 'Instead of supposing the love of nature necessarily connected with the faithlessness of the age, I believe it is connected with the benevolence and liberty [1] of the age. So he writes in the passage in a note to which appear the first quoted words. But he cannot sufficiently abuse the present age. Neither Carlyle nor he could or can find vials large enough to contain all their disgust and wrath. They exhaust all the resources of objurgation and anathema. And lesser men feel, or assume, a like horror and desperation. A poet is the mouthpiece of his time ; and how can sweet or harmonised sounds issue from him when the time is out of temper or out of heart?

But the republic is not to be despaired of. It has passed through dark days before, days not less dark than are ours ; it has weathered storms not less malignant and dire. The flood may rise yet higher, but the ark shall go over the face of the waters—that is, if we keep it taut and trim, and steer

---

[1] Mr Ruskin says he forgets what he meant by 'liberty' here ; did he mean liberty-loving spirit ?

warily and wisely, if the English breed is not degenerate ; and why should we suspect so terrible a decay?   And when the present tyranny is overpast it shall set forth on a fresh career of enterprise and success and honour.   In other words, when the evolution, whose throes we are now suffering, is complete, and society is once more satisfactorily adjusted and settled, we may trust that the spirit of depression that now invades and usurps us will be exorcised, and poetry will recover its heart and its mind and its voice.

So Milton, amidst the confusion and antagonisms of his middle life, was unable to sing.   He could only dream of a day when he should be free to give poetic expression to the thoughts that arose in him.   To a noble recital of some of these thoughts he adds these concluding words: 'With such abstracted sublimities as these it might be worth your listening, readers, as I may one day hope to have ye *in a still time, when there shall be no chiding: not in these noises.*'

THE END.

COLSTON AND COMPANY, PRINTERS, EDINBURGH.

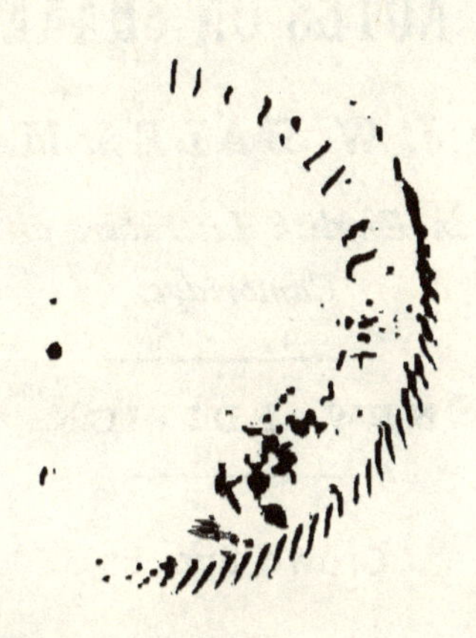

LONGER ENGLISH POEMS

WITH NOTES, PHILOLOGICAL AND EXPLANATORY,

With an Introduction on the Teaching of English.

(MACMILLAN & CO.)

First Issued in 1872.

Westminster Review.—' From whatever point of view we regard the volume, it is excellent. The selections are made with as good taste as Mr Palgrave has shown in the delightful '' Golden Treasury.'' . . . For the introductory notices, with their keen appreciation of each individual poet, and the beauties and characteristics of his poetry, combined with a liberal spirit, we are at a loss to find a parallel. There is nobody that will not be the better for this most enjoyable volume. . . . It should be in the hands of all lovers of poetry.'

The Examiner.—' Mr Hales has printed and carefully annotated twenty-eight choice poems, beginning with Spenser's '' Prothalamion '' and ending with Shelley's '' Adonais ''; none of them too long to be committed to memory, and studied line by line by an intelligent scholar, but all long enough to illustrate the spirit of their authors, and, to some extent, the spirit of the literature in which they are gems.'

London Quarterly Review.—' Teachers of English will find this a suggestive and serviceable book. . . . Mr Hales's notes are particularly good in their references to parallel and kindred passages, and they will suggest to the student how he may form a '' liber poetarum '' of his own.'

The Scotsman.—' Many an English master will find it a great service to him in the discharge of his duties. It is scholarly, thoughtful, suggestive and practical.'

EVENTS OF OUR OWN TIME.

A Series of Volumes on the most Important Events of the last Half Century, each containing 300 pages or more, in large 8vo, with Plans, Portraits, or other Illustrations, to be issued at intervals, cloth, price 5s.

Large paper copies (250 only) with Proofs of the Plates, cloth, 10s. 6d.

THE WAR IN THE CRIMEA. By General Sir EDWARD HAMLEY, K.C.B. With Five Maps and Plans, and Four Portraits on Copper. Fifth Edition. Crown 8vo. Price 5s., cloth.

THE INDIAN MUTINY OF 1857. By Colonel MALLESON, C.S.I. With Three Plans, and Four Portraits on Copper. Fourth Edition. Crown 8vo. Price 5s., cloth.

THE AFGHAN WARS OF 1839-1842 AND 1878-80. By ARCHIBALD FORBES. With Portraits on Copper of Sir Frederick Roberts, Sir George Pollock, Sir Louis Cavagnari and Sirdars, and the Ameer Abdurrahman; and with Maps and Plans. Second Edition. Crown 8vo. Price 5s., cloth.

THE REFOUNDING OF THE GERMAN EMPIRE. By Colonel MALLESON, C.S.I. With Maps and Plates, and Four Portraits on Copper. Crown 8vo. Price 5s., cloth.

*ACHIEVEMENTS IN ENGINEERING DURING THE LAST HALF CENTURY. By Professor VERNON HARCOURT. With many Illustrations. Crown 8vo. Price 5s., cloth.

*THE DEVELOPMENT OF NAVIES DURING THE LAST HALF CENTURY. By Captain EARDLEY WILMOT, R.N. With Illustrations and Plans. Crown 8vo. Price 5s., cloth.

Among the other Volumes to follow are—
THE LIBERATION OF ITALY.
THE OPENING OF JAPAN.
DISCOVERIES IN AFRICA.
THE AMERICAN CIVIL WAR.

Of Volumes so * marked there is no Large Paper Editions.

LONDON : SEELEY & CO., LIMITED, ESSEX ST., STRAND